DON'T TRY THIS AT HOME

Jonathon kicked himself up into a wheelie, slowing to about 45 kph. He leaned forward to keep his balance and stay focused on the closing distance between himself and the trio of oncoming lances.

When the distance closed to less than three meters, Jonathon braked hard and threw his weight forward, pitching himself onto his front wheel. And just as his rear wheel came up, he activated the hydrojack built into the front fork. He sprang up into the air, tucking into a forward flip. The stadium blurred past above and below him as he spun, and he heard shots over the collective gasp of the crowd. When his natural balance and gymnastic training told him it was time to come out of the tuck, he arched his back, laying out the final rotation to land again. Two wheels, no wobble.

Then it was time to elude the goalie.

The Buzzsaws' goalkeeper was a massive troll named Big Ed. Armored like a tank with huge polycarb plates. Armed with an autoshot riot carbine and twenty stun rounds, plus a tetsubo—a huge Japanese quarterstaff covered with densiplast bosses. Wicked nasty.

But Jonathon was faster. Quicker. And hopefully smarter . . .

SHADOWRUN

DEAD AIR

Jak Koke

A ROC BOOK

ROC
Published by the Penguin Group
Penguin Books USA Inc., 375 Hudson Street,
New York, New York 10014, U.S.A.
Penguin Books Ltd, 27 Wrights Lane, London W8 5TZ, England
Penguin Books Australia Ltd, Ringwood, Victoria, Australia
Penguin Books Canada Ltd, 10 Alcorn Avenue,
Toronto, Ontario, Canada M4V 3B2
Penguin Books (N.Z.) Ltd, 182-190 Wairau Road,
Auckland 10, New Zealand

Penguin Books Ltd, Registered Offices:
Harmondsworth, Middlesex, England

First published by Roc, an imprint of Dutton Signet,
a division of Penguin Books USA Inc.

First Printing October, 1996
10 9 8 7 6 5 4 3 2 1

Series Editor: Donna Ippolito
Cover: Doug Anderson

 REGISTERED TRADEMARK—MARCA REGISTRADA

SHADOWRUN, FASA, and the distinctive SHADOWRUN and FASA logos are
registered trademarks of the FASA Corporation, 1100 W. Cermak, Suite B305,
Chicago, IL 60608.

Printed in the United States of America

For Jonathan Bond,
my good friend and an excellent writer,
without whom I would never have had the courage
to write anything after college.

This novel is based on a short story
Jonathan and I wrote in collaboration;
the original core idea was his,
and I am deeply grateful that he let me use it here.

Acknowledgments

Many thanks to Seana Davidson for the multitude of sacrifices she made when my wrist was broken. She stayed up and typed for me, she put off her own work to help me get through the first half of the book, and her comments on the first draft prevented me from embarrassing myself more than once.

Credit should also go to Jonathan Bond, Marsh Cassady, Tom Lindell, and Mark Teppo for their insightful critiques of the manuscript, to my writer's workshop for its support and commentary, and to the staff at FASA for its help, especially Donna Ippolito whose unwavering encouragement kept me writing through even the toughest parts.

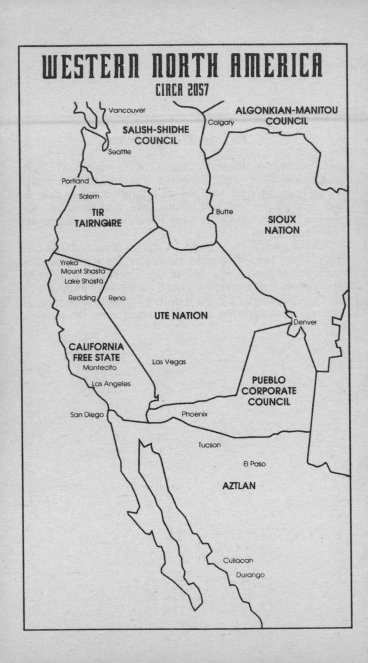

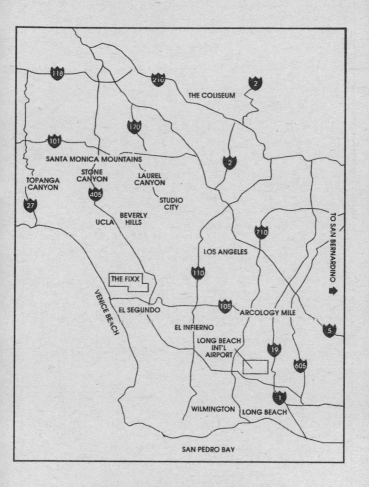

LOS ANGELES
AREA MAP

Prologue

First simtime. First day of release.

You are there.

It is the summer of 2057, and you've been waiting ever since they started showing previews on the trid—cuts of the catastrophic motorcycle wreck, the giant ball of flame erupting in the center of a crowded stadium. The adverts' staccato images and the tense voice-over hinted that this sim is based on the true story of Jonathon Winger and his deadly rivalry with fellow combat biker, Dougan Rose. That makes it all the more enticing; everyone wants to know what really happened in the days before Jonathon Winger died.

The harsh afternoon heat dissipates in a wash of cooled air as the line advances and you step inside the theater. The sweat on the nape of your neck grows cold, sending chills down your back. Glass doors close behind you, their mirrored surface blocking out the heat and the sun. The odor of burning asphalt and the choking scent of diesel exhaust lingers in the air for an instant before the theater's odor dampeners absorb them.

The real world is harsh, and you're glad to escape it for a moment. It is an Awakened world where powerful magic coexists with rapidly advancing cybertechnology. Where elves and dwarfs, orks and trolls share the streets with humans. Where megacorporations are more powerful than governments, and the global computer Matrix is the conduit through which all information is passed.

Today's simsense will take you away from a world where dragons can run for president, and creatures even more powerful can assassinate those dragons. Where reality is more shocking than fantasy has ever been. The sim will make you forget about the insanity of 2057, help you escape from the day-to-day grind. If only briefly.

A uniformed teenage girl with platinum blonde hair offers you the choice of an electrode rig or a datacord for straight jack. You slot your credstick into her scanner and grab a datacord. 'Trode rigs are for wimps. You can hardly believe anyone ever uses them.

The simsense in this theater is first release, primo urge, unlike anything you can get at home or on chip. It is Dir-X, a direct recording, untainted by the signal loss that comes with compression and decompression. Using a 'trode rig would dull the experience, like walking through life in a thick rubber suit. No, straight jack is the only way to fly.

You enter the theater and the world of noise and distraction gives way to the lush black carpeting of the aisle. The walls and the ceiling inside the room are lined with black, sound-dampening foam, and hidden subwoofers rumble with infrasonic white noise to prevent random vibrations from interfering with the sim. The last smells from outside disappear inside the chamber; there are to be no external distractions during the sim.

The chairs are self-adjusting recliners, all facing the same direction, but there is no stage. The chair fits you snugly as you relax into its comforting grasp. One end of the datacord clicks into the control panel by your right hand; the other end snaps into the silicon datajack in your temple.

Whatever remains of the real world dissipates as the sim begins and the sensedeck's RAS overrides kick in to dampen your own senses and muscle responses. The chair cradling you is gone, replaced by a wash of color and pulse of urge. The room fades, and the others around you vanish.

The opening music rises into your awareness as you stand in the body of a young elven boy in the throes of adolescence. Thin and tall with bones poking against skin. Heat blasts your face and your bare arms as you watch red and orange flames engulf an old wooden house. Wind rushes past to feed the fire, and you smell the black smoke of burning upholstery and bubbling plastic.

Through the melted remnants of the front window, you see a grandfather clock, its once polished hardwood blackened, its ornate face twisted from the heat. Across the room from the destroyed clock is a bassinet, and for the briefest of moments you think you hear the soft cry of a baby amid *the banshee scream of the fire. Then it's gone, and only the crisp anguish of loss remains.*

Adrenaline makes your heart pound in your chest. Fire-fighters rush to pump water over the blaze, but it is a futile gesture. The great roar of the fire seems to laugh at them as the water spray sizzles and vaporizes. Sadness wells inside you, bringing you close to tears. The house is too far gone to be saved. Too far gone. Such a waste.

A thin hand touches yours, and abruptly you realize that a crowd of people stands with you, everyone watching the fire. Gathered for the spectacle. You grasp the hand in yours and turn to see an elven girl of your age. The sadness wanes and a surge of affection rises in you. She is your best friend, your constant companion. You are happy she is here.

Her long hair is raven black, pulled back behind her sharply pointed ears. Her skin is the deep russet of an Amerind, and smudged with dirt. Her eyes are a dull copper color. Beautiful. She stands slightly shorter than you, but she is more fully developed. Rounded in places. She continues to stare at the fire.

You look back into the flames, their ravenous tongues licking black death into the wood around the doorway, the windows, cutting sharp grooves through the walls. The orange and red defocus as you stare, growing glassy and reflective. For a second you see yourself in the reflection.

You are tall even for an elf, but haven't put on the muscle to match your height. Your hair is a shaggy mane of auburn, straight as straw, unkempt and dusty. Your features are classic; prominent cheekbones, proud straight nose; up-tilted hazel eyes flecked with blue. The line of your mouth turns down at the corners.

The reflection of your face grows larger and larger until you can see nothing else. The sound of the fire fades slowly, replaced by the rising swell of orchestra music. Your face loses its color, becoming ghostly transparent, and the flickering orange of the defocused fire provides a backdrop for the opening credits. The words DEAD AIR appear and a simultaneous pulse of adrenaline rockets through you.

Time to fly.

Dramatis Personae

JONATHON WINGER, elf, regarded as one of the best professional linebikers in the entire World Combat Cycling League. He rides for the Los Angeles Sabers' combat biker squad and is the long-time close friend of teammate Tamara Ny.

DOUGAN ROSE, elf, the only professional linebiker who is rated better than Jonathon Winger. He rides for the New Orleans Buzzsaws and has been in the game for over ten years.

TAMARA NY, elf, teammate and close friend of Jonathon Winger. She loves Grids Desmond, a freelance simsense guru, but has been sleeping with high-placed Saeder-Krupp executive, Andreas Michaelson.

SYNTHIA STONE, human, hermetic mage and Jonathon Winger's girlfriend.

GRIDS DESMOND, human, simsense guru and boy-friend of Tamara Ny.

VENICE JONES, troll, Jonathon Winger's bodyguard.

MARIA NIGHTFEATHER, human, Owl shaman, ex-lover of Dougan Rose. She used to run with La Muerte, a Los Angeles gang and shadowrunning team that has long since broken up.

ANDREAS MICHAELSON, human, senior executive vice-president at Saeder-Krupp, plans to defect to Mit-suhama Computer Technologies. He is having an affair with Tamara Ny.

LUC TASHIKA, human, executive vice-president at Mit-suhama Computer Technologies in charge of the enter-tainment division. He has contacted the fixer known as

Cinnamon to arrange the extraction of Andreas Michaelson from Saeder-Krupp.

CINNAMON, free spirit, fixer hired to extract Andreas Michaelson.

HENDRIX, human, leader of a team of shadowrunners who are hired by Cinnamon. His team includes Layla, Juju Pete, and Mole.

ACT ONE

HIS FIRST DEATH

1

Jonathon Winger stifled a yawn where he sat in the board-room on the twenty-seventh floor of the Angelic Entertainment arcology in downtown L.A. Seated all around him in high-back synthleather chairs were men in gray or blue suits and muted ties, complete with discreet data-jacks and pocket computers.

Most of their faces were familiar to Jonathon by now. Ex-ecs and VIPs of Angelic Entertainment, which owned the Los Angeles Sabers, the combat biker team Jonathan rode for. There were also some promotion people from Saeder-Krupp, but Jonathon and Tamara were the only actual linebikers present. Everyone knew Angelic Entertainment was merely a shell company for the mighty Saeder-Krupp Corporation, which could technically not do business in California Free State. Too magical or too metahuman—or maybe both—for the folks up in Sacramento.

Coach Kalish was there too, and though she was a great coach as far as Jonathon was concerned, she was an aging dwarf and not the most trid-ogenic. The promoters were obviously not interested in using her in any special adverts.

Jonathon, however, they were most pleased to have rid-ing for them. He was large for an elf, bulked up by aug-mented muscle and a regimented workout to almost ork size, but with clean-line good looks. Superstar charisma, according to the promoters.

Whether they were right or not, Jonathon's mane of auburn hair, intelligent hazel eyes, and ten-thousand-nuyen smile had helped, along with his skill in the arena, to land him an unprecedented number of endorsement contracts for one so new to combat cycling. He certainly loved the publicity.

And that's what this meeting was all about—publicity. The promoters and producers and ad people wanted to hype up the relationship between him and Tamara. Wanted to imply something going on between them. Something intimate. *Sex.*

They could use that to sell millions of simsense chips and motorcycles and articles of clothing and whatever else they wanted to put Jonathon's name on. But it bothered him that it was a lie.

He and Tamara had never been lovers even though their relationship was deeper, closer than anything he'd ever imagined possible with another being. And sex had never been part of it.

Jonathon turned to look at her, seeing all the details of her face and posture. Reading her thoughts in those details. Her raven black hair, dark Amerind skin. The dull copper of her irises and the fine, beautiful line of her mouth.

He'd been in her mind so many times via the simsense link they shared. Feeling her emotions as though they were his. He knew what the tilt of her head meant, what she was feeling as she absently scratched the polished red-brown surface of the table in front of her. She was just as bored as he was.

She looked up at him and smiled, then rolled her eyes playfully. And in that smile, Jonathon read her thoughts. *She wants to get out of here.*

Jonathon stood up at the same time she did. "Excuse us," he said, interrupting the suit who'd been pontificating. "But we've got a tough match tomorrow night in New Orleans, and we'd like to get some rest."

The suit just stared at him, not knowing how to respond.

"I don't really think you need us anymore right now," Jonathon said. "Whatever you decide will be all right with us." He put his hand out for Tamara, and they turned to leave the room.

When they'd cleared the doors, Tamara burst into laughter. "Thanks," she said. "I was about to suffocate in there. How've you been able to sit through those meetings all this time?"

"Must be all the extra nuyen that comes pouring in with the deals," Jonathon told her. "Guess I've just built up a tolerance."

"Slot the nuyen," she said. "We make enough riding for the team. What I want out of it is the limelight. Maybe a chance to make a simfeature or something. But I hate this board meeting drek."

"It gets easier," Jonathon said as they reached the elevator. "You want to stop in the atrium for a cerveza? Venny's meeting me downstairs."

Tamara considered. "Sure, but I need to make it quick. Got a date tonight."

"Oh yeah? The dreamer again? Grids?"

"Grids will be there . . . sort of . . . but my main date is that S-K exec from Essen."

"Michaelson? I didn't think you were seeing him anymore."

"This'll be the last time."

Jonathon just shook his head. Tamara was scheming something, he could tell. But he didn't ask about it, didn't really want to know. Besides, she would elaborate if and when it suited her.

"I'll tell you about it tomorrow," she said. "In New Orleans."

"Just be careful," he said. "Playing around with powerful people is a dangerous business." Jonathan spoke the words even though he knew they weren't needed. Tamara already knew everything he felt, and she would either act on it or not.

Probably not.

She just smiled at him as he pressed the tab to call the elevator. A smile that told him everything was going to be fine. Just fine.

He only wished he could believe it.

2

High up the blue, steel-and-glass side of the Venice Beach Hilton, Grids Desmond stared out the window of his hotel room, watching the huge orange sun setting in an ocean of aquamarine green. A brilliant red streak reflected off the water, shimmering, glowing like a broad trail of fire between him and the sun. The Los Angeles smog had few redeeming qualities, but it did help turn the sunsets from merely beautiful into spectacular.

Grids was thin for a human, with little muscle on his bones and less fat. Maybe because he subsisted mostly on a diet of cheese crackers and soykaf. His pale skin showed no trace of amber melanin hue since he almost never ventured into the sunshine without his customary black jeans and Mickey Mouse T-shirt. Despite that, he was handsome in an old-fashioned film star way. Black, tousled hair, white skin. Thin face with delicate, almost feminine features. All but the eyes; his hawk-sharp, dark eyes hinted at what was behind them—a genius intelligence, and a quick, if detached, wit.

Grids watched and waited. Waited for the sting to begin.

Nearer, the daytime spectacles at Venice Beach were winding down, and the evening shows were about to begin. Grids brought his Ares CCD binoculars up to his eyes and scanned the beach. A team of hugely muscled joyboys performed acrobatics to a crowd of onlookers. The men had been surgically altered to look like clones—all natural flesh, identical deep brown tans, and blond wavy hair.

Grids scanned across the crowds. There were magic illusions, dance routines, basketball, volleyball, and sparring matches. People sold 'ware of every shape, size, and prescription. Venice Beach was safe territory, bounded by a huge desalinization plant to the south and the walled-off corporate beaches of Santa Monica to the north. It was also protected by the Mafia and thus considered neutral turf by the local gangs who prowled the toxic beachfront district south of the desalinization plant.

Grids brought his headclock into focus on his retina as he pulled the binox from his eyes. 07:18:24 PM. Almost time.

He'd been waiting for Tamara since just after one o'clock that afternoon, arriving at the Venice Hilton early to avert any suspicion. He'd checked into room 2305 seemingly at random, but had actually chosen it from a list stored in his internal headware memory of rooms within range of Tamara's simlink transmitter. He'd had plenty of time to set up the Truman Realink simrecorder and double-check the mods that would make the signals to and from the simrig implanted in Tamara's head look, at a glance, like portable telecon carrier waves.

Tam's simrig had been far easier to tweak than others Grids had worked with because it was UCAS military grade, from her years as a test pilot for the United Canadian and American States. Its virtual interface was clunky, but once he figured out what it could do, he marveled at its versatility.

Though most simware controls—the kind used by actors and simtech crews—were standardized for ease of use, Tamara's required fine-tuning. Even the most rudimentary features like adjusting range and EC/PC ratios required programming, but the sheer range of wiz options in the hardware made it all worthwhile. It was so flexible that the signal could be encrypted in any number of ways. Grids had found it harder to modify the Truman recorder.

But now, the time for action was near at hand. Even though, technically, he wouldn't participate in the flesh. Simming Tamara's wet feed from five floors away was as close as he wanted to get. He never took action directly if he could help it.

Better living through vicarious reality.

Grids turned from the window and sat on the bed next to the simrecorder. The Truman was a small quasi-portable unit in a black plastic box about the size of a briefcase. He set the small gray CCD binox next to the Truman, took the last gulp of cold soykaf in his cup, and double-checked that the chip in the slot was still the ten-gigapulse stack he'd popped in earlier. Wet-record simsense gobbled memory like a ghoul in a graveyard—one megapulse per second at baseline. That meant he had just under three hours' worth.

Unless Andreas Michaelson was some sort of sexual marathoner, three hours would be plenty for what Tamara had planned.

Grids jacked in and made another check of all the systems for lack of anything better to do. A few minutes later, as he was running a diagnostic on the on-the-fly decryption algorithm, the unit picked up Tamara's simlink signal and started recording.

A thrill of excitement shivered down his back as he reclined against a stack of pillows and faded himself into her feed. The signal was strong and clear, the decryption working perfectly.

Suddenly he was in a helicopter, feeling the resonating rhythm of the rotor blades as the machine descended toward the roof of the hotel. His body was tall and elven, lean and well-muscled. And female, very female.

He drank in the ecstasy of her scent—the primal sex of this new body, Tamara's body. Drekking tailored pheromones.

The signal coming from her was full-X, the entire spectrum of sensory and emotive tracks, but Grids had programmed the Truman to record only the baseline—the sensory tracks—to save on memory. Besides, Tamara had specifically requested that her emotions not be recorded, saying they weren't important or relevant to the task at hand.

She was the boss on this one. He was just technical support. It felt like old times, really, back when he used to run the shadows, decking for Grayson Alexander. Burning ice. Those were really old times. Before his stint with Brilliant Genesis, before Amalgamated Studios.

At least he wasn't dueling IC on this one. He hated decking, and had never really gotten good enough at battling intrusion countermeasures to suit his sense of self-worth. No matter that the Matrix was virtual, it was all too real for him. In the consensual hallucination of cyberspace, the virtual became realer than real. Data turned physical. The drek in there could kill you.

It was harder to die in sim. Not impossible, but harder. The technology was the same in both cyberdecks and sensedecks—Artificial Sensory Induction System Technology, otherwise known as ASIST. But commercial simsense chips were regulated and most sensedecks had built-in peak controllers. Cyberdecks did not.

In the sim, Tamara's svelte elven form sat poised on the edge of the helo's synthleather seat. Grids tasted mint and the faintest hint of garlic leftover from Tamara's dinner. It amazed him how fit she was, how good it felt to be able to move with grace and dexterity without strain or effort.

That professional athlete training really does pay off, he thought.

Tamara was broad-shouldered for an elf and strong for her size, though Grids knew she was acting the role of the female consort this evening.

Cool wind blew her long hair back, tugging at the loose hem of her sleek black evening dress as the helicopter door breathed open. The security guard holding the door for her was a troll of considerable size. Horns jutted from the top of his head, curling up and back like the rack on a huge mountain goat. The ends had been filed to a point and tipped with engraved silver caps. The troll wore a black tuxedo, mirror shades, and he smiled at Tamara as she stepped out.

Behind her came a large man, easily as tall, with a barrel chest and a graying brown beard. His name was Andreas Michaelson, and Grids knew he was an exec of some rank at Saeder-Krupp. He'd been seeing Tamara off and on since before Grids had come into the picture.

Michaelson wore an impeccably tailored suit of sharkskin gray, and a fancy datajack gleamed gold on his balding forehead. He took Tamara's outstretched hand, his palms rough against hers, and escorted her through the blustering wind of the helicopter to the set of double doors.

The troll took up a position behind them as they reached the edge of the helipad and passed through the doors, flanked by two Saeder-Krupp security guards. She flashed them a coy smile as they passed, all the while cozying up against Michaelson's shoulder.

She was really turning it on.

When the high whine of the helicopter's motor faded enough to hear, Tamara spoke. "I've missed you so much," she said. "LA is hardly bearable when you're gone." Her voice was breathy—a harsh rasp in the back of her throat. "And, of course, I can't come to Essen."

Michaelson laughed. "Yes, well, I'm sorry my wife is such a traditionalist."

Tamara smiled at him. "Is she?"

Michaelson nodded. "But soon, my sweet, soon I shall be spending more time here." He pulled her close and put his mouth over hers.

She reacted in kind, pressing her breasts against his chest and parting her lips slightly in the embrace.

Grids recoiled instinctively as the hairs of Michaelson's mustache and beard scratched against the edges of Tamara's mouth and the warmth of his tongue pushed past her lips. It tasted of cigar and beer. He was glad when Tamara pulled back and pecked Michaelson on the side of his mouth. She jerked her head in the direction of the troll with the mirror shades who walked behind them, simultaneously pulling at Michaelson's arm. "Let's get inside first," she said.

The hall led to another set of double doors adorned with antique-looking silver door knockers in the shape of lions' heads. A palm-scanner hung on the wall next to the entrance. Michaelson pressed his hand against the scanner's matte-black surface.

A second later, the lock released the doors with a sliding click, and Michaelson escorted Tamara into the plush suite. She kicked off her shoes and rubbed her stocking-covered toes into the thick gray carpet as she pulled from his grasp and danced away from him. Playing.

"Ruger," Michaelson said, addressing the troll who stood waiting to attend them, "please have Claudio bring up some chilled champagne and a sushi tray."

Ruger inclined his horned head. "As you wish, sir."

"And nothing local. The champagne should be French and the sushi from Japan or San Francisco."

A slight frown touched Ruger's face. "Of course," he said, "I'll tell him right away." Then the troll closed the double doors, leaving Tamara alone with Michaelson.

Grids took in the hotel apartment through Tamara's eyes as she looked around. The suite was massive and luxurious, with a full kitchen, a dining room, a sunken living room, and a large bedroom. The walls were adorned with paintings of beach or desert scenes represented in Southwest impressionist style—lots of browns and gray-blues, blurry images, and such. A wall-sized trideo filled one side of the living room and adjacent was a bay window offering a fantastic view of the ocean.

Tamara walked to the window and stood watching the blazing half-circle of the disappearing sun. "Grids," she whispered, "I hope you're getting this. I'm sure you'll enjoy it as much as I do."

Michaelson came up behind her and put his arms around her in a bear hug. His beard nestled up against her neck.

She moved her head against his, nuzzling him.

Shivers of the heebie-jeebies shook Grids, but he fought them and stayed locked into the sim.

Michaelson kissed Tamara's neck, and she responded by granting him access. His kisses were warm and wet, leaving a trail of cooling saliva on her neck and up to the point of her ear.

Grids fought down the urge to yarf up his soykaf.

But Tamara's physical body was responding to Michaelson's attentions. Her breathing grew deeper. Her lips parted slightly, her eyes closed.

Michaelson moved his hands over her body. One pressed low on her stomach, crushing the black silk of her dress against the sensitive skin of her abdomen. His other hand traced tiny circles over her breasts, causing her nipples to harden.

A knock at the door brought Michaelson's advances to a halt.

Grids breathed a sigh of relief.

"Yes?" Michael said.

"It's Claudio. Here to serve you, my executiveness." Even through the electronic modulation of the intercom, Grids could hear the affected, fake British accent.

"Come in."

The door clicked open and Claudio entered with a silver cart. Michaelson's aide was a fat dwarf, plump and aging; the stark white hair on his head had mostly migrated to his chin. He wore a traditional black tuxedo. "Ah, my dear lady, Tamara Ny," Claudio said, parking the cart near the dining table. "How good it is to see you again."

"Likewise, Claudio."

"I must say that I was impressed with my lady's performance last week against Atlanta. I particularly enjoyed the goal you scored on the hand-off from Jonathon Winger. That was—"

"Claudio!" Michaelson cut in. "Please set the cart by the couch. And then go."

"Yes, of course. So sorry."

Tamara burst out laughing, rich and full. And after a slight pause, Michaelson joined her.

"I will expect your assistance with the Magenics visit tomorrow," Michaelson said.

Claudio nodded and smiled his assent. "I will be ready." Then with a slight bow, he retreated through the doors.

As Tamara glanced after the dwarf, Grids caught a glimpse of Ruger standing alertly just outside the door. Several other security personnel stood with the troll, including a human woman Grids took for a security mage— a potential problem if the simlink signal was discovered and decoded.

"Now, where were we," Michaelson said, "before that rude interruption?"

"Right about here." Tamara put her arms around his neck and kissed him.

He reacted by lifting her into his arms. She laughed as he carried her into the bedroom, then laid her down on the king-size bed. Grids tried to get a sense of the room while Michaelson caressed Tamara's whole body as he slowly undressed her. Anything to avoid concentrating on what was about to happen. He thought briefly about jacking out for this next part, but Tamara would kill him if anything went wrong. So he clenched his teeth and tried to keep his attention on the periphery of Tamara's vision, on the decor and layout of the bedchamber.

The room was huge and had a desk along one wall, presumably where Michaelson worked late into the evening. Executive VPs were expected to work long, hard hours, or at least that's what Grids knew from his friends at Amalgamated Studios. On the desk was a cyberdeck and a small telecom unit as well as an open briefcase.

Tamara's vision was filled by Michaelson's hairy chest now. She was naked down to her black silk bra and panties. Her body, when Grids could catch a glimpse of it, was fantastic. Abdomen, arms, back, and legs cut with muscles hard as stone. Michaelson's, by contrast, was soft and pliable. She kissed one of his nipples, then the other, working her way down.

Grids knew what was about to happen and he cringed. She removed his pants slowly, teasing him. Driving him wild. Grids faded his senses out as she reached to brush

Michaelson's groin. Grids couldn't take any more. He dulled the input to where he could know what was happening, but he didn't have to experience it.

The fact that she seemed to enjoy it was bad enough.

Thirty-three minutes later, the two of them had finished and Tamara fell asleep. The Truman simrecorder recognized it and paused itself. Grids had faded himself in once or twice to make sure the signals were clear and strong. After the initial act, to which he had a particular aversion, the sex was more bearable. He even found himself having fun. Michaelson was no porn star, but Tamara knew how to enjoy herself.

By the time the Truman shut off, Grids himself was ready for sleep. Instead, he reviewed the chip. Tamara would be pleased; for a wet record, the chip was excellent. It would serve her purpose well. If Michaelson's wife was as traditional as the exec implied, Tamara now had a perfect tool for blackmail.

Grids fell into a deep sleep on the bed, and didn't wake until 09:28:43 AM the next morning. He went to pack up the Truman and noticed that another fifty-eight minutes had been recorded after the sex. The Truman had detected Tamara's signal in the morning and started recording again.

Grids prepared some instant soykaf, then jacked in to sim it. And as he experienced Tamara's morning, a sinking feeling took hold of him. She had done something stupid. Dangerously stupid.

Something that could easily cost them their lives.

3

Jonathon breathed deeply and took in the lazy morning. The Café du Monde was crowded as usual, filled with tourists and New Orleans locals enjoying the tastes and sounds of the French Quarter.

Even on this humid, cloudy mid-morning, the Vieux Carré was a feast for the senses. The rich aroma of freshly ground coffee filled the air. *Real* coffee, not soykaf. A lazy jazz melody drifted in from outside where a black-skinned ork wailed on a dented trumpet while his human companion picked accompaniment on an acoustic banjo.

Jonathon took a bite of his powder sugar-adorned beignet, then took a sip of his café au lait. *Damn, I like the feel of this old city,* he thought. *Timeless and vibrant. So serene compared to the insane rush and dirty air of Los Angeles. The people here know how to live.*

Across the polished hardwood table sat Synthia Stone. A petite human with shoulder-length red hair, Synthia's features were sharp and delicate, as though painted by some artist with fine strokes of a detail brush. Her irises were the color of faded denim, and her oval eyes were outlined with carmine-colored pencil.

She extended a delicate hand and laid it over his. The bones of her wrist were thin, birdlike beneath porcelain skin, but Jonathon knew appearances could be deceiving, especially in Synthia's case. Her thin hands could wield powerful magic, at least as powerful as any of her associates at UCLA's Department of Occult Studies. She wore a bracelet on her left wrist, crudely hammered from dull bronze-colored metal and covered with fine engravings. Jonathon had never seen her take it off, even at night. Even during sex.

She squeezed his hand. "Isn't this wonderful?" she asked. "The two of us alone in the French Quarter."

Her childish romanticism always brought a smile to his face. "It's great," he said. "As long as no one recognizes me."

"You're not all that famous, Winger."

"Shh, not too loud. They must hate me here."

"No one's going to recognize you; I've masked us with an illusion to make us look like Japanese tourists."

"And what about Venny?" Jonathon nodded toward Venice Jones, his troll bodyguard seated at the next table. A huge mug of coffee steamed in front of him, but Venny hadn't touched it yet. He was working, totally alert, his eyes scanning the crowd, his magically enhanced senses primed to detect danger.

"Venny looks like a huge troll with surfer blond hair, a goatee, and mirrored razor glasses," Synthia said.

Jonathon laughed. "Right, I suppose he looks touristy enough without masking." He munched down the rest of his beignet, and grabbed another from the plate. *Gotta feed the beast,* he thought. His gengineered hyperactive thyroid boosted his metabolism and gave him extra quickness and strength, but it also made him hungry all the time.

"You seem . . . pensive," Synthia said. "You nervous about the game tonight?"

"Not really," he said. "Just tired, I guess. But by bogey time, I'll be prepped and in a zone." Jonathon paused. "The only thing is . . ."

Dougan Rose. The name jumped into his head unbidden. Like a ghost from the past.

"What?" Synthia asked.

"It's Dougan."

"What about him?"

An image came to Jonathon. He was young, some time after the fire, after the funeral of his mother and sister. He'd gone away with Tamara and her band of gypsies when they'd left Lake Shasta, becoming part of their raggedy caravan of old rusted vans, junked cars, and a few motorbikes.

Jonathon had ridden with Tamara on her old Honda, and when the caravan stopped for the night to set up camp in some farmer's field, the two of them would weave the bike along gravel roads. They played a street version of combat biker with Ryan and Homey and the other caravan kids, all dreaming of being able to dodge and jump and flip the bikes like the great players. Like Dougan Rose.

"He psyches me out of the game every time."

"Why?"

Because he's been the greatest biker for the last ten years, and he still rides the line better than anyone.

"He was my idol when I was growing up," Jonathon said. "I even had a holopic of him and his Yamaha."

Synthia grabbed his hands and made him look at her. She stared into his eyes, unflinching. "You're better than he is," she said. "You don't know it yet, but you ride better, you're younger, stronger. You've got quickness and drive."

"You sound like the producers: 'Wingman and Sabers versus Rose and Buzzsaws.' I'm sick of the comparisons."

Synthia gave him a hard look, then smiled. "No, you're not," she said. "I know you. You eat up all the media type."

Her smile was infectious. " 'Tis true," he said. "As long as we keep winning, I'll continue to enjoy every minute of it." But even though Jonathon was smiling, and even though he was happy to be alone with his love, taking in the scent of fresh-ground coffee and the wail of lazy jazz, in the back of his mind he worried about the upcoming, must-win match. About Dougan Rose, and how in the Awakened world he was going to beat his childhood idol.

4

Andreas Michaelson hummed as he checked himself in the mirror. Tie straight, hair nearly perfect. Nice smile. Claudio would have to check his appearance for the luncheon, but all in all, not a bad bag of bones. Slick, elite. Definitely shark-proof.

"Still good enough for Tamara," he said to himself. Michaelson was amazed at how voraciously the elf responded to him sexually whenever he visited Los Angeles. He liked her, liked her almost too much. They romanced each other, but neither of them really expected the relationship to change.

He would never leave his wife, Nadine. And Tamara knew that, just as he knew from his sources that she had a boyfriend as well. An unemployed slot named Grids Desmond. It tweaked him that someone of her looks and money would consort with a type like that. From the Sabers alone, she must make at least a million a year.

Michaelson laughed at himself as he realized he should know exactly how much she made, because, technically, she worked for him. The Sabers franchise was ostensibly owned by Angelic Entertainment, which, among other Saeder-Krupp divisions, Michaelson oversaw.

That's what he was here for: to oversee. At least that was the official reason. In reality, he had come to discuss the so-called Magus File with the team at Magenics, another of S-K California's puppet corps. The research project was top-secret, and his boss, the dragon Lofwyr, wanted everything checked and double-checked. It was a testament to how twisted the world had become that a dragon could awaken from centuries of sleep to purchase and run the world's most powerful megacorporation.

But was Michaelson going to face the dragon down? Was he going to tell the worm to crawl back into its hole and leave people alone? No fragging way, *omae*. Like the marionette he was, Michaelson jerked when his strings were pulled. *As long as the dragon's in charge,* he thought, *I do what it wants. With luck, it won't be my fragging boss for much longer.*

The telecom beeped as Michaelson completed the finishing touches on his facial make-up, giving himself that smooth-skin appearance. Unmarred. Immutable. In control.

He stepped out of the bathroom and sat at his desk chair. "What is it?" he asked.

Ruger's huge warty face appeared on the screen. "Hello, sir," he said. "Sorry to disturb you, but the head of hotel security has uncovered something I think you should know about."

The only drawback to staying in the Hilton as opposed to the Angelic Entertainment facilities downtown was the security. Although the Hilton was own by S-K, and was as well-protected as any other elite hotel, even the highly secure penthouse suite couldn't match the sheer impenetrability of a corporate enclave. But the view here was much nicer, and the privacy allowed him to see Tamara. No price could be placed on such an advantage.

Michaelson looked into the telecom. "What did he find?"

"Last night, they detected a transmission, and they've narrowed down the source to your suite."

"What kind of transmission?"

"Well, it looks like an encrypted portable telecom signal. Nothing unusual there, but it lasted for almost an hour. And under the circumstances, I thought it unlikely that you were on your telecom for that length of time."

"I was not."

"And Miss Ny?"

Andreas smiled despite himself. "No, she was otherwise occupied."

"Just as I suspected. And that leaves me with a mystery." The troll frowned, a frightening look on his tusked face. "I don't like mystery, sir. Not at all. I like clarity. Cause and effect. I like neat and orderly."

Michaelson sank into the synthleather of the executive chair, and breathed a heavy sigh. "Give me your best guess, Ruger."

"Do you trust Miss Ny, sir?"

Michaelson thought for a second. "No, not really." It

was harsh to hear himself say it, but he knew the truth. She could be trying to use him, or steal from him, or blackmail him. He'd never thought she'd be that stupid; he'd hoped she was above such actions.

"We have a complete file on her, sir. She doesn't have a headphone, but she does have a simrig and a simlink transmitter. Perhaps the simlink was tweaked to disguise its signal."

"But how could she record with it?"

Ruger shrugged. "She'd need a simrecorder or a signal booster within range," he said. "Hotel security didn't pick up anything looking like boosted simsense or satellite uplink, but they've scanned their files and someone matching the description of Grids Desmond checked into room 2305 yesterday. He checked out late this morning, just after the helo took Miss Ny to Long Beach International Airport."

Michaelson needed a drink. It became all too clear to him now. She'd been nervous and anxious to leave this morning, claiming that her flight to New Orleans was leaving soon. Had Tamara recorded their sex, to blackmail him later?

Could there be any other explanation?

No. And that slotted him off.

Frag! I'll make that slitch pay. But what if . . .

Michaelson looked at his briefcase, sitting to the left of the telecom screen. The lid was open, the hardcopy of the Magus File resting inside. *Did I leave it open? Yes, I think so. What if she read through it?*

He checked to see if any pages were missing or out of order, but as far as he could tell, nothing had changed. *Maybe she didn't see it after all.*

Ruger's face peered from the telecom. "What should I do, sir?"

"Nothing. I'll handle it." Michaelson put on his impenetrable corporate smile. "Thank you for notifying me, Ruger. As usual, your thoroughness is unmatched. It will be amply rewarded."

"It's my job, sir."

Michaelson disconnected, and his smile evaporated instantly. He was up to his neck in drek. The sex was no big deal compared to the possibility that Tamara had seen the Magus File. If that got out, many lives, including his own, were forfeit.

I have to assume she glanced at the hardcopy and that now there's a simrecording of it. Spirits, I'm fragged!

He put his head in his hands and tried to relax. *I'll crush the slitch,* he thought. *If she's compromised my extraction, I'll watch her pretty face bludgeoned to a sopping red sponge.*

Slow breaths, he told himself. Relax. Think clearly.

After a minute his breathing was calm and steady, his anger abated. He meditated for a second, then knew what to do. He would call the headhunter he'd hired to get him out of Saeder-Krupp and tell her to find him a place with another megacorp. Yes, that was a good plan; he would contact Cinnamon.

He engaged the security protocol on the telecom, waiting for it to find a secure line, and then brought the fixer's number up onto his display. Once he was certain the line was secure, he tapped in the LTG number.

After a second, Cinnamon answered, her gorgeous face filling the screen. "Yes?" she said, her soft brown eyes narrowing in a barely discernible expression of distaste. "Ah, Mr. Michaelson, what can I do for you today?"

"It concerns the sale of certain talent which we discussed earlier."

Cinnamon's golden hair had fallen over one side of her face, and as she shook it back out of her eyes Michaelson reminded himself not to let her appearance deceive him. She was razor-sharp intelligent and quite resourceful. Her full lips curled down into a delicious frown. "Are you certain this is a secure line? My clients don't wish their acquisition of new assets to be made public until well after said assets have fulfilled the first contractual obligations."

"I'm confident this line is as secure as possible. And the matter is urgent."

Cinnamon looked off to the side, and Michaelson realized she was reading something from another window on her telecom screen. "No line is completely secure, Mr. Michaelson. However, I will listen."

"It seems that one of the . . . ah . . . items that was to have been part of the transaction may have . . ." He took a breath.

"Yes?"

Michaelson swallowed hard and dabbed his forehead with a handkerchief. He hated hitches and despised looking stupid. "I have reason to believe that one of the items may have been compromised."

Cinnamon pursed her lips in thought. "Is this one of the previously discussed assets that were part of the original agreement?"

"Yes."

"It has been stolen?"

"It may have been copied illegally."

"Do you still have a copy?"

"Yes."

Cinnamon ran a hand back through the shimmering gold of her hair. "Do you still wish to proceed with the talent transfer?"

Michaelson took a deep breath and tried to relax despite his pounding heart. "More than ever," he said.

Cinnamon smiled. "I see no cause for undue concern," she said. "I think my clients will agree to proceed with the transaction despite this setback. However, I'd like you to send me any information you have on the suspected culprit so I can investigate. Perhaps there is nothing to worry about."

Michaelson felt his muscles relax. He should have known that the headhunter would take care of it. That was her job after all. He hated feeling so impotent. In Essen and Berlin, his network of contacts was extensive, especially in the corporate world. But he couldn't risk disappearing there; only here in the jungle sprawl of Los Angeles would he be able to escape the vigilant eye of that fragging worm, Lofwyr.

And here, he needed Cinnamon's help. She would orchestrate his extraction and transfer. She came highly rated.

Michaelson told the telecom to interface with his private datafiles and send anything on Tamara Ny. When it was finished, he spoke, "She'll be in New Orleans this evening for a match against the Buzzsaws, but she should be back here sometime tomorrow."

"Say nothing further."

Michaelson nodded.

"For now, proceed as previously planned. I will contact you when I know more." Cinnamon cut the connection, turning Michaelson's screen black.

5

Cinnamon stared at the blank screen of her telecom and leaned back against the comfortable cushions of her blond leather couch. *Frag me!* she thought. *That dumb suit went and got himself ripped off just before his extraction.* She slid a cigarette from her gold case and lit it. In her other hand was a glass of Italian Chianti, vintage 2017. A very good year.

This should take the edge off, she thought. Cinnamon had acquired a taste for some metahuman vices of this age. Certainly, her human alias was much more palatable than her true manifest form, and the magic made dealing with the people go smoothly. She abhorred mess and often kept up the change even when she was alone, only giving in to nature when the hunger struck and she lost control.

The wine was like sweet nectar in her mouth, soothing in the back of her throat. At 500 nuyen a bottle, it better be. But at moments like this, the expense was worth it. The Michaelson extraction would not be easy; he was too valuable, too high up in Saeder-Krupp. The rumors told that he reported to Lofwyr directly. Extracting someone of such corporate power without compromising anonymity was going to be tricky under the most ideal of circumstances. And now some of the information he'd planned to take with him, a little incentive to get Mistuhama Computer Technologies to bid higher, might be worthless.

Cinnamon took another sip of her wine to calm her rising anger. *How could the slag be so fragging stupid?* Anyhow, she should notify Tashika at MCT. With a little subtle manipulation, perhaps Tashika could be convinced to commit his resources. He wouldn't want any of Michaelson's information compromised.

"Com," she said to the screen on the coffee table in front of her, "get Luc Tashika on a secure line."

The screen flashed green for a second as it routed the call through one of the thirty-two slave LTG numbers Cinnamon kept under aliases at various locations across North America. Then the call connected as Cinnamon sat forward to get a clearer look.

Luc Tashika appeared on the screen, looking somewhat suspicious. No doubt he hadn't been expecting her to call so soon. Tashika was a second-generation Asian-American, his Asian features blurred with the Anglo and Hispanic. He was a broad, stocky man with a prominent jaw, well-fleshed with pock-marked jowls and wiry black hair. He wasn't quite fat, but nearly.

Yakuza, Cinnamon knew. *An efficient, ruthless exec and not someone I want to cross.* His lack of a pure bloodline had kept him from moving any higher in MCT's corporate structure, and that gave him an angry disposition. Luckily, Tashika liked her.

"*Konichiwa,* Cinnamon," he said, and his head bowed slightly. "What can I do for you?"

Cinnamon gave him her most seductive smile. "I have news of a potentially unfortunate nature."

Tashika laughed, a high-screeching sound. Not at all pleasant. "To the point as usual," he said. "That's why I like you. Okay, I'm listening."

Cinnamon unraveled the situation to him, watching him carefully for a reaction. Tashika wasn't good at hiding his emotions. The chance to obtain valuable information without paying extra for it obviously thrilled him. Tashika wanted that file.

When she was done, Tashika bowed his head slightly. "*So ka,* my friend," he said. "I will find out what Miss Tamara Ny knows. Either way, Michaelson has the information and you will be paid the same. I will trim it from his new commission. You should not have to pay for his mistake."

"*Domo arigato,* Mr. Tashika. It is always a pleasure doing biz with you."

"You're welcome," Tashika said, and disconnected.

Cinnamon breathed a sigh of relief, and turned off the telecom. *With Tashika working on it, the situation should resolve itself in short order,* she thought. *Still, I should get a decker online to monitor things.*

She leaned back against the blond leather cushions once

more. Her work was nearly done. Or at least she hoped. She sipped the wine, then brought another cigarette to her lips. Michaelson's new salary at MCT was astronomical and would easily absorb any cost. Tamara Ny was the only person who would really pay the price, whether she was guilty or not.

6

Jonathon's headclock showed 03:27:46 PM and counting. Four hours to game time. The Louisiana Superdome
stretched above and over him as he ran the maze of concrete barriers that made up the playing arena. He always
ran the entire field on foot before a match, just to get that
extra sense, that extra edge which might prove to be the
tiny advantage he needed.

The corridors of the maze varied in width from one to
five meters, each side a uniform 2.5 meters in height,
curved into a half pipe so that the bikes could ride high on
the walls for acrobatics or fast turns. The lanes were
painted navy blue on this side of the arena and yellow on
the other—the colors of the Buzzsaws—and streaked with
black tread stains.

The stadium was quiet this early, only the faint echo of
the training room's sound system audible to Jonathon as he
increased his pace and concentrated on the details of the
maze. This was as tricky one. Few straight lanes, many
twists and curves that doubled across the midline. When
jittertime came, knowledge of location was crucial.

Jonathon was breathing heavily by the time he reached
the goal area on the far side—a two-meter-diameter circle,
painted yellow with a huge circular saw in the center. Only
three lanes opened up to the goal circle. Jonathon increased
his pace, running across to the corridor that led to the skyway—a ramp that traveled across the center of the maze
from one end to the other. This one was about two meters
wide, perhaps enough for two bikers side by side. Two excellent linebikers or one lancebiker.

Jonathon stopped at the apex of the skyway, about three
meters above the top of the maze. He took one last look at
the whole, letting his mind absorb the arena. Then he ran
down the other side of the elevated track and headed out

through the penalty bunkers and quickly past the communication bay where Terry was warming up the team's trideo and simsense equipment. Terry was a grotesquely fat ork with a crush on Jonathon. Luckily she didn't look up from her work as he ran by.

Jonathon breathed a sigh of relief as he slowed to a walk and made his way past the offices where he could hear Coach Kalish's raspy voice bitching at one of the promoters about too many reporters in the secure areas. Jonathon bypassed the check station where the referees would soon survey each player's motorcycle, armor, and weapons to make sure everything was consistent with World Combat Cycling League regulations.

The training area was underneath the actual playing arena, down a wide spiral ramp. It consisted of a locker room, exercise equipment, a warm-up track, and several simulators. Jonathon found Boges and Mason in the garage area, drinking hi-carb shakes as they watched Vic, the dwarf mechanic, work on Mason's BMW Blitzen.

Mason was an ork of uncommon ugliness, which was saying something because Jonathon found orks, as a rule, the ugliest of all metahumans. Mason was also unusually lacking in the intelligence department, but when it came to jittertime, there was no one else Jonathon would rather have gunning in front of him. Mason handled his bike with ease, was wicked nasty with a lance, and almost impervious to injury.

Boges was one of the goalies—huge even for a sasquatch, bulked up to nearly troll weight. His fur glimmered silver and black in the fluorescent light. Rumor had it that Boges was pretty smart, but Jonathon thought not; nobody with half a synapse would play goalie in this game at this level. Of course, he'd been super-equipped with skillsofts and other neural implants to make possible full communication with the rest of the team.

"Hoi, chummers," Jonathon said as he walked in.

"Hoi," they said.

"Seen Tam?" Jonathon asked as he picked a towel from the clean pile and wiped the sweat from his neck. Earlier, Tamara had seemed distracted and distant. Something was wrong, he could tell. He could always tell. And the feeling had bothered him, insinuating into his thoughts until he couldn't shake it. He had to find out what it was, get it behind him before the game.

"She's over at the simdecks," Boges said. "Going over some Dougan Rose pulses. Said something about looking for weaknesses."

"Dougan has no weaknesses," Jonathon said.

Boges laughed. "That's what I told her."

Jonathon crossed to the row of simsense decks where Tamara lay in a recliner, jacked in, simming one of the Buzzsaws' earlier matches. He dropped down into the simrecliner beside her and jacked in to the same recording, choosing Dougan's point of view from the menu.

Sudden disorientation, slight nausea pulling at his gut as he became Dougan Rose. Cold sweat ran down his back, soaked into his fireproof plycra unibody. Over the unibody was the thick Kevlar III armor, integrated with panels of slick polycarbonate like segments of an armadillo so that Dougan could maneuver inside. The segments were painted bright yellow and blue, with a huge buzzsaw on his plated pectorals.

The plexishield faceplate of Dougan's helmet was scarred, making Jonathon's vision slightly uneven for a moment before he adjusted mentally. A fiber-optic line integrated into his armor, letting the datajack at his temple connect through to the command module in the seat of the extensively modified Yamaha Rapier at his tailbone. He piloted the bike cybernectically, like an extension of himself, leaving his hands free for more important things like weapons.

Clamps on the Yamaha locked into hooks along the armor of his legs, making him inseparable from the light machine. The clamps were linked through the bike's dog brain into his mind and would release at his command. The Yamaha weighed less than he did; it was for high-speed moves and acrobatics. For showing off and scoring. Dodging and running, not fighting.

A concussion grenade exploded two meters ahead as Dougan accelerated toward the flying bogey. Dougan's cybereyes automatically compensated for the flash, something Jonathon's natural eyes couldn't do without special glasses. Dougan's transparent tactical display showed the clock at five seconds and an overlay of the arena maze, his teammates' positions showing as yellow motorcycle icons. The opposing team's positions were unknown, as per the rules.

Dougan mentally cranked the accelerator on his Yamaha.

Dougan's vehicle control rig wasn't as responsive as Jonathon's, but the millisecond of sluggishness didn't seem to affect his scoring ability. In the sim, Dougan flashed through the smoke left by the grenade blast and unleashed his polycarb whip, sending it cracking toward the bogey, which carried the red game flag.

Jonathon used the same type of tool as his weapon of choice; great reach, better for snagging the flag. Better for dismounting opponents at a distance. Just evil.

The bogey drone hovered just above the tops of the lane dividers, zipping along a quasi-random path, with the thin, flexible flagpole on it. The tip of Dougan's whip coiled around the pole and pulled the weighted flag from the bogey. With a quick jerk of his wrist, he snapped the flag toward him, then grabbed the pole and jammed it into the slot behind his seat.

Dougan slowed slightly to allow his teammate, Gorgon—a large human lancebiker—to rumble past into a blocking position. The lancebiker rode a huge, armored Honda Viking, his blunt plastic lance locked into the brace above the right fork of the front wheel. Dougan accelerated into formation, his front tire just to the left and slightly behind Gorgon's rear wheel.

A voice crackled over the headset. "Oncoming. Two lancers and one liner."

Dougan barked into his helmet mike. "Copy, T-bone. Lay suppression. Pollack and Webster run interference."

"Copy, Dougan." There was a distant *ka-thunk*, as T-bone fired.

The concussion grenade hit around the curve just ahead of Dougan and Gorgon. A blinding flash of white, dimming as his eyes compensated, followed by a ball of flame billowing up toward the stadium's rafters. Then the thunderclap hit, rattling the air around him.

A deafening cheer went up from the crowd, watching from behind the thick macroglass shielding. T-bone's voice filled Dougan's head: "Concussion ineffective. Pollack and Webster won't reach you in time."

Dougan took a deep breath. "Fragging-A," he muttered. The curve approached at breakneck speed. "Okay, Gorgon, this is gonna be tight. I'm going up and over. You scan, chummer?"

"Not enough distance, Dougan."

"I'm the flyer," he said. "Let me worry about it."

"It's your funeral."

Dougan stopped his bike for a second to let Gorgon move his big Honda into position near the curve of the lane. Cranking the throttle with a mental command, Dougan crouched low against the bike as the Yamaha squealed into a full-out run.

T-bone's voice boomed in his ear, "Five seconds to enemy contact. I'm gonna cross the skyway to declaw their thunderbiker."

Gorgon came to a full stop a few meters from the curve and unhitched his lance from its bracket. As Dougan reached forty klicks per hour, Gorgon braced his lance upright against his boot.

Dougan unleashed his whip, sending it cracking toward Gorgon just as the four enemy bikes rounded the curve, the blunt tips of three lances jutting at Dougan.

They'll hit Gorgon regardless, Jonathon thought. *But Dougan might just make it.*

The tip of Dougan's whip coiled around Gorgon's heavy lance, and Dougan locked the handle into the holster pin on his bike. The whip cord came taut as Dougan swung out wide, riding up the slope of the pipe. It pulled him into an impossible arc. His bike cut a sharp half-circle using the whip as radius, up the steep, half-pipe bank of the lane to shoot straight into the air.

Dougan threw his weight back as his wheels cleared the top of the barrier, sending himself and his bike into a backflip. The crowd gasped in unison as he tucked in close to the machine to complete the flip, then came down on the other side of the wall into a clear lane. He clamped on full brakes, skidding to a halt.

"Talk to me, T-bone," he said. "Where's the enemy? Where's backup?"

"Ion and Chibba are six ticks behind you. No enemy between you and ground zero."

Dougan checked his tactical. Clock ticking toward the thirty-second mark. Toward jittertime. "No enemy?" Dougan asked as he swung his Yamaha around and rocketed toward the Timber Wolves' goal circle. Ground zero.

Jonathon felt Tamara jack out of the sim. The slight discontinuity as she unplugged herself from the recorder. He stopped the simulation and jacked out.

Tamara hadn't moved. She sat stock-still in the simre-cliner next to him, her hands over her face.

Crying?

"Tam, what's wrong?"

She drew her hands from her eyes slowly. Then gave a heavy sigh. "Dougan Rose," she said. "He never makes a mistake."

But that wasn't it, Jonathon knew. "Come on, Tam. What's going on?"

"Mistakes," she said. Then she sat in silence for a minute. Finally, barely a whisper, "I fragged up."

Jonathon leaned in. "What is it . . . what's wrong?"

She just shook her head and wouldn't look at him.

"Talk to me, Tam," he insisted.

"It's bad."

"Is it something to do with Michaelson? We can fix it. I know we can, but you've gotta tell me if I'm going to help you."

"You can't help, Jonathon. Nobody can. You're going to have to let me fly solo on this one."

"But—"

"No. I won't drag you into it." She put her hands over her eyes again, trying to hide her emotions from him. "If I got you into another mess like the Multnomah Falls thing, I'd never be able to forgive myself."

"That was an accident," Jonathon said. But he knew that whatever she'd done must be serious for her to bring up Multnomah Falls.

Now she was murmuring to herself, "Grids was right, it's too big. Too dangerous. Too fragging dangerous."

"Grids? What did that dreamer—?"

"Leave him out of it!" she yelled suddenly. "It was all my idea so just leave him out!"

Jonathon held his hands up. "Sorry, Tam. I didn't . . ."

But she stood, wiping her eyes, and walked away. As he watched the retreating shape of her rigid back, the memory of the accident at Multnomah Falls came over him. The day everything changed in their lives.

After flight school, Jonathon and Tamara had flown proto-type Federated-Boeing fighter jets out of Fort Lewis in Seattle. He still considered that the best time of his life, and often dreamed of climbing into the cockpit of an FB1680 once more. Of sliding into the narrow, form-adjusting seat in his blue-gray flight suit, jacking himself through his helmet and into the powerful bird.

The FB1680 was code-named Falcon, and as such, it was smaller and faster than its predecessor, the Eagle. Sleek, single-wing design, painted a radar-absorbing matte black, nearly invisible to electronic detection. It had fully vectored thrust, VTOL maneuverability, and blazing speed. The only things quicker were a few elite cruise drones, and that was only because they could pull gees that would kill any metahuman.

Jonathon remembered the day of their sixth test flight as clearly as his breakfast with Synthia. How could he ever forget? He had strapped himself into his bird on an overcast day in mid-March. Wednesday, March 13, 2054. He tried not to think about the fifty-million nuyen price tag on this little military toy, and slotted the datajack. Mind to metal. The cybernetic kiss of electronic lips.

Suddenly he became the machine. Cameras and sensors embedded into the black metal skin of the bird gave Jonathon 360-degree vision, hearing, touch. Plus he had extra senses. Radar relayed from the tower showed him a 3-D view of the surrounding airscape. Digital information about wind speed and altitude were translated into taste and smell.

When Tamara jacked into her Falcon next to him, her simsense link synchronized with his, and they merged. Two planes and two minds becoming one entity. UCAS military headware made it possible.

When Jonathon and Tamara had enlisted together and volunteered for the special pilot-training program, Colonel Carmen Johansen had interviewed them. She was looking for non-magicians who were psychologically compatible and could survive the intense scrutiny of prolonged and continuous wet-feed simsense interconnection. Many previous attempts had ended in insanity or mutual addiction.

After their basic and advanced flight training, he and Tamara had undergone an extensive and grueling series of physical and mental tests. Then they were asked to participate in the test-pilot studies. They accepted instantly; it had been one of Jonathon's dreams to fly fighter jets, and this was that dream coming true in a way he could never have imagined.

After they signed the liability release, both he and

Tamara went under the knife. The headware they got was a prototype vehicle control rig, very fast. Very advanced. Plus the doctors installed a full-X simrig and a sophisticated transmitter that acted as a simlink as well as a single-channel remote control unit for the vehicle rig, so if Jonathon ever had to eject, he could still remote-pilot the expensive aircraft to a safe landing.

The simsense 'ware kept Jonathon and Tamara connected to each other during their flights; it allowed Jonathon to switch instantly to Tamara's point of view during a test move, then back. And over the course of months, they grew to know each other more intimately than he'd ever thought possible between two people. They knew each other's emotions, sensations, actions, responses. The technology had created as close to a telepathic link as could be accomplished without magic.

That thirteenth day of March, their sixth test flight of the Falcon, was their 213th mission together. And their last.

Their tactical officer was a dwarf named Theodore Rica. Theo was a brilliant mathematical mind in a squat, muscular body. Under his black curls, he was equipped with the same headware as Tamara and Jonathon, but he didn't fly with them. He remained in the control bunker in Fort Lewis, pulling together radar and satellite recon data to reconstruct an accurate taste of the airscape. He also took in the digital data flow from the two jets, flew the "enemy" test drones, and orchestrated the exercises.

That day, Theo directed them up and south of Seattle, over Salish-Shidhe territory. Burning fire rocketed through Jonathon as he throttled up his jets. His meat body sank into the cushioned seat as his mental body directed thrust down. With a searing push he was airborne, angling then hurtling then blasting across the forests of the Salish-Shidhe tribal lands.

Tamara nudged his left-wing space, flying just outside his slipstream. Jonathon knew from her stance, from her surge of adrenaline, her laughing, which he felt through the link. From a million tiny and subtle clues, he knew she wanted to lead this run. So he acquiesced, letting her slip past into lead formation.

They moved low and fast, edging down to skim the tree-tops, feeling the tickle of douglas fir needles as they blew past. Theo's voice crackled over the com, "Bogey at ten

o'clock." He highlighted the target on the tactical overlay—
an Aztechnology *Cheetah* class drone, a remote-rigged unit
that was no match for the Falcon speedwise, but could turn
on a credstick, and maneuvered through trees and canyons
like a cockroach through dirty dishes.

The drone flashed in and out of radar, but once Theo
had highlighted it, Tamara and Jonathon never lost track.
Flying as a unit, one or the other always sensed it. Simul-
sim-linked. One being made of two minds, two black
metal bodies in perfect unison.

"Closing," Tamara said as she narrowed the distance
with a spark of afterburner, and they found themselves
weaving through the fissures of the newly erupted Cas-
cades. The ice canyons around Mount Rainier, then the
scarred earth near Mount Saint Helens.

Tamara had the targeting array nearly locked down
when the drone made an unexpected move. It cut south in
a quick turn and bolted for the Columbia River, toward
the elven nation of Tir Tairngire. Later, Jonathon learned
that part of the test centered around their response to this
move.

The overly paranoid elven security forces were under
orders to shoot down any aircraft violating their airspace,
and any pilot would know that, but this was a drone. No
time for complex analysis. Their mission was to destroy
the bogey, and that's just what Tamara was going to do.
She angled her thrust and spun into a sharp carving turn.

Jonathon let his autopilot slave to her commands,
though he was ready to assume control if necessary. *She's
trying to play hero again,* he thought.

"Tam, we're too fraggin' close to civilians for anything
so risky," he barked into his headset, even though she
would know how he felt from the simlink long before she
heard the words.

Tamara always had a craving for ratings. Always wanted
to be admired, the center of attention. And that was her ulti-
mate dream, to feature in sims, to become a megastar whose
name was known to the whole world.

"Just three more seconds," came Tamara's reply as she
armed two of her Ares Rattlesnake III air-to-air missiles.

Jonathon readied his own with a thought as the air below them grew cool and moist. They dropped to skim just
above the surface of the broad river. Sun glared off blue

water, smells of fish and mist hit him, and the water flew up behind them into the vacuum of their wake.

"Abort," came Theo's voice. "Repeat, abort."

But it was too late.

In the split second before Tamara fired, a gathering of people on the far bank came into view. The drone cut sharp, downriver, its tiny wings glistening a dull bronze against the twinkling silver of the river's surface.

Ahead, a tall waterfall fell from the top of the gorge. Multnomah Falls. At its base, tourist buildings sat, crammed with unsuspecting civilians. The two Ares Rattlesnakes locked on target and flew from Tamara's bird. One hit the drone just as it turned downstream. The other missed.

Jonathon never discovered why it happened. Why the missile didn't track its target. Perhaps it encountered some electronic jamming from Tir Tairngire. That would be up to the elves' typical paranoid standards.

The other missile rocketed into the parking lot of the tourist attraction, retargeting on a huge bus full of corporate children, the sons and daughters of sararimen from Portland. Blew it to shrapnel in a huge mushrooming fire cloud. Jonathon saw the silver shape of the bus lift in the middle, split open for a brief moment before the whole thing turned to shrapnel engulfed in flame and smoke.

They learned later that nearly two hundred people burned to death in the explosion, but it was a number Jonathon could not comprehend. How could he and Tam have done such a thing, even by accident?

Tamara went into shock, and Jonathon had to take control of her jet. Fly them both back to Fort Lewis, with a growing sense of distance, the increasing numbness of unreality surrounding his brain. The Tir Tairngire government demanded prosecution of all the responsible parties. Theo, Tamara, and Jonathon were court-martialed, sentenced to five years in the military prison in Fairfax, and permanent ground. They'd only had to serve two years, but they'd never fly again; the elven High Council had warned the corporate world that any attempts to hire them as pilots would be considered a direct affront.

Jonathon and Tamara had decided to try professional combat cycling. And though riding the line was thriller chiller and another of his childhood fantasies come true, it couldn't compare to the rush of flying.

Now, Jonathon gritted his teeth against the frustration of the memory and pushed himself up from the simrecliner. He took a deep breath and went after Tamara. "Wait," he said, catching up with her. "Whatever happened, whatever trouble you're in now," he said, "I want to help if I can. We were a team back in Fort Lewis. And we still are."

Tamara bowed her head and stared down at the gray concrete floor. "No, Jonathon," she said, slowly shaking her head. "You know too much already." Then she looked up at him. She stared into his eyes with a dull, glazed expression.

He saw conviction in the flat color of her irises, in her dead stare. And he knew what her response would be.

"I fly solo on this one, Jonathon," she said. "Solo."

Jonathon had never felt more alone.

7

Luc Tashika stared out the window of his seventieth-story office at the infection that was Los Angeles. His building—the sleek, black MCT monolith—pushed up through the concrete and steel canopy of the urban blight. His building was a pinnacle of polished obsidian glass, shiny and clean against a backdrop of grimy concrete. Well, it wasn't his yet. But perhaps soon . . .

Tashika ran his fingers through his wiry black hair and contemplated his next move. *This Michaelson acquisition must not fail,* he thought. *He's my ticket out of the entertainment division.* Tashika had been left to stagnate by the purists in the corp, the oyabun distrusting the loyalty of his mongrel blood. Tashika oversaw subsidiaries such as Boromaker, Matrix News Corp, and the sports franchises, but entertainment was a dead-end track at MCT, and he had reached its terminus.

Michaelson will be my ticket back into electronics, perhaps even into the president's office.

Tashika's gaze tracked up toward the ocean from the crumbling concrete scourge that clung like guano to the feet of his building. The view was much the same all over Downtown and East Hollywood, but changed after a couple of kilometers as the sickly tenements gave way to the walled enclaves of Studio City–Beverly Hills, Bel Air, and the Palisades.

Even the tsunami of '45, which had ripped many of the mansions from their precarious perches along the ocean cliffs, hadn't stopped the ultra-rich from putting more grandiose houses and castles in their place. Now, the sea of beggars below crashed like waves against the walls of the elite, trying to erode away their hard-earned lifestyle and security.

He turned from the window and walked to his desk chair. *Well, it won't happen to me,* he thought.

The walls of his office were a tasteful antique white, unadorned except for two glass-framed holopics. One was a morale poster of Tiger Mitsuhama, the founder of the corporation, and the other was a portrait of Samba Oi, chairman of the board of directors. Samba Oi held the true power in the corporation. Each photo served to remind Tashika of where he was and where he wanted to be.

He sat at his desk and activated the flat-screen telecom. Bridget's lovely face appeared. "Yes, Mr. Tashika?"

"Get me Dougan Rose on a secure line," he said.

"Right away, sir."

Less than a minute passed before she had Dougan on the line. Tashika was treated to the elven face of one slotted-off biker. "Why the frag are you calling me? In case you didn't know, I'm trying to prepare for a playoff match." Dougan's features were those of an exaggerated elf—cheekbones so high they nearly blocked out his perfect almond eyes. The points of his ears, sticking up through his straight black hair, seemed sharp enough to cut.

On the side of Dougan's neck showed the death's-head tattoo that had become his trademark. It was large and unmistakable—a surreal vision of a metahuman skull with fiery wings.

It was a brilliant move to retain the tattoo, Tashika congratulated himself, *all those years ago when I discovered Dougan, changed him and brought him to the Buzzsaws.*

"Something very important has come up, Rose-*san*," Tashika said.

"What is it this time? Haven't I done enough for you?"

Tashika smiled, leaning back in his chair. "The debt you owe me has yet to be paid in full."

"I owe you nothing."

That burned Tashika up inside. *How ungrateful.* "Let's just say, *elf,* that what I've done for you—what I know—is worth more than you've paid."

"And probably will ever be able to pay, right?"

"Give the man a cigar. Have you been slotting those intelligence chips?"

Dougan sneered at him through the screen. "Just tell me what you want."

Tashika saw the hatred in Dougan's eyes, but Luc Tashika was used to dealing with people who hated him. All part of the biz of climbing to the top. "There is a certain individual who is known to you," Tashika said. "Her name is Tamara Ny, and she rides for—"

"Cut the gangster dialogue and get to the point. Half the world knows her."

"Yes, that's true. And I want you to make sure Miss Ny leaves this evening's match before it's over."

"In a body bag, right?"

"No. Most definitely not. But a DocWagon helo would be perfect. I will intercept it enroute."

"You want me to injure her?"

Tashika nodded. "Make it look like an accident."

Dougan breathed a sigh. "Of course," he said, irritated. "Is that all, corp-*san*? Or is there anyone else you'd like me to hurt while I'm at it?"

"No," Tashika said. Then he cut the connection and asked Bridget to get a certain DocWagon employee on the telecom—a fine artist in the practice of persuasion who Tashika knew through the yakuza. Doctor Franklin was not *kobun,* not part of the organization. And that was what made his involvement perfect for Tashika. Any yakuza involvement would trickle back to the oyabun, and Tashika did not want that.

I will allow no one to steal the credit for the Michaelson acquisition, he thought. *When I reveal Michaelson's stolen portfolio, they will have to move me up.*

Any of the portfolio would be valuable, but Tashika wanted one thing more than anything else. The Magus File. Cinnamon had promised that Michaelson would bring it along with him, and for Tashika that file alone was worth the nuyen. Combined with their own data, the research it contained could put Mitsuhama Computer Technologies years ahead of the other megacorps. It was Tashika's ticket to the presidency, with Michaelson as his top aide.

And maybe, just maybe, the Magus File was part of the data Tamara Ny had managed to steal. If so, Doctor Franklin would extract that information from the elf biker slitch. Tashika would know soon.

The prospect gave him a hard-on. Which was exactly the way he liked it.

8

In her three-bedroom house in San Bernardino, Maria Nightfeather cleaned up after dinner with Pedro and Angelina. She stood in the blue-and-gray tiled kitchen, rinsing the pots and pans and absently scratching the tattoo on her neck. The Muerte symbol—a death's head with wings of flame.

La Muerte was the El Infierno gang her brother, Jesse, had led so many years ago. She and Dougan Rose had both been Muertes, and stayed on when the gang had turned to shadowrunning. They'd been quite a force, all bound together by Jesse's dark, sharp eyes. By the strength of his leadership, which was never questioned. All tied by the symbolic bond of their identical tattoos.

La Muerte had been running the shadows for just a little over a year when the government had decided to declare war on the gang-ruled El Infierno. The California State Guard, Lone Star, and assorted merc forces had come pouring into its streets to bomb, burn, and smash everything in their path. Jesse had died that day, giving up his own life to save the rest. After that, La Muerte had disbanded. Maria stayed with Dougan for a few years, sharing his bed as they traveled out of California Free State, trying to escape from their past.

Now, Maria shook her head, trying to settle those memories back into the pockets and niches were they belonged, where they couldn't come out to haunt her. But her thoughts had been turning more and more to Dougan lately. And she knew why—the combat biker playoffs.

She didn't want to think about him after all these years of trying to forget him. But he was still there in her mind, still there every time she looked at Pedro's high cheekbones and almond eyes.

Dougan had disappeared before Pedro was born, forcing

Maria to sell her magical talents while caring for an infant. But it wasn't long before Dougan was a famous athlete and began depositing credit into her account. She never asked for it, but she certainly wasn't going to refuse.

"Pedro," she said. "It's your turn to clear the table. Get to it or you can't watch the game."

"Okay, Mom," came the reply. And soon the boy entered the kitchen carrying the dirty dishes. Pedro was almost twelve, with olive skin and black hair like Maria's, though he didn't seem to have her ability with magic. At least he hadn't shown it yet.

Angelina came skipping in behind Pedro. "Can I watch too?" she asked. Angelina was six and darker-skinned than Maria and Pedro, almost black like her father—a human named Wallace who passed through Maria's life once in a while.

"No, Angel," she said. "Talon will help you with your homework."

"Please, Mom. Please let me watch."

"No, it's too violent. No discussion."

Angelina gave her a scowl, but knew Maria's resolve was inflexible. She turned and walked out. Her footsteps echoed hollowly on the wooden stairs as she climbed up to her room where Talon, Maria's ally spirit, would supervise Angelina's homework.

"Hurry, Mom," Pedro said. "It's coming on."

Maria started the dishwasher and walked into the trideo room just as the pre-game hype began. "Millions are watching worldwide," said the plastic-faced man whose 3-D image hovered inside the trid box. "Biker bars are crammed full of combat cycling fans, all eyes focused on New Orleans. It's the fourth game in a best-of-five series for the WCCL Championship.

"The LA Sabers led by superstar Jonathon Winger has got to win to stay alive. But Dougan Rose is the greatest linebiker in the history of the World Combat Cycling League, and his Buzzsaws are at the top of their game. Here to give us an in-depth analysis of the two star players is Rand Anpretty. Rand?"

The angle shifted to a dark-haired, but just as plastic, elven face with perfect make-up. Enticing, but distant. "Dougan Rose is the most popular biker in the world," the elf said. "And most analysts believe he's the best linebiker in the history of the sport. But the younger crowd identifies with Jonathon Winger. He makes up for experience with sheer athletic ability and intelligent play.

"Hard-core Buzzsaw fans think Winger is still no match for Rose, but followers of the Sabers point to Winger's mysterious link with teammate Tamara Ny. Ny is a top-flight biker herself, one of only six female elves in the whole league. Passions are running high across the globe as millions tune to watch."

Maria felt some of that passion despite herself. A thrill of excitement coursed through her as she sat down next to Pedro. This was going to be fun.

9

The score was even at three points each. Jonathon took a slow, deep breath and tried to ignore the screaming of the crowd, crammed to the rafters inside the Louisiana Superdome. The roar was deafening, drowning out the drone of the rice burners and even the deep throb of the lance-bikers' Harleys.

Jonathon silently thanked the international rules for the ten-meter barrier of reinforced macroglass that separated the crowd from the combat maze on the stadium floor. The barrier prevented stray stun rounds from injuring the fans, but more important, it kept rabid spectators from mobbing the players.

Jonathon quickly checked his weapons as the officials prepared to release the bogey. Three shots of stun ammo in his Roomsweeper clip, holstered at his right thigh. The Roomsweeper was a shotgun with a short black barrel and almost no stock, outfitted with a smartlink interface and great for doing stun damage to a wide area. A standard-issue mace made from high-impact plastic and densiplast hung from the stripped frame of the Suzuki. In his hand, he held a polycarb filament whip. With a two-meter-reach and a wicked snap, the whip was his weapon of choice—delicate, tactile, and at the same time, deadly.

His blue and silver armor fit tightly against his augmented body, pumped and taut, prepped for the imminent release of the bogey. The rigid plates of Jonathon's armor dug into his skin as he wove his custom Suzuki Aurora into position. This bike was heavily modified, felt like an extension of his body as he controlled it cybernetically. Straight jack. He felt the engine purring like a second heart, the wheels gripping the concrete like another set of legs.

The bike had been stripped down to the titanium alloy frame to make it light and fast. Oh so fast off the line. No heavy armor for this dragon. But Jonathon had added a few extras—microbust hydrojack in the suspension for certain jumping moves. Extra sensors for improved rigging control, and all the necessary latches and holsters to lock down whatever weapons he needed. The bike's balance had been honed to perfection for Jonathon's size and weight when his armored legs were latched to the frame. It was as chill, as wiz a ride as the rules would allow, and he had six more just like it in the team garage because he never knew how many he'd destroy in a game.

The sensory details of the stadium faded from Jonathon's awareness as he steadied his breathing and focused on the here and now. The smell of exhaust and the scent of a hundred thousand sweating fans thankfully receded. The roar of the crowd faded to background static. Jonathon was ready.

He brought the tactical overlay of the combat maze into focus on his retinal display. Four Saber linebikers wove along this side of the midline. Jonathon held the straight corridor, which ran from goal to goal in the shadow of the skyway; Tamara and Bozwell patrolled sections of lane one, and the dwarf—Hragth—took his place in the tight arc of lane three.

Just across the midline from Jonathon rode Dougan Rose. Like Jonathon, Dougan wore semi-flexible Kevlar-3 armor slotted with narrow, rigid plates of high-impact polycarb. Like wearing an armadillo skin, except stronger and with more freedom of motion. Dougan's was bright yellow with a blue number "5" painted on his back and chest, and "ROSE" along the line of his shoulder.

All external distractions dwindled as Jonathon achieved focus. Dougan seemed preoccupied and was riding a little under his usual spectacular level of play. But even that did not break Jonathon's focus. His zen.

Only the linebikers could move before play began, and only on their side of the midline. The lancebikers had to hold their position until the flag carried by the bogey drone had been snagged and slotted by one of the liners. Riding lance for the Sabers were the orks, Mason and Webber, plus Tank, a fat black human, and Gnash, the troll. The thunderbiker was a dwarf named Smitty, and he too had to maintain his position until flagsnag.

The lancers were set, ready to rock'n'roll. Smitty revved

the engine of his Yamaha Rapier, a bike superficially similar to a linebiker's machine. But the thunderbiker had two distinct differences, first was the fixed-mount grenade launcher and second was the heavy ballistic armor. Smitty's role during play consisted of establishing a position on the skyway so that he could locate enemy riders, then relay that information to Jonathon and the team. The dwarf also got three chances per play to wreak havoc with concussion grenades. When used at key moments, those babies would take out three our four riders in a single shot.

Everyone was ready for play to begin. Clock reset.

Breath.

The officials in their turrets—protected crow's-nest platforms on three-meter masts—raised their green flags. Bogey release imminent.

Jonathon tensed.

Breath.

"Bogey away," came Bozwell's screechy voice.

Jonathon rolled, accelerating across the midline toward Dougan Rose, pulling his mace with his left hand, cracking his whip with his right. Trying to establish position for flagsnag.

Dougan feinted left and shot right, up the rounded slope of the lane's floor, around Jonathon and down the corridor.

Jonathon spun around to face Dougan again, expecting to see the bogey shoot by overhead. Instead he heard a shot.

Tamara's Roomsweeper.

"Bogey down," came her voice over the com. "Blew that drone clean out of the air. Flag in play. Repeat. Flag in play."

"In position." That was Smitty.

Jonathon saw a flash of white highlight the top of the wall on his left as a concussion grenade exploded in the next lane. Then the sound hit, shaking the air around him. *That's Tamara's position,* he thought.

"Tam?"

"I'm wiz," she said. "Dodged at the last second."

Smitty came on. "Two lancers approaching, Tam. Retreat for backup. Mason and Gnash, swing over."

"On it." Mason.

"Rollin'," growled Gnash.

"Retreating to skyway," Tamara said.

"Negative," came Smitty's voice. "Pick up Mason and

Gnash at turn seventeen. No time for skyway. Crunch in twenty seconds."

There was a *ka-thunk* and another explosion shook the lane on Jonathon's left. Then Dougan Rose approached, moving back toward his goal circle to help his team. Jonathon stashed his mace and pulled the Roomsweeper from his thigh holster.

The induction pads in his gloves synched with the smartlink in the gun's grip to show a dim red circle over his vision. The center of the circle corresponded with the gun's barrel, and the perimeter was the smartlink's estimate of damage scatter at Jonathon's focus distance.

Jonathon focused on Dougan, targeting his approaching shape. Then he fired, gel pellets spraying at the other biker. Dougan snapped his whip as he rocketed past, trying to make Jonathon alter his shot. The whip cracked against Jonathon's shoulder with a sharp shock, the distraction giving Dougan a split second to dodge the main force of the blast.

Jonathon had no time to lament as Dougan faded behind him. He had to get to turn seventeen. The count was up to nineteen seconds. The most he had left were eleven seconds, but any one of those could be the last. That was the thrill of jittertime.

Tamara's voice came over the com radio, "I'm cutting to skyway for crossover. Mason will front for me. Jonathon underneath. The rest of you slags block the ramp behind me."

"Bad idea, Tam," Smitty said. "Not enough time. Take Mason through lane three and jet. Better chances, and you can cross over to lane two if any major drek-fraggers find you."

"Too late, Smitty," Tamara said. "I'm there, and I've got six seconds to spare."

Suddenly, a concussion grenade blew Smitty off the skyway. Jonathon saw the dwarf get knocked back from the ball of flame, then fall five meters and hit the edge of a concrete barrier under his bike. Jonathon winced inside.

"Jonathon," Tamara said, "run ground shadow. Mason, you're up."

Jonathon watched as Mason's huge, armored BMW Blitzen cranked up the arc of the skyway. Approaching from the opposite direction were three Buzzsaws. T-bone on his thunderbike, Gorgon with his lance, jousting on the narrow path, head-to-head against the big ork—Mason. Behind them was a linebiker named Pollack.

Tam'll never make it across midline, Jonathon thought.

The Buzzsaws' maze was set up such that only three lanes crossed the midline between territories. Two lanes crossed it three times each, snaking in a series of hairpin curves. Jonathon's corridor was straight, and it crossed the center only once, running exactly below the skyway as it stretched from one goal area to the other.

"I'm here," he said, accelerating beneath Tamara as she shot onto the skyway behind Mason's block. Gorgon and Mason clashed as the big ork's lance connected dead center with Gorgon's chest. The rending of metal and the sharp crack of macroplast armor rang out above the roar of the crowd. Both bikes stopped.

Gorgon flew clear of his bike and missed the narrow strip of the skyway, plummeting to land hard against the edge of Jonathon's lane and slide limply down the curve of the half-pipe. Motionless.

Mason's bike slid out from under him, and he went into a skid as Tamara edged around him and shot on toward the midline.

Jittertime approached as Jonathon moved around the hulking form of Gorgon, lying next to his big hog.

"I'm not going to make it," Tamara said.

"No drek," came Smitty.

Jonathon looked up, riding exactly beneath her, matching her speed. "Ready for drop when necessary," he said.

Tamara pulled the flag from its latch and held it out at arm's length, over the edge of the skyway ramp as she approached T-bone and Pollack. They must have known what she was about to do because they started to turn around. But she pulled the flag in close to her to lure them back. They would have to force her to pass it.

At the last second she dropped the flag and skidded to a halt in front of them. Jonathon focused on the falling shaft. Intentionally dropping the banner pole meant ejection from the match, but only if the pole's base actually hit the concrete.

Jonathon saw T-bone fire his last concussion grenade down at him, while Pollack turned away to intercept. But Tamara let fly her polycarb net, which tied up Pollack all nice and neat and tangled in his spokes. All that happened

in the background, and Jonathon was barely conscious of
it. His focus was on the flag, its weighted end leading its
plummet. He was in position; his velocity matched it.

Jonathon caught it in both hands just as the concussion
blast seared the air around him, deafening him with its explosion. The grenade sent him sprawling, but he never
lost his grip on the flag.

No penalty.

Jonathon pushed himself up onto his wheels and shook
his head. He was in one piece. Whole. He jammed the flag
into its latch and made straight for midline.

"Three, two, one. Jittertime, chummers!" It was Smitty's
voice.

Jittertime was a random amount of time between zero
and thirty seconds, after which the bell sounded the end of
the play. The team whose territory contained the flag
when the bell rang forfeited a point to the other team.

Simple, *neh*? Only, nobody ever knew how long jittertime was going to be.

Jonathon had a clear lane to midline and into Buzzsaw
territory. He only needed three seconds.

Null perspiration. He cleared the line and zoomed onto
the blue-painted concrete toward the Buzzsaw goal area,
pushing his little Suzuki toward the 100 kph mark in an
all-out sprint. Going for the three-point conversion. Wind
rushed past, hot and humid with the heavy smell of sweating bodies. "Talk to me, Smitty," he said. "Where's the
enemy?"

"I'm trapped groundbound. Try Tam."

Tamara's voice came on. "Go for the score, Jonathon.
Strike that, you got three lancers coming online in . . .
well, now actually."

Even as she was speaking, three Buzzsaws on Harleys
rounded the corner at the end of the lane. They took up
formation, side by side by side, their lances locked and
pointed at Jonathon. Then they began their run, hoping to
force him and the flag back across midline before time ran
out. If he could get past them, he'd be in the clear. Free
run to the goal circle. Just him and the goalie.

Time for the Winger special—a move he had patented.
Don't try this at home.

Jonathon kicked himself up into a wheelie, slowing to
about 45 kph. He leaned forward to keep his balance and

stay focused on the closing distance between himself and the trio of oncoming lances.

When the distance closed to less than three meters, Jonathon braked hard and threw his weight forward, pitching himself onto his front wheel. And just as his rear wheel came up, he activated the hydrojack built into the front fork. He sprang up into the air, tucking into a forward flip. The stadium blurred past above and below him as he spun, and he heard shots over the collective gasp of the crowd. When his natural balance and gymnastic training told him it was time to come out of the tuck, Jonathon arched his back, laying out the final rotation to land again. Two wheels, no wobble.

Null strain. Stupid dreks had their lances locked or they might've got me.

He had cleared the lancebikers by four lengths, and his momentum carried him toward the goal circle.

De-fense! De-fense!

Time to elude the goalie.

The task of scoring wasn't easy, even though the flag could be placed anywhere inside the two-meter-diameter circle, and the goalie was on foot. The Buzzsaws' goalkeeper was a massive troll named Big Ed. Armored like a tank with huge polycarb plates. Armed with an autoshot riot carbine and twenty stun rounds, plus a tetsubo— a huge Japanese quarter-staff covered with densiplast bosses. Wicked nasty.

But Jonathon was faster. Quicker. And hopefully smarter.

Jittertime was down fifteen seconds and counting. This was his only shot to score.

"You're all alone on this one," Tamara said. "They've got us pinned down. No way we could reach you in time."

"Loud and clear, my love. Loud and clear." Jonathon began his final acceleration, swerving erratically to give Big Ed a harder time targeting. The riot carbine sputtered once, twice, missing. The third burst hit Jonathon's leg. Pain shot from his knee. One last swerve, then he rushed the goal circle, full throttle.

He aimed straight at Big Ed.

The riot gun fired and fired, over and over, but Jonathon locked the throttle at full and steered into a skid, using the machine as a shield. At the last second he released the bike from cybernetic control and jumped away, taking the flag with him.

The troll swung his tetsubo, trying to deflect the on-coming machine.

Jonathon hit the concrete, hugging the flag pole to his body, and rolled. It was a semi-controlled landing; he'd done this more times than he could remember. Big Ed would be busy with the bike as Jonathon planted the flag on the far side of the circle.

Big Ed, however, was faster and more agile than he looked. He side-stepped the oncoming cycle and lunged at Jonathon, swinging his tetsubo.

Jonathon reached toward the arcing line of yellow paint that signified the goal, holding the flag in his outstretched hand, just as the big quarter-staff slammed into his ribs. He gasped for air as several plates of his armor buckled and a sharp crack of pain shot through his chest.

Big Ed swung the tetsubo again.

"STOP!"

The flag in Jonathon's right hand was just inside the goal circle.

"Three points for—"

Big Ed's tetsubo came down hard again, this time catching Jonathon in the side of the head, ricocheting off his helmet and slamming into his shoulder.

More pain. Briefly.

Then blackness.

10

Synthia stood in her box seat and watched helplessly as the medics and techs carried Jonathon's unconscious form into the locker room. She knew she shouldn't worry; this had happened many times before. But she did worry. She always worried.

She wanted to slip into astral space. To project so that she could pass down into the locker room and see that Jonathon was all right. But she couldn't; astral projection during the game was against the rules. Once, the watcher spirits had let her roam astral space *before* play had actually started, but she'd never tried it during a game because it could disqualify the play, and they'd kick her out of the stadium.

Synthia sighed and sat down on the hard plastic seat. Then she pulled the portable trideo unit from her shoulder bag and turned it on. A male-biff commentator with slick black hair and a painted-on face looked out from the screen.

"Just moments ago," he said, "Jonathon Winger brought the count to six and three in favor of the LA Sabers. It was the first real goal of the match and will make it very difficult for Dougan Rose's Buzzsaws to come back and win this game. Let's take a look at the replay."

Just fragging tell us whether he's all right or not, she thought.

An image of Jonathon filled the screen, weaving his bike erratically as he barreled toward the camera. He crouched on one side of the bike as he approached, trying to stay out of the goalkeeper's line of fire.

Synthia saw a portion of the armor over his knee rip away in slow motion as a burst from the troll's carbine hit him. She winced and turned away from the rest, listening to the screeching and crunching and amplified moans of pain that came from the small unit.

Finally it was over, and the commentator returned. "Jonathon Winger's Sabers need to take this match to force a fifth and final world championship game in Los Angeles. It looks like they're on their way back to LA. But is Winger out for good? I'll give you an update when I come back."

Come on.

An ad came on and Synthia listened absently as she sat among the screaming, predominantly pro-Buzzsaw crowd. "You're watching TSN, the Total Sports Network, you can pick up our live simsense and experience the match from the point of view of your favorite combatant. The cost is only—"

Synthia muted the trideo, wishing she didn't care so much. These were the times when she regretted her relationship with Jonathon. These were the times when she thought that maybe, just maybe, she loved him too deeply.

11

Sharp, acrid. Jonathon's nose burned and he jerked awake. He snapped his eyes open to see the smooth baby face of Ducky, the team trainer. Brown human skin, innocent smile, razor-cut afro.

"Where am I?" Jonathon said. "What happened?"

"You scored a fraggin' goal, chummer. Put us three points up. That was one wiz move. Silenced the crowd; you could hear a fraggin' chip drop. Ratings have gone stratospheric."

"Yeah, well, I'm glad you enjoyed it." Jonathon tried to sit up, but a sharp pain in the side of his chest cavity made him gasp. "That makes one of us."

Ducky pressed him back down onto the plastic-coated mattress of the examination table. "I injected your broken ribs with coral gel," he said. "It'll straighten them and make a framework for the bone to heal, but you still have to wear this." He proceeded to wrap Jonathon's chest with a band of fiberglass tape that immediately began to harden around him.

"Will this be strong enough for me to—"

"Don't even think about going back in. Your trauma damper will dull the pain, and I've given you some Syndorphin, but Big Ed cracked you a good one. Right between two plates of your now defunct armor. Broke two ribs and bruised three more. The good news is—"

"There's good news?"

Ducky smiled. "Most assuredly. The MRI shows no major skull damage, and your headware is fine."

"You still won't let me back in?"

"Jonathon, the team makes more money when you're riding. The producers want me to send you back, but I've got to think of the long term. Unless a miracle happens, there *will* be a game five, and we need you healthy by then. Now, I want you to rest."

"Should've had my ribs laced," Jonathon said. He eased himself slowly into an upright position. It ached to breathe, but the Syndorphin was starting to kick in and dull the sharpness. "Since I'm useless anyway, can I sim Tam's feed?"

"Fine by me," Ducky said.

"Thanks." Jonathon stood carefully and limped out of the infirmary. He was bruised and battered, but with each passing step his strength grew.

The infirmary led to the team bunkers, where the players readied themselves to ride. Jonathon hobbled across the painted concrete toward the simsense decks. Here substitute riders could straight jack with simrigged teammates in order to learn their moves.

Through the bunker doors came the rumble of the crowd as the bell sounded the release of another bogey. New play.

Jonathon settled into a recliner and slotted his jack, punching up Tamara's feed. He'd been worried about her concentration since the crying episode that afternoon. But she seemed as aggressive as ever, perhaps more so. Jonathon strove for zen in his game, but Tamara used anger to fuel hers.

Jonathon felt the anger flow through him as her feed came online and flooded him. His aches and pains dissipated, forgotten as he synchronized with Tamara's senses.

Feral power coursed through her as she accelerated after the bogey, which had swooped into her lane and dipped toward the floor. She brought her Roomsweeper to bear, the red targeting circle on her retina flickering to life as the smartlink engaged. She fired, but the spray missed as the bogey dodged right, then up.

Dougan Rose appeared out of the corner of her left eye as she fired again, this time downing the small drone. The flag hit the concrete and rocked to an upright position on its weighted base.

Tamara gunned her engine to snag it. One second. Two.

Dougan flashed past on her left. He would reach the flag first unless . . .

She cast her net, a two-meter square made of high-tensile polycarb cabling and weighted at the rim. A wrapping filament looped through the edge to draw the whole thing closed.

Dougan grabbed the flag just as Tamara's net entangled him. She tried to let go, but Dougan was too close; the net caught the handle bars of her bike and wrenched her front wheel, pulling her off balance. Jonathon felt the weight of Tamara's Suzuki come down on her left leg as she fell.

Dougan jammed the flag into the slot behind his seat as Tamara pushed her bike off, and stood. She stepped up to him, targeting her Roomsweeper on his head. But before she could fire, he knocked the gun from her hand with a quick jab from his mace.

Then she heard a faint click, barely audible over the banshee scream of the crowd. Everything closed on slow motion as she turned to grab the flag from Dougan's Yamaha, wondering what had made the noise.

She saw the crystal silver glint of the cyberspurs arcing out of his forearm. Flailing wildly, he used the blades to slice his way out of the net. The razors cut the polycarb with ease, sending fragments of netting fluttering to the concrete.

He looked at her then. Through the macroglass of his visor, he stared right into her eyes.

What the frag?

His bladed arm connected with her neck, the monofilament-edged metal piercing the armor at its weakest point, up and under her helmet.

Tamara tried to jerk away but was too slow. She felt a cold sharpness against her throat. Then warm blood came gushing out. The iron smell of it filled her nostrils. The salt taste of it was sharp in the back of her throat.

Time slowed.

She's dying, Jonathon thought.

Blackness engulfed her, seeping like ink into her vision as she slumped. The suffocating blood choked her, making her helmet heavy with its weight. At the last second she reached for her tear-away trauma patch. And as she tugged at it with numb fingers, she felt its cybersnake needle penetrate her chest and jab her heart.

Adrenaline pumped through her, momentarily clearing her head. Her vision returned, and she saw Dougan Rose above her, a horrible look of false remorse on her all too elven face.

Jonathon was buried deep into Tamara's mind when her life shattered into a million frozen moments. Her emotions hit him. Surprise. Pain. Regret.

"Jonathon," she tried to say. "I . . ."

Love.

Then the dizziness washed away her sight, and her breathing gurgled to a halt. The blackout fringe approached in jerks and starts as the scream in her head arced through him.

Over the edge of fadeout.

Unconsciousness clawed at Jonathon's mind, digging, scrabbling to take him along. And he felt Tamara's darkness ooze into him like sweet molasses.

Flatline.

12

Grids bolted upright when he saw Tamara go down. He'd been watching the whole thing on the trid in Tamara's Beverly Hills apartment, his sweaty T-shirt sticking to the synthleather couch as he gaped at the image. The trid coverage kept showing the accident over and over. Dougan Rose snapping out his cyberspurs, the amplified click as they locked into place. Even in the slow-motion replay, Grids heard the intent in that click.

Dougan had made it look like an accident while trying to cut through Tamara's net, but Grids knew otherwise. The chances that Dougan could have breached Tamara's armor by accident were astronomical. He had known exactly where to strike. And yet the commentators blathered on as though Dougan must feel awful about the unfortunate accident.

The DocWagon paramedics had taken Tamara away in a helicopter, but none of the trid reports gave any update on her condition. Dougan had been slapped with a three-play penalty for using cyberspurs, an illegal weapon. He would sit out for a while, but that was the extent of punishment.

Grids' heart pounded; he could hear it in his ears. *She looks dead*, he kept thinking. He fell back against the soft cushions and stared distractedly at the 3-D images. Though he tried to focus on the game as it continued, the accident scene replayed itself over and over in his mind.

He couldn't concentrate. He saw the grimace of surprise and pain of her face, viewed in super close-up through the scratched face plate of her helmet. He could hear her amplified gurgles and gasps as she struggled to keep breathing despite the gush of blood.

Michaelson must know about the simrecording, he thought. *And somehow, he got Dougan Rose to kill for him.*

Grids took a slow breath. *No. Null chance.*

The visions in his mind returned. Dougan's monofilament-bladed spurs glinted in the white glare of the stadium's phosphor lights. Slicing through Tamara's net to plunge up into her neck. Slow motion. Close-up. Gigantic rivulets of her deep red elven blood cascading over the grotesquely magnified silver blades.

The images on the trid had shown Dougan Rose draw back in horror as Tamara clutched at her trauma patch, then slumped into unconsciousness. Then the DocWagon parameds had rushed in to get her out.

Gone?

Now on the trid, the gorgeous blonde with the impossibly full lips spoke. "Still no word from DocWagon on the condition of Tamara Ny, linebiker for the Los Angeles Sabers. Miss Ny, having a fabulous season this year, was inadvertently stabbed by veteran Dougan Rose in this earlier play."

"Trid off," Grids told the machine. He couldn't stand to watch any more. The images dissipated as the trideo went into sleep mode. Grids put his head in his hands. *Got to concentrate. Got to assume the worst.*

"Which is . . ." he said aloud.

Tamara is gone. Scragged because she read the stuff in Michaelson's briefcase.

"Which means . . ."

Michaelson probably knows about the simrecording. And people are probably coming after me right now.

"Fraggin' spirits!" Grids leaped to his feet. "What to do? What to do?" This was not some fantasy or simsense adventure. This was real. Too fragging real.

Grids took a deep breath and tried to remember his conversation with Tamara just before her flight for New Orleans. Tried to recall what they had said to each other.

The terminal at Long Beach International Airport was packed, but they'd found a small table in a bar near her departure gate. LBI was LA's only facility for suborbitals and transcontinentals, built on a swamp in Long Beach, floating on giant pontoons so that it swayed and rocked whenever a heavy suborbital touched down. It was strange to be motion sick in an airport, but a necessary evil ever since LAX was destroyed in the '28 quake.

"You think you can reconstruct the text?" Tamara had asked him. "That document looked important."

Grids grimaced, then took a sip of his soykaf and stared out at the runway before answering. "I don't think you understand, Tam. The document was clearly marked as Alpha-level security. Not to mention that it's drek Saeder-Krupp wants kept secret. Either one means just looking at that file might get us both geeked."

She put a finger to his lips. "It also means that Andreas will pay dearly for its return." The smile she gave him was edged with sadness. "I'm really sorry I dragged you into this."

Spirits, she was gorgeous. Even covered up and in disguise as she was then. Traveling incognito. She'd even convinced Rolph, her human bodyguard, to dress like an Amerind too and pretend to be her husband. Rolph sat at the bar right now, his obvious cybereyes glowing a dull silver in the tawny yellow light.

"Well, you can reconstruct it?" she asked again.

"Probably. Did you see every page?"

"Think so, but some of them only for a second. I didn't have time to read it."

"Null sweat. A second is eons in sim. I can program a smartframe to crunch on the text recognition." He grew serious. "But I don't like it, Tam. I think we should bail."

"No, I'm sure we can cut a deal, persuade Andreas to get me started in some simfeature or other in exchange for our copy of the file."

Grids stared at her in disbelief. "Michaelson is a senior executive veepee for the most powerful megacorp in the world! He eats people like us for breakfast. If he finds out, either from us or from someone else, we're as good as dead."

"Chill down, Grids. You're overreacting."

"Just promise me you'll contact Grayson Alexander if something happens. You remember me talking about him. He's a runner and can find you a place to hide."

"I promise." She smiled at him again, cocking her head to one side as she listened to the airport's intercom announcing that her flight was boarding. She picked up her red synthleather carry-on and stood looking at him for a moment. "Now you're getting me worried. But this is my big chance and I don't want to lose it. As soon as you've got the text, I'll give Andreas the ultimatum. He'll have to go along."

"I hope you're right." Grids thought she didn't sound anymore convinced than he was.

"Me too," Tamara said as she leaned over to kiss him goodbye, long and sultry, pressing her soft lips against his. Then she straightened up and gave Rolph the signal. They walked out, leaving Grids with his soykaf, growing cold and gritty.

The memory faded.

Now, in Tamara's apartment, Grids brushed his fingers across his lips, trying to keep the sensation of her kiss from evaporating. He wiped tears from his eyes with his other hand. *No time for that now. Gotta move.*

Time for action.

Grayson Alexander That's who I need to contact.

Grids activated the trideo, selected telecom voice-only, and placed a call to what used to be Grayson's message line. After two rings, the line picked up, but no one answered. No message. No beep, just the faint crackle of blank memory.

"It's a ghost from the past, chummer," Grids said. "Urgent biz for you." Then he hung up, knowing that Grayson's machine would have read the return LTG number from Tamara's phone. Grayson would call back on a secure line.

Of course, line security didn't mean drek if someone had already tapped Tamara's side. Then again, if someone had been here to tap, they'd already have come after the chip.

The chip!

Grids ran from the den to the garage; his joints snapped and cracked as he moved, protesting the motion after sitting idle for so long. Tamara had let him convert her garage into a freelance simsense studio. The guts of old computers, simsense decks, cyberdecks, and simsynths lay strewn across the astroturf-covered cement floor.

Grids instantly felt more comfortable as he closed the door on the overly tidy apartment and entered his work space. Scattered fiber-optics and carcasses of gutted electronics sprawled like roadkill. Stacks of compact disks, memory chips, and skillsofts littered the floor and shelves. There was even some old second-hand cyberware that he intended to scavenge for parts.

His actual workspace was compact and well organized.

The heart of the operation was a big Fuchi RealSense sim-synth that had been a Christmas gift from Tamara. The Fuchi simth pumped the electronic blood of his system, and Grids had been using it for all his most recent editing gigs. The Fuchi was assisted by three ingeniously pro-grammed smartframes and a huge library of modular plug-in effects, including emotive enablers, sense-patch samples, and EC/PC modulation controllers.

A Fuchi Cyber-7 cyberdeck, which he'd heavily modi-fied back in his old decking days, held the code for the smartframes and patched the whole rig into the Matrix for remote accessing. Even an off-the-shelf Cyber-7 would be overkill for that task, but occasionally Grids broke his own rules and decked into Amalgamated Studios or Bril-liant Genesis for some contraband simsense properties—bits of sense, chunks of just the right urge, and the like.

On the floor, next to the stack of CDs, was his Truman Realink simrecorder. He bent and opened it, quickly check-ing the recording bay. The chip still lay exactly where he'd left it. He breathed, then popped the chip and slotted it into the chipjack behind his ear. It was the safest place he could think of.

Then he closed the case of his Truman and gave his studio another look around. He'd never been forced to move the entire rig at once, but the components were moderately small, and at a glance he figured it would all fit into the rear hatch of his Jackrabbit. He went to work, tearing it down, and was nearly finished when the telecom beeped.

"Yeah?" Grids said, blanking the video.

"Ghost from the past, this is Gray Shadow. The line is secure."

"Gray, thanks for the quick comeback. I need a hidey-hole."

After a pause. "For an old chummer, I got three avail-able. All temporary, prices vary by location."

"Any in Beverly Hills?"

"East Hollywood."

"East Hollywood it is. And I need protection. You got that for rent too?"

"Everything's for rent."

"The cred's no problem."

"Then, your reservation is confirmed, Ghost. Meet me at the usual haunt for directions and accompaniment."

"Thanks, Gray."

"None necessary." The line went dead.

Grids finished packing his equipment, then threw some clothes into a travel bag. It had been a long time since he'd run the shadows, and he'd have preferred it to be longer still.

No choice.

When the Jackrabbit was completely packed, he drove away as nonchalantly, as inconspicuously as he could. He still didn't know if Tamara was alive or dead—or worse. But there was someone who would know.

Jonathon Winger.

Winger didn't like him, but Grids had to find out if she was still alive. Chances were that even if she'd survived all that blood loss, she'd probably have sustained brain damage. She might be a vat case.

Grids shook his head. He didn't want to think about it. He tried to concentrate on his driving as he passed through the well-protected gates that separated the mansions of Beverly Hills from the Hollywood filth. He continued down the hill into the sea of streetmeat and pornshops. BTL chip parlors and drug dens squeezed into the cracks between the legit theaters and tourist drek.

He'd escaped from this place years ago, and it slotted him hard that it was where he had to go back to now.

When was he going to be able to jack out of this nightmare sim?

Grids hoped it was soon, but something told him this was only the beginning.

13

Jonathon came to with a start, sucking in a huge gasp of air. And as he breathed in and out, he realized where he was. Still sitting in the simrecliner. Still jacked through to Tamara's feed, though no signal came from her. Where Tamara's emotions and senses had been a moment before, now there was only a low hiss.

Static in his head.

Dead air.

Jonathon straightened up and pulled the datacord from his temple to disconnect the feed. Tamara must be out of range or her simlink been damaged. At least the static meant she was still alive. But when the plug released from the datajack, the static crackled on in his head. He felt phantom tingles across his skin like a frayed edge to his nerves.

What the frag?

He jacked in and then out again. *Maybe my cranial memory hasn't cleared.*

No change. Only the faint hiss in his mind.

Suddenly the memory of her last moments coursed through him. The scream from her mind echoed in his ears, and he knew she was gone.

He doubled over in pain, clutching his stomach as bile rose in his throat. He had thought it would always be the two of them, from the gypsies through the military, through prison, to riding the line together. Always the two of them. Always together. But now she was gone, and all that remained was the distant crackle like wind trapped in a box.

He swallowed and stood up, feeling a surge of anger. His headclock showed that five minutes had passed since he'd blacked out. The crowd outside cheered violently, and Jonathon heard the loudspeaker announce that Dougan Rose's penalty time was up.

Jonathon remembered once standing in the gypsy tent

with Tamara at his side staring into a holopic of Dougan Rose. His idol's face had peered from the cube directly into Jonathon's eyes with a look of sheer hatred. It was the same look Rose had given Tamara just before his cyberspurs had sliced her open. His intent was clear.

Death.

Jonathon tried to ignore the pain in his chest as he walked to his locker and put on new armor. He moved methodically, purposefully, focusing on each task in sequence. His Plycra unibody. His polycarb-slotted Kevlar chest plating. His boots. Until he was armored and ready to rock'n'roll.

Payback time.

The noise of the crowd grew faint as he dressed. Distant. The questions of his teammates fell on deaf ears. Their sidelong glances ignored. None of that mattered.

His helmet went on last, locking into position. Then he strode into the garage, fired up one of his bikes, and grabbed a full complement of weapons from the racks by the corrugated metal doors.

"What the hell are you doing?" Coach Kalish yelled after him as Jonathon pulled up into the team's cycle bay. Coach was a dwarf with a drek eating disposition. In her youth, she'd go-ganged with the Marauders out of Fontana. Before combat biker had become an official sport.

"I want in," he said. He didn't wait for her approval; instead he jacked himself into his Suzuki and roared out into the maze.

"Winger!" It was Smitty's voice coming over the com. "Vacate before the refs frag us for a penalty."

Jonathon barely heard; his head buzzed with the frayed whisper of static. "Tamara," he mouthed.

"Tam's gone, chummer. DocWagon team took her. No news yet."

"Sorry 'bout Tam, Winger," came Webber's voice, "but you're gonna cost us unless you bail. We got too many bikes in the maze."

Smitty's cut in. "You exit, Fallon. Winger's in."

"But—"

"Move! You scan?"

"Where's Dougan?" Jonathon asked.

"Center lane, straight shot, but—"

Jonathon raised his Roomsweeper as he accelerated to

take the curve high on the side, then rolled back to vertical down the stretch.

Dougan roamed on his side of the midline, weaving. Waiting for bogey release. *Unaware.*

Jonathon cranked the throttle to full out, hitting fifty, seventy, then one hundred klicks per hour. In the seconds before he reached Dougan, he cracked his whip.

Dougan never expected the hit. Clearly against the rules, no pretense of fair play at all.

Jonathon fired the Roomsweeper over and over as he approached. The whip in his other hand snapped out to wrap around Dougan's neck while Jonathon anchored his end into the latch on his bike.

Dougan reached up, activating his cyberspurs in an attempt to cut the whip that coiled like a polycarb anaconda around his neck. But his razors never made it. The whip snapped taut, pulling Dougan into the air by his head.

Decapitated?

No, but his helmet snapped off, flicked into the air like a champagne cork.

Dougan hit the concrete on his side, his right ear grating against the pavement as his Yamaha Rapier, which was still locked onto his body, crashed on top.

Dougan's weight on the end of the whip jerked Jonathon's bike down too, flipping the cycle out from under him. Concrete rushed up like the belt of a power sander to grind against his armored thigh as he skidded to slam into the barrier.

Then the motors of both bikes went dead and the wheels locked as the referees in their turrets keyed the transponders to shut off. Jonathon was dimly aware of Dougan groaning, of the hushed awe of the crowd. He lay on his side, unable to push the weight of his bike off his chewed-up leg, barely able to breathe through the pain in his chest.

Still, Jonathon felt some satisfaction in that pain. Dougan Rose had been made to pay a small price. But it wasn't enough yet. Only Dougan's death would even the score.

Yet, the injury to the other biker served to dull the phantom echo of static in Jonathon's head. At least for the moment.

If only he could see Tamara's face once more.

14

Luc Tashika stared down from his office window. Far below the monolithic silver and black heights of the MCT headquarters, the night breathed and moved like an entity, a living creature crawling through the jungle of concrete and steel.

And crouched in the shadow of the megacorporate sky-towers of Arcology Milc were the SINless and the destitute. No System Identification Number meant untraceable, outside the ordered machine of society. Effectively nonexistent.

At this time of night, many of those were just beginning their biz down there. They were the shadowrunners, the street docs, the fixers . . . *Scum for hire,* thought Tashika.

Some sold 'ware, others services. And some were the real garbage—the chipheads and the BTL junkies, the beggars and the petty thieves. These were the largest in number, and before the night was over many of them would clog the sewers and dumpsters with their worthless flesh.

Tashika had almost stopped seeing them at all, but tonight his thoughts had been forced down into the shadows because of this unpleasantness concerning Tamara Ny. Tashika sighed, taking a handkerchief from his pocket to wipe the sweat from his brow. He tried to retain his calm; he didn't want to repeat his outburst of a few moments ago.

When Dr. Franklin had called from the DocWagon clinic in New Orleans to tell him of Miss Ny's death, Tashika had flown into a rage. He'd thrown the telecom across the room and nearly broken his hands pounding his fists against his desk. *That fragging incompetent had killed her.*

But that was minutes ago. Now, he was calm. And he struggled to stay that way despite the fire in his head and the shakes that threatened to take control of his shoulders. He breathed. Slow.

He didn't even know if Ny had actually stolen any

important information from Michaelson. Dr. Franklin had scanned all her headware for hints of a file or simsense record, but had found nothing.

Tashika sighed and picked up the remains of his telecom, which he placed on his desk. He could get Cinnamon to find Miss Ny's accomplice, this Grids Desmond, and take care of the situation, but it would cost him. If Mr. Desmond could be found for free . . .

Hmm, he thought, *perhaps there is a way Mr. Rose can remedy the situation.*

Tashika asked Bridget to get Dougan on a secure line. After a moment of blackness, Dougan's face filled the screen, a pained expression on the elven features. He was sitting in a bed in the DocWagon clinic, the call having automatically been forwarded to his room. The interlocking plates of a blue plastichrome exoskeleton fit snugly around his neck, holding his head straight and immobile. A bandage also covered the right side of his head where it had scraped against the pavement.

"Ah, Mr. Tashika," Dougan said, grimacing in pain as he spoke. "I've been expecting to hear from you."

Tashika tried to gather up his anger, but it was cold and distant. Used up. "Explain yourself," he said.

"It was an accident," Dougan said.

Tashika noted the change in Dougan's tone, almost subservient. Much different from their last conversation. "You cannot know how crucial a mistake you have made," Tashika said.

"I'm really sorry, sir."

He is trying to manipulate me, Tashika thought. *That is clear. Could he be lying? Perhaps he deliberately killed Tamara Ny. No, that doesn't make sense; he merely wants to appease my anger.*

Dougan's expression was one of atonement. "How can I amend my error so that—?"

"So that I reveal nothing?"

"Yes."

"Perhaps there is one thing . . ."

"What?"

"According to my sources, Miss Ny worked with an accomplice—a Grids Desmond. I want you to find him or hire someone else to do it. Someone discreet, you understand?"

"A shadowrunner?"

Tashika nodded. "Retrieve the simchip intact and destroy all copies. Mr. Desmond and anyone else who has knowledge of the chip's contents will have to be neutralized."

"Killed?"

"Yes."

"That is no small task," Dougan said.

"Neither was the magnitude of your error." Tashika glared at Rose, peering into the biker's dark eyes, framed by frowning black brows. "Do something like that again, and your secrets will hit the newsfax so fast you won't know your drekhole from a . . ." Tashika smiled and caught himself. He was sure Rose understood the situation well enough.

Dougan just stared wide-eyed from the screen. He was obviously still in some pain from his confrontation with Jonathon Winger. "Don't worry, I scan. I know some . . . people in LA who handle this sort of thing."

"I thought you might."

"I'll be in touch," Dougan said.

"Goodbye." Tashika disconnected and leaned back. A smile crept over his face and he kicked himself around in his chair, pulling his knees in for a 360-degree spin. *Ah, the pleasures of blackmail.*

15

Her face hung before his eyes. Smooth, olive skin, high elven cheekbones, copper-colored eyes, bright and full of life. Her lips were a dark red, almost brown, and her hair shone raven black in the glow of the fire . . .

"Tamara?"

"Mr. Winger? You're in recovery. DocWagon clinic." The voice was distant, as though filtered. And into the silence that followed, the hiss rose like a tsunami of static crashing in his skull.

Jonathon opened his eyes to a small room, lit overhead by fluorescent fixtures. He lay on a hard mattress, an IV needle taped to his arm. The woman above him looked like his mother. Human features, red hair streaked at the temples with gray. Freckled face, blue eyes.

"I'm Doctor Mitchell," she said. Her face became round and plump as she smiled, unlike Mom's. Wider, older than Mom's. The doctor's face wrinkled at the corners of her eyes, dimpled at the edges of her mouth.

"Where's Tamara?" he asked.

"I'm sorry, Mr. Winger," the doctor said, dropping her smile. "Miss Ny is dead."

Jonathon blinked. "H-h-how?"

"Mr. Winger, are you sure—?"

"Tell me!"

The doctor straightened up at the abrupt vehemence of his tone and took a step back.

"I need to know if it was an accident or not," Jonathon said.

"Miss Ny died from blood loss, according to the report, but I wasn't the attending doctor so I'm not sure—"

"Then get him in here!" Jonathon was screaming.

"Please calm yourself, Mr. Winger." The doctor looked concerned, very much like his mother again. Too much.

Jonathon took a breath. "I'm sorry," he said. "But I've got to know for sure. There's a buzzing in my head ever since the accident. I was jacked through to her, you see, when it happened."

"I know, I know." The doctor dabbed his sweaty forehead with a white towel. "We've done all we can. We've erased your headware memory and rebooted your simlink and vehicle rig, but our brainwave scans still show a faint background like a dead area in your mind.

"It seems to be part of your organic brain, but truthfully, Mr. Winger, none of us has seen anything like it. All we can do is hope it fades with time."

Jonathon said nothing, merely rolling to his side and bringing his knees up into a fetal crouch. Sharp pain shot through his chest as he turned, and his right leg burned with agony.

"I'll get Dr. Abramson." Then she opened the door and squeezed out.

Jonathon heard loud voices—a crowd of reporters and fans pressing against the door, trying to get a comment from the doctor or a quick glance inside for a headcamera photo.

Tamara's dead, he thought. *Really gone.* Then the memory of her emotions shook through him. Surprise. Pain. Regret. "Jonathon, I . . ." Love. He pulled his knees closer into his chest to ease the emptiness in his gut. To suppress the nausea.

He had first met her when he was thirteen, the year before the fire. His father was still alive then, and their orchards outside Redding produced olives and almonds by the truckload. That was just before the war with the elves, who say the Northern Crescent area belongs to Tir Tairngire. Just before Dad died.

Tamara had come through town with her caravan of gypsies, an unlikely melange of metahumanity. The caravan numbered about forty or fifty orks and dwarfs and trolls, sprinkled with a few elves and humans. Bound for the shores of Lake Shasta where they camped for the summer.

Jonathon was water-skiing up on the lake when he saw her swimming naked, the blue-green water cascading down her adolescent body. He stared at her and her ork friends as they swam, and when they looked up, he turned away. Embarrassed.

Later, two of the ork girls nearly beat him drekless before Tamara stepped in and made them stop. Feeling sorry for him, she helped him up and asked his name, even offered him fish for lunch.

They became best friends over the course of the summer. Nearly inseparable. He thought he would never see her again when the elves of Tir Tairngire attacked. The Battle of Redding they called it now.

More like a slaughter.

The gypsies fled the area in a panic, and Jonathon's father took up arms with the other locals to defend his land. But that act cost him his life, leaving Jonathon's mother pregnant and with only Jonathon to run and farm the land.

But unlike his human father, Jonathon was an elf, and no one would work for him. No one would buy from him. After the massacre by invading elves, none of the locals trusted him. Hatred of elves continued to grow for nearly a year before the Native Californians came—a human supremacy policlub with ties to Humanis. Shortly after the birth of his elven sister, they came, dressed in dark clothing and stocking cap masks, and set fire to the house.

Tamara and the other gypsies had returned to Lake Shasta by then. So Jonathon was off with her when it started. But his mother and newborn sister were not. They had been napping.

They burned to death in that fire.

When he finally got there, all he could do was stand and watch the blazing house, his heart cold inside, his gut empty. Skin burning from the heat. Tamara had stood there with him, holding his hand. And after the firefighters finally gave up on trying to beat the inferno, the torchers returned in their masks. Tamara took him, ran with him back to the caravan. And Jonathon had lived with them until he was old enough to enlist in the UCAS military.

Jonathon still owned the orchards and the remains of the house, but he'd never been back since.

"Mr. Winger?"

Jonathon rolled over as a human doctor squeezed through the door. The man stood tall and lanky, sporting the custom cybereyes and elongated finger extensions of a surgeon.

"I'm Doctor Abramson. You wanted to talk to me?"

"Yes. They say you were there, that you can tell me how Tamara Ny died. She's the closest thing I have to family."

"Actually, Mr. Winger, you are the only person I *can* tell. She left you as next of kin on her platinum account records."

"Well?"

Dr. Abramson ran one hand through his graying brown hair. "Plain and simple blood loss, Mr. Winger. Followed by cardiac arrest."

"Nothing suspicious?"

"No, not really."

"Not really? What does that mean?"

Dr. Abramson rolled his reflective green eyes. "It's probably nothing, and I won't go on record for its validity, but . . ."

"What? Don't play games with me, Doc."

The doctor stared at Jonathan for a moment. "I have to ask you not to repeat this because it isn't conclusive. In fact it's highly speculative and would never be considered valid evidence in any corporate court."

"I'm listening."

"It's not something I found, really. But a lack of something." Dr. Abramson started to pace around Jonathon's bed. "Miss Ny was in excellent physical health, and she had no record of hemophilia, and yet we found very little evidence of clotted blood around the wound."

"What does that mean?"

"Normally, blood coagulates when exposed to air, but Miss Ny's did not. Or not much anyway. Now, the wounds she received may have killed her despite that, but . . ."

Jonathon shot upright, wincing against the grating pain in his leg. "Is there another explanation?"

The doctor frowned. "You should lie down, Mr. Winger."

"Just tell me."

The doctor sighed. "If she had an anticoagulant in her system, even a small wound could have resulted in excessive bleeding. Perhaps even death."

"Are you saying—?"

"I repeat, Mr. Winger, I am not saying anything except that her blood didn't clot normally. We detected no known anticoagulants like Heparin or Parclo-V, but there are similar drugs that can be made to degrade in minutes."

Jonathon sank back into his pillow. *Oh, Tam, what did you get yourself into? Damn you!* Tears rose in his eyes, and he turned from the doctor's gaze. What was it she couldn't tell him before the match? Did it involve Michaelson? Had Dougan Rose killed her intentionally? And if he had, then why?

Too many fragging questions.

The hiss rose in his head and dried up his tears, grated at the raw edges of his nerves. He would find out the truth of what happened. That much he vowed to do. And afterward, he would destroy those responsible.

16

Cinnamon sipped her mocha, made from real coffee and Swiss chocolate. Only the best ingredients would satisfy the hunger of her human form.

The dwarf sitting across the etched glass coffee table was trying unsuccessfully to sip his drink as delicately as she did. She knew how he loved the sensual pleasures; his soft round body reflected that.

"Help yourself to some biscotti and chocolate," she said, tossing her golden hair back over her shoulders.

The dwarf's name was Frank Rupert, but he hated it. He preferred to go by his Matrix handle of Mole. Like most deckers, he was only truly at ease flying the electronic skies of the Matrix. Moving his persona icon through restricted systems, burrowing for data. Digging in electronic dirt.

Which was precisely why Cinnamon had demanded a face-to-face meeting. In her line of work, every edge mattered. The extra bit of discomfort gave her the advantage, and that was the way she liked it.

Mole grabbed a small palmful of biscotti and crunched it with his dirty teeth.

Cinnamon sipped her mocha again, savoring its rich taste. She gave the dwarf a moment to finish chewing, then leaned forward in her leather recliner. "Let's have it," she said finally. "Give me the short form; I'll read your full report later."

Mole brushed crumbs from his black beard and gave her an apologetic look. He had to gulp his drink to swallow what was in his mouth. "Sorry, Cinnamon. It's just that your treats are so wiz."

She gave a small shrug. "Thank you, Mole, but I didn't bring you here for your lovely company. Now, just sum up what you've discovered."

"Okay, okay. Tamara Ny is dead, as far as I can tell. The New Orleans DocWagon Trauma Center is pretty tough to crack, but I got in thanks to my own special sleaze arsenal, a wonderful little—"

"Mole!" Cinnamon felt the scales on the back of her neck bristle. *I might just eat this halfer right now,* she thought.

"Sorry, Cinnamon. Anyhow, I got inside and took a glance around. Tamara Ny was never admitted, but the records of her death were on file. She never made it to the Trauma Center. Died on life support in transit. Loss of blood, heart failure, brain death, the works."

"What about Dougan Rose? Why would he kill her?"

Mole tried to smile, but it was an ugly expression on his pimpled, red face. "Rose works for the Buzzsaws, which are owned and operated by Pollster Sports, Inc., a subsidiary of Mistuhama Computer Technologies. Tashika is the veepee of MCT's entertainment division. His promotion to that position roughly coincides with Rose's appearance on the combat biker scene ten years ago."

Cinnamon nodded. "Perhaps Tashika brought Rose into the game, or 'discovered' him, then used Rose's success to get his promotion."

"That's what I thought. Before that, Tashika was in a semi-secret division called special projects, whatever that means. And there's only sparse information on Dougan Rose prior to 2046, just rumors about how he came out of the El Infierno gangs before they stopped letting people out of that hellhole. His file is very shadowy, notably lacking in specifics like parentage and the origin of his death's-head tattoo, but that's all consistent with the gang story. He probably didn't have a SIN until after he started riding for the Buzzsaws."

"Good work, Mole," Cinnamon said. "What does his SIN indicate now? Any blemishes, any little slips?"

Mole shook his head. "Not one, that's what bothers me. He's been squeaky clean. As it stands, the connection between Tashika and Rose is purely circumstantial. Too intangible to say for sure why Rose might agree to kill for him. Tashika did place a call to a New Orleans LTG, but that could be more coincidence; I couldn't get an exact trace."

"Too many coincidences," Cinnamon said. *Still,* she

thought, *Dougan might be dancing to Tashika's tune. But why?* There were too many unanswered questions.

"Perhaps the death was accidental," Mole said.

"Is that what you think?"

"No."

"Me neither," Cinnamon said. "That's why we have to ask what possible motive Luc Tashika could have for wanting Tamara Ny dead even though she might have information extremely valuable to him."

"Perhaps he already has the information."

"Did he have time for that?"

Mole shrugged. "Given the time frame, I don't think so. But we could be underestimating him."

Cinnamon smiled. She liked this decker, despite his lack of refined manners. "Noted," she said. "I won't do that again. Now, tell me about Grids Desmond."

Mole sat upright and nearly bounced on the couch. "Yeah, Grids," he said, gesticulating in broad motions. "Grids is known among the shadow community, but he faded out of it about eight years back when he landed a corporate job with Brilliant Genesis. Before that he did some decking. Rumor said he was wiz with the hard, wank with the soft. A brilliant dock tech, but mediocre ice cutter."

"Get to the point."

"He most definitely checked into the Venice Hilton the day Tamara Ny was there with Michaelson. Room 2305, under the alias of Joe Smith. Who else would Ny have used as her technician for the simrecording? He's been living with her in Beverly Hills for about a year now, according to his SIN data, off and on freelancing on big simsense productions for Amalgamated Studios."

"Has anyone else tried to track him down?"

"As far as I know, he's at their condo in the Hills, only about ten kilometers from here in the meat world."

"We are in the meat world, as you call it," Cinnamon said, finishing off her mocha and setting the mug on a ceramic coaster. "Is there anything else I should know? Any others who might be involved?"

"Nothing conclusive," Mole said. "But she and Jonathan Winger have a very sordid history together."

"Elaborate."

"Records show they entered UCAS military service

together in 2049 and flew experimental jetcraft out of Fort
Lewis for a few years."

"So what? Is there any real evidence to implicate
Winger in the scam with the others?"

"Nothing except their history together. They've been
nearly inseparable for over ten years, including time before the military, then prison, and now they ride for the
same combat biker squad." Mole sniggered. "At least one
still does . . ."

Cinnamon scowled at him, finding him a distasteful
creature at the moment. "All right," she said, "here's what
I want you to do. Keep digging into the connection between Tashika and Rose. And find out what you can about
the Winger connection, but drop it if there's not much to
go on; I don't want to be paying you to hunt down dead-
ends. Meanwhile, tell Hendrix to contact me. I've got
some more easy work for him."

Mole nodded, shifting uncomfortably. "Standard rates,
I assume," he said, then gulped what remained of his
mocha, knowing the conversation was nearly over.

"As always," Cinnamon said, rotating the telecom on
the coffee table toward her. "Goodbye now. Contact me
when you learn something."

Mole stood to leave, finding himself flanked by Bardolf
and Githon—two earth elementals. Cinnamon could not
directly control other spirits, but the more intelligent ones
found her goodwill rewarding since her commerce was
often in favors—life force, income, and other goodies. They
could also find her anger a hindrance to their continued
existence.

Bardolf and Githon served as bodyguards, very large,
very intimidating, when they manifested. They escorted
Mole outside.

"Com," Cinnamon said when Mole was out of the
room. "Open a secure line to Luc Tashika."

A minute later, Tashika's face glared at her through the
telecom's screen. "Why are you calling me?"

Cinnamon smiled sweetly, hoping to charm the man
into a calmer state of mind. "*Konichiwa,* Mr. Tashika. I
merely seek a moment of your precious time."

"For what? I'm a busy man."

And a rude slag, Cinnamon thought. *Fine, if that's how
you want to play . . .*

"Since Miss Tamara Ny is . . . shall we say 'metaboli-cally challenged,' I take it that you have acquired the in-formation you sought regarding my client."

Tashika blanched. Then he composed himself, taking a deep breath. "No, Miss Cinnamon, your information is in error. Miss Ny's predicament was an accident, and I know nothing about any information she may or may not have stolen from your client."

Cinnamon scanned the inset screen on her telecom, which showed a voice-stress analysis of Tashika's voice. It showed that he could be lying.

Why would he lie?

"Very well," she said. "Then you remain committed to our earlier arrangement?"

"Of course."

"Good. I will commit some resources to containing the stolen information." She paused deliberately. "If it exists."

"Get back to me," Tashika said before disconnecting.

He must know more than he's saying, she thought. *Maybe he already has the information from Ny, but doesn't want to pay for the mop-up work of hunting down Grids Desmond. Perhaps he is telling the truth.*

Either way, she had to spend nuyen to track down Grids Desmond. Ice him and get rid of the chip. That slotted her off. *This Michaelson extraction is getting out of hand,* she thought. *And Michaelson isn't even out yet.*

Cinnamon changed, letting her human form give way to her true shape, the one given her by her former master. Slamming her fist—now a reptilian claw—through the glass coffee table, she released the roar that had been building, causing the walls of her home to shake.

The glass table shattered with a crash, spraying shards into the plush carpeting. She watched the tiny cuts on her knuckles heal to closure. "Dorian!" she bellowed, arcing her neck and swinging her huge dragon head from side to side.

A spirit manifested across the room. Dorian took the form of a human male of moderate build, white hair, and crisp blue eyes. "I am here," he said.

"I need to feed soon," she said, feeling the uncontrol-lable rush of hunger flow through her. She must control herself. "Could you please prepare something?"

"In the kitchen, my dear. A small swine awaits."

"Always the faithful," she said. "Thank you for that."

Dorian said nothing as he led her to the kitchen. Cinnamon wormed her way across the floor. And as she entered the kitchen on her blue-scaled belly, the smell of the piglet's fear drove her to a frenzy. Building and building until she ripped into the soft, red flesh of the tender animal. She ripped out its neck, then swallowed the thrashing body in three delicious bites.

17

Hendrix ran his hand over his shaved skull, wiping the sweat from its smooth surface. Four skillsofts bristled from the softlink behind his right ear. The softlink wired him into the changes of an increasingly bizarre and dangerous world. His activesofts and knowsofts kept him on the cutting edge. At least that was the idea.

Hendrix stepped into the warehouse's shower to examine his body for abnormalities. In the wake of the Giribaldi run, he needed to be certain he was still in perfect condition, just in case he'd picked up an unwanted eavesdropper or some slow-acting poison. He found nothing more than the usual—a large, cybernetically modified body encased in smooth skin as brown as semi-sweet chocolate, Chiseled musculature, wired reflexes. He was as strong and as fast as nuyen could buy.

Still alive after all these years of killing, he thought. A boast not many shadowrunners lived to make.

After determining that the Giribaldi run had left nothing more than bad memories, Hendrix let himself enjoy the sting of hot, clean water against his skin for a few minutes. Then he dried and dressed in jeans and the armored black synthleather jacket he'd stolen off a Barrens ganger who'd been unlucky enough to wander too close to his hidey-hole here in Wilmington.

The warehouse was a low-slung building made of black corrugated metal. It was part of the ancient oil refinery outside; sludge-covered metal pipes snaked and twisted along the ceiling. Hendrix walked past the old offices and into the central area where Juju Pete sat watching the trid. The offices now served as bedrooms for him and his runners: Layla, who shared his bed, the dwarf decker Mole, and Juju, an ork mage who'd been wounded in the Giribaldi run.

Juju glanced up from the trid as Hendrix entered. A

couch and a few chairs had been set up in one corner of the huge central room, which had once been a dock area. Juju was very tall, very black with a mustache and a goatee. His tightly curled hair was woven into long, thin braids, each tipped with a bone fragment. Despite his name and his appearance, Juju practiced hermetic magic and he thought shamans were deluded.

"How's the leg feel?" Hendrix asked.

"Not wiz. I've stabilized it, but I'm not gonna be rolling with the team for at least two or three weeks."

Juju's leg had been chewed up pretty savagely by a fragmentation grenade. Bone fractured in several places, shrapnel lodged deeply into his flesh. It had taken the street doc five hours to patch him up, but Juju had refused any sort of mechanical implants, so the healing process would be slow indeed.

"Null sheen," Hendrix said. "We pulled down enough nuyen to keep us going for a while."

Suddenly Juju's mouth went slack and his eyes rolled back. That was how he looked when his spirit left his body to travel in astral space. Hendrix didn't really understand all the intricacies of magicians and their art, but he did know that the effects of spells and spirits could be as deadly as a bullet through the brain. A second later the ork sat up straight again. "Mole and Layla are back," he said.

As if on cue, the door slid open and in they walked. Layla's laughter brought a smile to Hendrix's face. She was as close to a friend as he'd ever let himself have. A little overconfident during runs, but lovely to look at, fun to be around, and great in bed. She flashed him a smile as she removed her Ingram SMG from under her coat.

Mole was already talking. "Okay, okay," he said, rubbing his palms together excitedly. "We got biz if we want it, Hendrix. Cinnamon wants you to call her."

"Can we run without Juju?" Hendrix directed the question to both Mole and Layla.

"Sure," said Layla. "From what Mole tells me, sounds like a stroll on the boardwalk."

"Maybe," said Mole. "But that could change real fast."

Juju looked up. "I can ride shotgun in the astral," he said. "As long as someone's here to watch my body."

Mole laughed. "Well, I'll be right here the whole time."

"You'll be jacked in to your machine, dead to the world," said Juju.

"I can monitor you on the internal cameras," Mole said. "I'll jack out if anything happens."

Juju snorted. "All right," he said, though it was obvious he wasn't convinced. He looked at Hendrix. "I probably won't be that much help anyhow. I won't be able to cast spells at physical targets, but I can scout for spirits and watchers and such. I can let you know what's happening through Layla; she and I can talk when she's perceiving astrally."

Hendrix nodded. Layla was a physical adept who had the magical ability to see into the astral but lacked the ability to go jandering around in it. "Yeah, better than nothing," he said. "I'll give the fixer a call." Then he went back into his room and sat down in front of the telecom, activating Mole's line scrambler to avoid a trace. He punched up Cinnamon's LTG.

Cinnamon answered, looking as beautiful as ever. Golden blond hair. Deep, bronze tan. Even white teeth. But she seemed too relaxed as she slouched in the couch, almost tired.

"Hello, Hendrix," she said. "I'm glad to hear from you. I've got work." She drawled the words as though she were drunk.

"I'm listening," Hendrix said.

"I want you to find a human named Grids Desmond," she said. "Mole has the data on him. I need you to find him and a chip he may have. Bring the chip to me, him you can geek."

"Null perspiration, shadowlady. Except that our image is wounded from the Giribaldi extraction."

"Yes, sorry about that," she drawled, "but this work must be done expediently. Do you wish for me to offer it to another party? Or perhaps I can hire a freelance mage to replace Juju Pete?"

Hendrix frowned. "I'll conduct a preliminary recon of the terrain," he said. "Layla and I can probably infiltrate without tripping any alarms."

"No doubt you can. If you are discreet and secretive until the time comes for action. Then move quickly, decisively."

"As always."

"Yes, and that's why I pay you so handsomely." Cinnamon's expression became serious. "This run may be easy, but it is also crucial. Don't make me worry."

Hendrix just laughed, deep and full, then disconnected. He was still laughing when he returned to central room. "We've got work," he told them. "Let's get prepped."

Layla looked at him. "Do we get to play geek-the-dumb-slag again?"

"Yeah." Hendrix couldn't help but smile. "And he goes by the name of Grids Desmond."

"Goody, goody," Layla said. "I love that game."

18

Jonathon yawned and rolled onto his side, staring at the ochre print wallpaper of his clinic room. He hated that color now, had hated it for hours. Yearning for sleep to come.

The crackled fray to his nerve endings showed itself as a flash on his retina, a projection of a grainy image of trideo static on a dead channel. A gray-textured ghost overlaid on his normal vision. And in that textured static, Jonathon saw images—Tamara in the final throes of life reaching for the trauma patch.

The twisting blur of the crowd was a kaleidoscope of color in the background, a static radiance of metahumanity. Then up close, the bright white gleam of the stadium flood lamps reflecting off razor-edged cyberspurs. Suddenly dulled with red blood. Gushing everywhere.

Jonathon closed his eyes, but the rumble in his head worsened. And if that weren't bad enough, the crowd outside his door barked and panted to gain access like hounds finding the hole of the fox.

Venice Jones stood just outside the wide, metal door. On crowd control. Some of the reporters had given up trying to get inside and were barraging the troll bodyguard with their questions instead. But Venny remained impassive. A wall of stone.

They'll never get him to talk, Jonathon thought. He smiled for the first time since waking. And it felt good.

A murmur passed through the crowd outside and the door cracked open. Venny pushed his huge, tusked head through. He wore mirrored wrap-around sunglasses. Wavy blond hair floated down around his wide-set jaw, and two horns pushed from his skull, both curving up and out, one painted white, the other black in imitation of a yin-yang symbol. A light brown mustache and goatee pushed from his wart-marred lip and chin.

"Synthia's here, chummer," he said. "You want to see her?"

Synthia? Yes, he wanted to see her. "Of course," Jonathon said. "Thanks, Venny."

The troll stood aside for a second, and Synthia squeezed through under his arm. Her petite form was garbed in a flowing red summer dress, and she carried a bouquet of yellow roses.

"There's a load of flowers piling up outside," she said, giving him her delicious half-smile. "But Venny won't let them in."

Jonathon propped himself up into a sitting position as she put the flowers on the window sill, then came over to kiss him. She smelled of hot summer wind and roses. He was glad she was here.

"I told him I wanted to rest," he said. "No disturbances."

She grew serious. "How do you feel?"

"Not up to specs," he said, and he told her about the hiss in his head. About being jacked through to Tamara when she died. And about Doctor Abramson's remarks concerning Tamara's lack of blood clotting.

"You think Rose killed her on purpose?"

"That's what I'm going to find out as soon as I get out of here."

"He was released, you know."

"Dougan?"

"Yeah, you torqued his neck out pretty fierce, according to the newsfax. He'll be in an exoskeleton for a couple of days, but they say he'll ride in the final match on Friday." Synthia put her hand into his. Her thin fingers seemed so fragile, yet . . .

She reached over to the window sill and pulled a single rose from the bouquet. "Hold this," she said.

"What are you doing?"

"Giving you a little magical edge."

She focused on him for a few heartbeats, then crushed the rose into his bare chest. A rush of warmth overtook him, emanating out from his solar plexus to fill him with energy.

When it passed, the rose was gone, and much of his pain with it. "Wow, do that again," he said.

"That should be enough. You need rest more than anything."

"I can't sleep with all the commotion," Jonathon said. "What I need is . . ."

A huge yawn interrupted him. He sank against the pillows and closed his eyes. The last thing he saw was Synthia's delicate face, framed by her fire-red hair. He heard soft singing from all around, and saw her lips move slightly. Then sleep took him in a wash of relief.

The sun was just coming up when Jonathon finally opened his eyes again. How many hours had passed since the terrible events of last night? It seemed a lifetime. Venny still stood guard outside. *I've got to get hospital security to relieve him,* Jonathon thought.

Synthia slept in the chair next to his bed, looking as innocent as a baby. Of course, appearances could be deceiving. Jonathon smiled to himself. Innocent was one thing Synthia definitely was not.

He propped himself into a sitting position just as the telecom next to the bed beeped. That wasn't supposed to happen. Unless it was the hospital staff checking on him.

"Yes?" he said.

"Winger?" The face on the screen was an apparition from the past, broad and lined with deep wrinkles. A thick black beard and matching head of curls. Three datajacks adorned his left temple, the hair shaved close over them to provide easy access.

It was Theodore Rica, a dwarf of many talents. He used those datajacks. At least he had before prison, when he was the ground-bound tactical officer for Jonathon and Tamara.

"Theo, my long-lost chummer. How's biz?"

"It's good to see you up and awake, Jonathon. I saw the accident on the trid . . ." Theo's rough voice cracked as he trailed off. "They're saying Tam is dead. Is it true?"

Jonathon felt water rise in his eyes as he tried to hold Theo's gaze. "I don't know how it could have happened. After all these years, after . . ."

"Don't blame yourself, Jonathon. That won't bring her back."

Jonathon felt Synthia stir awake and squeeze his palm. "I don't," he said. "Not really. I just wish I'd been out there with her. Maybe I could've prevented it."

Theo frowned, but said nothing.

"How did you get through to me anyhow?" Jonathon asked after a long silence, trying to change the subject.

"Well," Theo said, the edges of his mouth hinting at a smile, "I *am* head of proactive security for MCT North America."

"You got the promotion. Congrats."

"Thank you," Theo said. His smile had emerged completely now.

"I can't believe they'd let a halfer get into such a high position."

"I'm no ordinary halfer."

"Verily," Jonathon said. " 'Tis true."

"I just showed them they had weaknesses I could either exploit or fix, depending on the kind of offer I got."

Jonathon laughed, and it hurt. It had been too long since he'd laughed full out, and despite the pain, it felt good.

After a minute, Theo lost his smile and gave Jonathon a serious look. "Gotta go," he said. "Back to work and all that. But listen, my friend, if there's anything I can do to help, just—"

"Actually, I thought of something."

"Name it."

"Could you get in contact with Anna and the gypsies for me? I think they'll want a funeral."

"It's as good as done, chummer. I'll be in touch." Then Theo's face was gone, replaced by the DocWagon logo.

Jonathon stared at it for a minute, thinking about the funeral. About seeing all the gypsies again. Seeing Anna. The big motherly elf had always blamed him for stealing Tamara away from the *vista*, the big family. Now she would blame him for Tamara's death as well.

And he wasn't looking forward to that.

Jonathon glanced over at Synthia, who had fallen back asleep, her head resting on the edge of the bed. *So lovely. So strong. What would I do without her?*

What if she died too?

He shook his head to clear those thoughts and punched commands into the telecom, instructing it to slave to his unit at home. He had sixty-two messages. *Frag!* He scanned the headers. Fifty-eight were from people he didn't know, most likely reporters or snoops or fans. Three were from his agent, and one was from Grids Desmond.

Maybe he knows something.

Jonathon hit a key to play back the message. And chills shook him as he listened to what Grids had to say. And after, Jonathon decided it was time he got out of this fragging clinic. Time he did something about Tamara's death.

19

In her San Bernardino home, Maria slept. Isolated from the sun by blinds and heavy curtains, her bedroom was a sanctuary, a dark nest where she could catch her daily sleep. Quiet, peaceful, and all hers.

Maria awoke to loud pounding. Thudding that shook the house. "Wake up! Wake up, Maria! It's important!" The voice was faint, distant as though she dreamt it.

Maria rolled in her bed, in her nest of pillows, patchy quilts, and clothing. She buried her head in the soft fabrics and cushions, trying to get away from the pounding.

Thud. Thud. Thud.

The noise never relented. The pounding continued until finally Maria opened her eyes, fully awake. She sat up in the bed and removed the blinding mask, feathered to look like an owl's face. Long black hair fell down to the small of her back, and she squinted against the daggers of sunlight filtering through around the curtain edges. She stood and placed the mask on its mannequin.

She walked toward the bedroom door, debating whether to cover her dark skin with clothes. "Quit pounding or I'll fry you," she yelled through the door. A fireball itched in the back of her head, just waiting to burn up the annoying culprit. "Who is it?" she asked. She expected Pedro or Angelina, perhaps home sick from school. Maybe even Wallace rumbling in on his bike. But Talon, her ally spirit, would never have let Wallace inside the house. And the kids knew better than to wake her up before dusk.

It must be an emergency, she thought.

The pounding had stopped, but nobody had answered her question. She activated the glass eye in the door to see who it was. Fear shot through her. The form standing in the hall outside her bedroom was out of place, not someone she immediately recognized.

She called for Talon, thoughts that her ally might have
been destroyed by this elf racing through her mind. Then
as she examined the man's features—the sharply pointed
ears, straight black hair, lean muscular body—she realized who it was.

Dougan Rose.

He was dressed in a long, black synthleather duster
over a dark blue suit. Looking very corporate. Except for
the bandage over his right ear and the hard segmented
polycarb exoskeleton that hugged his neck and covered
his Muerte tattoo. The exoskeleton was done in metallic
blue with silver sparkles, and it looked like another layer
of skin, except thicker and less flexible.

Maria unbolted the door and opened it. "Dougan, what
the frag do you want? I nearly fried you with a fireball,"
she said. "And I still might if your explanation isn't good
enough."

Dougan stood on the threshold and stared at her, an ap-
praising look on his face. His eyes scanned her dark human face, her doe-brown irises. Down her neck, pausing
only briefly to look at her matching tattoo, to her clavicle,
her breasts. Lower.

Suddenly she remembered she was naked, and though
she and Dougan had once been intimate, that was another
lifetime ago. She smiled and backed into the room, but
left the door open. "This had better be some crucial drek,"
she said, crawling back into bed to cover herself with a
quilt.

Dougan stepped inside, a faint whine coming from the
servos in his exoskeleton. He pulled the door shut behind
him, plunging the room into sweet darkness again, though
with light enough for her to see.

"Okay, Dougan, now that you've got me up, spill it. Or
get out." She smiled and held the covers up. "Or get in if
you want."

That brought a smirk to his face. He was obviously
tempted. "I wish we had time for that," he said. "And
maybe we will, after this is all over. But now . . ."

"Yes."

"I want to get La Muerte back together for a run."

Maria laughed. Deep and full, throwing her hair back.
It was the funniest thing she'd heard all week.

"I'm serious," he said.

After a minute, she gained control of herself. "I can see that," she said. "Maybe that's why it's so funny."

"It's important," he said. "And very lucrative."

Maria laid her head back against a soft pillow. "Go home," she said.

Dougan sat on the bed. "Maria, if we leave now, we can get Maurice and Bob Henry out before the El Infierno curfew."

"Dougan, you're loco. El Infierno security won't let them out. Nobody gets out of there anymore."

"I've already contacted them, and made plans to get them out."

Maria pushed up onto one elbow. *He is insane.* "Why should I help you? We're both many years out of the shadows. The biz is different now. Lot's of wetwork, no sense of honor. Besides, I have kids, and they'll be home from school in a couple of hours. Even if I wanted to, which I don't, I can't just leave and go back into the gang jungle."

Dougan sat on the bed and looked at Maria. "Tashika knows about me, and knows we used to run together."

"He's blackmailing you?"

"That would be the nice term for it, yes. He's got data on our last run—the lost election job. Twelve years, and he still won't let me forget it."

"Would you anyway?" Maria asked. Her brother, Jesse, had died in that run. Jesse with his dark, haunted eyes. His gaunt cheeks and whipcord physique, his bronze skin stretched tight over lean muscles.

She missed his reassuring presence, security and command emanating from him like heat from a kerosene burner. She dreamt of him often, during those days when sleep came slowly. And she could never get the events of his death out of her mind, despite years of trying.

Even now, she still saw that school building in Compton where they'd tried to hide from the Calfree forces— the state guard plus Lone Star special ops and corp mercenaries. Maria had crouched in the predawn stillness of the school's library. Jesse, Dougan, Maurice, and Bob Henry sat next to the hulking shadows of their big bikes, silent and waiting. Leaning their backs against the bookshelves, holding their automatic weapons ready.

Combat mages sent fire elementals racing down the

school's corridors lined with old-style lockers. Heavy battery drones rolled on thick treads and blew holes in the walls with their cannons.

Maybe those forces didn't know that orphans and homeless families lived in the school. Maybe they were unaware that gang wars had destroyed most of the houses and apartments in the neighborhood, that over four hundred people slept on the floor in the abandoned classrooms and the gymnasium. Maybe they were uninformed.

Or maybe they didn't care.

Children went screaming out into the halls, running for their lives. Trying to find a safer place. Many people burned to death when the fire elementals engulfed their soft flesh, turning it to bubbling black gelatin. The smell of burning corpses filled the air with its thick stench.

That smell permeated Maria's hair and her dark feathered suit, and it never came out. Later, she pulled all the hard-won feathers from her body suit and burned them. She cut her waist-length hair to the skull and threw it onto the fire.

Those people were innocent. The hardest lesson. Innocence is no protection. They had been killed because of her and Dougan. Because of Jesse, Maurice, and Bob Henry.

The Caltree forces fried the place to find them. Because they were La Muerte, a gang. And because they'd been smart and daring; they had branched out from gangbanging to shadowrunning. Shadowrunning was more to Maria's liking; more subtle and technical. Purposeful. And it paid much, much better.

On their last run, La Muerte had been hired to help get a team of cybersamurais and deckers into the California election computer base. The job was risky, but it paid well. How were they supposed to know that the insertion team was going to wipe the databanks clean, erasing the gubernatorial election results? It was an action that slotted off a whole drekking lot of powerful people. People who wanted anyone involved to pay.

Maria and the others were hunted for almost a week before they were cornered in the Compton school building. And by then a full-scale war on gangs had begun. State troops, Lone Star, and merc forces poured into the godforsaken streets of El Infierno, bombing, shooting, burning. Maybe La Muerte's involvement in the lost election was just the pretext the bigwigs in Sacramento needed for their dirty work.

Maria didn't know, but in less than a week, the edict was proclaimed; all gangs were to be purged from Compton and Gardena. The jungle must be purified. The war was on.

What the frag did the suits know about the jungle anyhow? *Nada. Zero. The big nothing.*

The suits looked down from their towers and saw violence and strife, thought they could bring order to chaos. But what they didn't know was that order was already there. Order of the baddest certainly, but order nonetheless.

El Infierno had its problems, perhaps more than most, but force was no way to solve them. Nuyen perhaps. Cred for jobs and schools. Self-confidence.

Hope.

Now, Maria felt tears resurface as she pulled her pillow close. She remembered how Jesse had sacrificed his life. As leader of the gang, and her older brother, he felt somehow responsible for them. So he did the fragging noble, heroic, macho thing. He rode his Honda Excaliber through the library's double doors and across the asphalt basketball courts. He yelled and whooped, trying to draw attention.

Maria had cast an illusion on him, to make it appear that all of them were making a run for it. Jesse only made it thirty meters before the assault cannons and miniguns blew his body to shreds. But it was enough time for Maria and the others to escape into the night under the cloak of invisibility.

Jesse had saved them and the remaining families and orphans that night. And afterward, Maria and Dougan left the jungle, left shadowrunning. Maria had no other family really, except Theresa, her mentor, so she did a quick fade with Dougan. She'd never have survived without him. They bailed together, and had stayed together for a while before Dougan changed his face and got the gig with the Buzzsaws.

"How could Tashika know?" Maria asked.

Dougan shrugged. "He's the one who helped me disappear," he said. "Got me the opening with the Buzzsaws, but I never told him anything about you or the others." He took a breath. "He shouldn't know about the election run, but he does. He knows everything. Somehow he found out who we are. And if we don't cooperate, he'll reveal it. For Maurice and Bob Henry, that doesn't mean much, but I'd be ruined if the fans and the public ever found out. And you . . . you have a family, a stake in this community. We could still be jailed."

Maria felt her shoulders sag under the weight of his statement. The daylight outside fogged her mind; Owl didn't help her until the sun went down. "Talon," she called.

The ally appeared before her in the shape of a birdman, taller than she was with large round eyes and feathered ears. "I'm leaving with Dougan," Maria said. "You will take care of the children."

"As you wish."

"Good." Maria looked at Dougan, who seemed suddenly tired. "Tell me about this plan of yours," she said. "We can go as soon as I dress."

Dougan talked about the run as she searched her closet for her old gear. He told her about Tashika's request that he injure Tamara Ny, and his reluctant acceptance. Then how he had accidentally killed her. If she hadn't moved her head at the last second . . .

In the back of the closet, Maria found her old nylon go bag. And inside were her old skins and a gelpack armored vest to protect against the occasional bullet. She had attached new feathers to the suit, replacing those she'd burned twelve years ago, but she hadn't actually worn it since. Maria had continued her magic over the years, but for herself only, and to stay close to Owl. Not for tricks and combat.

Dougan seemed very upset about Tamara Ny's death. Now, Tashika was forcing him to get Muerte back together to tie up the loose ends. "After we get Maurice and Bob Henry, we're to find a slag named Grids Desmond," Dougan said. "Plus some information he and Tamara Ny stole from Tashika."

Maria gathered her foci—a wide gold choker inlaid with orichalcum and studded with rubies and emeralds, and three silver rings that she wore on the last two fingers of her right hand. Then she opened her waist pouch to check her fetishes. There was a bag of down and four dried mice. Excellent.

"Are we to kill this person?" she asked, slipping into

her vest and skins. Everything still fit even after two kids and twelve years. Amazing. "I won't do wetwork anymore."

"Uh no, I don't think we'll have to."

"Tashika doesn't care?"

"I guess not," Dougan said. "He just wants the data."

Maria snorted. "Good."

"But if we did have to kill the slag," Dougan said, "it would just be part of the biz. No big deal."

She gave him a hard look as she finished dressing. "Shut up," she said. "Just shut the frag up, and let's go get the others."

ACT TWO

HIS LIFE AFTER DEATH

20

It was late afternoon by the time the skycab helicopter dropped Jonathon off at his estate just outside of Montecito. He stood at the edge of the helipad and waved at Synthia, who smiled back through the glass of the skycab's window. His hair flattened in the wind from the Hughes Airstar as it powered up. Jonathon ducked instinctively as he stepped further back to let the 'copter lift into the air.

The Airstar crested the top of the big oaks of his grounds and angled south, out over the water and toward LA, taking Synthia back to the heart of the sprawl. Jonathon took a moment in the aftermath of the helicopter's hurricane simply to stand with his eyes closed. He breathed deeply and felt the heat of the sun against his face.

Calm after the storm.

And then, into the calm, under the gentle breeze, came the low hiss. Ever-present. Tamara was still there in his head, and he found himself getting used to the constant frayed edge to his nerves.

He opened his eyes and walked slowly up the brick path to his house. He'd endeavored to recreate his childhood home when he'd purchased the ten-acre plot of land in the hills above Montecito. It covered most of a small, grassy hillside, shaded by old oaks planted eighty or ninety years before. He preferred oaks to the ever-popular palms that grew ubiquitously in Southern Calfree.

The house, which had been finished only a few months ago, was much larger than his childhood home in Redding, but the look was the same. Two-story, wooden farmhouse-style structure with wrap-around porches on both stories, painted white. But the architect had convinced him that such a meager house would devalue the property, and Jonathon knew how much nuyen he'd paid for the land.

Too fragging much.

He took one last glance out across the water in the distance, wondering if he could see Synthia's chopper. He loved her; that much he knew. She was warm and intelligent, fascinating and unlike anyone he had ever known. She wanted to be with him just to be with him. No ulterior motive. No agenda.

Oh, she had her secrets, her own life at UCLA, teaching young wannabee mages. But he liked that. He enjoyed discovering things about her that he never expected. He didn't know her inside and out. Unlike Tamara . . .

Now that Synthia was gone, Jonathon would contact Grids and learn why Tamara had been killed. He'd been waiting, impatiently, for this moment ever since he'd played the message from Grids.

The recording had been short and concise. "Jonathon, you're the only one who can help me. I've got to know what's happened to Tam. On the trid they're saying she's dead." The video was blanked and Grids' voice wavered as though he were agitated. Rushed.

"If that's true, I know why," he said. "Call this LTG. But use a public telecom or a secure line. Leave a message for Tamara's real mother. That's how I'll know it's you. Not Anna, but the other. You know who. Then give a meeting place and time. Make it a public place with a lot of people. Come secretly. Come alone."

Then Grids had disconnected.

Venny was asleep in the guest room, exhausted after keeping watch all last night while being besieged by reporters and lawyers and fans. *PR work was never Venny's biz,* Jonathon thought. *But since he's asleep . . .*

Jonathon moved through the massive kitchen, tiled with large white and black squares. He passed by the broad, hardwood staircase in the main entryway and into the garage.

Four vehicles awaited their turn to roll at high speed over the twisting, turning mountain roads along the coast and through the forested terrain east of Santa Barbara. There was a vintage 1988 Jaguar XJ12 with retrofitted cybernetic interface. Pristine condition. And next to it, a Mitsubishi Nightsky rested like a gentle giant.

But neither the Jag nor the limo was appropriate for his errand this afternoon. He needed something subtle. Some-

thing that might blend into the flow of traffic—his new
Eurocar Westwind 2000-turbo. *Hah,* he thought, *as discreet as an ork at a Humanis rally.* The Westwind was
uncommonly flashy for most occasions, but it would still
be less noticeable than either of the other two.

The fourth vehicle was a motorbike—a custom, built-for-
the-road Harley Scorpion. Not appropriate for a trip into the
city. Jonathon walked over to the sleek Westwind and
punched the combination into the door lock. With a muffled
click the lock released and the door swung upward. *Have to
hurry while Venny's sleeping.* The bodyguard would never
allow a solo jaunt into the sprawl. Especially now.

Jonathon checked the storage compartment to make sure
his drones were fully charged and loaded. The remote birds
rested neatly in position. One was a Cyberspace Designs
Stealth Sniper, gleaming on its spring-loaded launch rod
like a cat-sized beetle. Equipped with a rudimentary sensor
package and a sniper rifle. The other was an AeroDesign
Condor, inflatable, solar-powered, and excellent for long-
term recon and info-gathering. He hoped he wouldn't need
them, but since he had the toys, he might as well play.

Nestled neatly next to the drones was his box of emergency rations, hi-carb energy bars and a case of chocolate
protein shakes. *Gotta keep the beast at bay.* He pulled a
can from the case, peeled away the top and drank half of it
before closing the trunk. Then he climbed into the driver's
seat, wincing against the stiffness in his knee and the pangs
in his chest.

The car's internal trid unit linked with the surveillance
cameras to show a couple of trid reporter vans waiting
outside the front gate. Luckily the underground rear entrance was still secret enough to elude unwanted scrutiny.
Jonathon fired up the Westwind and made his way out
through the short tunnel.

The unmarked private road joined the main road three
kilometers from his front gate, and the cameras showed
no traffic. Within minutes he was down the road and out
onto the CalTrans expressway, bound for the LA sprawl.
Jonathon drove manually for a while, losing himself in
the physical mechanics of it. He hadn't jacked into a machine since attacking Dougan, and he didn't particularly
want to any time soon.

He tried to give himself to the road, the muted growl of

the pavement under the wheels—nearly in harmony with the hiss of his head. The stretching flickers of the dashed white lines disappearing into the distance, forever over the curving horizon.

He stopped at a rest area to place the call. Stepping up to a telecom that smelled of urine and vomit. He activated the telecom, voice only, and punched in the LTG number Grids had given him.

No message. No beep. Just the faint whine of empty memory.

"This message is for Jennifer Sanborne," Jonathon said, using the codename Grids had asked for.

When Jonathon and Tamara were in prison, after the Multnomah Falls accident, Tamara had hired the services of a genealogist to track down her real mother. Evidently, the gypsies had found her as a baby, abandoned on Freeway 10 in Pueblo territory. Anna had adopted her and raised her, but Tamara had always longed to know her real mother.

The genealogist took some DNA from Tamara and scanned the databanks for a SINner with a close match. Jennifer Sanborne was one of the closest, and since she lived in Phoenix, smack in the Pueblo lands, Tamara was convinced the woman had to be her real mother. But Tamara had never confronted Jennifer Sanborne to learn if she'd abandoned her six-month-old daughter on a freeway in the desert. She'd been too afraid of finding out this wasn't her mother after all.

Then Tamara would have no real mother.

Very few people knew about Jennifer Sanborne. Grids had been smart to pick that name. "Jennifer," Jonathon said, "meet me at Venice Beach. The Dockweiler Gardens." Jonathon focused on his retinal clock, which showed 02:48:21 PM. "At five o'clock," he said, then disconnected.

He quickly climbed back into the car and accelerated out onto the freeway.

About an hour later, Jonathon parked the Westwind 2000-turbo in a Mafia-controlled gravel lot between Grandma's Pharmacy and Survival and a giant, hotdog-shaped food shack called The Big Weenie. Venny had tried to get him on the car's telecom more than once, but Jonathon wanted to be on his own for this one. Venny's presence might make Grids bolt, and Jonathon needed to find out what he knew about Tamara's death.

Jonathon felt like a shadowrunner as he stepped out of the Westwind, activating the auto lock-down mechanism and leaving the car in ready mode so he could rig it or launch the drones remotely if necessary. Since he'd never again be ejecting from experimental aircraft, Jonathon had reprogrammed the transmitter of his head rig to communicate with the car and its drones.

He flipped up the collar of his armored black duster. He was in disguise. Undercover. It wouldn't do for anyone to recognize him.

But the coat was pristine and too clean. Frag, it was almost new; he didn't do this kind of drek very often. Anyone with a sharp eye would slot him for a newbie runner or a wannabee, but it was all he had.

On Venice Beach it wouldn't matter. Here, everyone was in a disguise of some sort.

The large right pocket of his duster held the cool weight of his Ares Predator II pistol, loaded with gel rounds. Probably not good enough if the drek really came down, but Jonathon wasn't expecting this to be a set-up. And if the time came to put up or shut up, he had several clips of armor-piercing ammo.

His fedora covered the tips of his ears, and his wide mirrorshades blocked much of his face. The glasses jacked in through his temple with a very fine wire hidden under his hat, giving him infrared, thermographic vision if need be. *Finally a good use for all my toys,* he thought.

He walked the short distance down the road to the boardwalk, surrounded on all sides by the mob of tourists and local vendors. No one recognized him. Excellent.

He passed custom cyberware vendors, street docs, krill fryers, surf shops, costume rentals. The beach on his right was packed to overflowing, the crowd thickening near the spectacles of magic and acrobatics.

As Jonathon walked, he watched a dwarf on three-meter stilts. The dwarf wore a huge, mushroom-shaped hat and a white shirt that shimmered orange in the light from the setting sun. Red-and-blue striped pants extended to the ground, and huge clown shoes had been attached to the base of the stilts.

The dwarf was juggling miniature chainsaws as he balanced. The crowd drew back in front of him as he walked, and the dwarf seemed to stumble for a second, but it was all part of the show; he regained his balance easily, and never dropped his chainsaws.

Jonathon smiled; he loved Venice Beach and felt a tinge of sadness that he was here for business and not the sheer fun of it. He passed a street mage performing an intricate dance with seals and gulls, which Jonathon suspected were illusions.

Dockweiler Gardens was an old-style bar and grill just off the boardwalk. Time showed 04:42:16 PM when he entered. The place was full, but he requested a table on the redwood deck, overlooking the beach and surf. Twenty minutes later, he was sitting, nursing a cold Pyramid cerveza and scanning the flow of people for Grids Desmond.

Grids arrived about five minutes later, his thin body covered in black denim. His dark hair slicked back as though he'd applied grease to it. "You alone?" Grids asked.

"As specified," Jonathon said. "I even ditched my bodyguard for this."

Grids looked tired; the lines of his thin face were drawn tight, wrinkles deepened as though he hadn't slept in days.

"You look like drek," Jonathon said.

"What are you, the fashion police?"

Jonathon laughed. "Whoa, calm down, chummer. It just looks like hiding out has affected you, that's all."

"You ever lived in East Hollywood?"

"Places like it."

"I doubt it," Grids said, then paused to call the waiter to order a soykaf and some nachos. When the waiter had left, Grids popped a chip out from behind his ear in a smooth and rapid motion, palming it.

Even Jonathon almost didn't notice.

Grids placed his hand on the table, palm down. "You sure Tam is gone?"

Jonathon heard the static growl in his head, very faint. He nodded. "Her funeral is tomorrow. Lake Shasta."

"You can go there? I thought it was protected. Dragons and shamans and drek."

"I've got a permit."

"What?"

"Sorry, not a good time to joke around," Jonathon said. "Shasta is a no-man's-land, and there's a dragon—Hestaby—but it never shows up unless there's a war. I've never seen it. Anyhow, Tam's family, the gypsies, are there for the summer."

"Can I come?" Grids asked.

"You want to?"

Grids stared at Jonathon with his black eyes. "I know you don't like me," he said. "I've never understood why, but—"

"You're unstable. You have a history of bailing out when the drek gets too deep. Women, jobs—you can't keep 'em. You always retreat into the sim or something like it." Jonathon held up his beer to show Grids what he meant by that.

Grids just stared at him and said nothing for a minute. Then softly, "I loved her. I loved her more than I've ever loved anyone." His voice cracked and he looked away, out at the ocean.

Jonathon sighed. "I know," he said. "And I know she'd have wanted you to come to the funeral. So you can come. Now, tell me why I'm here."

Grids took a deep breath. "The night before the game in New Orleans, Tamara and I made this sim."

"What—?"

Grids held a finger to his lips for silence. "Maybe you know she'd been sleeping with a Saeder-Krupp exec named Andreas Michaelson." Grids quickly glanced around, but the place was bustling; no one was paying them any attention.

"Yes," Jonathon said. "She thought he was going to make her a simsense star."

"Bingo. Well, Michaelson kept putting off her requests to arrange an audition, so Tamara got tired of waiting."

"Patience never was one of her virtues."

Grids gave Jonathon a sad face. "She thought a more direct approach was necessary."

"Blackmail?"

Grids nodded. "She had me record their sex that night." Jonathon frowned.

"So she could threaten to reveal it to his wife and the corp if he refused to get her a deal."

"So he killed her? Seems a tad harsh."

Grids shook his head. "There's more." The waiter arrived with the soykaf and nachos. Grids sipped the black liquid and gobbled down a few bites of the cheese-slathered chips.

Jonathon sipped his cerveza.

"You got a chipjack?"

"No."

"Null sheen. I brought a Senseman." Grids pulled a tiny simsense deck from his black leather satchel. The unit was about the size of his hand, could take CDs or chips. Grids pulled the thin fiber-optic cable from the unit and gave it to Jonathon.

Jonathon snapped the 'trode into place while Grids faded him into the sim.

Satin sheets caressed Tamara's naked body as she awoke in the huge bed. The chip was a wet record, though not as crisp as Jonathon got from the team's equipment. Plus, here there were no emotive tracks, only sensory, which left him feeling empty, like he was simming a hollowed-out person, a shell devoid of soul.

A ghost.

The bed shook and a huge, bearded face filled her vision, then the stench of stale morning breath filled her nostrils, and his mouth was over hers.

Jonathon cringed and nearly sprayed his cerveza.

"Good morning, my pet," the man said. "I'm going to get a shower."

Tamara mumbled, rolling away from him and closing her eyes.

A minute later, the distant sound of spraying water came through the bathroom door. Tamara snapped open her eyes, wide awake, and got up. She pushed her long, black hair from her face and walked, stark naked, to Michaelson's desk.

Jonathon wondered at that moment why they'd never made love. She was the most beautiful woman he'd ever known. A goddess. But this wasn't really her; this was only her body, her sensory tracks. Tamara was like a sister to him; he felt a tinge of guilt at this sudden burst of desire.

She was gone forever. And she had taken part of him with her.

Tamara scanned the desk. "Grids," she whispered, "you better be getting this." Most of the stuff on the desk was mundane—memos, chips, the telecom. None of that was important.

But then she was searching through the briefcase. Inside were documents. Some progress report on a corporation called Magenics, Inc. based in Long Beach. And underneath, what was obviously a top-security hardcopy in a magnetically sealed binder.

Tamara tried to open it, her heart racing. Her breath coming quickly.

The seal wasn't locked. She opened the binder, reading the cover page. "The Magus File: A compilation of data concerning genetic loci relevant to the Magus Factor, and how those loci might be incorporated into a stable AZ54-type biocomputer."

Jonathon had no idea what it meant.

Tamara quickly paged through the document, not pausing to read each word, but looking at every page. "I hope you'll be able to decode this," she whispered.

She finished just before Michaelson emerged from the shower. She closed the file and brushed away any fingerprints with the corner of a pillowcase, her hands shaking and sweaty. She left everything as she found it.

She jumped back into the bed just as the big, hairy man lumbered from the bathroom, his white cotton robe flowing around him, open in front.

Tamara rolled lazily between the sheets staring at Michaelson's rejuvenated body. He smiled then and climbed back into bed.

Click; the sim stopped. Tam was gone again. The ghost dissipated, and Jonathon felt whole once more.

"That should be far enough," Grids said, popping the chip out of the Senseman unit and back into the slot behind his ear.

Jonathon snapped out the 'trode and let the wire retract into the tiny player. He looked at Grids. "What do you know about this Magus File?" he asked.

Grids sipped his 'kaf. "At first, nothing," he said. "But I've been scanning Shadowland for data on the text I could read. Still don't have too much, but it looks like the Magus Factor from the title has something to do with genetics and magic. I have a subroutine scanning the databanks for info on it, but I already know that most of it's way too technical for me.

"I do know a little about biocomputers though. At least in theory. From decker hearsay, some megacorps, especially Aztechnology, are pouring metahuman brains into vats full of an electrolyte solution and wiring them as processors to create some sort of higher, artificial intelligence."

"You're drekking me."

Grids shrugged. "I'm just telling you what I heard."

Jonathon stretched, then downed the last of his cerveza. "Can you reconstruct the text of Magus File?"

"I've got Goofy working on it now."

"Goofy?"

"A smartframe I whipped up."

"Oh," Jonathon said. "Well, good. I want to get that bastard Michaelson. There must be a connection between him and Dougan Rose." Jonathon stood to go, then looked at the pale human in black denim. "Grids," he said, "I may not like you, but I need your help. Are you with me?"

Grids stood as well. "All the way," he whispered, almost to himself.

"Good," Jonathon said. "Because that's the only way I'd allow. Now, come on, we've got a funeral to go to."

21

Hendrix cracked his neck with a quick, precise tensing of his shoulder muscles, then piloted the van around a slow corner. He snatched a glance at Layla, sitting in the van's passenger seat. She wore a hat with the Sprawl Repo, Inc. logo on the front patch. The ponytail of gold hair that hung out the back of her hat caught a ray of the fading sunlight.

Dusk approached—the perfect time for shadow work. Twilight, when colors lost their hue, becoming gray and indistinct. When shade and light fused into one.

"Checkpoint," he said. "Get ID ready."

She nodded, then handed him a flat plastic card with a holopic likeness of her and a scanbar. Like Hendrix, she wore a gray pinstriped uniform over her urban camouflage armor.

Hendrix put on his best biz face as they pulled up next to the guard booth protecting the entrance gate to Beverly Hills. The guard inside the booth looked bored, probably because he never saw any action at this post.

Hendrix had come in through Brentwood for that very reason. This guardpost had minimal security back up. Unlike the section that separated Studio City from East Hollywood, the three-meter-high plascrete wall was free of graffiti, and the pointed wrought iron spikes that jutted from the top of the wall were clean of dried blood. Cameras and gun turrets were also sparse.

Hendrix straightened his seat and activated his headphone, opening a connection to the temporary LTG number that Mole had set up so that Hendrix could upload data, including voice and images, directly to the Matrix. One of Mole's smartframes scanned the virtual space every hundred milliseconds, then encoded and forwarded the data to Mole's deck.

"We're approaching checkpoint number two," Hendrix said.

Mole's response was quick. "I've got you on visual. No worries."

Hendrix grunted. That was Mole's job. He'd better have control of the video. Hendrix looked over at Layla again. "Anything in the astral?" he asked.

"Nothing I can see right here," Layla said, shaking her head slightly as her eyes focused on him. "Except for Juju. He just made a quick scan of the etheric and says it's all clear. No watchers."

Hendrix nodded. It was a testament to the strange nature of the Awakened world that two of his team could operate without being present physically. The meat bodies of both Juju and Mole were back at the warehouse where they would be safe.

Hendrix pulled out his own ID holopic as the bored guard actually stepped out of the booth and walked up to the window. *He must really be hunting for action,* thought Hendrix. *Never seen that happen before.* Normally, the guards just looked through scratched macroglass and punched the gate open if the card scanned true.

Hendrix thumbed down the window and handed his and Layla's cards to the man. The guard glanced at Hendrix's face, then at the card. Hendrix smiled at him.

"Destination?" the guard asked.

"Stone Canyon Condos," Hendrix said.

The guard was a plump salaryman, unused to trouble and certainly not prepared for Hendrix and Layla should they decide to go for their weapons. The man straightened his hat and scanned the Sprawl Repo logo on the side of the van. "What's the take today?" he said.

"Just some fancy simsense 'ware," Hendrix said. "Real 'spensive drek."

When the ID scan came up green, the guard handed the cards back to Hendrix and Layla, then resumed his bored look. "Have a lazy one," he said. Then he was back into the booth, punching the code to open the steel door.

Hendrix pulled the van through, smiling to himself. Next to him, Layla burst into laughter, and it was like sweet music to his ears. For a minute he let her humor infect him and he laughed as well.

"We're through," he told Mole. "Proceeding to destination."

"Okay, okay," came Mole's synthesized voice. "I'll be scanning some data on Mr. Winger. Contact me when you're approaching ground zero."

"Check."

Layla's laughter subsided and she glanced at Hendrix. "This one's easy money," she said.

"Perhaps."

"What could go wrong?" she said. "We've checked the angles; the run is easy. The cause is just. This Grids slag stole the information; he should return it."

"But we're supposed to retire him as well," Hendrix said. "And we don't know anything about the data he stole. Perhaps it should be disseminated."

She laughed again. "You think too much, babe."

Hendrix just smiled at that.

The drive to Tamara's apartment went without incident. The traffic lights were flickering to life outside the Stone Canyon Condos as they pulled up. Layla was giddy from watching all the huge, sprawling houses nestled behind manicured lawns and sculptured landscaping. Huge old trees and hundred-year-old ivy almost made them forget they were in the sprawl at all, only a kilometer from shadows so black they'd geek you for a fragging cigarette.

The Stone Canyon Condos were new, set among some evergreen trees along Stone Canyon Reservoir. The structure was built from real redwood and mirrored gray glass so that the trees and sky reflected off the windows.

Hendrix parked in plain sight and scanned the condos, clicking the magnification up on his cybereyes. With their low light and thermographic vision, he could tell nearly everything happening on the grounds.

There was a palm scanner on the front gate, but no actual guard. Null sweat. Nada. Zero opposition as far as he could see.

Lights were on in one of the apartments, but the residents seemed to be watching the trid. Tamara Ny's apartment was dark. "Mole," Hendrix said, "we're on site and ready to roll."

"Give me five seconds to get back into the node, and I'll intercept any alarm calls."

Layla looked over at Hendrix, her fine features shadowed

by the van's overhead lamp. "Juju says there's a watcher and an air elemental guarding the apartment complex. Nobody's home otherwise. No Grids Desmond. No nobody."

"Will the spirits disturb us?" Hendrix asked, wishing Juju Pete were here in the flesh.

"Juju says it depends on what they're tasked to do. Most likely not, unless we have to force entry."

"We'll be discreet."

Layla grinned at him with white teeth as she slapped the ammo clip onto her silenced Ingram SMG. "Of course," she said, "discretion *is* the better part of valor." With an impossibly quick move, she slid the Ingram into its holster under her uniform. Accélerated by magic.

Hendrix relied on more mundane ways to keep up. The latest technological advances in bioware and cyber. He'd never gone toe to toe with Layla to see who was faster, stronger, but he had more experience by a long shot. Not even close. Each day that he ran the shadows and lived, he realized with more clarity that experience was what kept him alive. Making the right decisions. Maintaining the right contacts.

Shadowrunning had come fairly easy after his years as a merc. Years he tried to forget. Desert wars. Yucatán. Then the El Infierno invasion as part of the Calfree forces. What a joke that was, but he'd survived again, saved when his conscience and experience told him to bail out of his contract. The army had no right mowing down civilians in the name of keeping the peace. His unit had been captured by a marauding go-gang later that same day. All of them gutted and hung on lamp posts.

But bailing on a corporate contract had its own catches. As part of the Calfree deal, Yamatetsu had injected Hendrix with nanites—symbiotic microorganisms that increased his ability to heal. But they'd also been tailored to produce a neurotoxin in the absence of a certain compound that was provided in the food. When Hendrix left, he no longer got the food, and without the chemical he was a dead man.

It was only because of Sergio, a street doc chummer, that Hendrix lived through the experience. Sergio took all of Hendrix's nuyen, but he specialized in bioware and was able to destroy the symbiotes and clean the toxin from Hendrix's blood. Another testament to the value of maintaining good contacts.

Now, Hendrix straightened the cap on his shaved head, checked to make sure his armor was in place, and stepped out of the van. The plan was simple. Since nobody was home, they would enter the condo on the pretext of repossessing Grids's simsynth. Mole had doctored some payment records to the Corporate Bank of Calfree where Tamara Ny had borrowed the cred to purchase the expensive Fuchi box.

Once inside, they would scour the place. Try to find the chip Cinnamon wanted. Gather clues to help them find Grids. Perhaps Juju could locate him magically when he'd healed up. Plus there were always other clues—holopics, telecom messages. Hendrix was confident they'd eventually track down Mr. Grids.

Hendrix's own gun rubbed against the callus just below his ribs as he walked. The weapon was an Ares Alpha Combatgun, not subtle but a die-hard favorite. With its integrated grenade launcher and built-in recoil reduction, Hendrix could shoot his way out of an all-out assault with it. His other gun was a silenced Ares Predator II for the more discreet situations.

They moved across the street and passed easily through the outside gate, thanks to Mole. Then up the stairs to number seven. His favorite number. Layla walked with him, snickering slightly to herself. "Can't wait to see inside this doss," she said.

Hendrix glared at her to stow it, which she did. Then he reached up and pressed the intercom button.

A tiny icon of a blind, ugly rodent appeared on the intercom's small screen, and Mole's voice came through the speaker. "Please come in," he said.

The lock inside the door clicked, and Hendrix pulled the door open with a gloved hand, then stepped through.

Layla suppressed an excited laugh as they passed through a natural redwood-paneled foyer and into the living room. Plush gray carpeting. Southwestern-style furniture. Very expensive. "Wiz," said Layla. "I could live here."

"Stay sharp, chica," Hendrix said. "Seems safe enough, but we've got an elemental and a watcher tracking our movements, just waiting for us to make a mistake."

"We'll just fry them if—"

"Better to pretend we belong."

Layla put on a mock serious face. "Let's get rolling then."

The two of them searched the entire apartment. Hendrix capturing the images of each room in digital perfection with his cyberoptic camera. They quickly determined that Grids had left, packing in a hurry. It looked like he'd taken some clothes and some food. Unfortunately he'd purged the telecom's memory so they couldn't pull off the last outgoing calls. The incoming messages revealed nothing.

Their search for the chip was systematic, even though Hendrix suspected that it was gone with the target. Layla scanned the astral with her special sight, all the while listening to Juju give updates on the spirit. Hendrix took the lead, moving as fast as his boosted reflexes and augmented musculature would allow. Juju had reported finding no auras doing his astral recon, but that didn't mean there weren't surveillance cameras or track-running security drones. Hendrix had seen too many mercs kiss death by such killing machines. And to him, that would be the worst way to go—by the mindless autofire of a drone.

Hendrix had been hit by such a beast only once, and he knew that wasn't how he wanted his number punched when the time came. He wanted to be able to stare into the eyes of his executioner. To know who it was had beaten him at his own game. The killing game.

"Paydata!" Layla said when they reached the garage.

"Mole," Hendrix said into his headphone. "You scan this?" He uplinked his cyberoptic camera data, then slowly panned around the room.

Old cyberdeck cases lay scattered, fiber-optics and motherboards jutting like decaying teeth from the wreckage. "Junk," Mole said. "Most of it anyway."

Hendrix came to a vacant area where the floor was free from electronic refuse. Stacks of chips and compact disks lined the shelves at the edge of the area, and a datacable lay loose, one end dangling free.

"He's taken his drek and gone," Mole said. "Take the chips and CDs if you want, but I seriously doubt he's left the sim we want."

Hendrix nodded. "No, he wouldn't be that stupid."

"What do you think, babe?" Layla asked, grinning. She had removed a satchel of radio detonators from her waist.

"We need a material link for Juju first," Hendrix said.

Layla bent down to the floor and picked up something. "Fingernail clippings good enough?" she asked. But she wasn't talking to Hendrix, she was talking to Juju Pete. She nodded in response to whatever Juju was saying from astral space, then pulled a tiny plastic baggie from one of her many pockets and sealed the clippings inside.

Hendrix took one last look around the room, recording it in case they needed to reexamine it later. Then he nodded to Layla. "Okay, set the charges quickly."

He removed his own satchel and placed three charges of plastique throughout the condo, carefully inserting a detonator into each. Layla did the same, and when they were done, Hendrix gave the order to move out.

Then they were back in the van, rolling for East Hollywood Gate. In ten minutes they had passed through and back into the shadows. Hendrix finally breathed a sigh. *Mission accomplished,* he thought as he pressed the transmitter to blow the charges. Even from a kilometer and a half away, he heard the explosion.

"I saw the flash!" Layla said. "Wiz."

On site, the windows blew out in a spray of glass, showering over the nearby houses. Hendrix imagined it in his mind. The walls ripped like rice paper and a searing hot sheet of fire flashed for a moment, just before a huge black cloud erupted from the dead shell of Tamara Ny's apartment. It was just too bad he wasn't close enough to see it for himself.

After a few breaths, he called Mole on his headphone. "Any leads on where the target might have gone?"

"Nothing solid, but I did find something when I broke into Jonathon Winger's home system. There was a message from Grids on Winger's telecom."

Hendrix smiled to himself. "Good job, Mole. We'll go after him next."

"He just returned to Montecito a few hours ago. I'll monitor his telecom just in case he contacts our man."

"Excellent," Hendrix said. "Layla and I will rendezvous with you and Juju at the safehouse, then we'll arrange to shadow Mr. Winger."

"Till then," Mole said, disconnecting.

"Hendrix," Layla said. "Look here." And when he turned toward her, she leaned across and put her lips against his, soft red against rough black. Then she leaned back and smiled. "Winger's involved?" she asked.

"Yes."

"That makes me sad," she said, dropping her smile for a beautiful pout. "I like him."

Hendrix hadn't thought about it. Like or dislike didn't come into it. This was biz. "Me too, I guess."

"If we have to geek him," Layla said. "The elf, I mean—Winger—I want to do it," she said.

"Sure."

She threw her head back and laughed. And laughed all the way to the safehouse.

22

Night came like a benediction. Maria breathed in the darkness, feeling Owl waken and give her strength.

Getting inside was easy. No one cared who went into the El Inficrno jungle. It was getting out of that war zone that was the problem. Anyone who tried to escape risked being gunned down by the powers that be.

Gunned down like Jesse, Maria thought as she sat in the passenger seat of the hijacked Pacific Foods truck. Hijacked with Dougan's nuyen; the rigger who piloted the truck didn't get paid enough for this route and had taken Dougan's cred willingly.

Dougan crouched between the seats, trying to avoid being recognized by the security guards. El Inficrno was isolated by a four-meter-tall cyclone fence topped with razorwire and surveillance cameras. There were motion detectors and autofire turrets, but they all faced inward, toward the city streets inside.

The rigger piloted the food truck past the sentry and into Compton, a blasted wasteland of low, dilapidated houses, built way back before the turn of the century and long ago blown to splinters by gang warfare.

The Pacific Foods truck had four guards who clung to the bumpers on each corner of the vehicle. The guards were armed with automatic weapons to prevent gang attacks between the gate and the Safestore on Avalon, the truck's destination.

The turf wars had never stopped; they'd only intensified when the walls had gone up because now room for expansion was limited. The top gang in West Compton was 'Hood Watch, which kept some order as long as the proper tributes were paid.

Maria heard the distant chatter of automatic gunfire and saw the faint glow of a burning building, reflected as an orange glow off the clouds and billowing black smoke. The smell of burning flesh grew as they approached the fire, and Maria swallowed hard to keep her stomach down, fighting the memory of the school raid twelve years ago.

They rounded the corner and for a second Maria was years younger, crouching behind the cinderblock barricade in the old boiler room as the Lone Star attack squad blew the drek out of the elementary school around her.

Now, the gutted school stood like a husk, a ghost in front of them as Dougan directed the rigger to pull the truck into the lot next to the old gymnasium doors. Maria was taken aback at how little it had changed over the years.

Across the asphalt basketball court and the dead football field, the house fire crackled and burned. A large crowd of onlookers had gathered to watch it—the primal draw of the flame holding their attention. Better than a show on the trid, better than simsense.

From the black rectangle of the open gym doors stepped two shapes. Specters from the past. They were human, large and bulked up with old cyber. They wore trenchcoats that bulged at sharp angles from the guns they carried.

Maria opened her door and stepped down from the truck. Dougan followed.

"Well, well, if it isn't Mr. Pointy Ears, daisy-eater himself." That voice was familiar, deep and resonant. Rich and humorless. Maurice's voice.

"Nice to see you too, Maurice," Dougan said. "I'm glad you missed me."

Maurice laughed, full and bass like a rumble through a subway tunnel. "I missed the nuyen you got me," he said. "Looks like that might change, neh?"

"You scanned it, chummer."

Bob Henry stepped around Maurice and out into the dim light. His ghostly white skin a contrast to Maurice's black flesh. Both razorguys stood two meters at the shoulder, gigantic for humans, and both still had their death's-head tattoos, though the wings of fire were dull against Maurice's dark skin. Bob Henry's large head and spike of white hair added another half-meter to his height. Maurice's head, by contrast, was squat and nearly square, his do cut into pinstripes along his scalp.

Maria marveled at their sheer bulk. *Too bad their brain size doesn't translate into intelligence,* she thought. "You chummers ready to fly?"

"Maria, you're a sight for horny eyes," Maurice said, the same resonant chuckle in his voice. "Your beauty makes me as mute as Bob Henry."

Bob Henry put a huge drek-eating grin on his face and nodded his head up and down. Up and down.

"You guys want this gig?" Dougan asked. "If we can get beyond our past, I think we could make a good team again."

"Muerte," Maria said. "For the last time."

"Bob Henry and I are in for two reasons," Maurice said. "One: escape to the outside. And two: the promised nuyen. Our dandelion-eater *elf* here has given his word for twenty kay each. True, neh?"

"True," Dougan said. "Now let's roll."

"What about the truck rigger and the guards?"

"They get the truck back after we leave," Dougan said. "Plus a nice cred bonus from me."

"We could just geek their pussies right now," Maurice said. He pulled out a machine gun to punctuate his sentence. Typical macho drek.

"No," Maria said. "There are to be no unnecessary kills on this run. We're already responsible for too much death."

"Well, listen to our shaman. Change of feather, eh, Maria?"

She felt the fireball itch in the back of her mind. *Just push it a little farther,* she thought. Then she relaxed. "Owl is not afraid to kill," she said, glaring at Maurice. "But doesn't slaughter needlessly."

"And I agree," Dougan said. "Now, scan these wiz Artemis Nightgliders." He rolled open the back of the truck. "Four of them with remote ops package. They can be slaved to mine so that I can fly us out. Maria puts us under an illusion and we fly silent as a desert night."

Maurice and Bob Henry crowded in for a closer look, smiles lighting up on their big dumb faces. "Keep treating us this well," Maurice said. "And we'll have this slag geeked, skinned, and spitted before you can say 'Dunklezahn is dead.' "

Maria smiled too, but behind the facade she was thinking of the last time they were together, of Jesse's blazing form as the combat mages hit him with hellblasts so fierce he exploded. His flesh blew out from the inside. Then she thought of the children who had died then. And she thought of her own kids back in San Bernardino.

And she wished Dougan had never come back.

23

The weight of Jonathon's Predator II pistol grew in the pocket of his armored duster as he stepped from the rented Landrover. He closed the door, leaving Synthia inside with Grids and Venny. He wanted to do this alone. He needed to face up to his past now that Tam was gone. He hadn't returned here since the fire. Since the funeral for his mother and baby sister.

Hot, dry wind gusted around him, carrying dust and dead leaves. The smell of memories. The memory of the fire so many years ago. Jonathon absently put his hand in his pocket, his fingers brushing over the hard edge of the gun's metal. Caressing the brutality of it. He could almost feel its darkness, the black of the steel barrel, the murderous weight of its fitted handle.

Static hissed angrily in his ears as he crunched gravel under his boots, walking the distance from the Landrover to the blackened remnants of his childhood home. And as he came around the bend of the gravel drive, out of sight of the Landrover, the remains of the house came into full view. The twisted and charred bones of the old house jutted from the rubble like those of a burned corpse, overgrown with brown brambles and dead, graying grass. And as Jonathon looked at it, the static grew until he could hear nothing else.

The wind was gone, the birds disappeared. Only the static remained, a banshee scream crackling like the fire. Then he was sixteen again, standing in just the same spot, watching the ravenous tongues of flame lick black death to his house. To his mother and sister, both of whom had been asleep when the torchers had struck.

The Native Californians policlub. Night riders. An organization with a vicious hatred for non-humans, and elves in particular ever since the Battle of Redding the year before. Kill the daisy-eaters! Kill the daisy-eaters! they'd chanted, parading around in their stocking-cap masks. Jonathon had seen them near the house many times, like some recurring nightmare. Destroy the elven spies! Pointy-eared scum!

The chanters had forgotten that Jonathon's father had been one of those who'd fought and died in the Battle of Redding, fought for California Free State, trying to save his own land. Both Jonathon's parents were human, even though Jonathon and his baby sister had expressed the elven morphology from birth.

Jonathon had been away when the policlub torchers came to the house; he'd been off motorcycle riding with Tamara, trying to perform tricks on her Honda. When they'd noticed the black smoke billowing up through the trees on the north edge of town, he and Tamara went after it. Unaware. To watch the fire. They would travel for kilometers to see a good fire. Always had. The show of destruction and death broke up the summer's monotony.

By the time Jonathon realized it was his house, it was too late. The house was too far gone. *Beyond salvage.*

His mother and sister had followed his father to the grave, only a year behind. And Jonathon was alone in the world. Alone except for Tamara, who stood beside him, strength flowing from her young beautiful body. Reassurance passing through the connection between her hand and his. Her strength saved his life that day, held him back when he was about to plunge into the fire. When he was teetering on the verge of giving up the final sacrifice. His own life.

Now, she was gone, and her strength had gone with her. Their connection was broken, and the banshee howl of the fire became the scream of static in his head. He stood alone. Flying solo.

His only comfort was the smooth grip of his Predator II, its smartlink coming online as he clasped it tightly in his hand. As he drew it from his pocket. As he removed the safety.

Cocked it.

Time to end the static. Time to silence the screams. Time to embrace the long, eternal loneliness.

He started to bring the weapon up toward his head.

"Jonathon!"

The barrel's metal felt cool against his sweaty brow.

"Jonathon!" Synthia's voice in the distance.

Such sweet music, he thought. *So out of place here.*

"Jonathon!" she called again, from inside the Landrover. "We should roll soon if you want to make the lake for the funeral."

Yes, he thought, *the funeral. One last goodbye.* He dropped his arm, letting his muscles go limp suddenly. Then he released the gun's weight into the large pocket of his duster.

He took a deliberate breath and squeezed his eyes tight. Then he turned his back on the skeleton of his childhood and walked away from the dead memories, crunching gravel until he reached the big, off-road vehicle.

He climbed in and Venny accelerated, rumbling out, heading up old Highway 5. That morning they'd flown into Oakland, then rented the Landrover to take them the rest of the way to Lake Shasta. They traveled north and into the Northern Crescent, that beautiful, disputed territory claimed by both the CalFree government and Tir Tairngire.

The Landrover wound up into the mountains, among huge evergreen trees flanking the roadway. The old interstate was in need of serious repair in many places, but was clear of fallen trees for the most part. They saw only one or two other vehicles, both of them old pickup trucks packed with shamans or talismongers.

The shamans of Shasta, or shaman wannabees, had been drawn to this region ever since the dragon, Hestaby, made her emergence—or whatever great dragons do when they suddenly appear. The talismongers merely came here to scavenge the area for magically active souvenirs or trinkets. The area was rumored to be strewn with arcane elements.

Jonathon rode in silence, not really listening to Synthia and Venny chatter on about shamanism versus hermetic magic, about the nature of astral space. About the meta-planes and initiation.

Synthia was in teaching mode and Venny loved to learn. The troll with beach blond hair and a surfer goatee was underestimated by many. He had saved Jonathon's life more than once. Mostly by his prudence and sense of danger. But he could dance with the fastest samurai if he

needed to. Jonathon had seen the big troll work out;
they'd pumped iron and run together often, but Venny
was faster and stronger. Maybe the troll couldn't perform
a triple forward flip on a motorcycle, but Jonathon would
always need his help in a fight. And the prospect of fighting seemed extremely likely before this was all over.

The gypsy camp was in its usual place on the south
bank of Lake Shasta near Squaw Creek. They came upon
the collage of old cars, junked buses, and tents set among
the tall firs and pines next to the lake. The water shone
a deep blue, glinting golden where the sun reflected off
its surface. Jonathon suddenly envied his life with these
people; so carefree and wayward it had been. *Why did I
leave?*

He knew the reason as soon as he stepped out of the
Landrover and started down toward the gathering of people
next to the shore. He recognized each one, and knew their
families. He and Tamara had left to explore the world,
meet new people, pursue their dreams.

The people here had given up on fulfilling their dreams,
or edited them down so that they could realize them without leaving. He saw the ork family of Gahalp, the dwarven
group called Brumington, and from them came a face
he hadn't seen in the flesh since he'd left prison. Not a
Brumington face. Not a gypsy face at all. No, this face
was the ruddy, black-bearded visage of Theodore Rica.

Jonathon's old tactical officer wore a blue-gray business suit that even the most traditional megacorps would
accept without a second glance. Theo's datajacks gleamed
on his temple. "Jonathon," the dwarf said. "Good to see
you." Theo pushed his small hand into Jonathon's.

"Theo, my friend." Jonathon reached down to embrace
the dwarf.

Theodore responded in kind, then stood back and
smiled, a little surprised by the gesture of affection.

"It's rare in these times to have a true friend," Jonathon
said.

Theo was stunned into silence for a second, then he
took a breath. "You look as though you've healed well,"
he said.

Jonathon sighed. "Not all wounds are on the outside."
His voice was barely a whisper.

Again, Theo was left without a reply. He looked over at

the others who'd accompanied Jonathon. "I don't believe I've had the pleasure . . ." Theo said, inclining his head toward Synthia, Grids, and Venny.

"My apologies," Jonathon said, then he introduced them. Afterward, as they continued down through the trees to the edge of the lake—to the funeral pyre—Theo questioned Jonathon about Tamara in the years since prison, when they'd parted ways.

"Too bad I've been so preoccupied with my work," Theo said. "Can you believe it? Theodore Rica promoted to a supervisory position in proactive security for MCT. Me, a convicted felon. Funny, *neh*?"

Jonathon felt a smile tug at the edges of his mouth despite his mood. "What does proactive security mean anyway? Are you a corporate spy?"

"Not exactly," Theo said, laughing. "But I decide who and what security resources go where, based on classified data. A lot of that data is obtained by special ops people."

"Spies."

"You scanned it."

"They give you full control?"

"I'm a fragging halfer," he said. "Working for MCT, one of the most racist corps." But he was smiling. "Sure, I've got full control. A lot of enemies, too, but full control, and as long as I have that, I can deal with the enemies."

Jonathon was silent, listening to Theo, but not looking at him. Instead he watched Tamara's body lying atop the stack of dried kindling on the small beach. She was draped in one of her old silk dresses, dyed a rich brown. Jonathon remembered when Anna had dyed the garment.

Next to the unignited pyre, five or six gypsies danced on a temporary parquet floor, accompanied by guitar and a lamenting and intensely sad song. The beautiful voices hit high tones and drew the anguish out of them, the sound of it nearly bringing water from Jonathon's eyes.

Theo tugged on his arm. "Jonathon," he said. "I know her death is hitting you hard. Harder than any of us." He paused long enough to get Jonathon to look at him. "If you need anything . . . just punch up my number." Theo's dark eyes were intent, deadly serious. "*Anything,* Jonathon. I mean that."

Jonathon held Theo's gaze. "Thank you."

Theo reached up to slap Jonathon on the back, then

turned to join the crowd. Jonathon went to find Synthia and the others. "I want to see her once more," he said. "And I need to talk to Anna before the fire begins. She still blames me for taking Tamara away from the *vista*—the clan."

Synthia had been quiet since they'd left the car, and Jonathon wondered if he'd done the right thing by bringing her along. By bringing anyone. He didn't want to have to deal with introductions and social convention.

Synthia gave him a sad smile and nodded. Maybe she was worried about him. Maybe she was bored.

Jonathon pushed the worry from his mind as he turned away and stepped up to Tamara's body, resting serenely on the high pile of dry wood. He stood facing down at her and pulled back the brown and black silk scarf that covered her head.

Her once olive skin was ghostly pale, and her lips were cracked and white. The doctor who'd removed her headware hadn't done a clean job of replacing her skull; it jutted slightly where the cut had been made.

"Oh, Tam," Jonathon whispered, his throat a tightened ball. "How did we end up like this?"

Then he couldn't hold it any longer; the sobs came from deep in his chest, wracking through him. Tears flowed down his cheeks. *Damn.*

He felt an arm encircle his waist. Then another, covered in customary black wool, reached around to replace the silk cloth over Tamara's face. "Jonathon," came a familiar voice, with an old inflection. "She is with God now. Come."

Anna led him to a blanket spread in the sand a few steps away, next to the dancers. "Sit," she said.

"Hello, Anna," Jonathon said, accepting the woman's embrace. He wiped the tears from his face and paused for several breaths before taking a good look at the woman who'd been his surrogate mother for four years after the fire had taken his real one.

She was human with black hair, streaked with gray, and the chocolate skin of an Indian. Wide, dark eyes stared into his, and the lines of her face had been etched from smiles instead of frowns. She had gained weight, and it looked good on her, gave her a solidity that her frail frame had lacked before. Everyone knew she could hold her own in an argument, and now she had a bit of mass to help. Jonathon approved.

"It's wonderful to see you again, Anna," he said. Then before she could interrupt, he continued. "I'm sorry for taking her away, but you know I couldn't have stopped her."

She put a finger to her lips. "No apologies, please. I was wrong to accuse you."

A wave of relief spread over Jonathon, and his muscles relaxed. He felt tired, more tired than after a hard match. Exhausted.

Anna supported his weight with her shoulder. "Watch," she said. "The dance has ended and Tamara's soul will soon be released to God."

As if on cue, a giant ball of fire erupted from the kindling beneath Tamara's body. Soon, flames crackled and leapt, ripping away her mortal coil. The flames hissed and snapped, occasionally matching pitch with the static in Jonathon's head so that as he watched, he imagined that he heard echoes of her whispers in those flames.

Fatigue weighed upon him like a lead suit. But despite his exhaustion, he knew that Tamara's soul could not be fully released until the hiss in his head faded. Perhaps killing Dougan Rose would accomplish that. Perhaps geeking Michaelson would. Perhaps nothing would.

Nothing short of a bullet through his own skull.

24

In the parking lot of Long Beach International Airport, Hendrix sat in the driver's seat of his modified Americar and watched Layla stifle a yawn. Jonathon Winger was scheduled to arrive on the shuttle jet from Oakland, but that should've landed a while ago.

Hendrix and Layla had been sitting in airport parking for nearly two hours, watching and waiting. And as the sun made its inevitable way toward the horizon, Layla had turned on the car's tiny trideo to pass the time. Now, a brunette biff with glittery gold eye shadow was reading the news.

"In the aftermath of the bombing at the home of former LA Saber, Tamara Ny, Lone Star is still searching for suspects," the biff said, her voice smooth and melodic.

"In related news . . . the whereabouts of LA Sabers' star linebiker, Jonathon Winger, is still unknown, but an unidentified source claims he attended the private funeral of teammate Tamara Ny in the Shasta Lake area of the Northern Crescent today. Coach Kalish of the Sabers had no comment about Winger's ability to play in the upcoming final match against the New Orleans Buzzsaws for the world championship."

A clip of a dwarf with a green mohawk and about fifty piercings on his face—ears, nose, cheeks, eyebrow, lip—came on. "Winger'll show. No pansy-peckered slag could keep 'im from ridin'."

Then the biff was back with her smooth tones, saying, "Jonathon Winger's rival, Dougan Rose, also seems to have gone into seclusion. Neither could be reached for comment. Meanwhile, the rivalry between the fans has escalated, resulting in riots across the continent . . ."

Hendrix tuned it out and focused on Jonathon Winger's Mitsubishi Nightsky limousine—a sleek black vehicle, sitting in a row of identical limousines. Nothing distinguished Winger's Nightsky from the others; the only way Hendrix knew they were watching the right one was the number on the license plate. Mole had slashed his way into some CalTrans node to get that data.

The Nightsky limos rested like black beetles in their patrolled elite parking stalls. They had satellite uplinks and dark tinted glass, plus two sets of rear wheels for an exceptionally smooth ride. It also made them harder to disable.

"Mole," Hendrix said into his telecom, "can't you get anything from the security cams inside?"

"I told you," came the dwarf's synthesized voice. "No can do. Too risky to crack into. The airport is crawling with black ice. Even though there's no cred to steal, the big corps don't like their flight schedules made public, and they pay heavy to keep that drek locked down. Don't worry, the elf will show, and I'll wager Grids Desmond is with him."

"Here's Juju coming back from the terminal," Layla said, bristling in her seat. She'd been sitting there with that faraway stare that meant she was seeing the mage on the astral plane.

Hendrix slapped the button on the trid to turn it off. "He's back? What did he see?"

"He says Winger just got off the shuttle. Grids is with him, plus a female mage of some power and a big troll who Juju thinks is an adept. The mage wasn't perceiving astrally, but the troll nearly spotted him."

"That'd be Venice Jones," Hendrix said. "Winger's bodyguard. Physical adept, an initiate, according to the scan sheets Mole gave me. He's going to be tough."

"Pah!" Layla spat out the car's open window onto the asphalt.

"Just remember the objective," Hendrix said. "We track them discreetly, devise a plan of attack, then hit them."

Earlier, Hendrix had tried to get one of his microburst transmitter pods to attach itself to the underside of the vehicle, but several of the Nightskys had sophisticated proximity alarms that detected the pods and went off, blaring and auto-dialing Knight Errant. Hendrix and Layla had retreated to the far side of the parking garage until the team of cops had left, hopefully under the impression it was a false alarm. Personal-response service from Knight Errant must cost Winger some heavy nuyen.

So now they'd have to resort to the old fashioned tracking method—following in a car. It was more reliable than using a drone. And besides, Hendrix didn't trust drones; they could give a distorted picture of things. Distances seemed skewed and sensations like smells and touch were difficult, if not impossible, to get from a drone.

Besides, even the most stealthy of drones couldn't blend in as well as their car. It was an old model Americar, modified to be faster and more maneuverable without looking out of place. Plus, Hendrix himself had installed a few choice bits of weaponry.

"Grids mustn't get killed," Hendrix said "until we know what he's done with the simsense recording."

"What about the others?"

"Expendable if necessary," Hendrix said. "Especially that mage. I don't want her around when we hit them. That's gotta be Synthia Stone, Winger's girlfriend. She's an unknown quantity. Without Juju Pete online, we're vulnerable to magic."

Layla snorted. "Have it your way."

After a few minutes, four people who looked, at a glance, like Japanese tourists approached Winger's limousine. They got in, one of them taking the driver's seat while the others climbed into the rear compartment.

"Let's roll," Layla said, a wide grin on her face. She was happy for some action after the long wait.

Hendrix fired up the Americar and pulled out, keeping two cars between them and the Nightsky. Layla brought a pair of Ares binox to her eyes. "It's hard to see through the tinted macroglass," she said, "but I think they've dropped the illusion. That was a troll arm that slotted the credstick in the paypole."

Hendrix merely nodded. *Drekking mages,* he thought. He hated not having the edge, and without Juju here in the flesh, he and Layla were potentially overmatched. Juju could engage in combat with spirits and astral creatures while projecting astrally, but his ability to affect the physical world was limited.

They followed the Nightsky up the Cal 405, then onto the Santa Monica freeway. They were three cars back, sandwiched between a Eurovan and a go-ganger wannabee when the limo suddenly accelerated. The sleek black machine leaped forward and swerved across three lanes.

Hendrix punched the gas, and the engine roared, shooting them into quick pursuit around the Eurovan and into an open lane. That limo wouldn't be able to outrun them with speed.

The Nightsky lunged left, then cut right, across two lanes to take a quick exit. Hendrix followed on its tail, pulling the wheel sharply to careen around a Chrysler-Nissan Jackrabbit before jumping the edge of the exit ramp. They landed firm on the pavement, only seconds behind Winger's car.

"Chase in progress," Hendrix told Mole through his head telecom. "Repeat, chase in progress."

"So much for stealth and guile," Layla said, laughing as she pulled out her laser-sighted Ingram smartgun and slapped in a clip of armor-piercing rounds.

"I don't like this," Hendrix said. "But we can't lose them now. Full frontal. Repeat full frontal. Take them all down if you have to, just leave the simdecker alive."

"My pleasure," she said, then aimed for the tires and fired a burst.

"Mole, you copy?"

"Here."

"We're engaging the targets. You're on."

"I've got a couple smartframes active and ready to intercept emergency calls, but I can't do much about direct-to-satellite connections. Should give you ten, maybe fifteen minutes."

"Eons," Hendrix said, pressing the button to activate the Vengeance minigun recessed into the Americar's front grill. The weapon fired seconds later, shaking the whole vehicle as it sprayed sparks up the roadway and off the armored hull of the Nightsky.

Two of the rear tires went flat, but the limo sped on, screeching around a corner and accelerating down a garbage-strewn street. They were in East Hollywood, the porno district. The area was filled with BTL junkies and cyberwhores, surgically altered to look like Honey Brighton, Maria Mercurial, or anyone you wanted.

Hendrix kept up easily. The modified Americar was quicker and more maneuverable than the limo. He fired the Vengeance gun again, chewing up the rear of the limo. But most of the rounds went wide as the troll driver swerved back and forth.

As they hit a straight section of road with no turns, Layla fired her Ingram and flattened one of the remaining rear tires just as the limo tried to pull a quick turn into an alley. The driver cut the corner too sharply, tipping up and sideways. It skidded on its left side, grinding sparks from metal against asphalt, then crashed into a lamppost before slamming back down on all its wheels.

The streets vacated around them, the residents sensing a fire fight. Some watched from the windows and alleyways as the smell of gunpowder mixed with the stench of human refuse. Others merely shrugged and tried to ignore the scream of the minigun and the rending of twisted metal.

No one tried to stop it. Happened all the time. People here knew the rules of the street. Get in the way, die. Stay clear, live. Even Lone Star rarely made it down here, and when they did, nothing changed.

Hendrix readied the minigun for another burst, sighting the plexan-shielded macroglass of the rear window. Perhaps the plexan would hold for a few seconds, but this *was* a minigun. He fired, rocking the Americar again, hearing Layla curse because it ruined her aim on the driver. Then the sound of the Vengeance gun deafened him, just before his audio limiters cut it off.

Layla missed the driver and hit someone in the rear. Hendrix could see now through the chewed hole that had been the rear window. Layla had hit a wiry norm with black hair and white skin. Grids. *Fragging great, just what we need.*

Blood poured from the man's shoulder, and he was screaming as though electrodes had been clamped to his testicles. But Hendrix could tell he would live for at least an hour more. *Good.*

Hendrix thumbed the minigun to remote rigging via his smartlink. Another burst would kill everyone inside, and he didn't want that. At least not until he pulled Grids out of there. Hendrix reached for his Ares Alpha Combatgun, a bit more precise than the Vengeance.

Mole spoke in his ear. "Knight Errant security's on its way," he said. "ETA: four minutes. Sorry, I can't—"

"Null sheen," Hendrix said, hefting his rifle. "This is almost over." Then he pushed open the car door and stepped out into the bright light and noise.

25

Andreas Michaelson stepped from his private helicopter onto the roof of the Venice Beach Hilton. He'd spent the whole day and much of the evening at Magenics, going over the details of the Magus File. Numbers and scientific theories about genetics, magical aptitude, and artificial intelligence spun around in his mind as he crossed the helipad to his suite. Giving him a headache.

Ruger and the security team flanked out around him as he entered the cool of the hotel corridor. He breathed deeply—clean, filtered air—then activated the palm scanner and stepped inside.

Why can't the labcoats simply give me a time frame? he wondered. He hated dealing with science types, because they would never commit to anything. Engineers could promise to have a bridge built in a specific amount of time with a predetermined amount of nuyen. But not researchers.

No, they always spoke in theoreticals. Talking about proving this hypothesis and that theory. Never about practical applications.

Inside the suite stood the white-haired Claudio, dressed in a dwarf-sized tuxedo and cummerbund. "Ah, my executiveness," Claudio said, greeting him with a low bow. "How are the trials and tribulations of the upper echelon?"

Michaelson smiled, setting his briefcase on the floor and prying off his leather Armanté shoes one foot at a time, then wiggling his silk sock-covered toes into the plush carpeting as he walked to the couch. He plopped down in a slumped position and activated the huge trid. "The trials outweigh the tribulations today, Claudio," he said.

"I'm so very sorry to hear that," said the dwarf. "Maybe you'd like some dinner?"

"Yes, please." Michaelson waved a tired hand. "Just bring me whatever you have."

"How about foie gras, followed by poulet cordon blue and a rice pilaf?"

"Fine, whatever."

"Very well." Claudio turned to leave. "Oh, one other thing."

"Yes?"

"Check your messages right away. The new secretary, Johan, called from Essen. He said something about Mr. Brackhaus arriving tomorrow."

Michaelson bolted upright in his seat and turned to look at Claudio. "Brackhaus is coming here? Why?"

"I don't know." Claudio suddenly became serious, losing all hint of affectation. Then he smiled. "I just work here," he said.

Michaelson stood. "Just what I need, a fragging spy from the head office breathing fire down my neck." Then he noticed that Claudio still stood there. "You can go get my dinner," he said. "Thank you."

Claudio nodded, then walked out.

Why the frag would Brackhaus be coming? Unless he suspects something . . .

Hans Brackhaus was a mysterious figure around Saeder-Krupp. He seemed to have his hand in a number of operations, though even Michaelson wasn't sure exactly what his title or position were. All he knew for sure was that Brackhaus seemed to get around a lot. It was said that his speciality was covert ops and that he reported directly to the dragon, Lofwyr. There were even rumors spinning around that Brackhaus *was* Lofwyr, though who could ever be sure of anything like that? Michaelson had dealt with both the human and the dragon, but had never discerned any similarities.

Michaelson walked into the bedroom and sat at his desk to play back his messages. The face of the new secretary came on—a typically skinny elf with short dark hair, a narrow black mustache, and a haughty disposition. Michaelson listened to what the elf had to say about this unexpected visit by Hans Brackhaus. On the surface it seemed to be a routine check on the Magus Project, but Michaelson saw through it. Things were coming apart. Ever since that slitch elf had gotten too curious for her own good. And now this. Brackhaus on his way here.

It could only be because he suspected something. And

that meant Lofwyr might have gotten wind that somebody had stolen his secrets. The dragon's fury could come to strike him down any minute. From any direction, from anyone.

When the message winked off, Michaelson punched up Cinnamon's number on a secure line. He put on his best face for the beautiful blonde, but she didn't smile at him.

He took a deep breath and said, "We've got a problem."

26

The crash of shattered glass and the staccato spray of heavy gunfire rang in Jonathon's ears until he could hear no more. He was crouched on the floor of the Nightsky, his shoulder pressed against the panel separating the driver's seat and the limo's rear compartment. He shook the shards of glass from his hair and watched, stunned, as Grids's shoulder exploded.

Blood erupted like crimson lava through the black denim on Grids's back, spraying the door and upholstery. In slow motion, the man's body lifted up from the bullet's impact, then slammed into the electronic console. He slid to the floor, leaving a trail of blood all the way down, and lay there.

Dead?

Jonathon's heart beat once. Then twice, pounding like a bass drum.

Grids looked up then and screamed, wailing like a stuck pig as the color drained out of him. "I'm gonna die," he yelled. "They fragging killed me!"

Jonathon reached across and clapped his hand against the wound to stop the bleeding. Hot sticky liquid gushed over his knuckles and down the underside of his arm as Grids screamed.

Synthia swallowed hard next to Jonathon, then reached over and touched the wound. Warmth rushed over the area, growing in heat until Jonathon had to pull his hand away.

Grids moaned, then stared at Synthia with a look of exhaustion, before gritting his teeth and bowing his head. Synthia nodded to him, then turned away and concentrated. She began to chant something and gestured once or twice in the air.

"Jonathon," bellowed Venny. "Don't move!"

Jonathon didn't have to be told twice, but reached into

the wide pocket of his duster and pulled out the Predator II just in case. Their attackers hadn't fired again. *Why?*

Venny crouched low in the front seat, trying to sight through the ragged hole that had been the rear window of the Nightsky. In one hand, the troll held his laser-sighted Uzi III, in the other was some sort of black ball.

The Uzi's laser flashed in and out of the car as Venny leaned for position. "The driver's getting out," Venny yelled. The Uzi sputtered as the troll fired.

Jonathon risked a look up the street, and for an instant he saw a dark blur near the door of the other car, moving faster than he thought possible. Coming straight for them.

The man was black-skinned and bald with multiple skill-softs bristling just above one ear. His eyes were chromed, and his motions were blindingly fast, but jerky, not like the smooth movements of Venice Jones. In armored synth-leather he came like a robot, first firing a blast from the grenade port of his rifle. Then, as the grenade flew toward the hole where the rear window had been, the man's eyes locked with Jonathon's and he fired a pulse of his rifle directly at Jonathon's head.

"Get down!" A heavy hand shoved Jonathon to the floor.

But it wasn't Venny's push that saved him. As he fell, Jonathon saw the bullets ricochet off something invisible. A transparent barrier less than a meter from his head. Bullets that would have hit him between the eyes. *I should be dead,* he thought.

Venny gave Synthia a quick glance. "Thanks," he said. Then he, too, was moving, out the driver's door and into the street.

Jonathon felt adrenaline and anger rising inside him. *They nearly killed me.* But as he breathed, seeing an image of the bullets in his head, time slowed. He found himself focusing, searching for that feeling of unreality that gave him the edge in biker matches.

The grenade had bounced off Synthia's shield and landed on the pavement behind the limo. But it never exploded; instead a white hazy gas billowed from it. *Smoke? Tear gas?*

Venny disappeared out the side door, throwing his black ball in a lightning-quick motion, almost too fast to register. But as the zen came over Jonathon, as he focused his mind, he found himself able to follow the accelerated movements.

The black ball split into two weighted spools that gradually grew farther and farther apart as the nearly invisible fiber of a monofilament thread unwound between them. They revolved around an imaginary point as they spun toward the black man with the combat rifle.

The man glanced at the oncoming weapon for a second, then fired a burst at Venny, before diving to the left at the last possible second. The rotating monowire weapon missed by a hair, flying past.

Venny grunted in pain as one of the rounds hit him. "Jonathon," he said, "you're gonna have to rig this boneshaker out of here. I'll stay and handle this."

"But—"

"Just do it, the tires will hold."

Jonathon pulled a datacord from the console in the panel separating the front and back compartment of the limo. The Nightsky came equipped for rear-seat and remote rigging in emergencies. Like now. Jonathon slotted the jack into his temple.

"Wait!" Synthia yelled at the same instant a huge fireball exploded near the other car. Red glow and heat flashed against the black interior of the limousine as bits and pieces of the Americar rained down on the street around them.

Jonathon became the vehicle, activating the cameras and road sensors. The car's dog brain was intact, and the forward inputs worked perfectly. He could see, feel, and hear the road in front. But the signals from the rear were nothing but static and dull ache. The internal microphones picked up the gunfire and the sound of Grids moaning in pain, but nothing Jonathon could use to get a clearer idea of what was behind the limo.

The wheel sensors and the dog brain told Jonathon that the runflat tires had been brutalized, but they might hold for a few kilometers. He revved the big engine and mentally slammed the limousine into gear. The internal sensors let him feel the presence of the passengers. He could feel Grids and Synthia, plus his own weight, sitting on the floor of the rear.

Venny was still outside.

Another blast shook the street behind them as Jonathon urged the car forward. *Synthia.* Then gunfire thrummed from the burned hull of the Americar, and in the silence that followed came the rocking weight of a troll's body thrown into the front seat.

There was no time to glance with his meat eyes to see if Venny was still alive. And the internal camera was off-line. Jonathon accelerated, peeling down a side street. If anyone followed, he had no way of knowing.

Then the troll weight in the driver's seat shifted and sat upright. The door closed and Jonathon felt Venny's hands on the steering wheel. "I'm all right," he said. "Just a few scratches."

"Just tell me if they're following," Jonathon said.

"Nope, Synthia's blast fragged up their car."

"Good."

Jonathon eased the limousine back up onto the freeway. Once they were out of danger, he shut down the transponder and the auto-distress call. He didn't want anyone knowing where they were going, including Knight Errant. Or DocWagon. If Grids needed surgery, they'd find a street doc to do it.

Jonathon's zen lasted several minutes longer, and in that time he decided what to do. Obviously, their attackers were professionals. Mercenaries or shadowrunners since they didn't seem to have corporate affiliation.

Shadowrunners hired by Michaelson, no doubt.

Jonathon knew they needed a place to hide out. To rest and decide what to do next. And he had just the spot. One of his old riding buddies, Chico Rodriguez, had a house up in the hills off Laurel Canyon Boulevard. A secluded place where he used to stamp BTL chips.

At the moment Chico was sitting in an Aztlani prison awaiting trial for smuggling charges. It wasn't likely he'd be coming home or needing his hideout for a while. Not for a long, long while.

They could use the place to hide out and recover. They needed time. Time for Grids to heal. To learn more about the file that seemed to have everybody trying to frag their hoops. Time to think about how Dougan Rose was connected to Michaelson.

Time to make a plan.

A plan to take down Michaelson.

27

The sky stretched forever in all directions around Maria. In the west the deep red sunset glowed; in the east, the first stars showed as tiny diamonds, twinkling in a midnight blue firmament. And below, the colors of the city sparkled beneath the smog layer like hazy fireflies. Red, yellow, green fuzzy dots.

Maria breathed in the clean air, filling her lungs with it. Owl loved flying at night, searching the air and the ground for hapless prey. Searching with the parabolically focused night vision, seeking out prey with sound. Owl had shown Maria how to track with her ears, and once she'd mastered the technique, she no longer relied so much on sight.

Owl could hear the movement of a mouse from sixty meters. Could pinpoint its location, its direction, speed. Could *see* it from the skittering, scratching noises it made as it moved.

Two flights in two nights. Maybe there was something good about this run after all.

They had spent yesterday at Dougan's summer condo in Laguna Beach. After the flight from El Infierno, cloaked in invisibility. Dougan had spent the day jacked into a deck, gathering data on Grids Desmond and Tamara Ny.

Maria had slept through all that, waking earlier this evening when they unfolded the Nightgliders again. Dougan had taken them back up, wind singing beneath the thinly stretched polycarb weave of the wings. Maria had never been so anxious for a run. It had almost been enough to take her mind off Angelina and Pedro, home alone with only Talon to care for them.

Dougan had piloted them out over the ocean so they wouldn't risk colliding with any sky-scratching arcologies. Then he'd banked them inland over the Santa Monica Mountains, settling down on a narrow beach next to Stone Canyon Dam. An incredible feat of flying.

"We leave the Nightgliders here," Dougan said.

Maria nodded in the darkness. She stretched and flexed inside her tight bodysuit, then walked back and forth, feeling the solid ground beneath her boots. Disappointed to be on the ground again. Above, the stars were now blocked by a covering of smog, underlit by the city lights.

Maurice and Bob Henry came up behind them. "Where's the hit?"

"Grids lives in one of those condos," Dougan said. He pointed at a building of glass and dark wood. The condoplex was built into the hills, with many balconies overlooking the reservoir, but the entrance must be on the opposite side, by the road.

"Number seven," Dougan said. "It's the one where the explosion and fire happened last night."

"What kind of security we facin'?" Maurice said.

"Unsure," Dougan said. "Maybe Maria can help us scan it."

"I'll project," she said, "and search the building. Watch my body."

Maurice grunted. "I been watching it all day," he said. "Why stop now?"

Bob Henry chuckled.

Maria ignored them and sat down on the dry grass. Then she lifted her awareness up and out of her flesh, shifting from the physical to the glowing plane of the astral. And she was there, flying over the others.

She saw their auras from above, their bodies a swirl of red, green, and blue except for the dead areas where cybernetics had violated the flesh. Gray and black dimmed the auras of all three of them in places, but in Dougan the effect was disturbing. Only a flicker of life remained.

Dougan, what have you done to yourself? she thought.

But she didn't have the luxury of time. She flew up and across the street. The dull landscape of the buildings and concrete blurred slightly as she moved. Only the trees seemed vibrant from the astral plane.

She saw the results of the explosion right away—massive trauma to the structure. Destruction surrounded her; support beams had been demolished, windows shattered. Much of the natural wood was severely burned. And the aura of the place echoed the trauma, tiny splotches of red and orange glowed where the wood had been severed.

It looked like one or two people had died in the explosion. Maria had assensed death enough times to know what its astral afterimage looked like.

Suddenly, a watcher spirit in the form of a basketball-sized eye floated by on her right. When it saw her, its eye grew larger, unblinking. But in the time it took the watcher to decide whether she was a threat, Maria had banished it. The eye winked out of existence without a sound.

Then she moved through the decimated apartment toward the front of the building. There were two guards near the entrance to the condoplex, speaking in low voices. They carried pistols and shock batons. Parts of their head and arms were cyberware. *These boys won't be a problem,* she thought.

Suddenly, a large spirit raced toward her. "Who are you," it asked in a voice like the whooshing of wind.

Maria spun to face it, recognizing the creature as an air elemental—a moderately intelligent spirit. Sometimes it was possible to confuse them. "I'm part of a security team investigating the explosion."

The elemental blustered. It did not understand. "Who are you?" it repeated. "I must report you to my master."

"Never mind," Maria said. Then she called for Stoney. A fraction of a second later, the spirit called Stoney appeared beside Maria. It was a concrete and riebar city spirit hulking with weight. "Would you be so generous as to destroy that?" Maria pointed at the air elemental.

Stoney rushed it.

The air creature turned to flee, but Maria created a mana barrier to prevent its escape. The elemental slammed into the barrier and stopped.

Stoney loomed up behind it, swallowing it in an embrace of flowing concrete and jutting steel.

The air elemental turned and attacked, but it was no match for Stoney. The city spirit pressed the elemental against the mana barrier until it spread along the barrier like a stain—thin and white. The elemental tried one last time to break through, but it was weakened, and in a moment the creature was gone. Disrupted.

Stoney turned toward Maria, smiling.

"Thank you," Maria said. "Your task is complete."

Stoney disappeared.

Maria dropped the mana barrier and turned from the entrance and flew back into the condoplex. She searched the whole structure and found no one. The place was deserted, except for the guards who must have been there to prevent any residents from risking their lives trying to get back in. *Probably hired by the insurance company,* she thought.

She dropped quickly back into her meat body, feeling her chest rise and fall. Her heart beating firmly. She opened her eyes. "There are two guards in front," she said. "I got rid of a watcher and an air elemental, but nobody else is home. It looks like the fire crews left no more than two or three hours ago."

Dougan gave her a hand up. "Any dead bodies inside?"

Maria stretched again, and took a deep breath. "Not anymore, but I'm pretty sure some people died in the explosion. I can't be positive, but the aura of the place read moderately high background."

Bob Henry laughed.

"Yeah," Maurice said, slapping Bob Henry on the back. "You hear that? Aura read moderately high background. Whatever the frag *that* means." His laugh rolled from his chest like a freight train.

"Shut up," Dougan said. "Time to toss this place." He lifted some sort of shotgun into the crook of his elbow.

"Why?" Maurice said. "What if Grids Desmond is one of the dead? What if the explosion took out him and the chip?"

"Guess again, chummer," Dougan said. "The news said two people died in the blast, and their names were mentioned. Neither was Grids Desmond."

"Too bad."

"Maria," Dougan said, "can you still do that trick of finding people using personal items?"

Maria sighed. "I suppose so," she said. "But the items have to be fresh."

"Null persp," Dougan said. "We'll find something. Okay, chummers, let's scale this puppy."

Less than an hour later, they had scoured apartment number seven in silence, cloaked by Owl's invisibility. The four of them were black from soot and sweaty from the effort, but the take was better than Maria had hoped.

Bob Henry had found a man's razor in the bathroom, seemingly untouched by the fire. Dougan had discovered some holopics in the closet, mostly intact. Three of them showed both Grids and Tamara. Plus, from the dirty laundry, Maurice had pulled some dirty underwear complete with tiny strands of pubic hair.

That was the best prospect, if the samples weren't too old. If the detection ritual works, Maria thought, I'll have Grids Desmond by the short hairs—quite literally.

28

Jonathon's zen had all but dissipated by the time he pulled the Nightsky into the hidden drive of Chico's place. The anger threatened to return, but it seemed weak. Tired.

And as he stopped the car and jacked out, he took a look at what the assault had done to the limo. Shards of glass littered the seat and floor, tiny odd-shaped fragments that weren't sharp but stuck to flesh like large sand grains. The air in the car recked of blood iron, so strong that Jonathon could almost taste it. Splatters of blood soaked the seat and the floor under Grids.

Grids himself sat in silence, breath rasping, his face ash-gray. Behind him, the trid console was dented and streaked with blood.

Venny shifted slowly in the front seat. Jonathon saw only the blurred shape of the huge troll's back through the separating glass. He had no idea what injuries Venny had sustained, but it looked like he could hardly move.

Then Jonathon's gazed settled on Synthia. Lines of exhaustion creased the corners of her eyes and wrinkled her forehead, but she was looking straight at him with her denim blue eyes. Her gaze intent, unrelenting. She would require an explanation.

She deserved an explanation. So did Venny. *What kind of drek have I dragged them into?* Jonathon wondered. *Even I don't know.*

"We should be safe here," he said to fill the silence. "For a while."

Synthia released his gaze, then pointed at Grids. "He needs a doctor."

Jonathon nodded.

Grids didn't move.

"I know a good street man," Venny said. "Or maybe you could get Ducky to look at him."

Jonathon thought about it. Would the team's trainer know enough surgery to patch up Grids? Maybe, but it would be risky to let anyone know their location. "We can't take any chances," he said. "We need someone who doesn't know us and can't reveal where we are."

Synthia broke in. "Why? What's this all about? Why are we hiding out? And why did those thugs attack us? They were professionals. Not some random gang-bangers out for a joy ride."

Jonathon frowned. "I'll tell you everything as soon as we get inside."

"You sure will," she said.

Jonathon climbed out of the limo. His legs wobbled under him as he walked around to help Venny pull Grids from the other side. Behind him Synthia stood and brushed herself off.

Jonathon nearly fainted when he saw Venny. The troll had been hit at least ten or fifteen times. Some of those hits had been stopped by his body armor, but several places were crusted with dried blood.

"Don't look so worried, chummer," Venny said. "It's not the first time I've been in a fire fight." The troll hefted Grids's nearly unconscious body over his massive shoulder and started inside.

Jonathon hurried to beat him to the door. The drive ended at a short cobblestone pathway that wound through some trees and overgrown brush to the front door of the house. Jonathon had to fight some of the bushes to get through. "Gardener's been on vacation," he said.

Venny laughed. "As long as the maid is still here," he said. "I hate washing dishes."

Jonathon smiled. At least Venny seemed to be taking the situation in stride. He even seemed to be enjoying the whole thing. Maybe he liked action better than waiting for action.

The front of Chico's house looked like a modest, single-story white structure with a flat roof, but because of the steep slope of the hillside only the top floor was accessible from the front. There were two more stories below this one.

Jonathon listened at the door to make sure nobody else had decided to borrow the place. He heard nothing.

Synthia came up behind them. "I've already scouted out the house astrally," she said. "Nobody's home."

Jonathon nodded. "Thanks."

She gave him one of her half-smiles, which meant either she was half amused or half irked. Jonathon guessed the latter.

The door opened with the correct five-digit code that Jonathon had, fortunately, tucked away in his head memory. And they were in, smelling the must and the mold of years of disuse. Still, the place wasn't in such bad shape. It had power and running water; Chico must have had a custodial account set up to keep the utilities going for emergencies. Just like this. The pool hadn't been cleaned in a long time, and was host to a vibrant algae population, but the deck gave a great view of downtown LA. Hollywood, Century City, the Arcology Mile. Even the hint of the ocean in the distant haze on the right.

Chico had been a man of exotic taste. His music collection rivaled the most anal of connoisseurs, especially stuff from the 1970s and '80s. And some newer tunes that recreated the same sounds with polycorders and synthlinks.

Mirrors adorned nearly every wall and ceiling, reflecting the deep, deep shag of the burnt orange carpet so that it seemed to stretch for kilometers in every direction. And there were the paintings of sunflowers and psychedelic swirls of color in the shapes of mushrooms and human faces.

"Strange chummer lives here," Venny said, setting Grids down on a green couch in the room with the trideo. "I'll call the street doc," he said. "Unless Synthia thinks he won't need it."

Synthia frowned, a sad look on the delicate features of her face. "I think the bullet went clean through," she said. "I've healed the wound, but I'm no doctor. He still might get an infection."

Venny nodded. "I'll call him."

While the troll spoke on the telecom, Synthia grabbed Jonathon's arm and took him out by the pool. He'd never seen her this insistent. This slotted off.

The last remnants of the sunset glowed a faint red behind the layers of smog to the west, the glimmer giving an edge of crimson to the sleek black glass of the MCT arcology. The Mitsuhama building was the closest structure of the Arcology Mile. Its black needle towered over the slums of East Hollywood to one side and central LA around the corner.

"Look at me, Jonathon."

He turned to see her, eyes hard as ice. The flowing

summer dress she'd worn on the plane was splattered all over with Grids's blood, and torn in myriad places from glass shards. "I'm sorry, Syn," he said. "I didn't mean for you to get involved."

"Well, I *am* involved, Jonathon. Now, are you going to tell me what's going on?"

So he told her about the telecom message from Grids and about the simsense Tamara had made of her and Andreas Michaelson. He told her about the Magus File and what they knew of it, which he realized was nearly nothing. "I had no idea we'd be tracked down so soon," he said. "I never meant to get you into this."

"It's too late for that, isn't it?"

Jonathon nodded. "I'm sorry, Syn. I don't know what to do."

"You could have been honest with me up front."

"I know." Jonathon went to explaining that the hiss in his head seemed to be growing, that it was driving him to find out why Tamara was killed. Like an obsession. He had to figure out how Dougan Rose and Andreas Michaelson were connected.

All the while she listened intently. Surprise and fear giving way to concern for him. Her gaze grew softer as he spoke.

Synthia had to know she couldn't go home without risking further assault. "Those were shadowrunners, all pro," she said. "If they were targeting Grids, and perhaps you because they traced his call to you, then they've also gathered as much data as possible on anyone associated with you two. *I* am known to be your . . . girlfriend. You aren't a very low-profile personality."

"I know."

"But even if I could go home, I wouldn't. I'm in this now, too."

Jonathon said nothing.

She looked at him, blue eyes tender now. "I know how much she meant to you," she said. "That's why I want to help. And because . . ."

Jonathon couldn't take his eyes off her.

"Because if I ever lost you, I would do the same." She came in close to him, putting her arms under his, encircling his body. Nuzzling his chest.

Jonathon turned to watch the lights of the city in the distance. He sighed, clutching Synthia's body to his.

After a minute, Venny opened the sliding glass door and stepped out onto the patio. "I'm taking Grids to the doc now," he said. "I've got a taxi on the way. I told the driver to pick us up down the street. He's an old chummer and very discreet. After, we'll swing by Grids's hideout to get his simsense gear. He keeps mumbling about it."

Jonathon nodded. "Any chance you can get the Westwind or the Jag from home?"

"I've already got that scoped," Venny said. "Hired an old samurai buddy to steal the Westwind and drive it into the plex. I've given him the lock code, the one that makes the combination cycle. Don't worry, even if I didn't trust him, which I do, the code will only work once. He'll meet us at the clinic in the Valley where we're going."

"Good plan, Venny. Thanks."

Venny just shrugged it off, but Jonathon knew they were lucky to have the troll's experience. Jonathon had thought of some of the same things, but not all of them. And he certainly didn't have Venny's contacts to call upon. "Just promise me you won't leave," the troll said. "Neither one of you. Stay here until I get back."

"How long?"

"Three or four hours."

"We promise," Jonathon said, looking at Synthia. "Don't we?"

She squeezed him tight. "I'm sure we can think of something to pass the time."

"And I'll even go shopping for some chow." Venny smiled as he turned and left, sliding the door closed behind him.

When he was gone, Synthia straightened up and pressed her lips against Jonathon's, holding the kiss for a long breath. "Let's find a bed," Synthia said.

Nearly an hour later, after soaking together in the huge jacuzzi tub filled to the brim with scalding hot water, they found the kingsize waterbed beneath a mirrored ceiling. They put clean silk sheets on it, and climbed in together. Tired and sore, but unwilling to release each other from the embrace.

They rolled and moved together, and Jonathon soon lost himself to the rhythm of their dance. Lost himself to the tickle of her hair, the softness of her white breasts. The roughness of her teeth against his chest. The scratch of her nails on his back.

He danced the edge with her. Balancing on the delicate and taut tight rope of orgasm.

Until finally . . .

Over the edge. Falling . . . falling.

Into the afterglow came the warm evening breeze, carrying the smell of fire and the distant sounds of the city. And closer, the sweet smell of her body, hot against his. The soft sound of her breathing.

He rolled onto his back and looked up at the ceiling. At the shadowy reflection of them in the dark. She put her head into the crook of his shoulder and kissed his cheek. Minutes passed and exhaustion pulled him toward sleep. It seemed like years since he'd last slept.

"I know something about the Magus Factor," Synthia said suddenly.

Her words hung in the darkness, solid entities that refused to be carried off by the breeze.

"What?"

"The Magus Factor," she said. "Didn't you tell me the file Tamara copied said something about it?"

"What do you know?"

"It's a genetic explanation for magic," she said. "I've read some about it. Scientists believe that the ability to channel magical energies is genetic. They call it the Magus Factor." She shifted to stare at the ceiling. "But not much is known about which genes are involved. At least not much is *publicly* known."

"Maybe Saeder-Krupp is conducting research into it," Jonathon said.

"No doubt. Perhaps they've located some . . . what did that title say? Loci. Genetic loci that are tied with magical ability. It's a scary prospect, 'cause if anyone figures it out, they could manufacture magi just by giving an unborn child the right genes. Or they could try experiments like putting more than one copy of the crucial locus into someone, hoping to get a super mage. Who knows what the frag they're up to."

Jonathon nodded agreement. Nobody could ever predict what a megacorp might have up its sleeve.

"One thing's for certain," Synthia said. "If that file has details on S-K research into the Magus Factor, it's no wonder Tamara was killed. And now we're in the same game."

29

The rocky cliffs over Topanga Canyon proved a difficult landing site for Dougan, but he finally managed to bring the four Nightgliders in with only one incident. Bob Henry's glider caught a wing against a young eucalyptus tree, tearing a wide gash in the fabric.

Maria unbuckled herself from the wing as soon as her feet touched the ground. Midnight rapidly approached, and she wanted to get going. She needed to use the medicine lodge of her old mentor, Teresa Darkhunter. Her own lodge was back in San Bernardino, and they didn't have the time to make that trip. The ritual itself would take several hours.

"You should remain here," she told the others. "Teresa won't welcome us all."

Dougan's dark face nodded in the dim moonlight. "Right," he said. "I'll work on fixing the wing on Bob Henry's Nightglider. How long you gonna take?"

"I'm not certain. Two hours at least, maybe as much as four or five."

"Well, we'll be waiting for you," Dougan told her, then went off to work on the torn wing.

Maurice was seated on the ground, his back leaning against a large sandstone boulder and his eyes closed. Bob Henry did the same.

Maria stretched for a minute, then started toward the grove of giant eucalyptus trees that held Teresa's lodge, picking her way through the sandstone rocks and the thorny chaparral underbrush. Topanga Canyon was essentially desert, though its proximity to the ocean kept it more humid than most deserts, providing enough airborne water for chaparral and some succulents like icicle plant.

Maria entered the grove of giant eucalyptus, noticing the watcher spirit at the base of the trees wink out. Then a nature spirit appeared to block her way. It looked like a boulder of solid rock, except that it flexed and moved and had bits of plantlike material which appeared on its surface, traveling across the rocky skin for a moment before being absorbed back into the creature. The trees behind the spirit bent slightly toward it, almost as though deferring to its judgment.

Maria waited. The cool breeze ruffled the feathers adorning her unibody as she stood stock still. Not afraid, but not daring to pass.

Then Teresa manifested. She was brown-skinned like Maria, black hair cut to the shoulders, dark eyes. But she was older by ten or fifteen years. Maria could see tiny wrinkles at the corners of her eyes and mouth, even though she knew this wasn't Teresa's physical body, but a manifestation of her astral projection.

"Maria, my child," Teresa said. "It has been many nights. Years of nights since I've seen you." The older woman gave Maria a warm smile.

At the age of nine, Maria had been taken from her family in Mazatlan to live in the *teocalli* pyramid in Ensenada. And, three years later, it was Teresa who'd saved her from death at the hands of the priests. Teresa had kidnapped her and fled to California where Jesse was living.

Jesse had run away from home, making for Los Angeles in hopes of realizing his dream of becoming a music star. But then he'd been pulled into the turf wars, and by the time Maria showed up, he'd formed Muerte and given up his music.

Maria later learned that the Aztlani priests had been planning to sacrifice her as soon as she achieved her magical ability. It was a story she'd pieced together from bits and pieces of revelations Teresa let slip over the years. Maria had been one of many magically adept virgins the priests kept under the pretext of apprenticeship. To be sacrificed for the blood magi.

Maria owed Teresa her life, and her magic. It had been too long since they'd seen each other. "I've missed you, mentor," Maria said.

Teresa smiled. "Me too, child. Me too."

The moon inched across the sky. "But I come not to visit, I'm afraid."

"I thought not. What brings you?"

"I need a medicine lodge tonight," Maria said.

"Of course." Teresa spoke a few words to the nature spirit. "Carro will let you pass."

"Thank you."

"You're welcome, my child. Perhaps you will come visit me when you have time."

"I will."

Teresa's smile creases deepened. "May Owl fly with you." Then she was gone.

Maria stepped past Carro, the nature spirit, and into the eucalyptus grove. The air stilled under the trees, and sounds of night creatures disappeared. No small animals would enter this place.

A rope ladder hung against the trunk of one of the tallest trees, leading up about fifteen meters to a wooden platform. It had been years since Maria had been here. This was where she'd first beaten the Dweller on the Threshold, the first time she'd crossed over to the realm of Owl.

The platform was triangular and about three meters on a side with no walls. It was high enough in the trees that Maria could see the tiny pinpoints of stars in the sky above. Feathers and twigs lined the edges of the triangle, and the trees supporting it were decorated with dried skins of small mammals—raccoons, mice, rats. The skeletons of crows and snakes and lizards hung in the branches and off the edge of the bier.

Maria felt instantly at home. She wanted simply to meditate; to cross over and seek out the company of Owl for no other reason than to fly with her and learn. But she had no time for that now. She brought out the items they'd taken from the burned-out apartment.

The underwear would be their best bet, but even so, she'd have to build the power of the spell to the very edge of her ability. She must not fail, for failure would mean the loss of crucial time. Time and the material link. She wanted to get back to her children. No, failure was unacceptable.

Maria perched on the platform and steadied her breathing. She focused herself, bringing in the sounds and the sights of the grove. The starry sky above. The deep black below. And when she had achieved focus, she began to channel the currents and eddies of magic toward her, to build the ritual's strength.

Time stood still for her. Only the protection of the trees and the swirling, entwining ripples of the spell penetrated her focus.

And when she was done, when the spell had as much power as she knew how to draw into it, she touched the man's hair that she'd laid on the wood platform in front of her. And she saw his image in her mind as she slipped into the astral and took flight.

Flew out across the night, in ever-widening circles. Owl might've been with her, just behind her awareness, helping her search. She scanned the astralscape with her senses, her acute hearing, her sensitive night vision.

She rode the power of the spell as she soared out across the sky. And the spell weakened the farther she got from the medicine lodge. Then, like a flare in a dark cave, she saw him.

Grids Desmond, mundane human.

He was in a car, traveling up a hillside somewhere in the sprawl. Maria followed his progress from a distance, for there was an adept with him and she didn't want to be discovered.

The human and the adept came to a house. Maria recognized the location easily even though she couldn't read the exact address. The house was in the Santa Monica Mountains above Hollywood, off of Laurel Canyon Boulevard. Overlooking downtown.

There was a mage in the house, seemingly asleep. And someone else with her. Four of them in all.

When Maria had determined that Grids Desmond was not going to leave the house, she decided to return to the medicine lodge. She didn't want to tarry, to risk being discovered. She stopped in front of the residence only long enough to memorize the look and feel of the road and the other buildings so she could find it later.

She came back to her body, exhausted and weak. Her watch read four-twenty in the morning. She climbed down slowly, and made her way out of the grove and back to the landing site. "I know where he is."

Dougan smiled. "How far?"

"Close," she said. "Very close."

30

Hunger woke Jonathon from a deep sleep, and he found himself in Chico's kingsize waterbed, snuggled next to Synthia. His stomach grumbled. *Damn suprathyroid beast telling me it's time to feed.*

His eyes opened to a dark room, dim shadows reflecting off the mirrored ceiling. Distant sounds of the city drifted in on the warm breeze coming through the open screen door. Careful not to wake Synthia, he slipped from the bed and walked, naked, up the half flight of shag-covered stairs and into the kitchen.

As he walked, the jagged crackle in his brain faded into his awareness once again. Always there. Though it had let him sleep untroubled for a few hours. His headclock read 03:55:34 AM.

The kitchen matched the decor perfectly; even in the dim light Jonathon could see the avocado and gold flooring, the matching appliances and counter top. A full refrigerator said that Venice Jones had returned. Jonathon grabbed a can of Prohydrate liquid energy, and popped the top.

Gulping the thick brew, he made his way back downstairs for a quick check of the other bedrooms. Both Venny and Grids were asleep in separate rooms, just down the hall from Synthia. *Nobody is keeping watch. Would Venny leave us unprotected?*

He suspected not, and he searched with his headware for a signal. Sure enough, his vehicle control rig detected the Eurocar Westwind, outside and ready for remote rigging. The Westwind's dog brain indicated to Jonathon that one of its drones, the AeroDesign Condor surveillance craft, had been launched. The other drone—a CyberSpace Designs Stealth Sniper in the trunk—remained at ready.

Jonathon took another gulp of the thick, vanilla-flavored liquid and mentally switched to the Condor's frequency.

Suddenly he was floating high above the house, a sensor pod hanging below a huge helium-filled balloon, held in position by electric turbo fans. His eyes were sensitive holo-cameras, and his ears were algorithm-enhanced microphones. The night was as bright as day through the low-light and thermographic sensors; he zoomed in on the exterior of Chico's house.

The Westwind sat behind the Nightsky limousine in the driveway. The Nightsky's tires had been repaired, he noticed, but the rear window still gaped like a jagged-toothed mouth. The heat-vision highlighted the engine of the Westwind, and the house glowed a cool blue, with strips of yellow leaking out around the windows.

Everything was peaceful and quiet. As it should be. As he hoped it would stay long enough for them to do what they needed to do here. *Good.*

Venny had set the drone to autopilot, to maintain continuous surveillance of Chico's property. It was to notify him if any large animals (including people) appeared outside the building. The balloon's power cell had plenty of energy to last until daybreak when the solar panels would recharge it.

Jonathon released control back to the autopilot. Then he made his way back to the kitchen, taking another gulp of his Prohydrate. They were safe for the moment. It was time to make a plan.

A plan to discover the connection between Dougan Rose and Andreas Michaelson. Then take the next logical step. Killing everyone responsible for Tamara's death.

Tamara's ghost required no less.

A tide of fatigue washed over Jonathon. And then a wave of disappointment in Dougan—his childhood idol—the man who was now his arch rival, according to the trid reporters and the newsfaxes. Jonathon had been in awe of Dougan Rose for years, admiring his awesome moves and ruthless fighting tactics, and wishing all the while—desperately wanting—to be just like him.

Jonathan crushed the Prohydrate can in his hand. All that time his admiration was misdirected. Dougan might be a great linebiker, but he was also a thug. Nothing more than a murderer.

He's not larger than life, Jonathon thought. *He's small.* And that was a disappointing thought.

Once Dougan was dead, Michaelson would be next. The S-K exec would probably be even harder to get to. And connecting him to Tamara would require the help of a drek-hot decker. Yeah. Jonathon would have to hire some shadowrunners. *A fragging brilliant idea!* he told himself. *But where?*

Then suddenly he realized he knew where to contact runners. The Fixx.

He pulled another Prohydrate can from the fridge and walked toward the bathroom as he thought about it some more. He sat on the toilet and sipped his drink. The Fixx was a place as well as an event—a sort of continual party for shadowrunners, hosted by Dexter Hemmingway—a paranoid ex-military type with nuyen out the wazoo.

Hemmingway was not a fixer, nor a shadowrunner of any kind, except in his own mind. He was a shadowrunner wannabee; he didn't run any shadows himself, but he liked keeping tabs on the shadow community. The party at Hemmingway's fortress at the old LAX airport never stopped. Hemmingway had the nuyen to blow and he liked the company of shadowrunners, even though he never left the safety of his fortress. The Fixx had become a constant in the LA sprawl.

All they had to do was get inside. And with Venny's help, Jonathon didn't think it would be too much of a problem.

Jonathon downed the last of his drink and was reaching for the toilet paper when he heard the Condor's alarm go off. Something was approaching the house. *Fragging-A!* he thought, *I'm naked and sitting on the drekker.*

He concentrated to bring calm, then picked up the Condor's signal and switched to remote rigging so he was now looking down on the house. He focused in quickly, and noticed several people-sized heat signatures crawling along the outside deck by the pool. Seemed to be about four, but they were invisible to the low-light cameras.

Magic.

Jonathon finished with the toilet paper and stood, contacting the Westwind to give it the launch command for the Stealth Sniper. The Condor was only a surveillance drone and did not mount any weapons. The Sniper, though, was another story.

As the drone went through its launch sequence, Jonathon ran down the shag-carpeted stairs calling out, "Venny!

Intruders, intruders! I saw four of them coming through from the pool patio. One must be a mage; they're cloaked by some sort of invisibility spell."

No answer.

The Sniper drone's autopilot informed Jonathon that it was in flight and hovering in near silence, waiting for him to take control.

"Venny?" Jonathon reached the troll's room and stuck his head in.

Still no answer.

A huge, rough hand pulled Jonathan off his feet. "Quiet," rasped the big troll as he pulled Jonathon into the room with one smooth motion. "You'll give us away." Grids was sitting on the bed, looking dazed and pumped full of painkillers. He was awkwardly holding a huge Colt Manhunter as if he could barely lift it. Synthia was nowhere to be seen.

Jonathon whispered, "Have you woken Syn?"

Venny shook his head, and Jonathon started to move back into the hall to get her when a barrage of automatic gunfire suddenly blew out the windows down the hall. "Frag!" Jonathon yelled as more glass crashed down amid the chatter of machine guns. "Synthia, wake up! Get down on the fragging floor!"

Venny's hand clamped down on Jonathon's shoulder as he tried to lunge into the hallway. "You stay here," he said. "I'll go. You rig the drones. I can't do that."

Jonathon nodded, then crawled into a corner, trying to hide behind a huge orange beanbag chair as Venny clicked into hypersense mode. Jonathon concentrated as the troll checked the hall with the aid of a small mirror. Then Venny plunged into the hall with his Uzi III and was gone.

Jonathon remote-interfaced with the Sniper and became a sleek beetle, about a half-meter long, with a rotating set of turbines that kept him in the air. The world was warped through the Sniper's cameras, flattened and focused forward. He moved silently forward, hearing the sound of guns and screaming voices through the Sniper's pickup mikes.

As the Sniper flew in rushed silence to a position just off the patio, Jonathon quickly switched to the Condor to see where the intruders had gone. High above, looking down with clarity and perfect hearing, he saw only heat signatures huddled against the sliding glass door.

His awareness came back to the room. "Two are out-side," he whispered. "The others must be—"

Before he could finish, an explosion shook the house, a flash of red lighting the walls and etching shadows on Grids's frightened features. Then a wave of heat and smoke rolled through the hallway.

Grids ducked behind the bed, fumbling with his pistol.

Jonathon popped his awareness back into the Sniper, hovering off the edge of the patio. He readied the sniping gun, a silenced Barret 121-like weapon with a 24-round armor-piercing clip. Once the mounted weapon was acti-vated, Jonathan saw a target superimposed on the view in front of him.

He targeted one of the heat signatures and opened up, the single-shot weapon giving off a muffled spitting sound as it fired.

The bullet was on target, but was deflected at the last second by an invisible magical barrier. *Frag!* Jonathon fired again, moving the drone as the gun coughed a sec-ond time.

One of the runners fired a shotgun blast into the space where he had been. Missed.

And Jonathon's armor-piercing round hit homo this time, passing clear through the runner's shoulder and shattering the glass door behind him. Jonathon circled up and around as the shotgun went off again. Way off the mark.

Jonathon targeted and fired once more, but in the split second before the gun went off, a massive shape appeared between the Sniper and the two people. It was a towering monstrosity made of metal and concrete. The round was lost in the hard flesh of the summoned creature.

He moved again and continued to fire at the pair, hit-ting the wounded one once more before forcing them both to duck inside. They tried to see him, but couldn't make out the matte black beetle-shape in the dark. The house behind them was burning, flames shooting from the bed-room window where he and Synthia had slept.

Syn?

Bringing the Sniper around to the side, Jonathan tried to focus through the sliding glass doors, but he couldn't see through the orange flames. Then someone was shak-ing his meat body, and he barely had the time to click the drone to autopilot before Venny lifted him to his feet.

"We've gotta get out," the troll said, wrapping the duster around Jonathon. "The place is going to burn."

Jonathon nodded. "Did you get Syn?" he asked.

"I'm here," came Synthia's voice, sounding tired. All she had on was one of Venny's huge tuxedo shirts, which came down to her knees. "I'm a little shook up, but that's about all."

"You take the lead," Venny said. "Take Synthia and Grids in the limo. I'll follow you in the Westwind."

Jonathon nodded quickly, then he pulled his Predator II and glanced into the hall.

Nothing but the hungry tongues of fire lapping at the dry wood.

He took two seconds to switch into the Condor's aerial view, checking the path from the front door to the car. Nobody, but he did see three figures rappelling down some ropes from the pool patio to the ground below.

"Let's go," he said, then he was running through the smoke and the fire. Up the stairs and across the living room, then out through the front door and down the flagstone path to the drive. He jumped into the driver's seat of the limo and jacked in.

Next came Grids and Synthia, panting and struggling to keep up. Then Venny sprang from the burning building, sprinting at an unreal speed. Grids and Synthia jumped into the Nightsky's cabin and pulled the door shut behind them as Jonathon accelerated down the drive and away.

Venny drew up behind him in the Westwind, and soon they were heading back down into the brown smog of the sprawl. The troll's face appeared on the limo's telecom. "Where to?" he asked.

Jonathon thought for a second. "The Fixx," he said.

"Hemmingway's?" Venny asked.

"Dexter is a part-owner of the LA Sabers. He knows me, *likes* me even. He might help us out."

The troll nodded. "Sounds primo, chummer. The Fixx is a better place than most for what I think we're about to do."

Jonathon breathed a sigh. He was naked except for his duster, which no longer looked too new; it was taking on the look of the genuine article. *Well,* he thought, *they certainly won't have any problem searching my body for weapons.*

31

Michaelson couldn't sleep. He lay, fully clothed, on his unmussed bed and stared, wide-eyed, at the plaster ceiling. Thinking about his last conversation with Cinnamon and the upcoming events. Events that would change his life forever.

He recalled Cinnamon's beautiful face. Her brown eyes narrowing, the smooth white skin around the edges of her mouth crinkling as she frowned. "Moving the extraction to tonight creates some enormous problems," she told him, tossing her golden hair. "The runners I've hired are on another job. Plus I have yet to arrange for an appropriate hiding place."

Cinnamon did not have to elaborate on that last. Michaelson had heard tales that Lofwyr kept tissue samples of his high-ranking employees in magical stasis. Samples that could be used to locate or destroy their donors by ritual magic. Insurance against defection.

The original plan was for Cinnamon's team to get Michaelson out, then immediately make the transfer to MCT and their heavy security. Mitsuhama should have the capability to protect him. If he had to wait a day with Cinnamon, he'd be vulnerable.

Lofwyr would find him and take him back. Or perhaps kill him outright.

Michaelson had pleaded with Cinnamon. "I'm about to be discovered," he said. "I'll pay whatever you ask, just get me out of here."

"I must remind you that this line may not be fully secure."

"It's too late to worry about that, isn't it?" he told her.

Cinnamon frowned. "Let me make some calls. The cost is double what we agreed upon originally." She paused as if to give him the chance to object.

He simply nodded.

"You will not hear from me until just before I want you to move." She disconnected.

Now, five hours later, Michaelson sat up on the bed. He was fully clothed in his midnight blue pinstriped Zoé suit. On his desk, his briefcase was packed and ready. He told the lights to come on, then walked to the wet bar in the living room and poured himself a tall glass of ice water. The cold, clean liquid was the best water Claudio could find. Very expensive in this part of the world. But worth every drop.

"You're up quite late, aren't you, Andreas?" The voice came from near the door, smooth and congenial.

Michaelson jumped, spilling water down his front. *What the frag?*

"Oh, did I startle you?"

Michaelson turned to see Hans Brackhaus standing in the doorway. Brackhaus was a handsome human, moderately built and with black hair, blue eyes, and smooth white skin. His features were Germanic, the jaw strong, the nose straight and thin. The suit he wore matched the deep blue of his eyes exactly.

Michaelson's heart leapt into his throat, and for several seconds he couldn't speak.

Brackhaus strolled down the two short steps into the sunken living room and across the carpeting, his hand extended in greeting. "It is good to see you, Andreas."

"Hans," Michaelson said, shaking the other man's hand. Then he took a towel from the bar and dabbed at the water stain on his shirt. "What a surprise. What brings you here in the middle of the night?"

"Urgent business, I'm afraid. You're needed in Essen as soon as possible."

"In Essen? But I haven't finished evaluating the Magus Project. The scientists at Magenics are on the verge of some big breakthroughs, I think. But I've got several more days of work at least."

Brackhaus shook his head. "I hate to be the bearer of ill tidings," he said, "but my orders come from on high, Lofwyr himself. I am to take over the Magus Project until you can return."

The man's blue eyes bored holes into Michaelson despite his congenial demeanor. "So, pack up right away. Just the essentials; the helo will take you to the airport in an hour. Claudio can follow in the morning with the rest of your things."

Brackhaus paused, but didn't release Michaelson's gaze. "Oh, and I'll need everything you have on the Magus Project."

Michaelson nodded. What choice did he have but to consent? He walked to his desk and gathered up his briefcase. Then he went back into the living room and sat down, clicking the case open on the cherrywood coffee table.

The Magus File hardcopy rested inside its binder. It was an Alpha-level security document, and only three copies existed—all of them on paper. Still, he couldn't believe that Brackhaus didn't have his own.

"Thank you, Andreas." Brackhaus reached into the briefcase and took the magnetic binder. He punched in the access code to open it up. "Hurry," he told Michaelson, glancing at his old-fashioned wristwatch. "You only have fifty-five minutes now."

And as Michaelson turned to walk back into the bedroom, hoping beyond hope that Cinnamon's plan would somehow be able to get him out of this, brilliant orange light flashed behind him, reflecting red against the walls. He heard a searing crackle, like fire.

He spun to see what had happened.

Brackhaus held the smoking remains of the Magus File binder in his hand. Gray smoke wisped up from the blackened ash remnants of the pages that had fallen from the binder to the floor.

Magic fire? Or . . . or something else?

Brackhaus reached out to shut the lid of Michaelson's briefcase. "The Magus File," he said, "is too sensitive to carry on a public suborbital, and we didn't have time to get a company jet for you." The dark-haired man stood and brushed his hands together as if to remove the ashes, though Michaelson could see no black smudges or gray flakes.

Then he realized he was just standing there, his mouth agape. *Brackhaus must know,* he thought. *He must suspect I plan to defect. Frag me, the best I can do now is play along, do as I'm told and hope for mercy.*

His hope was faint; everyone knew that mercy flowed like a glacier from the cold heart of the dragon.

32

Maria wiped sweat from her brow and climbed into the GMC Bulldog stepvan that Dougan had brought up from his condo in Laguna Beach. The van was a black delivery truck that Dougan had modified to carry his dirt-biking equipment. Wide and squat, with double doors on the side, it was perfect for shadowrunning.

Behind Maria, Maurice let Bob Henry's body down from his shoulder to the floor of the stepvan, laying the huge man's dead mass as gently as he could. "I'm gonna pop that elf, but good," Maurice said, mostly to himself. He'd been mumbling about how many different ways he was going to geek Jonathon Winger. "It was him, I know it. Had to be, rigging a fragging drone or some drek like that."

Dougan was outside collapsing the Nightgliders and packing them into the back of the stepvan. Showing no emotion, no remorse. All biz.

Bob Henry was dead, cold flesh. His aura gone.

Maria had tried to heal him after he took two hits from an unknown, unseen sniper, but one of the bullets had passed through his neck and spine. His heart had stopped, his breathing erratic.

Bob Henry's death was just beginning to register for Maria. The hit on Grids Desmond and his associates had been a fragging disaster. Somehow, Grids and company had seen through Owl's cloak of invisibility; they'd been warned and ready.

The run that Dougan had claimed would be easy was turning out to be a nightmare. They still hadn't gotten the chip, had nothing that would appease Luc Tashika—the man who could reveal their criminal involvement in the so-called Lost Election. Tashika could destroy Maria's life. Put her in jail. Away from her children.

I won't let that happen, she told herself. *I'll do what-*

ever it takes to prevent it. She had never met Luc Tashika and she already hated him. She hated him for what he was making her do, for bringing her past back to haunt her.

When Dougan was finished packing, he took the driver's seat. "Ready?" he asked.

"What now?" Maria said.

"First," Dougan said, "we get rid of Bob Henry's body."

"Then I kill Jonathon Winger," interrupted Maurice.

Dougan smiled. "You might get that chance," he said. "I have a plan to get Winger to come to us *with* the information."

"Then we shouldn't have to kill him," Maria said.

Dougan glanced at her. "That's right, we shouldn't, under ideal circumstances. But we might. He's dangerous and we've got to be ready to use lethal force if necessary." Dougan stared hard into Maria's eyes. "Can you do that?" he asked. "If we have to?"

Maria didn't have to think about it. She hated killing, but she *would* kill to save her children. If it came down to that.

"Of course, I can kill when I must," she said. But it wasn't Jonathon Winger she was thinking about, it was Luc Tashika. He was the one she wanted dead.

33

Jonathon wound the limo along the twists and curves of Laurel Canyon, heading down to Sunset Boulevard and the strip, which was still packed with tourists and night partiers out for a wiz time. Synthia and Grids sat in the back, sullen and quiet.

In the rearview mirror, Jonathon caught glimpses of the two. Synthia's arms wrapped around herself, clutching Venny's huge white tux shirt as if it could warm her. Grids still wore his black jeans, but he'd replaced the black Mickey Mouse shirt with a cleaner white one. No blood on it, though Jonathon noticed black smoke stains on his chest, and he could make out the bandage on his bullet wound underneath. Grids had never really come fully awake, and Synthia was lost in thought.

Earlier, they'd stopped by the side of the road for a few minutes while Jonathon remote-piloted the two drones they'd left behind. The Condor turned up no sign of their attacker, but Jonathon could see Chico's house burning down below like a giant bonfire. *Sorry, Chico,* he thought. *I'll make it up to you if you ever get out of Aztlan.*

Then he scanned the whole area. Finding no one in close pursuit, he told the autopilot of each craft to fly to his position. And when they landed, Venny helped him pack the two drones into the Westwind's storage compartment. Afterward, they'd resumed their drive to Hemmingway's.

Now, Jonathon accelerated up onto the 405, heading south toward the old LAX. They drove in silence for almost half an hour before Synthia looked up. "You know, those were different runners than the first ones," she said. "This bunch had a shaman—a second- or third-grade initiate. Maybe higher."

"Of course they were different," Grids said. "You destroyed the first group."

Jonathon and Synthia both laughed.

"What?"

"You've been chipping too many action sims," Jonathon said.

Synthia spoke, "My hellblasts might've wounded them, but I was targeting the car. So we could get away. I know the black fragger isn't hurt, and the blond, she was some sort of adept, I think. We might've slowed them down, but they'll be back. And if they find us . . ."

Grids's voice was hoarse. "They were after *me*," he said. "They must know about the chip and are trying to kill me because of it."

Jonathon shook his head. "I don't think so," he said. "They could've killed us all with another pulse of that minigun. I think hitting you was an accident. They were obviously professionals. If they wanted us dead, they wouldn't have followed us, they'd have killed us outright.

"They probably know about the chip, but don't know where it is. They need us alive so they can force us to tell them how to find it." Jonathon took the old LAX off-ramp, weaving in and out of the CalTrans barricades and the signs releasing the Free City of Los Angeles from liability.

"Entering the Coastal Restricted Area," Synthia said, looking through the glass. "Where only the deranged and insane go in the middle of the night without a corporate army."

After they were past the barricades, Jonathon accelerated onto the dark freeway and tried to catch the shadow of Synthia's face in the rearview mirror. "Do you think it was the shaman who found us?" he asked.

She nodded. "Had to be," she said. "How else?"

"So we have two separate groups of shadowrunners after us . . . why?"

Neither Grids nor Synthia could answer that. "Not enough data," said Grids.

"Speaking of data . . . Did you get a chance to check if your smartframe—Goofy—managed to translate any more?"

Grids nodded. "Venny and I stopped by my hidey-hole for my stuff. But Goofy hasn't got the whole manuscript finished. More than half is still left."

"Did you bring what it got so far?" Jonathon asked. "And can I see it?"

Grids sighed. "Might not do you much good," he said.

"A smartframe doesn't process it linearly; it's finished translating the image in the center of Tamara's vision because the focus is better, so we have the middle part of each page converted to text, but not the words on the top, bottom and sides."

"What a fragged-up way to—"

"That's how a parallel machine works, chummer," Grids said, an edge to his voice. "Try getting an old Cray III to crank on it one instruction at a time. Take till fragging Christmas."

"Whoa," Jonathon said. "Okay, I scan. I scan. You're the hardware guru."

"Fragging right."

Jonathon glanced into the rearview again. "Syn, next time Grids gets shot, remind me not to argue with him. Puts him in a foul state."

"I am *not* in a foul state!"

Synthia and Jonathon laughed.

A few minutes later, the freeway ended at the wrecked old airport. A three-meter-tall cyclone fence topped with barbed wire blocked their way. The husks of old burned-out cars and trucks were piled up in front of the fence, stacked two or three high to form a near solid wall of rusted steel and cracked macroplast. An effective barricade.

The freeway curved left, but the narrow gap in the barricade was on their right. Jonathon turned on the pitted asphalt and came to a stop about five meters from the fence. He flashed his lights, then turned them off, signaling the security that they wanted in. Venny stopped the Westwind behind the limo.

A minute went by before a couple of orks with padded synthleather jackets and obvious combat shotguns appeared and approached the limo. On the surface they looked like gangers, maybe part of the Steppin' Wulfs, but they were too much alike; their armored synthleathers were nearly identical except for the designs. Like uniforms.

One had a multicolored thunderbird up his front, and the other some dripping red Japanese characters. Their black boots matched perfectly. And the weapons gave them away; each carried a combat gun—a bulky Mossberg CMDT—plus a Scorpion machine pistol in a thigh holster and sword for up-close work. Everything was too clean for gangers, too pristine to have been used recently.

Thunderbird stood in front of the car while the other came up to Jonathon's window, shining the bright beam of a flashlight into the car. "I don't know you and this car neither," the ork said. "So sell it to me, chummer. Make me believe I should let you through."

Jonathon looked into the light and smiled. "You like combat biker?"

The ork gave him a puzzled look for a second. Then he stepped back, a doubting sneer on his tusked face. "No," he said. "You ain't . . ."

"Yes, believe it, chummer. I'm Jonathon Winger. And I need to speak with Dexter."

The ork broke into a broad smile. "Well, I'll be fragged," he said, then turned to Thunderbird. "Reece, this be Jonathon Winger. Right here in this fragging limo."

Reece disbelieved at first, but when he realized his friend wasn't joking, he lost his composure. He stepped around the car and approached Jonathon. "Man, you're the greatest. I can't believe you's here, what a fraggin' mind blow. You've gotta kill Dougan Rose tomorrow, frag him up the daisy-eatin' hoop of his." Reece paused for a breath. "Nuthin' 'gainst elves, y'know. Just Rose, he thinks he's the best. But you's wiz, primo compared to him."

Jonathon smiled, and said, "I plan to destroy him." He wasn't lying. "But right now I need to speak with Dexter."

"You know Mr. Hemmingway?"

"We've met once or twice at parties; he's got a big share of the team."

"I'll call him," said Reece. Then he started subvocalizing, his lips moving but not saying anything. No doubt he was getting authorization on his headphone. After a minute, he looked down at Jonathon. "You got any ID? You know, just for the boss."

Jonathon searched the pockets of his duster, feeling the panels of hard polycarbonate armoring. He hoped he still had those credsticks. He was relieved to find everything still there.

Jonathon handed the credstick to Reece, who walked over to a nearby car. He reached in, apparently to slot the stick, then was back within a few minutes.

"Convinced me, Mr. Winger," the ork said. "Follow me."

"The car behind is with me," Jonathon said.

"Of course."

Reece and the other ork led Jonathon through the gap in the wall of junked cars and trucks. Then a wide gate in the cyclone fencing opened inward to let them through. Jonathon noticed the track-mounted security drones that patrolled the fence, complete with cameras and guns. This place was tight.

"You stay between the yellow flags, Mr. Winger. Nice car like yours wouldn't want to test out the 'crete. We lost a truck to a new sinkhole just t'other day."

"Thanks, chummers," Jonathon said. He drove slowly out onto what used to be a massive expanse of concrete on what was once LAX. Most of the buildings and runways had buckled during the '28 quake, and what was left standing had been flooded in the tsunami of 2045. Now, wide areas of cracked runway had collapsed into polluted sinkholes filled with ocean water. Many places were below the waterline. The water itself was black, but Jonathon caught glimpses of garbage and machinery in the water.

"Toxics must love this place," Synthia said.

"Oh, that's reassuring." Grids sounded apprehensive again.

After a half-kilometer or so of winding around and between large puddles or mini-lakes, Jonathon pulled the limo onto a wide stretch of concrete in front of a massive metal building. The wall of the building stretched left and right as far as he could see. Rows and rows of cars and motorcycles, all in operating condition, rested there with several tractor rigs, one or two helicopters, and several large stepvans.

"This place looks like it's rocking," Jonathon said.

"Now, why is it we came here, again?" Synthia asked.

"Shelter and safety first and foremost. Hemmingway will probably oblige me because he wants me to stay alive, at least until after the final match tomorrow night. Secondly, I want to hire some runners to help me hit Michaelson."

Both Synthia and Grids turned to face Jonathon. "What?" Grids said.

"Excuse me?" said Synthia.

Jonathon parked the limo next to a Toyota Elite, not quite as nice as his Nightsky, but the rear window wasn't shattered either. Venny pulled the Westwind's small but powerful frame into the spot on the other side of the Nightsky.

"You heard right," Jonathon said. "We need to start putting some pieces together, and the best way is to strike at the heart. Michaelson."

"You want to try to take down a senior exec of one of the most powerful megacorps on the globe?" Grids sounded baffled, as though such a thing was beyond possible.

"Not take him down, at least not right away. Just raid his office, get some data that will connect him to Tamara's death."

"Don't you think we should wait until Goofy finishes deciphering the Magus File?"

Jonathon got out of the car. "No," he said. "I can't wait. We wait, we get killed. It's time for a little turnaround. Come on, let's go see The Fixx."

Synthia put a hand on his arm as she stood up from the limo. "Can I get into the trunk first, my suitcase? As much as I love Venny's shirt, I'd like to change before we go in to dance among the shadows." She fluttered the tail of the massive shirt around her knees.

"Uh, good idea," Jonathon said, feeling conspicuously underclothed himself. The duster was beginning to chafe.

Venny got out of the other car and assumed a protective posture next to Jonathon. The big troll provided a good screen behind which they changed into more appropriate attire. "Just in case anyone wanders by," Synthia said.

To go under his duster, Jonathon chose jeans and a loose dark blue shirt with lots of pockets. Synthia put on her slitch-from-Hell outfit—black synthleather pants and matching jacket over a low-cut cherry-red halter. None of it was armored like Jonathon's duster, but at least she looked the part.

A few minutes later, Jonathon led the way to the entrance. The building was an old jet hangar, built from thickly corrugated sheet metal covered with peeling white paint. It was huge, stretching up at least ten stories, and five times as long as it was tall. Facing them as they approached were the massive double doors of the original hangar, seven or more stories tall themselves, built to accommodate the giant jumbo jets of the last century.

Built into the massive hangar doors were smaller doors, one of which stood ajar, the sounds and lights of many people and music escaping through it. Jonathon headed for that one and was greeted by a heavily cybered dwarf woman wearing obvious body armor. "Greetings, chummers," she said. "Dexter said he'd be right out. Meanwhile, mingle or do biz or whatever you wish."

Exactly one-half of her head shone a brilliant chrome in the florescent lights. The other half was natural skin sprouting greasy black hair. "The rules are simple: weapons are allowed for demonstration purposes only. Kill anyone on the premises and you will be killed. We're all professionals, and no one will tolerate a disruption of the biz. There will be no remorse."

She smiled to herself, then extended her cyberarm to Jonathon. "That's the spiel I've got to give everyone," she said. "But with you it might be different. Everyone loves you. And I thought your riding in the last match was some of the most butt-kicking wiz moves I've ever seen."

"Thank you," Jonathon said, trying to push past her and into the hangar. Inside, he'd expected to see only an oil-stained concrete floor and steel girders holding up the sheet metal walls and roof. But Hemmingway had remodeled the interior.

A short set of stairs that looked like real wood led to a huge deck that surrounded a large indoor pool. Tall palm trees and flowering bushes surrounded the pool and made the place smell like a tropical paradise. Jonathon noticed that much of the roof, thirty or so meters overhead, had been replaced with tinted glass to let the sun in for the plant life. *Remarkable,* he thought.

About a hundred or more people spoke in hushed conversations in the shadows of the trees or sitting in private booths and tables along the walls. A massive bar served drinks at one end of the pool, and a few bikini-clad biffs and one or two steroid-muscled joyboys swam in the water, but Jonathon suspected they were being paid to contribute to the atmosphere. No professional shadowrunners would strip down and go swimming in a place of biz.

The chromed dwarf walked along with him. "So tell me . . ." she said. "What brings you here? You need some muscle? Some force to get back at Dougan Rose? Revenge for killing Tamara? I can't believe he got away with that drek." She shook her head disparagingly. "Anyway, if you need someone, just let me know, 'cause I'm a top-rate samurai, and the price would be reasonable for a chummer like you . . ."

"Look," Jonathon said finally, wanting to ask her if she ever shut up, "Dougan Rose will pay for what he's done," he said. "I plan to get him in tomorrow night's match. I'm just here to see Dexter." Jonathon saw a large golf cart making its way around the pool. "And here he comes. Thanks for the offer—"

"You can call me Halfchrome."

"Thanks, Halfchrome. I'll let you know."

The vehicle rolled up to them. Much longer than a normal cart, it had five bench seats. At the wheel sat another ork who could have been a twin of Reece and his chummer by the main gate. Except this one was female and more heavily cybered. She looked quicker, smarter maybe. More deadly.

Next to the ork sat a human male with peroxide-white hair and the acne-ridden skin of a teenager. He wore synthleather pants and a tank top, but his skin was tattooed everywhere except his head. Tattooed with arcane symbols.

Venny whispered in Jonathon's ear, "Mage. Probably responsible for the water elementals we saw on guard by the road in."

Jonathon shivered. He hadn't seen any elementals.

In the second seat was Dexter Hemmingway. He was a thinning human who looked to be in his late fifties, though he was rumored to be much older. Graying brown hair, gaunt face etched with hairline wrinkles. His face seemed to have undergone many cosmetic operations and Jonathon suspected that his eyes were cyber even though carefully masked to look natural.

The man stepped out to greet them. "Jonathon!" he said. "What a great surprise to see you here."

"Dexter," Jonathon said. "I appreciate your hospitality. This is—"

"Venice Jones I know," Dexter said. "And Synthia Stone is familiar to me, but I don't know . . ."

"Grids Desmond," Jonathon said. "A very good friend of Tamara's."

Dexter frowned. "I'm sorry about what happened to her." Then he waved at them. "Come, let's speak in private. Get on."

Hemmingway's cart took them past the pool and down a concrete path behind the trees to a guarded gate. As they rode, Jonathon told Hemmingway why they'd come, that he needed a decker and some muscle to help him raid the office of a corporate exec. Grids knew how to get there, but was unwilling to risk running the Matrix.

Past the gate was a ramp down to a tunnel that passed below the water outside and through several more checkpoints before emerging up into another renovated hangar. And by that time, Hemmingway had assured Jonathon that his needs would easily be met.

"Good," Jonathon said. "Then we'll make the run right away, before daybreak."

"Null persp, my friend," Hemmingway said. "I'll arrange for whatever you need. I'm more than happy to oblige. Nothing, you see. *Nothing* is too much for my star rider."

34

The hour was up and Michaelson still hadn't heard a word from Cinnamon. He'd packed a few things and pretended nothing was amiss as he listened to the deep thwup of the Hughes Airstar landing on the pad outside.

He turned to get his briefcase and bid Hans Brackhaus goodbye as if nothing strange were happening. But Brackhaus was nowhere to be found. Gone.

And as he walked out to the helipad, Ruger and the combat mage—Firnulan—falling into step behind him, he wondered about his new life in Essen. Perhaps he would get to see his wife again, perhaps not. He'd made arrangements with his contacts in Berlin to have her kidnapped and transferred to MCT custody. If he couldn't get a message through to stop that from happening, he might never see her again.

The thought twisted his heart with agony, the kind of breath-stopping apprehension he hadn't felt in a long, long time. Not since his early years in the corp, the days when he used to second-guess his every move, wondering if his boldness would suddenly bring down Lofwyr's anger. He'd heard plenty of stories about the dragon's wrath and how it was known to dismember underlings in a rage.

But Michaelson's boldness had caused him to advance, both his creativity and his ruthlessness been rewarded. Spirits, he'd devoted his entire fragging existence to Saeder-Krupp. But he'd always hated being under the constant, unblinking reptilian gaze of the worm. He could hardly bear the terror that one day he, too, would suffer from a massive claw slicing across his midsection to spill his guts.

Now it looked like that might happen.

Michaelson calmed himself and ducked as he made his

way across the painted circle toward the chopper. A uniformed human woman with blond hair pulled into a ponytail waved at him to hurry over.

When Ruger looked up at her, he hesitated for a second. "Hey, you're not the usual team—"

By then it was too late. The blonde had an Ingram SMG in her hand and was firing.

Firnulan started to cast some sort of spell, but he jerked as a staccato barrage of bullets pierced his body armor. The bullets came from the pilot's seat where a large black-skinned human sat, shaved head and a serious, barely human look on his sweating face.

Firnulan went down, but Ruger refused to fall even though he'd been hit. He tried to shield Michaelson. "Run," he yelled. "Get back inside!" The troll pulled an automatic shotgun from under his tux coat. "Backup's coming!"

Michaelson couldn't move. He heard a *ka-thunk* come from the black man's position, then a second later the hotel behind them exploded in flame, throwing him face-first onto the painted concrete.

Ruger fired twice before he went down. The first shot should've hit the blonde, but she dodged to the side in a blur of motion. The second one did get her, catching her leg. A blast of such strength should've taken her limb completely off, but all it did was toss her out of the way. Her black synthleather pants ripped into tiny shreds to reveal form-fitting body armor beneath.

She cried out as the blast threw her to the ground. "Frag it, Hendrix! I'm down."

The black man stepped out of the helo, his movements just as fast as the biff's, but jerky like a robot's. The big gun in his hand barked as he chewed even larger holes into the gore-spattered bodies of Ruger and Firnulan. Then with one hand, he reached down and lifted Michaelson off the ground.

"We're from Cinnamon," he whispered. "Get in."

Michaelson picked up his fallen briefcase and obeyed.

"Layla, can you walk?" the black man asked the blonde.

"Maybe," came the response. And as he helped her into the seat next to Michaelson, she said, "Let's move, I hear people coming."

"Check," said Hendrix.

Michaelson looked back at what was left of the entrance to the penthouse. The doors were gone and part of the entry had collapsed to the floor, swathed in a wall of flame that blocked the hall behind from view.

Then the black man jumped into the front seat and the helo lifted into the air. "Strap yourself in," he said. "This ain't no luxury ride."

"Yeah," the blonde said. "We might encounter some turbulence." She gave a short, sharp laugh.

The helo dropped abruptly as if on cue, and Michaelson strapped himself in. The next ten or fifteen minutes were spent hiding from and out-maneuvering pursuing aircraft until Hendrix finally brought them down in the Harbor District down by Long Beach, an area Michaelson recognized as the Barrens.

Not a nice place at all.

"This is where you're going to hide me?" he asked.

The blonde, who'd started to cut away her pants to get a look at her wound, glanced up at him. "Welcome to the fragging free world, Mr. Michaelson," she said. "May your brief stay be a joy ride and a half." Then she broke into a long eerie laugh that sent a shiver of ice through Michaelson's very bones.

35

When Jonathon saw Hemmingway's home, he forgot about the run on Michaelson, forgot about the hiss in his head. For the space of several heartbeats, he simply stood in awe.

The jet hangar was as large as the first one—thick, corrugated metal walls over a frame of huge steel girders. Except in this one, lush ivy climbed the girders. The metal roof and walls held expansive windows of tinted, one-way glass. Hazy, blue moonlight shone through the skylight.

But it was the building *inside* the hangar that took Jonathon's breath away. Hemmingway had brought in dirt and planted grass and trees over tiny rolling hills. But here there was no pool, no deck.

Here, a castle stood in the center of the hangar—an old-style French chateau from the age of knights and lords and drek. A fragging castle! There was no moat, but it had a draw bridge and a portcullis and wrought iron bars over the leaded-glass windows.

"Do you like my humble home?" asked Hemmingway, the finely etched lines of his face bunching as he smiled. "I had it brought over from the Loire Valley, stone by stone, and reassembled. Cheaper than you might think; castles sure don't cost what they used to." He chuckled.

Both Synthia and Grids stared in awe. Only Venny didn't react; he remained impassive as ever, his gaze on the kid mage and the samurai in the cart's front seat. They drove through the front gate into a medieval courtyard complete with suits of armor and fluttering banners.

"I'll have Montgomery set up some rooms for you," Hemmingway said.

"Thank you, Dexter," Jonathon said. "But I'm anxious to get on with this next bit."

"Ah, of course," Hemmingway said. "Shadowrunning."

"Yes."

"All right, let's sit down in the library and discuss what you need, but I do insist that you stay here until after the match tonight."

"It would be my pleasure," Jonathon said. "After the run, we'll stay as long as you'll have us."

Hemmingway smiled. "Excellent."

Less than an hour later, Jonathon had assembled a team and the equipment they needed. One of the runners, a human street samurai called Samantha, had run on the Venice Beach Hilton before. A veteran runner, all padded up in form-fitting body armor, she was ready to rock and roll at any moment. She helped Jonathon and Grids, who'd actually seen the inside of Michaelson's suite, to formulate a plan.

Jonathon's headclock read 04:46:55 AM when they lifted off—Jonathon pilot-rigging the jet-assisted Hughes Stallion helo. Synthia had insisted she come along as combat mage; Venny accompanied Jonathon as bodyguard, but Grids remained behind.

Grids wanted to set up his simsense equipment and his cyberdeck so that Goofy could continue crunching on the Magus File conversion. But he also planned to ride shotgun with the decker Jonathon had hired, a young kid who went by the handle of Noodle.

Halfchrome was brought in because Samantha trusted her; the two of them were the muscle. Jonathon had provided them with a choice of weaponry and ammo from Hemmingway's storehouse.

The whine of the Hughes helo rose like a wave of goose pimples over Jonathon. Then the rotors reached a deep harmonic pulse as he lifted off the tarmac. *Thwup. Thwup. Thwup.* The Stallion was a creature of metal and macroglass, a beast of sound and fury, modified with jet engines to give it that extra push in a flat-out run.

Jonathon rose to fifty meters and kicked in the jets. The whine of the turbines raised hackles on his neck as he flew the metal insect out across the flooded concrete that was LAX. The sky was a deep predawn blue, lightening ever-so-slightly on his right as he flew north along the coast.

Besides the macroglass frontshield, Jonathon had 360-degree sensors and cameras, letting him see and feel the surrounding airspace. A thrill of adrenaline pulsed through him as he rocketed the helo past a huge water-desalting plant and out over the open water, swaying left, then right beneath its rotors, testing the yaw and pitch.

Damn, it's good to be flying again, he thought.

"Grids," Jonathon said. "We're enroute. ETA Venice Hilton twelve minutes."

Grids's voice came into Jonathon's head. "Copy," he said. "Noodle and I are in position." He sounded apprehensive, almost scared.

"How you holdin' up?" Jonathon asked.

"Shoulder's okay, but . . ." Grids trailed off.

Jonathon waited until it was obvious the other man wasn't going to finish his sentence. "Yeah, I miss her too," he said.

Grids was silent and Jonathon was suddenly flooded with memories of flying. The test craft he'd flown with Tamara were much more powerful and destructive than this helo, but the feel of the wind caressing his fuselage was the same. The bounce of turbulent air, the screaming fire of the turbines, rumbling like excess distortion through his metal body; all were similar. Except that Tamara wasn't there to share it.

Now she's gone.

Jonathon gritted his teeth against the memories and bowed the Hughes. He throttled up the jets and dropped down toward the water's surface, almost touching the breaking waves full of sludge and debris.

The water changed as he passed the last desalinization plant and the arcing line of buoys that held an underwater micro-net to keep debris and garbage out of the area. Venice Beach lay clean and pulsing with life even this early in the AM.

Jonathon banked right and climbed, spotting the Venice Hilton—a shiny blue steel and mirrored glass building, elegant and dark against the backdrop of towering arcologies behind it. He brought the onboard cameras online and focused on the penthouse helipad.

The roof of the hotel was unoccupied, nobody in sight. Excellent.

"Grids, one minute approach," Jonathon said. "What do the internal cameras show?"

"Jonathon, you're not going to like this."

"Tell me anyway."

"All sec cameras covering the helipad are blacked out. Security reports a fire as the cause, but I've heard that drekking excuse one too many times."

"What about inside?"

"That's odd too. No one's home at our Mr. Michaelson's, and security seems way too porous. Noodle thinks something's going down, and I agree."

"Copy, Grids. I'll keep that in mind."

Jonathon swung the Hughes steeply left and down, zooming his camera-eyes on the roof below as he brought his machine toward the helipad. "We're going in," he told everyone. "Prep for landing and assault."

The low-light cameras showed that Grids was right. Not only had some sort of fire recently burned the drek out of the outside entrance to the penthouse, but it looked to Jonathon as if an explosion had been the cause of the fire. He saw chunks of fallen wall. Melted macroplast finish strewn like rubble. The thermographic filters revealed residual heat from the structure.

What the frag? This explosion had happened not long ago.

Synthia slumped in the passenger seat, just for a second, before sitting up and turning to Jonathon. "Something's going on in the astral," she said. "I can't get through the drek around the penthouse. It could be a ward of some kind, but it's probably just a mana bramble."

"Mana bramble?"

"It's an LA phenomenon," Synthia said. "Because of all those mages playing with magic at UCLA, astral space around here is full of interference that sometimes makes magic unstable, unpredictable. A mana bramble is a localized contortion of astral space. It won't stop us from going in physically, but it looks like a demilitarized zone in the astral."

Venny leaned forward from his seat behind Jonathon. "I've got a twitchy feeling about this run," he said.

Jonathon glanced back at him. "You want to cut out? The internal cameras show all clear."

Venny shook his head. "Magic can fool cameras, chummer. And Syn can't project inside to do an astral scan."

"Could be just a coincidence."

"Maybe, maybe not," Venny said. "Either way, I don't like it."

Jonathon lowered the Hughes Stallion to the tarmac. "Neither do I," he said, "But we're here. Shouldn't we have a look? I'll keep the rotor humming."

"If you say so."

Halfchrome popped the side door open and jumped out. "We're on," she said. "I'll patch my cyberoptic camera through my headphone."

"Copy," said Jonathon. Then he switched to her video feed, which the helo's communications relay picked up. The image was monocular, coming only from her single cybereye. The resolution was low and jumpy, like watching a rapidly changing set of still shots.

Samantha glided out after Halfchrome, carrying her combat SMG at ready, braced in the crook of her elbow. The human's movements were superfluid and oh-so-quick thanks to the move-by-wire implant that bulged slightly on her neck. She flickered to Halfchrome's vanguard position, slicing across the helipad to the rubble of the ruined doorway.

Halfchrome glanced inside, the red laser sight of her Berretta SMG tracking up the blackened walls for a second before she ducked back.

Nobody.

Nothing to see but scorch marks along an empty hallway.

Halfchrome waved Synthia and Venny to join them. "Seems clear," the dwarf subvocalized. And as Venny accompanied Synthia across the short distance to the twisted and shattered doors, Halfchrome followed Samantha inside.

The video jumped and hopped as she ran, giving Jonathon a brainache. The white walls were streaked with black burn marks. The carpeting was melted in a blast pattern. *Someone else has been here and hit Michaelson already.* "Grids," Jonathon said. "You sure this is the right place?"

Grids let out a short laugh. "This is it. Noodle says the hotel records show Michaelson never left. Of course, he comes and goes as he pleases because Saeder-Krupp owns the place."

In Halfchrome's video link, the red dots of the laser sights were the only lights in the hall. The short hall ended at a set of double doors, joining another dark hallway leading off to the right. Still no sign of security or hotel personnel.

The doors opened easily as Noodle accessed the locking mechanism through the hotel's security node. The decker had to bypass the printscanner and unlock the door. Then the four were inside, scanning the suite with their laser sights, trigger fingers ready. Coming up blank.

The cameras hadn't been lying; the suite was empty and clean. The bed hadn't been slept in; no clothes in the closet. Michaelson's stuff was gone.

Paranoia clamped strangling fingers on Jonathon's throat just then. *A trap,* he thought. "This is fragged," he said. "Back-track. Now! Full retreat!"

And just as the words left his mouth, he saw the brilliant flash of white light through the video linkage, overloading the dwarf's cybereye. There was no sound, though, and for a split second communication was out, and all he heard was the faint hiss in his head.

Then Venny's voice cut in, "—nathon, did you hear me? Synthia's gone."

"What?"

"She just fragging disappeared."

36

The ancient refinery stood dead in the early morning light. This was Wilmington, in the industrial Harbor District, just on the edge of the Barrens—an area of factory waste, quake-tossed concrete and steel, and insane gangs.

Not the most pleasant place in the Sixth World, thought Cinnamon as she looked at it from astral space—dead gray metal, a lifeless wasteland beneath the lightening haze. Bardolf and Githon, her two earth elementals, accompanied her, but they did not manifest when she did. She assumed her human guise—Cinnamon, a sexy blond in skintight synthleather pants and jacket.

Oil-blackened metal columns seemed to suck the sunlight from the air, darkening the cold spaces beneath the growth of ancient pipes and tubes.

"Hendrix?" Cinnamon called softly.

A metal door, large enough to admit a tractor rig, creaked open on her left, leading into a low-slung warehouse of corrugated black metal. Hendrix glanced out, and the light behind him caught the shining silver of the skillsofts that bristled from his shaved head. He waved her inside.

The smell of incense and scented candles rolled over her as she entered the warehouse. Normally, she would never have come in person to check on the progress of a run. Normally, she merely paid for success, withheld funds in the case of failure, and punished incompetence. But this was far from normal.

No, this was a fragging emergency. And not one she was happy about.

Sludge and blackened goo stuck out from the elbows of the old oil pipes that ran along the high ceiling and walls. Dim incandescent bulbs lit the black with their yellow globes. The floor was oil-stained duracrete, stretching thirty or more meters into the darkness.

A hermetic circle had been drawn in the center of the floor; Juju Pete's construction designed to hide Michaelson. To mask his presence from searching eyes, and to protect him from ritual spells until tomorrow when Tashika could take possession.

The circle was one of the largest Cinnamon had seen, ornately drawn with fluorescent powder of red and blue. Juju Pete had drawn patterns of happiness and melancholy, faces with painful eyes, but smiling lips. Deception inherent in the images themselves. Tiny voodoo dolls sat interspersed within the patterns, each simple yet different. Cinnamon noticed several dragon-shaped dolls among them.

Interesting . . .

The hermetic circle's astral image was a swirl of color and contradiction. Hints of powerful magic intermixed with a constantly shifting current of illusory elements that served to hide the whole construct. If she weren't so close, Cinnamon might overlook the astral image of the circle and the spell.

Which is the whole idea—to hide Michaelson from Lofwyr.

Hendrix skirted the circle, leading Cinnamon around to where Layla slept on a small cot, her broken leg in a tight brace. Hendrix seemed fatigued himself, stopping by Layla's cot and sitting in a vinyl seat he'd pulled from an old Eurovan.

Inside the circle was Juju Pete, hobbling around on his crutch as he continued to build the spell ritual. The mage looked like a relic from the past—his braids, tipped with bone, swayed and slapped against his back and chest, bare except for the intricate tattooing and the skeleton necklace he wore.

Over his blue jeans, Juju Pete wore a non-invasive brace on his wounded leg to allow him to walk. His leg had been severely damaged in an earlier run. Nearly blown completely off. It looked like it would be long in healing.

Michaelson slept restlessly on a cot identical to Layla's, except that it was inside the circle. He wore a blue-gray business suit and his briefcase rested under the cot.

Very good, Cinnamon thought. She stood just outside the circle and called to Michaelson, "Hello, Mr. Michaelson. Please wake up."

Michaelson stirred, then sat up when he saw her. "Hello, Cinnamon," he said.

"I trust you are not injured," she said. "This setup is inconvenient, but it should suffice until we can get you to your destination."

"I owe my life to you," Michaelson said. "And these very competent people." He indicated Hendrix and Layla.

"Your money will be adequate," she said. "I trust you have all the documents?"

Michaelson's face went white. He took a breath before answering. "Most," he said. "Not all."

"What do you mean? What's missing?" *This is not funny.*

"Lofwyr sent somebody to see me." Michaelson swallowed hard. "He suspected something, I'm sure. He burned the Magus File and was going to take me to Germany to have me killed."

"He burned *what*?" Cinnamon felt the edge rise inside her, the loss of control that sometimes came with the hunger.

"Don't be upset. I had no way of knowing he was already here," Michaelson said. "My secretary told me he wasn't expected until later today."

"Oh, I'm not upset," Cinnamon said, the surge rising like a tide inside her. "I am fragging slotted off!" Her voice rose until she was bellowing. She turned away from him and let out an inhuman roar to vent her frustration.

I will crush this puny human, she thought. *I'll take his weak flesh between my claws and pulverize him. Then slam the bits and pieces that hang limply from his dead form into the floor. Over and over.*

But she couldn't get into the circle without major effort, not without revealing what she was. *Besides if I lose control, I'll forfeit my chance for this man's spirit energy, the sweetest nectar of all.*

Cinnamon clenched her fists and tried to relax, to maintain her composure. After a minute she pulled a cigarette from her gold case. She lit it and took a satisfying drag.

"I . . . I'm . . ." Michaelson said. "I'm sorry. I'll make it up to you if I can."

She ignored his whining attempts to placate her while she smoked. Then when the edginess had retreated slightly, she turned to face him. "You have made me into a liar," she said. "I do not appreciate that."

"I never meant—"

"Shut up!"

"Sorry."

"I have promised that information to certain parties, and if it cannot be found, someone will have to pay."

Michaelson sighed. "I will compensate you for any inconvenience."

"Yes, you will, Mr. Michaelson. You will." Cinnamon gazed hard into his eyes. "And you just better hope your value doesn't keep slipping. You're a corporate, you should know the rules better than most. When an asset declines too far, the wisest course is simply to dump it."

Cinnamon tilted her head back and blew out a long plume of smoke. "Wouldn't you agree, Mr. Michaelson?"

37

"Look for her!" Jonathon screamed. "She must be some-where."

There was no reply for two, three heartbeats. Nothing but the rushed whisper of feet across the carpeting and the rapid scanning of the empty room through Halfchrome's vid linkage. Showing a room that was just as empty. Just as silent.

Like a tomb.

Grids's voice cut in, "Alarms are going off," he said. "Some tricky delayed thing we couldn't trap. Sorry."

"We're falling back," came Venny's voice after a minute. "With all this astral interference, I can't begin to trace her."

Venny led the retreat, followed by Halfchrome and Samantha, running the short distance to the Hughes Stal-lion. *Syn,* Jonathon thought desperately, *what happened to you? Why did I agree to let you come?*

The door slammed and he lifted off instinctively, flying by gut, down along the waterline and back the way they'd come. He felt detached from his body. Separate, isolated.

A cold melancholy seeped into Jonathon as he flew, feeling the cool wind off the ocean swells as he rocketed just above the surf. He cranked the Hughes Stallion, his metal body, to the red, trying to warm the freezing chill inside. The sinking sensation in the heavy pit of his gut that he'd seen the last of his love.

"Venny, tell me exactly what you saw," Jonathon said.

Venny gave him a sad look. "It's hard to explain," he said. "Synthia and I came up behind Samantha and Half-chrome. I glanced around in the near dark, but saw nothing.

"Synthia was standing next to me, just a step away, scanning the astral to make sure we weren't hit with a trap. I was trying to keep tabs on the astral myself, but the landscape kept changing. Suddenly there was a blinding white light like a flash grenade, but no concussion report. Just the light. I turned toward it, trying to blink away the glare, and saw . . ."

The sky grew yellow in the east as Jonathon angled the Stallion around the line of desalinization plants. The water was deep green, punctuated by floating debris and drek. "And saw what?"

"Nothing."

"What do you mean nothing?"

Venny frowned. "I mean, nothing. I didn't see the world at all. Not the penthouse suite, not the furniture and the walls with the afterglow of the flash on my retina. Instead I saw blackness, void. . . . Nothing."

Jonathon banked the helo in toward the old LAX. "That's it?"

"No. In the astral, I saw something. The ward that surrounded the suite fluxed just at that time."

"Fluxed? What the frag does *fluxed* mean?"

"I don't know how else to describe it. And I didn't really get a close look, but that ward wavered and moved. It closed down on the spot where Synthia was standing and collapsed."

Jonathon started bringing the helo down on the cracked and pitted concrete that had once been a runway. He parked it behind Hemmingway's modified jet hangar, and powered down the rotor.

"Then when my eyes adjusted," Venny continued, "she was gone. Vanished. No trace even in astral space."

As Jonathon stepped out, his legs nearly gave way beneath him. *I might never see her again.* He steadied himself against the side of the helo.

"Jonathon," Venny said, supporting the elf with his massive arm as they walked inside the chateau. "You need rest. Frag, *I* need rest. Please sleep."

The rooms inside were modern and lush despite the walls made of rough-hewn gray rock. Jonathon and Synthia had been given a room decorated with rich velvet curtains along the walls and a white tiger rug over hardwood flooring that looked like actual wood, not synth. Two white terry cloth bathrobes had been laid out on the king size, four-poster bed.

When Jonathon saw Synthia's dresses, pants, and shirts

hanging in the closet, he went blank. The hiss rumbled like background noise in his head and he just stared at the clothes as if his brain had gone into sleep mode.

Syn, what the frag happened to you?

Venny snapped Jonathon out of it a minute later when he opened the huge wooden door. "You're not asleep yet?"

"Huh? Oh, yeah, I'm getting there."

"Well, since you're up, there's a call for you," Venny said. "I turned your telecom off so you could get some rest, and I was going to take a message, but it could be important."

"Who is it?"

"Dougan Rose."

At the sound of that name, the hackles rose on Jonathon's neck. "Let me talk with him alone," he said. "Thanks."

Venny nodded and walked out, closing the door behind him.

"Telecom on," Jonathon said to the trideo unit in the enclosed oak cabinet. The doors of the cabinet powered open to reveal a screen divided into small squares, each one representing a telecom line. Dougan Rose's face showed on line three. Jonathon touched the screen below Dougan's image, and the other elf's face expanded to fill the whole screen.

Dougan smiled when he saw Jonathon. Dougan's elven features showed fatigue, and his exoskeleton sparkled a deep blue like a second skin around his neck.

"What do you want?" Jonathon said.

"I called to apologize," Dougan said. "And to offer you a job."

"Go fuck yourself."

"I'm serious," he said. "First of all, it was an accident that Tamara died. I meant to hurt her, not kill her. I *am* sorry she died."

"You're stuffed to the gills with bulldrek."

Dougan's green eyes sparkled as he held Jonathon's gaze. "You've got to believe me," he said. "I'm telling the truth. Perhaps her trauma patch was tampered with."

Jonathon felt his knees go weak. He stared at Dougan's face, into his almond eyes. Trying to see the lie, trying to piece together a gestalt of tiny clues that would give him proof that this elf was evil and must be destroyed.

He couldn't see it. He didn't believe Dougan, but neither

did he know for certain that the other elf was lying. *Maybe Dougan is right,* he thought, *Tamara's trauma patch could've been sabotaged.*

"I had no reason to kill her," Dougan said. "That wouldn't have been smart if my . . . associates wanted the information that she had."

"Is that why you wanted to injure her?"

"Yes," said Dougan. "Someone wanted her to leave the game early. Wanted to find out what information she had. That someone applied pressure on me."

"Who?"

Dougan shook his head. "I can't tell you. I can only pass along a warning; the people who did this aren't amateurs. They think you've got the data Tamara stole and they want it back. Which brings me to my next—"

"How did you know to contact me here?"

"Much is known to me, but frankly, too many people saw you enter The Fixx and go with Hemmingway. Now, may I finish?"

Jonathon nodded.

"I have reason to believe your tenure with the Sabers is limited. The team's major owner is Saeder-Krupp, and—"

"Yes," Jonathon said. "I can make the connection myself."

"I'm sure you can," Dougan said. "And that's why I called. To—"

"I'm tired of this conversation." Jonathon reached out a hand to disconnect.

"Hear me out," Dougan went on without missing a beat. "I called to make you an offer. An offer to join me and the Buzzsaws."

38

Synthia awoke to a world of silence and dark. She remembered nothing since the raid on Michaelson's penthouse suite, the flash of light, and the swirling hurricane of astral energy. Then everything went blank, until now.

Sensations filtered into her awareness slowly. The growing sound of muted tires on pavement. The unbalanced sensation of moving, the feel of a cushioned seat at her back.

She blinked open her eyes to the dark interior of a limousine. It was larger than Jonathon's Mitsubishi Nightsky and more luxuriously appointed. Even in the dark, she could make out the wet bar and the simsense decks.

"Welcome, Miss Stone," came a resonant voice. "I am called Brackhaus."

Facing her was a human of indeterminate age, slightly shorter than average stature and wearing a dark silk business suit. His aura was that of a mundane, at least it appeared so. *He could be masking it,* she thought.

"I must apologize for the rude manner in which you were brought here," he said. "But it was the easiest way, I assure you."

"Do I know you?" Synthia asked.

"Not directly, but my . . . employer is a benefactor of yours. Funds much of your magical research, if I'm not mistaken."

"Lofwyr?"

"Yes."

Synthia stared at the dark shadow that was Brackhaus. "What do you want?"

"Nothing much," he said. "Merely what is ours."

"Which is?"

"The simsense recording of the Magus File."

"I don't know what you're talking about."

Brackhaus snorted. "Come now, Miss Stone, don't insult my intelligence. I have conducted a complete mind probe on you."

"What? You . . ." Synthia couldn't believe it was possible. She remembered none of it.

"I assure you it's true. Many hours have passed since you were taken, and it's mid-morning now." As if to verify his claim, Brackhaus touched a button and let the black shielding glass drop five centimeters. The shielding had an interior layer of plexan as an extra security measure. Light poured in through the crack for an instant before Brackhaus flicked the shielding back into place. "My mages were thorough, and your memory of the pain had to be edited out."

Edited out? Synthia thought. *How much power can one person have?*

Synthia glared at Brackhaus. "Am I to understand that Lofwyr will cut funding for my research at UCLA unless I betray my friends and get this recording for you?"

Brackhaus nodded. "It's a little more serious than that, I'm afraid."

"What does that mean?"

"This chip must be retrieved before it is translated," Brackhaus said. "And all copies destroyed. We wouldn't want to have to kill anyone who knew too much. The less your friends know about the chip's contents, the better their chances of staying alive."

"Fine," Synthia said, trying to make herself comfortable in the too-soft seat. "I think you've made that clear. What I meant was—"

"What else have I done to coerce you?"

Synthia nodded.

"While you were unconscious, our doctor injected a suite of symbiotic nanites into your blood."

"What!" she yelled, her heart sinking. She struggled to breathe as her throat closed down. "You put machines inside me?"

"Little biological time bombs, to be exact. They manufacture a lethal toxin and store it. Without an injection of monoclonal antibodies, the molecular clock in the symbiotes will trigger the release of the toxin into your system. You'll die in a matter of minutes."

Bile rose in her throat. She doubled over, clutching the black hole in her gut. *Damn.*

"The molecular clock was set for twelve hours. Once we give you the antibodies, the symbiotes will die. No harm done."

Synthia looked up through bleary eyes at the little man. "You understand nothing," she said through clenched teeth. "What you have done to me *cannot* be undone. You have violated me. Raped my flesh."

The manabolt spell itched in her mind as she focused on it. She would fry this fragging exec to an oily black smudge on the seat.

"If there had been a choice—" Brackhaus began.

She let the spell fly, seeing the spell form in astral space and ground through Brackhaus. But the energy flowed around and over him, not penetrating his aura, which remained unchanged.

"As I was saying," Brackhaus continued. "We would have used another way, if there had been a choice."

Synthia cast another spell, trying to burn him with a hellblast. But Brackhaus moved at blinding speed, touching her forehead. "Sleep," she heard as she slowly sank into the abyss.

"I can't have you burning my limo." The words were fainter and fainter as she fell. "You will explain that you were caught in an astral vortex and slipped into unconsciousness. You don't remember anything." Brackhaus's voice was barely audible. "I expect to hear from you by early this evening."

Then her head fell against her chest and she remembered no more.

39

Jonathon saw Synthia's face in his dream, the delicate brush strokes of her features smiling under copper-colored hair that glowed red in the streaming sunlight. She bent down and kissed him, ruby lips pressing softly against his. Moist and warm.

Jonathon put his hand in her silky hair and pulled her head tight against his. He kissed her hard, turning to bring her into bed with him. Her weight felt real. Her smell, that scent of summer wind and roses, was strong and undeniably sweet. Everything about her seemed too real.

This was not a dream at all.

He held her tight against his chest and breathed, closing his eyes for a long moment before opening them again. Before breathing again.

Synthia was still there in his arms, her delicate nose nuzzling behind his ear. She was alive! How? "I love you," she said. "I just want you to know that I love you."

Jonathon couldn't let go. Refused. "Are you all right?"

"I'm a little scared," she said. "But I'll be all right. I just want this to be over."

"What happened to you?"

"I was caught in an astral vortex or a trap of some kind," Synthia said. "I thought I could destroy it at first, but whoever placed it has a lot more skill and power than I do. I went unconscious and woke up in the back of a corp security van about two hours ago."

Jonathon squeezed her. *Spirits,* he thought, *I've missed her.*

"But I escaped," she went on. "Summoned Ilopos and burned them and their drekking van to cinders."

"I thought you were dead," Jonathon said. "I thought I'd killed you too."

Synthia ran her hand over his naked chest. "You didn't do anything, Jonathon. I made the decision to go." She straddled him and began unzipping her synthleather halter. "I have to take responsibility for my own actions," she said, pulling off her top to reveal beautiful white breasts.

"Well, I'll certainly take responsibility for this action," Jonathon said. He lifted his head and took one rosy nipple in his mouth.

Synthia gave a barely audible sigh and leaned down over him, moving her hips. She smiled and pushed his shoulders down into the pillow. She kissed his forehead, his lips, neck, and chest. She trailed her hair over the hard muscles of his chest and stomach as she worked her way down.

Down until the heat of her mouth enveloped him, and for the next few minutes his mind went blissfully blank. His thoughts only on Synthia and his building ecstasy.

And after, he sat up and slowly undressed her, sending her clothes fluttering to the floor. Her body glowed under him, radiating passion as she moved against the soft silk sheets. He kissed her, slowly, gently at first, trailing his tongue across the succulent landscape of her flesh. Pressing his lips into the curves and hollows of her body.

He took his time, building her slowly to a frenzy. Until, finally, she shook with orgasm, bucking her hips, raking her nails into his scalp.

He moved slowly up to kiss her, lay with her a while. Their embrace calm, content. And sometime later, after closing his eyes, he entered her and they made love that way. Holding onto her as if this might be the last time he would ever have with her. Desperate and wanting. Urgent and impossible to quench.

And later, after sleeping awhile, they made love again, both tired but unwilling to release each other. Until they were too exhausted to stay awake.

It was several hours later when Jonathon's headware woke him. Someone was fragging with his remote rig, sending him something that felt like a gentle tickle in the back of his head. *Must be Grids,* he thought.

Jonathon disentangled himself from Synthia and crawled out of bed, careful not to wake her. Pangs of hunger jabbed him in the gut as he wrapped one of the thick, terry bathrobes around him and silently stepped out the door.

Jonathon met Grids in the next bedroom where the big

Fuchi simsynth was set up next to the cyberdeck. A cluster of fiber-optic lines connected the two machines. "Come in, come in," Grids said, also wearing a terry bathrobe over his thin, ghostly pale body.

Sunlight blazed through the room's two-meter-tall leaded glass windows. Beyond, Jonathon saw the wall of the hangar, verdant green ivy draped over the steel girders that held up the structure. The huge windows in the wall showed a view of water and flooded buildings that used to be part of the airport years ago, and beyond them, the ocean.

Jonathon pointed to his head. "Did you—?"

"Yeah," Grids said, a wide grin on his face. "A little wake-up call."

"What's up?"

"Goofy finally finished decoding the Magus File." Grids held up a datajack. "Here, I want you to keep a copy in your head, just in case something happens to these chips."

Jonathon took the 'trode and slotted it. A few seconds later the contents of the Magus File were safely nestled in his headware memory. He'd go over them in detail later, but now he was hungry.

"Good job," he told Grids as he unjacked and looked around the room for some food.

"Thanks," Grids said. "The only thing I haven't decided is whether to stash a copy on a Matrix-accessible site."

"I don't think so," Jonathon said. "At least not until we know what we're going to do with it."

Grids nodded. "That's why I hesitated. By the way, did I hear that Synthia was back?"

Jonathon smiled. "I don't know, what did you hear?"

"Just the usual grunting, screaming, and rhythmic squeaking of the bed."

Jonathon's smile broke into full laughter. "Sorry if we kept you awake, chummer."

"Don't be," Grids said. "I seem to have a knack for voyeurism these days."

"Well, she's back anyway. Got caught in a magical trap of some kind." Jonathon explained about the astral hurricane and Synthia's escape from the security van. As he spoke, he walked to a tray of french sourdough and paté on the bedstand.

He spread a thick layer of the paté on a slice of bread and took a huge bite to satiate the growling beast inside.

Grids sipped from a cup of soykaf while he listened.
"I'm glad she's all right," he said. "But this is far from
over. The Magus File is serious drek."

"You've read it?"

"Just the first part," Grids said. "And even that's
enough to know why we're fragged up the yin-yang."

Jonathon finished his bread in one bite and started to
fix himself another. "Tell me," he said.

"You want the short or the long version?"

"Short," Jonathon said. "I just want to know how much
drek we're into. I'll review the text myself later."

"We're in drek so high it's clogging our ears."

"Just give me the short scan, okay?"

"You remember the tsunami in 'forty-five?"

"The one here in LA?"

"Yeah," Grids said. "An off-shore oil rig blew its old-
style fusion reactor, remember?"

Jonathon nodded. The damage from the tsunami and
the fallout had destroyed the coast and the beaches from
Ventura to Oceanside. Some of the damage had been repaired, but many places, like LAX, had been left to floun-
der and rot away. "I wasn't here at the time," he said.
"But I heard about it." *Frag, who hadn't?*

"Rumors flew on Shadowland about who was responsible,"
Grids said. "But no evidence was uncovered. None. You
know how rare that is? To completely sequester all evidence
of something that big?"

It boggled Jonathon's mind to think about it.

"Part of the Magus File contains data on the cause of
that explosion," Grids went on. "Hard data. I've almost
been afraid to read the rest of it."

"What does it say?"

"The short scan is this: Saeder-Krupp hired some shadowrunners to break into an offshore laboratory run by Aztechnology. The lab had been there about ten years or so and
still ran on an old fusion reactor. Guess what kind of experiments they did there?"

"Just fragging scan it to me, okay?"

"Biological artificial intelligence."

"Is this what you were talking about before?"

Grids nodded. "The rumor on Shadowland was that the
Azzies were attempting to make a bio-AI with sections of
brain tissue. The Magus File not only confirms that, but it

has details on how to do it. They succeeded in creating
one over ten years ago!"

Jonathon sat on the edge of the bed.

"But it wasn't stable, at least that's what they think.
When the runners attacked the lab, trying to infiltrate and
secretly steal the Azzies' data, the AI detected them and
went paranoid. It took control of the fusion reactor and blew
itself up. Committed suicide."

Grids was silent for a minute, taking another sip of his
soykaf.

"How do you know this data is real?" Jonathon asked.

"To prevent the AI from gaining access to the Matrix,
Aztechnology kept the lab computers totally isolated,"
Grids said. "That's why the runners had to physically in-
filtrate the old rig. Once inside, they uploaded most of the
files via satellite link to an S-K databank. It's all in there.
Read it and drek your pants."

"Now, you think S-K is building one of these bio-AIs?"
Jonathon asked.

Grids shrugged. "It doesn't matter," he said. "They
could just be holding the info for later. But the fact that
we have it is a problem for them. They'll kill us to prevent
its dissemination, and others will kill us to get it. Either
way we're fragged."

A knock on the door interrupted them. Grids checked the
security camera. "It's Venny," he said, opening the door.

Venice Jones entered, dressed in his usual gear. Loose-
fitting black pants with lots of pockets, a black long-
sleeved shirt, synthleather gloves. Mirrorshades.

Jonathon scowled at him. "Have you slept?"

"Yep," Venny said. "Caught a good four hours of down
time, though I had to endure some noise coming from
your room." He laughed.

"Yeah, well, we had fun."

"I'm sure you did," Venny said. "Anyway, I thought it
might be time to head for the stadium. You did say something about competing tonight, didn't you?"

Jonathon thought about it. He wasn't sure anymore.
Synthia's disappearance had spooked him. Derailed his
momentum. And Dougan's offer was sounding more and
more tempting. Transferring to the Buzzsaws might just
solve all their problems.

Provided Dougan is telling the truth, he thought.

Jonathon looked up at Venny. "Yes," he said. "And I need to get there early to think. Let me get dressed, then you and I will head for the stadium."

Venny nodded.

Synthia was still sleeping soundly as Jonathon crept back in and put on some clothes. He silently packed a bag with some extras. Then he donned his duster, feeling the weight of his Predator II and the extra ammo.

Just as he was about to leave, he turned back to gaze at the sleeping face of the woman he loved. So serene. So beautiful and childlike she seemed.

I can't risk losing her again, he decided suddenly. *I don't care what I have to do to protect her.* He knew then that he would contact Dougan Rose and accept his offer to join the Buzzsaws.

Later, after everyone was safe, he would resume his quest to avenge Tamara's death. Neither Dougan Rose, nor his . . . associate would be exempt. Jonathon would kill them both. But first, he would bargain for the safety of his friends.

40

Synthia woke to a dim room, sunlight blazing through the cracks around the window shades. She rolled over and discovered that the big bed was empty. Jonathon was gone.

Where is he? she thought. A quick astral reconnaissance told her that neither Jonathon nor Venny were in the adjacent rooms. Then she checked the old-fashioned analog clock on the wall. It read a quarter past two. Jonathon might've gone to the new LA Coliseum to run the maze and begin warming up for tonight's championship match.

Synthia quickly got out of bed, showered and dressed in a flower-print summer dress before going to see Grids. She had no idea how she could get the chip from him without his knowledge. Perhaps a spirit could be told to steal all of his chips, then she would simply destroy them all. But even that couldn't happen with him in the room.

Perhaps he could be persuaded to join her for breakfast.

She knocked on the oversized wooden door. Grids answered, wearing only his white bathrobe. "Synthia, come in, come in."

"I thought you might like breakfast or lunch or something," she said.

Grids pointed to a tray of fruit, french bread, and paté. "I've been munching all morning," he said. "Besides I want to make some more copies of this chip. Goofy has finally decoded the whole text. Can you believe it?"

She could, but didn't want to. "That's wiz," she said. "How many copies have you made so far?"

Grids picked up two chips off the case of the simsynth. "Just these two," he said. "Plus the one in Jonathon's headware."

"Where?" Her voice rose imperceptibly.

Grids looked askance at her.

She forced herself to speak evenly, calmly. "Isn't that going to put him in danger?"

"Only if one of the bad guys finds out," he said.

Spirits! she thought. *That makes things a lot harder.* Then she remembered the symbiotes in her blood and nearly fainted. Without the antidote, she would die. Without the chip, there would be no antidote.

"Did Jonathon go to the stadium?" she asked.

"I think so," he said. "Venny went with him."

"Did he say for sure he was going there?"

"Yes, but—"

"But what?" Synthia said, her voice rising again.

Grids shrugged and took a drink of his 'kaf. "I don't know, it just seemed like he had something else on his mind. Like maybe he was going somewhere else first."

"What do you mean by that?"

"Well, he got this call from Dougan Rose while you were gone."

"Dougan? What did he want?"

"I don't know," Grids said defensively. "I didn't talk to him."

"Well, what do you *think* Dougan wanted?"

"It's just a hunch, but I think he offered Jonathon a deal. To get everyone out, safe and sound."

"And you still let him go? What a pixelheaded thing to do!" Now she was yelling.

"Hey, calm down," Grids said. "That astral hurricane or whatever must've hit you pretty hard. They'll be all right."

Maybe, Synthia thought, *but I won't. I need to destroy all copies of the data, including the one that's in Jonathon's head.*

She didn't have time to be nice, to be discreet. She had to move now. The spell slipped from her, forming in astral space and passing through her aura and into his as she reached to touch him gently with her fingertips.

She framed the first question in her mind, "Where are all copies of the simsense chip and the translated data?" And he yielded to her easily, collapsing to the floor as his memories washed over her like waves of surf.

She saw the original recording, Grids in room 2305 of the Venice Hilton. That was the same chip he carried in his own chipjack behind his ear. Goofy, the smartframe, had translated the text and there were two copies of that on two chips, and one in Jonathon's headware. That was it. Good, he hadn't been lying.

She sustained the power of the spell and probed further, asking where Jonathon went. Grids's memories of Jonathon and Venny leaving flowed over her. Jonathon said they were going to the stadium, but Grids didn't believe him.

Another memory filled Synthia's mind. Hours earlier, before she'd returned, Dougan Rose had called for Jonathon, and Grids had tapped into the telecom. He had watched the whole conversation through his Fuchi Cyber-7 deck, invisible.

After some preliminary sparring, Dougan had made Jonathon an offer to leave the Sabers and come over to the Buzzsaws. "MCT is prepared to pay handsomely for your transfer, plus protection and whatever else you might desire," Dougan said.

Jonathon's response was too quick. Too eager. "And what will they want from me in return?"

That smirk pasted itself to Dougan's face again. "Only that you ride the line with the Buzzsaws. We could make an unstoppable duo, chummer. Also, they want the simsense recording. They won't go for the deal without that."

"What simsense recording?" Jonathon asked.

Dougan just laughed. "Here's my private number. Think it over and get back to me." Then he disconnected and the telecom screen went dark except for the white alphanumerics of Dougan's LTG.

Fear crept icy fingers along Synthia's flesh as this memory poured through her. Dougan was convincing, and Synthia could see how Jonathon might go for the deal to switch to MCT even if he didn't believe Dougan. To protect her and the others.

Frag me blue!

She released Grids, who rolled to the floor, unconscious. Her head burned with the pain of the mind probe, and she sank to the floor as the effort of sustaining the spell hit her. She took a moment to gather her strength, breathing steady and slow. Then she decided what she must do. She'd already tipped her hand; it was time to strike.

She popped the simsense chip from the jack behind Grids's ear. Then she placed it with the other chips, against the wall with Grids's simsense equipment and cyberdeck.

"Iopos," she called. The fire elemental manifested, ablaze

and crackling. "Destroy that equipment," she said. "Burn it to cinders."

"Yes, mistress," came the response. Then the elemental engulfed the electronics, swathing them in red and blue flame. In a few minutes, everything was black and melted. Destroyed beyond salvage.

Synthia released Iopos, then drew up the astral energy for one last spell—an enhanced physical illusion that made the room look as if nothing had happened. No argument, no fire. She drew on the power of her bracelet focus and extended the illusion to mask the smell of burning, then she held the pattern of the spell in her astral sight and sustained it until her quickening power had fused it into place, making it permanent.

The whole effort left her even more exhausted and weak, but her strength would return in time, and her escape from Hemmingway's was crucial if she was to catch up with Jonathon. She took a minute to get her things together, another to make two telecom calls, then she rented a Saab Dynamit from one of the runners at The Fixx and was gone, out of the chateau and rolling along the highway in her new set of wheels.

She only hoped she could find and reach Jonathon before he passed the contents of the Magus File to MCT. She could almost feel the toxin building inside the symbiotes, waiting for the molecular clock to signal release into her system. She shuddered and pressed the accelerator.

ACT THREE

HIS FINAL DEATH

41

Jonathon went to Dockweiler Gardens for lunch with Venice Jones. He wanted to bring Venny over to MCT with him, but he wasn't sure what the troll would say. One way or the other, Venny always had the practical view, and Jonathon needed that right now.

The Gardens were crowded with the usual lunch crowd—upscale criminal types, semicorporate wageslaves anxious for a little risk outside the arcology, and overpaid pleasure-seekers from the entertainment industry who were just recovering from a late night of hot simchips and parmaceuticals.

Jonathon found himself worrying that his disguise wouldn't hold up to close scrutiny. He was dressed as before in the same mirrorshades and long duster, though now the coat was dirty and blood-stained like a real shadowrunner's might be. Still, it was the day of the big, finale match and everyone seemed to be talking about it.

No tables were available so they waited in the bar, a dark place whose walls were covered with holopics of pro athletes, including one of Jonathon. Everyone watched the huge trideo hyping the upcoming combat biker match and specifically the rivalry between Jonathon and Dougan. Jonathon and Venny huddled at a corner table while Jonathon reviewed the Magus File data Grids had downloaded into his headware. Venny was content to wait; he knew something was bothering Jonathon and kept silent.

The Magnus File was divided into three parts; the first discussed the AZ54 bio-AI that Grids had told him about. The second went into details about the Magus Factor, the genetic elements that gave someone the ability to use magic. And the third discussed ways to combine the bio-AI with magic. They called it the artificial mage project.

Most of the technical data was over Jonathon's head. But he thought he understood the significance of it. A bio-AI, like any artificial intelligence, would be alien and un-predictable. It might have extraordinary abilities in the Matrix, and could tip the balance of power between the megacorporations.

Likewise, if all the loci of the Magus Factor were discovered, a supermage could be engineered. The file had details and projections on how much the various megacorps knew thus far. Jonathon didn't really understand the intricacies of genetics, but he thought shamans and mages were powerful enough already. Magic scared the drek out of him.

The last section was technical information about how to build an artificial mage. The file warned that Aztechnology was working toward the creation of a biological AI with a potential magical ability far beyond what could be done within the known confines of a human or metahuman soul. Magenics was conducting research into finding weaknesses in such a creature, and its parent corp, Saeder-Krupp, had been organizing covert operations designed to ascertain the level of this threat.

The file contained all the details of what Magenics knew about the artificial mage, plus specifics on the covert ops staged by S-K and the information recovered from them. The gist was that the Azzies had a working prototype that was unpredictable, but had limited spell-casting ability. Its thought processes were alien and its magic power fluctuated.

Shivers shot through Jonathon as he scanned this. What would happen if he gave the data over to MCT? It was the age-old question; was it better that sensitive data be in the hands of a few elite or at the disposal of the masses?

Everyone knew that atomic energy had been used first and foremost for war. To blow people up. It had been developed for that reason, and once the principles were discovered it was impossible to contain. But afterward, it was used for good. To generate power. Its discovery led to others: fusion energy, atomic microscopes, magnetic resonance imagers, and quantum interference devices. All powerful tools, some of which were used to heal.

If MCT also has the info, Jonathon thought, *it might keep Aztechnology from getting too much of an edge. Something about the Azzies gives me the creeps.*

Besides, for me it's personal.

If he could save the lives of Grids and Synthia and

Venny by selling the data, it was worth it. That was the bottom line.

"Mr. Jones, your table is ready," said the hostess.

Venny nodded, then stood. Jonathon followed him to the table, ordering a tall mycoprotein chocolate shake for starters. Venny ordered iced lemonade.

"I'm thinking about taking Dougan's offer," Jonathon said when the waitress had left. "Joining the Buzzsaws in exchange for the protection of their parent corp, MCT."

Venny gave him a long, unreadable look. "Why?" he asked.

"I'm tired of running," Jonathon said. "When Synthia disappeared, I realized that what I'm doing is insane. I still want revenge; the crackle in my head keeps pushing me to get it for Tamara. Frag, I can't even remember what she felt like inside my mind. My memory of her emotions is fuzzy. All I have left of her is that hiss, the dead space in my mind.

"And for that, I'll find and destroy whoever killed her." Jonathon took a breath. "But at what cost? Synthia's life? Your life? Grids's? I can't risk that anymore. What Dougan is offering is an escape. Everyone will be protected. Then I can kill him later for what he's done, in a few months or years when he's forgotten."

Venny listened in silence, his eyes moving over the crowd as always. Alert for any possible threat to Jonathon's life.

"I want you to stay with me," Jonathon said.

"I will remain by your side as long as you want me," Venny said. "Wherever you go. There is and never will be a question about that."

"I know."

"Something about this offer from Dougan rings false. He may be lying."

"I know that too," Jonathon said. "But I don't see another way out."

"Just be ready for it."

"I plan to."

The waitress brought their drinks and took their order. The mycoprotein shake soothed the beast inside Jonathon, pumped him full of energy, and made him yearn for the biker match. "I'll be right back," he said.

Jonathon stood and walked to the restaurant's public

telecom. He placed his hand over the video pickup and dialed the LTG that Dougan had given him.

The elf's face appeared on the screen.

"Hoi," Jonathon said.

Recognition registered on Dougan's face. "Ah, it's you, my friend. I'm glad to hear from you."

"I want to make a deal."

"Of course. Have you got the data?"

"Yes."

"Wonderful, then we can proceed. Meet me—"

"First you must guarantee the safe transfer of my friends."

"I assumed that as well. My associates will agree, I'm sure."

"Where shall we meet?"

Dougan smiled. "I have a place in Laguna Beach."

"A neutral site, perhaps. Try Hollywood. Or Venice Beach."

"Isn't Venice yakuza territory?"

"Mafia, but it'll be safe enough."

"All right," Dougan said. "I'll meet you at Grandma's Pharmacy and Survival. Do you know where that is?"

"Yes."

"In the basement is a firing range. Meet me there in an hour." The line went dead.

Jonathon returned to the table and sat down. He stared at the ocean for a few minutes, mesmerized by the surf and the deep primordial roar. Then he looked up at Venny. "I hope I'm making the right move," he said.

Venny nodded. "So do I, chummer. So do I."

42

Luc Tashika sipped his tea and sighed. It was mid-afternoon Friday and he'd been wading through an insurmountable pile of paperwork pertaining to a new recording contract for some mediocre talent. When the phone rang, he was glad for the distraction. Hearing that it was Dougan, his breath caught. For a Friday, today was certainly turning out to be one of the drekkiest.

Tashika looked into the telecom. "This has better be good news," he said.

Dougan gave him a smirk. "I think you'll like what I have to say."

"Yes?"

"Winger's bringing the data to me," Dougan said.

"How—? No, don't tell me."

"I promised him a position on the Buzzsaws. And he thinks MCT will protect his friends."

"Do you know how much that'll cost?"

"Don't worry, Tashika-*san*. I have no intention of keeping my word." Dougan gave a harsh chuckle. "No, I'll take care of Winger. I just wanted you to be ready for the exchange."

A thrill of excitement coursed through Tashika. Dougan's plan was brilliant if Winger fell for it. "I'll be ready," he said. "What time should we meet?"

"I'll call you after I deal with Winger," Dougan said. "We can set a time and place then."

"Very well," Tashika said, then disconnected. *Dougan plays the corp game well,* he thought. *Almost as good as me.*

43

Hendrix pushed down the accelerator on his modified
GMC Bulldog stepvan, weaving between an old couple in
a beige Jackrabbit and a convertible full of chipped-out
teenagers. Trying to keep up with Synthia's Saab Dynamit as she zipped through the afternoon traffic on Cal-
Trans 405, heading toward the Santa Monica Mountains.
Her car was a sleek and sporty inverted bubble of macroglass and cherry-red steel. It was exceptionally fast, and
since his modified Americar was no longer functional, he
had to follow her in the stepvan.

The GMC Bulldog was a cross between a truck and a
van. It handled much better than a full tractor rig, and it
had a huge capacity for weapons and all the wiz equipment Hendrix could ever want to pack into it. The stepvan
was armored and outfitted with sensors so it could be
rigged cybernetically, but Hendrix didn't bother with all
that drek. The rearview screens and heads-up tactical display were all the tech he needed to pilot the truck.

Hendrix liked to use the big vehicle on runs because it
was better equipped for combat, but when it was just he
and Layla, he preferred the Americar; it was faster. Or
at least it used to be until the mage slitch burned the drek
out of it.

Hendrix kept the Saab in view, three cars ahead and looking to pass the little red Mitsubishi Runabout. *This Synthia
is in a mighty rush to get somewhere fast,* he thought.

After Cinnamon had shown up at the ancient Wilmington oil refinery and learned from Michaelson that he no
longer had the Magus File or whatever drekking info,
she'd called on a frightening group of spirits and elementals to help Juju Pete keep Michaelson secure. Then she'd
asked Hendrix and Layla to try to track down the data, offering them a ridiculous amount of nuyen. The whole biz

was getting a tad out of control, but Hendrix wasn't ready to bail just yet. Besides, the extra cred would come in handy for fixing up the Americar.

Layla's leg had been magically healed by Juju Pete, but it was still far from one hundred percent. She was in the back, arranging her weapons, grumpy because of the pain in her leg; she'd refused painkillers on the theory that it would affect her abilities.

Mole's synthesized voice buzzed into Hendrix's headphone. "I've cleared up the file," he said. "You're going to like what I got."

"Good," Hendrix subvocalized into his throat mike. "I'm patching it through the truck's telecom." Hendrix glanced back at Layla for a second. "You want to hear what Mole's got?" he said.

"Yeah," Layla said. She pushed her way past a pile of machine guns and a box of grenades to get into the front seat. "Go," she said.

"The Condor II laser microphone picked this up a few minutes ago," Mole said. "It's still somewhat staticky, but I've passed it through a digital signal-enhancer to make it as clear as possible. It's a miracle we got anything at all."

Hendrix smiled at that; he'd been the one who'd made the modifications to the laser mike. The laser beam was ingeniously polarized so that it was able to penetrate the reflective surface of The Fixx's huge hangar windows, then detect microvibrations on the surface of the leaded glass of the chateau's windows inside.

In the recording Synthia said, "How many copies have you made so far?"

"Just these two," came the voice of Grids Desmond. "Plus the one I downloaded into Jonathon's headware."

There was a rush of static, then a long silence. Synthia said, "Iopos, destroy that equipment. Burn it to cinders." Then the sound of fire crackled from the truck's speakers.

Then came the sound of someone placing a telecom call. "Hello, LA Sabers," came a modulated voice.

"Hoi, Terry. Syn here."

"How's biz, chummer?"

"Biz is wiz, Terry."

"Hey, Syn, you know if Jonathon is coming down for the match? Lotsa chummers been calling, wanting to know."

"He's not there?"

"Nope," Terry said. "Sorry."

"It's chill," Synthia said. "I'll find him."

Synthia disconnected and entered another LTG number. Hendrix could hear her pushing the buttons instead of using the voice interface. The reason became clear when the rumbling voice echoed into the room.

"Yes?" the voice said.

"I've destroyed the chips," Synthia said. "All but one copy."

"Good. Why not the last one?"

"It's in Jonathon Winger's headware memory, and he's gone."

"Find him," rumbled the voice. "Use ritual magic if you have to, but find him."

"I will," Synthia replied.

"Find him and erase the memory. You now have about six hours." The line went dead and the tape ended with the slam of a door.

"That's it," Mole said. "Winger has the only copy of the data. He's not at the stadium, and the only way we'll find him is by shadowing the mage."

Layla reluctantly agreed. "Fine," she said.

"Mole," Hendrix said as he tried to weave the stepvan between two tractor trailers. "Get a scrambled and coded line open to Cinnamon; she should hear this."

A second later, Mole came back on. "Okay, got it."

"Hello?" came a sultry voice. No video on this link.

"Cinnamon, this is Hendrix. We've got something you should hear. Mole?" Hendrix listened again as the conversation replayed for the fixer's benefit.

"Very good work," came Cinnamon's response. "You continue to impress me, Hendrix."

"Just doing my job."

"Of course. Now, when Synthia leads you to Winger, you must capture him since he has the last copy of the data. He must not be killed, just in case the memory is purged at death. Do you understand?"

"Certainly," Hendrix said, pulling the van onto Santa Monica Boulevard a few cars back from Synthia's. "We'll keep him alive."

"Good," Cinnamon said. "Keep me posted." The line went dead.

Hendrix followed Synthia's Saab up the hill and onto

the UCLA campus. The green landscape and the ancient buildings brought excited laughter from Layla. "So we don't have to kill the elf biker?" she said.

"Nope."

"Good, I want to see if he can stay alive long enough to grind Dougan Rose's face into the pavement at the match tonight."

"Yeah," Hendrix said, then gave a short laugh. "Hope you get your wish."

44

On his way to meet Dougan, Jonathon checked the West-wind's telecom for messages. He was surprised to see one from Grids, and even more surprised by what he had to say.

"Jonathon," Grids began, his hair messed, his face drawn in pain. "Synthia has changed. I don't know why or how exactly, but she's working against us now." Grids's blue eyes widened. His voice was edged with a kind of hysteria that Jonathon had never seen from him.

"She did something to me, used magic to sift through my mind, I think. Then she took the simsense chip from my head and destroyed all my equipment." He was almost crying.

"The fragging slitch burned it all!" Grids turned away from the screen and wiped his face with his hands. When he turned back to look into the camera, he regained some of his composure. "I hope you get this message before she finds you," he said. "I don't know where you are or what you're doing, but beware of Synthia. Watch your back, chummer. Trust nobody. Not a soul."

The screen went black and Jonathon sat staring at it for a minute before shaking himself back to consciousness. *What the frag was going on?* Jonathon realized he didn't want to believe Grids. He still didn't really trust him.

But could he trust Synthia? Apparently not. But then again, maybe there was an explanation for what she'd done. There had to be.

Venny brought him back to the task at hand. The meeting with Dougan Rose. "Leave your gun here," Venny said. "The door guards will confiscate it anyway, and if we have to leave in a hurry, it'll be easier to get it here than from them."

Jonathon nodded and pulled his Predator II from the right pocket of his duster and slid it under the driver's seat. Then he set the Westwind in ready mode and climbed out.

Grandma's Pharmacy and Survival filled an entire block. The first floor was packed with the most popular drek— chips, weaponry, and drugs, including a full pharmacy and a broad, quasi-legal range of over-the-counter chemicals and simsense. They had swords and bows, guns of all types, grenade launchers, and even guided missiles.

Upstairs was survival gear like tents and clothing, camp stoves, plus merc gear like BattleTac systems and combat drones. The top floor was the clinic where cyberware and a limited selection of bioware were installed.

Jonathon had spent meganuyen here, on drones and other chiller toys. But not today. The door guard scanned both Jonathon and Venny for weapons, but found nothing. He waved them through.

Venny insisted on leading the way to the basement, all his senses alert for any sort of trouble. They took the stairs instead of the elevator, more room to maneuver. "More dumb slags get geeked in elevators than anyplace else," Venny said. "Nowhere to run."

The sound of gunfire grew loud as they passed down the hall and through the macroglass doors into the firing range. There were about fifty or sixty lanes, each some fifty meters long, and most were occupied. An armory on the left supplied the weapons, each one with a smart guide that prevented it from firing unless it was aimed toward the target. That way any kind of live ammo could be used without risking anyone's getting shot, accidentally or otherwise.

Venny held Jonathon behind him as they walked behind the macroglass separator, scanning each firing lane for Dougan Rose. They found him in the last lane, firing a Colt Manhunter at the target. A Hispanic or Amerind woman stood next to him, wearing a black bodysuit adorned with brown and white feathers.

Shaman? Jonathon wondered.

As the woman's face came into Jonathon's view, he saw that she was beautiful, with olive skin and straight black hair that hung to her slim waist. She grimaced as Dougan squeezed off shots with the Colt Manhunter in his hand.

Dougan himself was outfitted in loose-fitting blue jeans and a black Maria Mercurial T-shirt. He wore studded synthleather gloves, a bandanna over his black hair, and mirrored glasses that made him harder to recognize.

Jonathon rapped on the glass, and the woman opened it

for him. Dougan turned to greet them, setting the pistol on the shelf. He was exactly the same height as Jonathon, but a tiny bit bulkier; he'd gained some weight over the years.

"Jonathon," Dougan said. "Glad you came."

The hiss rose in Jonathon's head, and he bit back the urge to strangle the elf. "Dougan."

"And this must be Venice Jones," Dougan said.

Venny inclined his horned head ever so slightly.

"Now, Maria!" Dougan shouted, his hands suddenly moving from behind his back. He brought up a plastic drinking bottle of some kind, aiming the poptop toward Venny.

Jonathon sensed threat and tried to move—a reflex to slap the bottle from Dougan's hand, despite its harmless appearance. But his hand hesitated; he stood motionless against his will. The shaman had somehow taken control of his body.

Time clicked to slow-motion as Jonathon watched Dougan's gloved finger squeeze the drinking bottle, spraying Venny with a clear liquid. But Venny was no longer standing there; he'd moved to the side, his hand striking out for Dougan's neck.

The spray missed.

Dougan nearly dodged Venny's blow, but the troll's fist glanced off Dougan's shoulder and sent him flying back into the wall.

A large black man suddenly appeared behind Venny. Heavy-set jaw, cybereyes, smartlink induction pads on his hands. The man's afro was cut in close stripes along the arc of his scalp. A squirt bottle, identical to Dougan's, appeared in the man's hands, the pop-top aimed at Venny's face.

Frag, he must've come from the adjacent booth.

Venny tried to duck, but the man caught him in the side of the head with the spray from another squirt bottle. Venny screamed as the liquid ran down his face, squeezing his eyes shut and covering his ears. He sank to his knees.

Jonathon tried to move again, struggling to break the hold on his body. Suddenly his muscles were his own again, under his control. His hand shot out and grabbed Dougan's wrist, aimed the tip of the bottle at the black man and squeezed. The liquid stream caught the man full in the face, and he, too, hit the ground a few seconds later.

But Dougan jerked his hand, trying to wrench the bottle

away. Jonathon held on, but some of the liquid spilled from the bottle's tip. Jonathon felt moisture over his knuckles, and seconds later he tasted garlic. *DMSO,* he thought. *Drek* . . .

Then light grew to a blinding brilliance, stabbing through his brain like hot spears. As the DMSO carried the drug—hyper—through his skin and into his blood, gunshots in the hall became unbearably loud, each crack splitting his skull with its volume. He tried to block it out, tried to retreat into silence and darkness, but even the scratch of his clothes on his skin burned him. Tortured him.

He sank to floor and crumpled into a ball.

The torture went on for what seemed like hours, though Jonathon's headclock told him only fifty minutes had passed before it finally receded enough for him to concentrate coherently on his surroundings. He found himself handcuffed, sitting in a chair in the back of a stepvan that wasn't moving. He kept his eyes shut for a moment, wanted some time to think before he let his captors know he was awake.

Moans and cries came from two individuals next to Jonathon. The one on his left he recognized as Venny. The other was in front of them, most likely the huge black chromer he'd hit with the spray.

A door opened up front and Dougan climbed into the driver's seat. Jonathon kept his eyes focused on the floor, feeling the scrutiny of Dougan's stare. Then he heard Dougan's voice. "Okay, Maria, I've set up the exchange with Tashika. Are you prepped?"

"I'm solid," came the soft reply. "When Maurice comes off the hyper, we'll be set. I can't wait for all this drek to be over so I can get back to my life."

That's just what I was thinking, Jonathon thought. The residual effects of the drug amplified the crackle in his nerves.

"The meet is set for four o'clock, El Segundo plant," Dougan said. "After that, we collect payment and you can go home."

Venny seemed much calmer now; he'd quit yelling and his hands had dropped to his sides. "Sorry 'bout this, chummer," he whispered to Jonathon.

"Just think of a way to get us out."

"When I can think, I'll let you know."

Jonathon almost laughed. His own thinking processes were just coming back online. His head ached as he stared at the grooved metal of the floor between his knees. He thought about what had happened. Dougan had betrayed him. *But why?* He had no idea. *And how do we get away?* Again, he had no idea.

Better get some fragging clues soon, he thought, wondering exactly where they were. It couldn't be too far from Venice Beach. But the van had no windows in the back, no way to look out and try to get a fix on their location.

"Maria, please step outside and keep watch for a minute?" Dougan said.

"If you insist."

"I do."

Jonathon heard the door open and close, then Dougan climbed from the driver's seat into the back. An Ingram SMG in hand, he pushed past the moaning hulk that must be the Maurice they'd been talking about, and came up close to Jonathon and Venny.

"You've recovered well, Jonathon," Dougan said. "As I knew you would. Accelerated metabolism has its virtues, *neh?*"

Jonathon said nothing and glared up at the other elf. The hiss roared in his head, searing his nerves and bringing a flush to his face. He wanted to spit at Dougan, but his mouth was too dry.

"I just wanted to let you know a few things before I kill you," Dougan said. "Oh, yes, I plan to kill you just as I killed Tamara." Dougan sat on the floor, keeping the Ingram trained on the two of them.

"I lied earlier," Dougan continued. "So sorry, chummer. I have a tendency to lie. It's pathological really. Not something I can control. I geeked Tamara very much on purpose. You can't accidentally kill someone like her, you know. Have to plan drek like that. Adplaquin, you know what that is? Anticoagulant, leaves no trace. Very effective, very deadly."

The words hit Jonathon's ears, and on some level, he actually registered what they meant, but the roar in his mind was deafening. "Why?" he said.

"What? Oh, that's simple. Because Tashika, that's my associate—the one who so desperately needs the data in your head. Because he wanted her injured." A look of sheer hatred flashed across Dougan's features. "I killed her because he wanted her alive, plain and simple," he said. "And I'm going to kill you because you've got the information he needs. But first, I plan to—"

Outside, Maria screamed. "Drek! Look out!" Then she let out a long, loud screech that scissored up Jonathon's back.

Something impacted with the side of the stepvan and exploded, rocking the vehicle up on two wheels. Dougan's eyes went wide with surprise as he slid into the tilted wall. As the van crashed back down onto all four wheels, Jonathon kicked with all the quickness and strength of his augmented muscles, lashing out for the Ingram gun in Dougan's hand.

Dougan's eyes narrowed on Jonathon, and he squeezed the trigger. But Jonathon's foot had already connected with Dougan's wrist, making the Ingram jerk to the side. The gun sprayed bullets against the inside walls of the van.

Another blast rocked the van, and the searing heat struck Jonathon as the double doors in the side rattled. Dougan tried to stand, but Jonathon was faster, stomping on Dougan's hand, grinding the fragile bones of his knuckles into the metal floor of the stepvan.

Dougan's other hand moved in a striking motion toward the soft of Jonathon's knee. *A knife? A gun?* Jonathon heard the snick of extending cyberspurs almost too late. He pivoted and dodged the blow at the last second, again trying to kick the Ingram out of Dougan's hand.

No luck.

Dougan brought the gun to bear as he struck again with the shiny chrome blades that extended along the bone of his forearm. But Venny had stepped around Jonathon; the troll hit Dougan with a blow that made Jonathon wince. In a lightning-quick motion, Venny's handcuffed arms came pummeling down on Dougan's head.

The gun sputtered for a second, bullets singing past Jonathon. Then the weapon flew from Dougan's hand and skittered across the floor.

Jonathon noticed a wide, spreading crimson patch under Venny's arm; the troll had been hit. But the wounds didn't seem to affect him. Venny planted a front kick into Dougan's gut and sent the elf careening off the wall to land halfway out the open door. Dougan gasped, then began to scramble into the front, reaching for the bottle of hyper next to the seat.

But it was far too late. Venny grabbed his wrist and jerked him back onto the floor. "Cuff keys," he said.

Dougan heaved several breaths before answering. "In my pocket," he said. "Let me—"

"I don't think so," Jonathon said. Then he reached into Dougan's pocket and pulled out a small magnetic bar. Jonathon inserted the bar into his cuffs and they popped open. Venny's did the same.

A searing crackle raised the hair on Jonathon's arms. *Incoming!* The doors blew open and twisted on their hinges like foil as the heat of the blast burned Jonathon's eyebrows. *Another one like that and we're all fried.*

Venny ducked and threw Dougan out of the van and onto the pavement in one smooth motion. Dougan landed next to the woman, Maria, who lay slumped with her back against the graffiti-smeared concrete of a retaining wall.

"Get in front and drive us out of here!" Venny yelled.

Jonathon moved toward the driver's seat as Venny tossed a nearly catatonic Maurice out the side doors. Broken glass crunched under Jonathon's boots as he fired up the stepvan and slammed it into motion.

"Jonathon!" called a familiar voice, barely audible behind them. Synthia's voice.

And as he watched her in the rearview, standing beside her Saab Dynamit, Grids's words echoed in his head. *Trust nobody. Not a soul.* Synthia looked haggard and spent, and Jonathon suddenly realized the blasts of fire had come from her. She'd nearly killed them all in the attack. *Why?*

Behind Synthia, the monstrous pipes of a cold fusion plant reached toward the ocean like black tentacles. And seeing the alien curve of the desalinization facility, sitting like a mutant kraken made of concrete and a tangle of oversized pipes, Jonathon knew where he was. He ignored Synthia and drove on, accelerating to full speed.

Sorry Syn, he thought. *When this is all over and done with, we'll talk and sort it out. For now, it's me and Venny and the whisper of Tamara in my mind.*

45

Hendrix risked a quick glance at Layla. "Paydata!" he said. "She led us straight to him." He pulled their stepvan out into traffic, making sure the vehicle carrying Jonathon and Venice Jones was in clear view. Not too close, but not too far.

"Did you have any doubt?" came Mole's voice in his ear.

Hendrix didn't respond to that. He always doubted. Skepticism and caution had kept him alive longer than many of his cohorts. It was either a blessing or a curse; he wasn't sure which. He was alive, but nearly everyone he'd ever run with was dead.

It had gotten to the point that losing a chummer was routine. Par for the course. He expected it.

If Luylu goes, though, it will hurt. It will tear me up like a belly blade.

Layla sat forward in the passenger seat, like a cat ready to pounce. She'd been getting more and more antsy ever since the long wait at UCLA where Synthia had stopped. Probably to do her location magic, Hendrix guessed. And now Layla was ready for action, especially after watching Synthia nearly destroy Winger in that succession of fireblasts back there. Patience was never really one of Layla's virtues.

Hendrix just stared at the road and shook his head. He'd almost given the order to take out the mage, but seeing Winger take off in the stepvan, they abandoned Synthia so as not to lose Winger. The Bulldog stepvan that Winger drove was similar to Hendrix and Layla's machine, except for the blown-open side doors and the blackened scorch marks over the white paint. And Hendrix had made a few modifications to his, just to maintain the edge in case of a fire fight.

Freeway traffic was light as Hendrix followed Winger's truck up onto the 405. *He's heading back toward Venice*

Beach, Hendrix thought. *Probably going for his car.* That would be bad because the Westwind would be able to outrun the stepvan.

"They're looping back toward Venice Beach," Layla said. "What say we take them down now?"

"Soon, my love," Hendrix said.

"Oh, come on," Layla said. "Broad fragging daylight, middle of traffic." She let out a short laugh. "Why the frag not?"

"As soon as they exit the freeway, they'll be in Culver City for a klick or so. It's an uncontrolled zone. No Mafia, no regular Lone Star patrols. We'll hit them then."

"So ka, omae," Layla said.

"Nice japspeak."

"You like?" Layla gave a mock bow.

Hendrix just laughed.

A few minutes later, the black-streaked van angled for the exit to Venice Boulevard. "They're exiting as predicted. Mole, you in virtual position?"

"I've got the Lone Star grid crunching on a loop," Mole said. "They won't get any calls from this area for a good ten or fifteen minutes."

"Chill," Hendrix said. "Layla?"

"I'm on it." She lifted a rocket launcher from the space on the floor between the seats. A swivel mount on the barrel clamped to the door. "Get us a little closer."

"Remember that Winger lives," Hendrix said. "You can injure him, but don't kill him."

"The troll?"

"Expendable."

"I like when you say that," Layla said, then straightened her hat and sighted the missile.

Winger pulled onto Venice Boulevard, a road that was supposed to be four lanes wide each direction, but had been under heavy construction for years. *Under demolition is more like it,* Hendrix thought. "Fire when ready," he said.

The missile flew with a burst of flame and a loud hiss. And when it hit Winger's stepvan, just over the rear axle, the explosion threw the stepvan forward and sideways. The rear of the vehicle ripped open as it plunged onto its side and skidded through the construction markers before hitting a concrete barricade.

Hendrix pulled his Ares Alpha and stopped the van

while Layla jumped out, carrying her Ingram. *We won't be smoked by any surprise magic this time,* Hendrix thought. Then he too stepped out onto the street amid the sunlight and the noise of passing traffic.

Using his door as a shield, Hendrix brought the Alpha up and sighted on the only two openings in the overturned stepvan, the passenger door and the double side doors, both of which were now on top of the vehicle. The flaming rip in the rear wasn't large enough for anyone to squeeze out.

"Layla," Hendrix said. "Use a tear gas grenade to flush them out."

Layla nodded and pulled a grenade from her belt with a smooth motion. She heaved it the five or six meters into the stepvan.

White smoke billowed from the stepvan's openings, blowing away in the wind as it drifted up and out. A minute later, a huge shape jumped from the side doors, diving head-first in an arc. Hitting the pavement fast and rolling to a crouch. Firing shots from the shotgun as he rolled.

The door in front of Hendrix rocked into him as the shot-gun slugs hit. He aimed at the fast-moving target of Venice Jones, chewing up pavement with the combat gun's ammo. *Damn, he's fast.* But several rounds hit home on the troll. And Layla's did as well.

Then Venice Jones came for Layla, dodging and run-ning, very hard to hit. Hendrix pegged him two or three more times, but the huge figure, spattered and dripping with blood, would not go down. The troll dodged a last time and lunged, lightning-quick, for Layla.

Hendrix heard her yell, "Slotting tusker-frag!" Then the stepvan's door slammed shut and shots went off. Hendrix moved fast, glancing back toward the overturned vehicle to make sure Jonathon Winger wasn't about to pop out and open fire. The tear gas should've flushed him out by now, so he'd probably been knocked unconscious by the crash.

Hopefully, he's not dead.

Hendrix clicked into wired mode, rapidly stepping around the front of their stepvan, Ares Alpha combat gun in front of him. He cleared the hot grill and peeked around to see Layla and Venice Jones dancing the dangerous dance. Circling each other at close quarters.

Layla, the stupid slitch, had set her Ingram on the ground. Or perhaps Venice Jones had knocked it from her hands. The troll's shotgun also lay on the pavement a few steps from them. The troll hulked over her, his clothes shredded from gunfire to reveal form-fitting body armor underneath. Even so, several wounds bled, soaking his tattered clothing with crimson.

Hendrix moved quickly to a position that gave him a view of both the wreckage and the fight. Then, since there was still no sign of Jonathon Winger, he brought his Ares Alpha to bear on Venice Jones.

"No, Hendrix, don't shoot," Layla yelled. "Let me finish him."

Venice Jones moved then, almost too fast to see, his massive hand striking out for Layla's throat.

Layla blocked it and stepped lightly to the side. "Gonna have to do better, tusker-frag," she said.

But the strike was only a decoy for the troll to sweep Layla's legs. He must've noticed that one of them was recently injured. Layla fell back, and Venice Jones continued his motion. Pivoting insanely fast to strike down, a fist to the throat.

Frag this! Hendrix thought. He aimed his Ares Alpha at Venice Jones's knees, and squeezed the trigger, blowing out one, then the other with two quick bursts.

The troll screamed in pain, arching his back as his punch went wide. Venice Jones crumbled to the pavement. Incapacitated.

Hendrix smiled. It was an effective injury. Layla's pride would be wounded because the troll had bested her. She would want the kill for herself as a small redemption.

Layla pushed to her feet and kicked the troll in the face. "Frag you!"

Venice Jones said nothing. He merely lay still, his chest heaving as he tried to concentrate on staying alive.

Layla was slotted off. Nobody fragged with her pride. She gathered up her Ingram and targeted the troll's head. "You better confess your sins, tusker-frag," she said, "if you think you got a snowball's chance of not going to Hell."

No response from Venice Jones.

Hendrix turned and approached the overturned stepvan. In seconds, the troll would be dead, and Jonathon Winger's head would be theirs.

46

Maria came back into her body as quickly as she could, opening her eyes to see the broad, deep-chocolate face of Maurice looking down on her. The tiny rows of his hair glistened with sweat, and his expression showed concern. "You okay, shaman?" he asked.

Good question, she thought. Her astral struggle with the mage had nearly killed her. Maybe if it had been nighttime, Maria would have had a chance to beat that slitch. *Maybe.*

The mage had blindsided her with the rapid succession of hellblasts targeted on the stepvan. And then, when Maria put up an astral shield and confronted her with Stoney, the slitch called up a strange spell, the type of which Maria had never seen. A mana fog had surrounded Maria, filling the astral around her with a brilliant white glow. A radiance that blinded Maria's astral vision, her astral sense of direction. She tried to run, but the glowing fog stuck to her. She'd been completely blind and couldn't come back to her body.

It had taken her several minutes to shake off the spell and find her way back. And by then, Jonathon Winger was driving away, and it was all Maria could do to prevent Dougan and Maurice from burning to death in the alleyway. The mage slitch had run for her little Saab car when she saw Maria stand up, no doubt to finish her task of killing Jonathon Winger.

Maria told Stoney to pulverize the little Saab, and she watched with detached pleasure as the spirit materialized next to the car and crushed the tiny glass and metal machine to a crumpled mass. The mage stopped in shock a few meters from the vehicle, shaking her head at the sight of her destroyed car. Then she turned and stared back at Maria with a look of sheer despair in her eyes before running out of the alley and around the corner into the street.

Maria sat up now and looked herself over. Whole, complete except for some surface burns on the skin of her left hand. And she was tired, exhausted beyond her breaking point. "I'll live, I think," she said.

"That's good," said Dougan, walking up the alleyway toward them. He smelled of burning hair and soot. His black duster was scorched in several places and his face was smudged. "We'll need you for this last little bit of biz."

"No more biz for me today," Maria said. "I'm scragged."

"Just this last bit," Dougan said. "I've got some new data. I think you'll want to hear it."

"What now?"

"As you know, I hired this decker to do a scan on Tashika, trying to see if we could get some goods on him."

"You never said anything about that."

"Well, I did," Dougan said. "And she just found something. It's nothing we can use for blackmail, but it's worth mentioning."

"Spill it, daisy-eater," said Maurice.

"Yeah, spill it," Maria said.

"I think Tashika was responsible for the military attack on the Compton school," Dougan said. "He ordered the strike that killed Jesse."

"What?" Maria said, feeling the ground tilt beneath her. "Jesse? How is that possible? Tashika is a corporate suit; he had nothing to do with the Lost Election."

"Tashika is yakuza," Dougan said. "Has been all his life and will be until he dies. The yaks had informants in Compton, and that's how Tashika learned that some runners who'd helped with the election hit were holed up in El Infierno. He simply passed along the data to Lone Star and the Calfree National Guard as a gracious gesture." Dougan let out a sharp laugh. "A debt to be repaid at some future date no doubt."

Jesse's dark, haunted face hovered in Maria's mind. She had distant memories of the two of them, very young, swimming naked in a warm, crystal blue ocean. Before she'd been taken by the priests. Before he'd run away.

A wave of heat crested in Maria's head and she found herself on the dirty pavement. All that was so long ago that she wanted to put it to rest. And she thought she had. For so long, she'd set up a safe life for herself and Pedro and Angelina. Away from ghosts and distant memories.

She felt a hand on her arm, helping her to stand. "Are you all right, Maria?" It was Dougan's voice.

"No," she said. "I am not all fragging right!"

Dougan stepped back. "I think I have a solution," he said.

Maria narrowed her eyes on him. "You always have a slotting solution, Dougan," she said. "And it always gets us hoop-fragged."

Dougan held his hands up as if to ward off the sting of her words, to stop the onslaught of her vehemence. "I'm sorry, Maria," he said. "This is my last idea. But I think you'll like it."

She just stared at the elf for a minute. He looked back at her, but his gaze was soft. Entreating her to trust him. "Okay," she said finally. She had no more trust for him than she'd ever had; he was one of the smoothest liars she'd ever known. But at one time he'd cared for her, and she for him. Besides, she didn't have any brilliant ideas of her own. "Go ahead; spill this plan of yours."

"It's simple really," Dougan said. "We keep the appointment for the exchange as planned."

"But we don't have the data."

Dougan held up a chip. "We do," he said. "I downloaded the data from Winger's headware before he escaped."

"Seriously?" Maria didn't remember Dougan getting anything from Winger.

"No, because there wasn't time to wait until the drug wore off; hyper frags with data transfer. But Tashika won't know that. We could tell him anything."

"What for?" Maurice said. "He'll know the chip is belly-up as soon as he slots it."

"We don't let him get that far," Dougan said. "We geek him first."

"What?" Maurice said.

But Maria had been following Dougan's line of thought all the way. She'd known what he was going to say. Putting the suit on ice would solve their problems. Plus it would be perfect closure for Jesse's death. Revenge after all these years.

"Let's do it," she said. "Let's fragging do it so I can go home."

47

In the meat world, Jonathon huddled in a fetal crouch against the shattered side window of Dougan's stepvan. He squeezed his eyes against the rain of tears gushing from his eyes and held his breath to keep out the gas. He felt the zen of biker training slow his metabolism. His body might be here awhile.

But his mind wasn't in the meat world; Jonathon was a stealthy black beetle, zooming at high speed over the city. He was in a rigger's verisimilar reality, piloting his Cyber-Space Designs Stealth Sniper drone, launched from the Westwind's trunk before the accident. He rotored at nearly 100 klicks per hour, as fast as the drone's turbine could fly him. Through the towering skyscratchers, along the freeways and under bridges, dodging and darting to reach the accident.

Now, Jonathon saw the overturned stepvan in his holo-camera vision and readied his sniper rifle. *What happened to Venny?* he wondered. Then he saw the troll, lying on the pavement, blood oozing onto the concrete from wounds in his knees. A blond human woman stood over him, aiming an automatic weapon at his head.

A black-skinned man with a bald head was walking away from them. Toward the wreckage. *Are these the same runners who hit us in the limousine?* But the thought was fleeting. It didn't matter.

Jonathon sighted on the woman with the gun and opened up. The sniper rifle coughed, a barely audible sound amid the rumble and screech of traffic.

Perfect shot. The bullet hit her in the back of the skull, and went clean through. A bloody hole blossomed on her face, spraying bone and teeth and bits of brain as it flowered. She lurched forward from the impact, hurtled to the pavement like a ragdoll.

The black man turned, very fast. Very fragging fast.

Jonathon zipped up and sideways as the street merc sprayed bullets after him. Jonathon aimed the sniping gun again and fired. The bullet should have hit the merc's head just like the woman's, but the man wasn't there anymore. He was diving left, over and behind a concrete construction barricade.

Jonathon whirled the drone around into position and pivoted, bringing the sniping gun to bear once again. Target inline, dead-center on the bald black head. Fire. Such a small recoil, a whispered cough.

The merc didn't have much room to move, but he tried lurching to the side as the bullet hit his shoulder and tore through the armor plating to the flesh beneath. He was speaking subvocally at a frantic pace; Jonathon saw his mouth move. The merc moved to put more of the barrier between him and the drone, then aimed his combat gun.

Jonathon dodged the barrage of bullets, plummeting for half a second, then zipping laterally to bring the merc into aim again. The bullets missed, but just when the black head came between the cross hairs a blinding white flash overloaded the holocameras.

Flash grenade.

By the time the drone's holocameras had readjusted, compensating for the glare, the black man was gone. Jonathon scanned around, but couldn't find him. Then the merc's stepvan powered up and screeched off into traffic, leaving the sprawled bodies of Venice Jones and the woman runner lying side by side on the pavement.

Jonathon came back to his body, nearly out of breath in the real world. The world of meat and bone. He tried to maintain calm and focus as he took the Ingram SMG and quietly, quickly climbed up out of the stepvan, through the passenger window, and down onto the concrete.

His legs buckled under him as he landed, gasping for breath. He crouched there sucking in deep breath after deep breath, wiping the water from his eyes on his sleeve. After a minute he heard the rhythmic pulse of a helicopter approaching. He looked up and saw a white Hughes WK-2 Stallion with the DocWagon logo emblazoned on the side.

About fragging time.

Venny must've pressed the emergency call on his platinum account wrist band when he went down. Jonathon tried to stand, finding that he could walk. He made his way stiffly to Venny.

Jonathon could see the troll's massive chest heaving as he breathed. Still alive. "Can you hear me, chummer?" he asked.

Venny uttered something incoherent.

"You hang on," Jonathon said. "DocWagon's almost here."

48

In the grimy public telecom booth of a Hollywood Stuffer Shack, Synthia sat on sticky vinyl and stared at the blank screen. Though exhausted and drained, she fought off sleep, healing from the exertion of fighting the owl shaman.

The ghost image of Hans Brackhaus sparkled in the blank screen, haunting her. Watching her, always watching. Moments ago, Brackhaus had looked at her with his cold alien eyes and his hard-as-chiseled-stone features. He refused to discuss failure or anything else over the telecom. Said he was on his way, anger and cold menace in his voice.

Jonathon, Synthia thought, *why didn't you stop?* She felt the churning blade of despair in her gut, twisting and chopping her insides. *If only I could have talked to you, purged the data from your head . . .*

But that was past. She couldn't afford to dwell on it. She needed to look to the next step. Finding Jonathon again. Getting him to purge the data. *He's bound to show up at the match in a few hours,* she thought. *I can contact him then.*

The huge black Rolls-Royce Phaeton limousine pulled up into the Stuffer Shack's parking lot, Brackhaus's car. Synthia took a deep breath and stepped out into the heat and humidity of the late afternoon. She felt an ache in her bones and a sickness in her gut as she walked the few steps to the limousine.

A door opened for her and she climbed into the plush, air-conditioned interior. The too-comfortable seat enveloped her like a velvet glove, tempting her to just close her eyes. Forget and dream.

"I am disappointed in your progress," Brackhaus said. "Pained actually."

Synthia stared into the man's eyes, like chips of blue

ice. "I've done all I can," she said. "I've destroyed all physical copies of the data. Only one remains, and I plan to erase that as well. I'm sure Jonathon will show up at the stadium for the championship match. I'll meet him then."

"I can no longer afford to wait, Miss Stone. Because of your failure to contain the information, I have taken matters into my own hands."

"What do you mean?"

Brackhaus thought for a moment. "Well, I suppose I can tell you, considering . . ."

Synthia just waited, trying to ignore the tightening pain in her stomach.

"I can no longer risk leaving Winger alive. I have . . . made arrangements for him to be killed. It's not the way I would have preferred, but circumstances dictate immediate action."

A chill shook Synthia and she realized that whatever had remained of her composure was rapidly evaporating. "You hired an assassin?"

"Assassin is a nasty word," Brackhaus said. "But yes, more than one actually. They will hit him at the stadium. If Winger does show up for the match, he will die."

"Give me one more try," Synthia said. "I know I can get him to purge the data. I just need to talk to him."

"I'm afraid the arrangements have already been made. I'm sorry." Brackhaus shifted in his seat and reached toward the small bar unit adjacent to him. "It's a pity things turned out this way for you," he said. "Can I offer you a drink, a small pleasure. Wine perhaps."

Synthia shook her head as sweat made its trickling way down her back. "Am I off the hook then? You'll give me the antibodies?"

"I'm afraid not, Miss Stone. You failed."

Synthia fought down her reflex to fry this man. That hadn't worked before and it wouldn't now. She clenched her teeth against the frustration and took a breath. "I've done everything in my power," she said. "Please reconsider."

"Life is not fair, Miss Stone. Sometimes all you can give is just not enough."

"Frag you, Brackhaus! Can the philosophical bulldrck." She felt the tingle of a spell growing in the back of her mind.

"Miss Stone, this conversation is no longer informative, nor amusing."

She cast the manabolt, thinking, *I'm going to pummel this fragger.* And she cast another after that. And another. She kept on casting until the energy drained from her and she had no strength left.

And through it all, Brackhaus merely glared at her with his ice blue eyes, a disappointed frown on his face. The energy channeled around him and away, having no effect.

The blackness of unconsciousness swelled over her like a dark and comforting blanket. A prelude to her final oblivion, and right now she welcomed it. Relief from the gnawing pain and the fatigue. She gave in to the exhaustion and slumped forward, nestling under the dark blanket of peace and passed out.

49

As Jonathon waited for Venny to come out of surgery at the UCLA Medical Center where DocWagon Los Angeles operated, memories of prison washed through his mind. After the Multnomah Falls incident, Jonathon and Tamara, along with the dwarf, Theodore Rica, had been shipped to a medium-security federal penitentiary in Fairfax, Virginia. Most of the inmates were low threat: deckers or spies.

The hardest thing for Jonathon had been his withdrawal from Tamara's link. He'd been so used to sharing mind and emotions with her four or five times a week that the sudden isolation gave him the DTs—the shakes, sweating, and vomiting. It hit them both pretty hard.

But now, it had been several days since Tam's death and Jonathon expected the symptoms to hit anytime. But they didn't. Perhaps the ghostly hiss in his mind was keeping the shakes at bay. Perhaps the DTs just hadn't set in yet.

Either way the dead static seemed to be growing. Now it howled through his mind like a banshee, hissing and growling in his ears. And it made the tips of his fingers and toes tingle.

Jonathon stood up from the sofa in the waiting lounge and walked to the vending machines along the wall. The doctor had been kind enough to let him into the private waiting area since someone had recognized him and reporters were starting to show up and hound him for an interview. Jonathon had been grateful for the privacy.

He slotted a credstick and punched the code for a chocolate-flavored mycoprotein bar. Make that two. He was hungry, and he needed food to think. The beginnings of a plan were coalescing in his head, but the details were still vague. It was hard to think with so much static.

Jonathon would have to contact Grids, let him know what had happened. Grids could still help, that was certain. In fact, his help was crucial. And as Jonathon chewed the last of his mycoprotein bar, part of his plan solidified and clicked into place.

He stepped up to a public telecom on the wall and punched in the number for Hemmingway's chateau. He knew this line was by no means private or secure, but he didn't have the time or the resources to seek out another telecom.

After a brief conversation with security on Hemmingway's end, he was patched through to Grids, who was having a late lunch with Hemmingway beside the pool.

It was Dexter who answered, the microthin lines of his face edging around his smile. "Hello, Jonathon," he said. "Grids has just been telling 'bout all the wiz drek he does with simfeatures. How's it going with you?"

"Not great, Dexter," Jonathon said. "Venny's been hurt, and I need to speak with Grids before I head down to the stadium."

Dexter frowned. "If there's anything I can do . . ."

"Grids may need some supplies."

"My arsenal is at your disposal."

"Thank you."

"Just smoke them tonight, Jonathon," Dexter said. "Smoke 'em and I'll be happy. Especially Dougan Rose."

"I intend to do just that," Jonathon said.

"Here's Grids," Dexter said, then the image tilted wildly and swiveled around to show a harried, but healthier-looking Grids Desmond.

"How's biz?" Jonathon asked.

"Not too chill," Grids said. "I'm still in shock over all my fragged-up equipment, but I'm gonna hang with you. All the way, chummer. That's what I said when we started and that's what I plan to do."

"I appreciate it more than you can know."

"It's what Tam would have wanted," Grids said.

Jonathon nodded. "I need you to get some things together."

"What?"

"For starters, a small hunk of plastique, C-12 if possible, and a digitally timed detonator. Dexter should have what we need. Also bring a couple of certified credsticks, each with ten-kay nuyen on them. And put together a set of tools for making changes to some simsense hardware."

"What hardware?"

"Don't know exactly, but it's a live-feed, multiple-input system with on-the-fly editing for a mass market."

Grids nodded, staring off into space as he mentally tallied what he might need.

"I want you to pack everything into the Nightsky and drive here, UCLA Medical Center, and pick me up."

"Null sheen," Grids said. "I've got it chipped."

That almost brought a smile to Jonathon's lips. Almost. "Good," he said. "I'll expect you in less than an hour."

Grids nodded, then disconnected.

Jonathon stepped back from the wall telecom and took a breath before placing the next call. The crucial link in his plan.

Jonathon turned to the sound of a door opening. "Mr. Winger?" said a middle-aged elven doctor. She was black-skinned and quite attractive, wearing green surgical scrubs, booties, and a mask that hung around her neck. Jonathon stared into her eyes, looking for a sign. And he could see it there, even before she spoke.

"Venice Jones will live," the doctor said. "But he must remain in ICU for another twenty-four hours minimum. We removed five bullets, and replaced five liters of blood. He's lucky."

Jonathon breathed a heavy sigh. "Thank you, Doctor," he said. "You've made my fragging day."

She smiled. "He's amazingly resilient. I've lost patients with less damage. They just didn't have the will to survive. But him, he held on."

"Can I see him?"

"No, I'm afraid ICU is a high-security area and no visitors are allowed," she said. "You can observe him on the closed-circuit screen if you'd like, but . . ." She paused for a second. "Don't you have to be someplace in a few hours?"

Jonathon laughed.

"I'll contact you when he's moved out of ICU," she said.

"Thank you."

The doctor turned and stepped through the door. And as soon as it was closed, Jonathon tapped in Theo Rica's private number. He wanted to get it over with.

Theo answered, his dwarven face a pleasant sight to Jonathon's eyes. "Winger, you daisy-munching fragger. It's good to see your face again so soon, chummer."

Jonathon smiled. "Likewise, halfer."

Theo's expression grew serious. "What's biz?"

"At Tamara's funeral you said if I needed your help, I should just ask."

"And I meant it too."

"Well, I'm asking," Jonathon said. "And it's not a small thing."

"Hold on," Theo said. "Let me get a decker to scan this line for any traces."

Jonathon waited while Theo spoke to someone on another part of the screen. After a minute Theo looked back at Jonathon. "All right, we're clear. Spill it."

So Jonathon did. He outlined his plan to Theo, watching the dwarf for a reaction. He knew it was a long shot, but he didn't see any other choice. And when he was done, Theo considered for a moment. "I think it's madness, chummer," he said, scowling at Jonathon. "It'll probably get you killed. Is drek really that over the top?"

"Yes," Jonathon said.

"Then, I'll make the arrangements. I'll have to call in quite a few marks, but the plan should work . . ." Theo paused for effect. "*If* you survive the match."

Yeah, Jonathon thought. That was one huge fragging "if."

50

Maria crouched in the long shade of the desalinization plant's fusion dome, enjoying the reprieve from the sunshine as much as she could. She hadn't slept today and she was more than a little slotted off at Dougan for not postponing the exchange until after sundown. Then, under the cover of night, she would have Owl's complete strength.

But Dougan had nullified that program. The meet had to happen now so that he could make it to his combat biker match. Saying he needed to prove he was a better linebiker than Jonathon Winger. Lay all the hyped speculation to rest along with Winger's body.

Originally, Dougan had wanted the meet in El Infierno, and Maria had liked the idea of killing Tashika in the old burned-out husk of the Compton school, where Jesse had died. She could appreciate that kind of irony.

But Tashika had rejected the idea, suggesting Watts or even Downtown, both corporate-controlled areas. Dougan had just laughed at that; they'd finally decided on the coast, in the open lot just outside the three-meter-high cyclone fence that surrounded the El Segundo desalinization plant.

The lot was oil-soaked gravel, filled with broken glass and the smell of seagull guano and rotting fish. The roar of the ocean was soothing, lulling Maria toward sleep. She just wanted this over and done so she could see her kids again. She shook her head and concentrated on the task at hand, astral reconnaissance to watch for Tashika's approach.

Shifting into astral space, she let her body slump against the metal wall of the warehouse that bordered the gravel lot. Then she stepped through the wall, checking on the five Steppin' Wulfs Dougan had hired for backup.

Four humans and one ork crouched behind the sliding metal door. They were cybered to the teeth and antsy with their guns. Ready, in their tattoos and obvious chrome, to ambush the suits when they arrived. *Hopefully, they'll be enough,* Maria thought. The Steppin' Wulfs generally didn't hire themselves out, but Dougan had played on their hatred of the corps and on their love of bloodshed and nuyen. The coast district was their turf, and they were rumored to be deadly and ruthless, especially to trespassers.

The distant sound of an approaching limousine. Make that two—Toyota Elite limos, skittering toward them like sleek, black cockroaches. Maria returned to her body as the limousines stopped just steps away from where Dougan and Maurice stood. The big human carried a large automatic gun of some sort, crooked into his elbow. Dougan's gloved hands were empty.

After a minute, two huge bodyguards stepped out of the front limo. Private security types. Rented for just this occasion most likely. The bodyguards were both human, distinctly Nihonese in appearance, and looked to weigh a good hundred kilos each. A slight rigidity to their business suits hinted at body armor beneath.

The two made a quick scan of the area, then stood on either side of another man with somewhat Asian features as he stepped out of the rear limousine. There was a slight curl to his black hair, and a hint of roundness to his eyes. *Must be some Euro-blood in Mr. Tashika,* Maria thought. He stepped up to Dougan Rose. "I take it you have the chip?"

Dougan nodded. "You have destroyed the data you have on me?"

Tashika reached slowly into the pocket of his suit. "It's all here," he said, extending a chip toward Dougan. "The rest has been purged."

Dougan pulled his own chip, the one that contained the false data. "This wasn't easy to get," he said. "I lost a chummer because of it."

Tashika took the chip from Dougan's hand and let out a harsh laugh. "Not my concern, slot," he said. "You made your fragging bed a long time ago."

Maurice's shoulders tensed and he nearly struck out at Tashika, but Dougan put his hand out and grabbed the chip from Tashika's hand. "That concludes our biz, then," Dougan said.

That's the signal. Maria whispered, "Now, Stoney. Now!"

The huge city spirit manifested behind one of the body-guards and grabbed him. Stoney crushed the man in a mass of living concrete and riebar. Dougan dove out of the way, and Maurice brought his gun to bear on Tashika and unloaded.

At precisely the same time, the warehouse door on Maria's right slid open and the Steppin' Wulfs released a barrage of bullets and rockets. Several rockets hit the limos and exploded, launching one into the air in a gout of flame and a concussion of shrapnel. The other lurched and caught fire.

Tashika's bullet-ridden body flew forward from the blast, landing near Maria. Bleeding and burned and all twisted up like a ragdoll that had landed wrong.

It was all over in a matter of seconds. The other body-guard managed to get his weapon out and blow a hole in Maurice before doing down, but they were all lying twisted and bleeding, the burning corpses of the limousines a flaming backdrop to the violence.

Maria lost Stoney during the second explosion, the big spirit disintegrating in the wave of heat and flame. The Steppin' Wulfs advanced on the scene with lust in their eyes, then proceeded to gut the corpses, Maurice among them. Dougan didn't even try to stop them, and Maria was too tired to argue.

So much death.

She stepped over to Tashika's body, and bent down. His aura still clung to the mangled and leaking flash. *Still alive.* She leaned close to his ear. "This is payback for my brother," she said. "And for all those families you killed in Compton when you told Lone Star where we were."

Tashika tried to turn his head, bone showing silver through the red gore of his cheek. Breath hacking up through him. "Not me," he said. "Not . . . *only* . . . me."

"What?" She put her ear down close to what was left of his face.

"Dougan," he spat out, "betrayed your . . . position to me." He pulled his knees up into a fetal crouch.

Chills crept spidery tendrils across her back, and she shivered despite the waves of heat coming from the burning limos.

"In exchange for . . ." Tashika coughed up some bloody flesh from his throat.

"What?" Maria whispered, her voice barely audible even to her. "In exchange for what?"

"Buzzsaws," Tashika said. "Fame."

Could it be true? But even as the question formed in her mind, she knew the answer. The myriad small inconsistencies in Dougan's story, in his excuses for things, all coalesced in her mind. He'd been lying to her all these years. And now, she had killed more people because of it. Murdered innocent people for him.

He's fragged up my life for the last time.

She started to stand, but Tashika's hand caught hold of her collar with a death grip. He pulled her head down by his again, and the smell of burnt flesh made her stomach lurch into her throat.

"Kill me," he said. "Please, before they . . . My body."

Maria looked over to see the Steppin' Wulfs bathing in the eviscerated remains of the dead. The two Nihonese bodyguards and Maurice had been torn to shreds with cyberspurs, and the gangers had clothed themselves in the bloodied strips of their flesh. The Wulfs were dancing in a pseudo-ritualistic circle, celebrating their kill.

Dougan, who'd been thrown down by the explosions, just watched. A frown of distaste showed on his face.

Maria turned away. She couldn't watch anymore.

"Let . . . me . . . go," came the ghost of a whisper from Tashika.

But as Maria stood up and prepared to hit him with a manabolt that would send him over the edge of fadeout, she saw with her astral sight that he was already there. The last tatters of his aura had fluttered away.

She formed a spell anyway, not a manabolt, but a cold blue flame. She let it loose, bathing his body in blue fire. And she sustained the spell until he was no more than ash. Then she turned to do the same with the bodies of the others, not caring what the gangers might do to her for messing with their kills.

Dougan stopped her as she approached them. "What the frag are you doing?" he asked. "They'll kill you."

She stopped, looking up into the face of the man who'd once shared her bed. She had loved him then, but all the while he'd been using her. "You betrayed me," she said, her voice soft. But as she continued, her whisper rose to a scream, "Tashika told me everything. Jesse died because you sold us out!" She pushed against his grip and focused her power. *I will destroy him,* she thought.

Suddenly Dougan spun her around and held her. A gun appeared in his hand, he pressed the cold metal against her temple. "Don't, Maria," he said. "Don't try magic now. My finger is slippery on this trigger, and I'd hate for an accident to happen out here." Then he reached into his pocket with his free hand and pulled something out. He pressed it against her neck, just above her Muerte tattoo.

Within seconds, her vision blurred. A dermal tranquilizer patch.

"I'll see you dead, Dougan," Maria said, then her knees buckled, and she fell into his hard embrace. Drawn down into the dark caress of oblivion.

51

Jonathon pulled his thoroughly abused Mitsubishi Nightsky up to the security gate of the Sabers's garage. A big ork in a gold and navy blue uniform that looked about a size and a half too small stepped up to the driver's side window.

"Hoi, Nick," Jonathon said, holding out his team ID card. "Having a wiz one?"

The big ork guard shrugged and scanned the card as a matter of protocol. "And who's your passenger?"

"He's a new simsense tech. Terry's training him tonight."

"Well, don't let her tear his head off like she did the last one," Nick said.

"This one doesn't make mistakes."

Nick smiled at that. "All right," he said. "You're clear. All the chummers and I have nuyen on you, Winger. Don't let us down."

"No chance of that," Jonathon said.

Then the ork flicked the switch to make the cyclone fence gate roll to the side, and Jonathon drove through. The ramp down into the underground parking beneath the rebuilt LA Coliseum welcomed him with familiar smells and sounds. This was one of the places where he felt at home. Comfortable.

Jonathon realized suddenly that Grids had been speaking to him for the last minute. And that he hadn't heard a thing. Words drowned out beneath the hurricane roar in his mind.

"Then she burned everything I own," Grids was saying. "My simth, my cyberdeck. Everything. I don't have anything now. Nothing."

Jonathon welcomed the seclusion of the underground parking garage. Most of the team's cars were already parked there. His headclock read 05:20:34 PM. A little more than two hours to game time. Still plenty of time to

make the modifications to his bike and run the maze before bogey release.

"What do you think happened to her?" Grids asked.

"Who?"

"Synthia, for frag's sake. Haven't you been listening?"

Jonathon parked the limo. "Sorry, chummer. I can't think
about Syn right now. There's an explanation for what she did,
I'm certain of it. But it's past now. When this is all over, I
want you to find her and sort it out."

"I don't know."

"Promise me, Grids." Jonathon turned to face him. "Promise
me that whatever happens tonight, you'll find Synthia."

Grids breathed a sigh. "Okay," he said. "I promise."

"Tell her I still love her."

"You can tell her yourself."

"Just tell her," Jonathon said. Then he stepped out of the
car and into the cool subterranean air of the parking garage.
"Come on, I'll show you the simsense equipment."

Grids put an Angelic Entertainment jumpsuit over his
Mickey Mouse T-shirt, then retrieved his satchel of tools
and chips and whatever other drek he'd brought. He followed Jonathon through the metal door and into the team
garage where the motorcycles were parked. They walked
past the bikes and up the ramp into the locker room area.

Most of the team was there, lifting weights or stretching
or warming up on the small track. Jonathon saw Vic, the
mechanic, and Boges and Mason, plus Ion and Chibba.

"Hoi, Winger," came Smitty's voice. "You showed,
chummer."

"That's right," Jonathon said, looking at the bulked-up
dwarf with his feet in gravity boots and doing upside-
down abdominal crunches.

"You've got *cajones*," Smitty said. "I'll give you that.
Cajones the size of cantaloupes."

Jonathon laughed and let the mood of the locker room per-
meate him. Let it focus him on the match. He wasn't in the
best condition for a championship game, considering the past
few days, but he wouldn't have to last long to execute his plan.

Jonathon showed Grids the simsense decks and the simre-
cliners against the wall. Grids gave the equipment a once-
over, shaking his head. "No go, chummer," he said. "Can't
make the modifications here; none of this drek can transmit."

"Didn't think so."

"Tell me again," Grids said. "What data is received by the bikes when they're in the maze?"

"As far as I know, just the positions of the other riders. It's projected onto the retina as a heads-up display."

"Anything else?"

"The time and verbal communications, but that's about it."

Grids pursed his lips. "Hmm," he said. "What about in emergencies?"

"There are transponders in each bike that let the referees shut the engine down to prevent excessive aggression. Basically to keep anyone from repeatedly running over someone else or pummeling them with their bikes."

"Nice," Grids said.

"It's not a game for the weak and fair-minded."

Grids grinned. "Guess not," he said. "So, where are the transmitters that send the data to the bikes?"

Jonathon turned to lead Grids to the communications bay adjacent to the coach's office. "Each side has the same setup," he said as they approached the bank of screens, holo-projectors, and electronic drek. Terry was inside, sitting in front of a complex-looking console. Terry was a gigantic ork woman with more fat than a hippo and a complexion to match.

Jonathon stopped just outside and whispered to Grids. "We get all the signals, but we can only send the locations of our own bikes."

"That's what you think," Grids said.

"You got the little incentive stick I asked you to bring?" Jonathon said.

Grids nodded.

Jonathon smiled, then he stepped through the door to the com bay. "Hoi, Terry," he said.

Terry turned from her screens, smiling as she saw Jonathon. "Winger, it's good to see your sexy bod, chummer." She gave him a huge, tusky grin.

"Likewise, Terry," Jonathon said. "Look, I've got an Angelic Entertainment tech out here who needs to make a few adjustments to patch my simlink feed directly to Dexter Hemmingway's booth. Can you give him some room for a few minutes?"

The ork considered. "You sure this is legit?" she asked.

"Sure it is," Jonathon said. "As legit as it gets. Hemmingway's spending a load on this direct feed. I'm sure this young man could see fit to share a little of his newfound nuyen."

Grids stepped forward. "How about ten kay?"

"Ten kay to walk around for a few minutes?"

Grids nodded, and held out a certified credstick.

Terry yawned, showing the dark saliva cavern of her mouth, a truly repulsive sight. "I think I need a little refreshment," she said. "Before the game starts." She stood, taking the credstick from Grids and slipping it into her pocket before walking out.

"Thanks," Jonathon said, then motioned for Grids to get moving. "I'm going to get to work on my bike," he said. "Come back down to the limo when you're finished."

Grids nodded and took a small black device from his satchel. Then he removed the face plate over onē of the consoles.

Jonathon turned away and walked back down to the team garage. He went up to his cache of Suzuki Auroras, seven of them in pristine condition. He pulled a temporary datacord from a wall rack and jacked in to one of the Suzukis. He fired it up and listened to its purr. Checked all its components and systems. *Yes,* he thought, *this will do nicely.*

He killed the engine and dismounted. Then he stepped out through the door and walked back to his limousine to retrieve the brown duffel that held the small cube of C-12 plastique and a digital fuse. He hefted the duffel and walked back with it to his bike.

Tamara's ghost whispered incoherently to Jonathon as he pulled on the skin-tight surgical gloves Dexter had graciously included. The explosive was an opaque color. Off white. It didn't really match the blue or silver paint of the Suzuki, but he didn't need much. Jonathon pressed a thumb-sized hunk of it into the space under the seat, next to the bike's electronics.

The detonator fuse had a cybernetic interface, and through the bike's dog brain, Jonathon was able to access the timer. The digital readout was displayed on his retina in small white numbers. Jonathon set it for five seconds, then he carefully buried the detonator into the soft explosive, leaving the microthin wire jacked into his bike so that he could activate the countdown when it was time.

The seat fit back nicely, and Jonathon carefully cranked up the Suzuki again to make sure the bike was still working properly. Yes. Perfect. Now, he would run the maze. After which he'd be ready and prepped to ride.

52

Inside the dripping, stinking warehouse at the ancient oil refinery, Cinnamon felt the hunger gnawing at her as she paced the outer circumference of Juju Pete's hermetic circle. Michaelson and Juju Pete were inside the circle, Michaelson looking bored as he sat and stared at Cinnamon with a scrutinizing eye. Juju Pete continued pacing the interior, sustaining the complex formula of his spell. He limped more noticeably now, hours into the ritual.

Less than an hour had passed since Hendrix had returned with the news that Layla was dead. He'd been withdrawn, cold and distant. Her death had hit him hard, and he was unwilling to go on with the run

Cinnamon didn't understand why. The physical adept's death was a loss certainly, but she could easily be replaced with another. Hendrix was usually all biz, no remorse. Not one to let emotions cloud his senses. He was always dedicated to any run he accepted, and totally efficient to the end.

Cinnamon was starting to have her doubts about him now. She'd seen the symptoms in other runners, less experienced mercs who'd lost someone close. They all knew death was a risk, part of the hazards of the job. And everyone took the responsibility for his or her own skin.

But in their hearts, they believed death would never touch anyone they cared about. And when it did, it could hit them hard. Make them want to stay out of the risky biz—which destroyed their edge. *A shame for that to happen to Hendrix,* she thought.

That was why she'd asked him to go to the LA Coliseum for the combat biker match. Not only was that the most likely place for Winger to show up, but it would keep Hendrix thinking about work. About biz.

In the long run, that was the best thing he could do for

himself. Move beyond history, past his insubstantial attachment to the memory of Layla.

Hendrix had almost refused. Cinnamon sensed his reluctance like a palpable smell in the air. But he'd gritted his teeth and gone, dutifully. Just as he should. Business winning out over his emotions.

Cinnamon was glad; she had other problems to think about. Tashika hadn't returned her last two calls. Was he reconsidering? Had he obtained the data himself and decided he didn't want or need Michaelson at all? *Frag,* she thought, *I need to slaughter something before I eat one of these nice people.*

The dwarf decker, Mole, emerged from his room where he'd been jacked into the Matrix. "I've got the data," he said. "But you aren't going to like any of it."

Cinnamon ground her teeth together, but on the outside her illusion showed only a smiling face. "Go ahead anyway, please."

"First of all, Tashika is dead."

"What?"

"Lone Star is seventy percent certain that a Steppin' Wulf gang attack near the El Segundo desalinization plant killed Luc Tashika, formerly of Mitsuhama Computer Technologies," Mole said. "I scanned it off one of the Star's communications relays."

"Seventy percent is far from incontrovertible," Cinnamon said.

"The only reason they limited the stats to seventy percent was because the bodies were mutilated and burned beyond recognition, but DNA from one of the limos at the scenes scans positive as his. Two of the other bodies match the identities of his bodyguards. If he's not dead, the fabrication is pretty fragging solid."

Frag me!

"And before you recover from that bit of news, there's more in the same vein." Mole tried to remain emotionless, but she could smell his fear. "The data you had me double scan . . ."

"What about it?"

"I couldn't check it all, too well . . . protected. But what I was able to access—"

"Yes?"

"It's drek, Cinnamon, pure and smelly," Mole said.

"None of your data scans true. It's all close, but some of the important details are wrong, inconsistent, or missing from the stuff I've been able to get from the Matrix."

"Michaelson!" Cinnamon yelled, very unladylike of her. She turned to see a startled Michaelson looking at her with a dumbfounded expression on his face.

Mole looked at her. "Would this be a bad time to discuss my fee?"

"Shut the frag up! I'll talk to you later." Cinnamon disconnected and turned from the telecom. The hunger surged inside her and threatened to break her illusion, but she didn't fragging care. This dumb suit had brought her false data.

"What is it?" Michaelson asked, standing now, just inside the near edge of the hermetic circle.

"The supposedly secret data in your briefcase is fabricated and false."

"What?"

"The data you carry is worthless. Someone must've suspected you were leaving and fed you distorted intelligence."

Michaelson was obviously stunned, but his mental wheels were turning. Obviously considering the validity of what she was saying.

"Didn't that ever occur to you?"

"No," Michaelson said, a concerned look on his face. He knew what it meant that all his precious data was worth no more than drek.

"Does that include the Magus File, Mr. Michaelson?" Cinnamon asked. "That fragging data that has cost me meganuyen and the life of one of my shadowrunners?"

Michaelson shook his head. "No, I've had that for years, tucked away in my files. This other stuff . . . more recently, but still—"

"Yes? I can't wait to see you explain your way out of this one."

"Either my info is false, as you say. Or the data your decker scanned is false. Maybe Brackhaus changed the databanks *after* he learned I was leaving. To make it look like my info is inexact."

"You mean Brackhaus altered his own data to make you look less credible?"

"Exactly."

Cinnamon thought about it for a second. "Doesn't matter either way," she said. "No one's going to trust the information you've brought."

Michaelson's forehead creased in frown.

"Oh, and there's another bit of news," Cinnamon told him. "The MCT exec who was funding your transfer just turned up dead."

Michaelson sucked in a breath.

"What that means," Cinnamon went on, "is that without the Magus File data, you are worthless. The integrity of your other data is suspect, meaning it's worthless, too. Keeping you here costs me nuyen I may never see."

"Can't you find another corp who'd want me? Certainly a senior S-K exec has value. Come on, Cinnamon, someone will pay you to get my expertise and knowledge."

"No, I'm afraid not," Cinnamon said, feeling the hunger break through the veil of illusion. Her petite blond human guise gave way to a huge sinuous, scaly body. Her animal form. Her voice boomed and hissed as she spoke. "Brackhaus could have been feeding you false information for a long time. No corp will risk taking you."

Michaelson staggered back, falling to his knees. Speechless.

Hunger overcame her, and she lunged through the veil of Juju Pete's hermetic circle. She had to push hard and exert a considerable force to make it across, but once she broke the circle, pain washed over her and the spell broke.

She walked toward Michaelson's prostrate form, thrashing with her scaly wings. He shrank away from her as she towered over him. "I can think of only one final use for you," she said, running her forked tongue over rows of dagger-sharp teeth. "To satiate my appetite."

"No, I—"

"Unless you're willing to part with life force to pay me off?"

"Life force?"

"Your energy. Your experience. Your—"

"Yes, anything. Just don't kill me."

"Open your soul to me," Cinnamon said. "And I will drink from it." Then she touched Michaelson's aura with hers, and she took great gulps of his life force. White hot flashes of his memory pulsed through her, filling her. The transfer took only seconds.

And when it was complete, Cinnamon came back to her manifest form to see the human's prostrate body under her. He was bewildered and drained, confused.

He screamed as she struck suddenly; her jaw opened and engulfed his head and neck, then bit down, crunching bone and sinew beneath her teeth. She was no longer hungry, physically; it was her anger at his incompetence that drove her to kill him.

Michaelson's scream was swallowed as the salty warmth of blood gushed over her tongue. She lifted his body off the ground with her bite, and thrashed her head back and forth to tear off his head. He was a big boy; it took her six or seven bites to finally finish him off.

53

Synthia flashed her season pass at the stadium security guard, then ran past him into the Coliseum. It was thirty minutes to game time and she needed to warn Jonathon about Brackhaus. About the assassins he'd sent.

If I can convince Jonathon to erase the data in his head, Synthia thought, *maybe there's one last chance Brackhaus will let me live.* She refused to give up. If she failed, she died. Any minute now, the toxin would be released.

Security was tight and wouldn't allow Synthia into the locker room, but that didn't deter her. She went to her usual seat in the premier club box, then shifted into the astral plane, leaving her body slumped in the comfortable chair. The game hadn't started and the watcher spirits should let her pass without warning.

Synthia didn't really care, though. If they tried to stop her, she would destroy them without a second thought. She traveled through the macroglass barrier and down onto the stadium floor.

Jonathon was standing next to his locker, removing his grimy duster and stained jeans.

Synthia moved close, a few steps behind him as her form became visible in the physical world. "Jonathon," she said. "Can we talk?"

He turned slowly, deliberately, and when she saw him a trickle of fear passed over her. His aura looked cold and resigned. He nodded to her. "Yes," he said.

"You must erase the Magus File data from your headware," she said. "Or they will kill me."

"They?"

"Saeder-Krupp; it's their data."

Jonathon nodded slowly. "In a few minutes everything will be all right."

"What do you mean?"

"The data will be destroyed . . ." Jonathon trailed off. "After that, there'll be no reason to kill you."

"Destroyed? But how?"

Jonathon didn't respond, but his aura flared red for an instant.

"How, Jonathon?"

"It's best you don't know."

"You don't plan to survive that match, do you?"

No response.

"Jonathon?"

"If I live," he said. "Too many will die. You, Grids, Venny . . ."

"You don't have to die," Synthia said. "Just purge your headware memory."

"And they'll take my word for it? I don't think so, Syn. They'd have to check to make sure, and they're not going to make the effort. Not now. Things have progressed too far for that. I've read the file, too. No, it's easier for them to kill me. Cheaper."

Synthia remembered what Brackhaus had said about his assassins. "So, what . . . ?" she said. "You're going to save them the trouble and suicide? Good fragging plan."

Jonathon didn't respond, but Synthia could see that he was resolved. Unmovable. "I have one more thing to do," Jonathon whispered. "But I wanted to say goodbye to you."

Synthia felt a wave of vertigo wash over her. Sadness, manifesting in her physical form as tears. *I can't even hold him in my arms,* she thought. *Can't even kiss him goodbye.* She waved at him, letting her physical manifestation slip away as she returned completely to astral space.

His last words hung in the air as she disappeared. "I love you, Syn. Don't ever forget."

54

Sweat poured down Jonathon's face as he ran the curves and corridors of the maze. His home maze. He knew its pits and hollows, the sharpness of each turn, the steepness of each half-pipe. He passed across the far goal area and made for the skyway.

He'd expected to need several complete circuits of the maze before being able to achieve the level of focus he needed for the game. He'd expected to be distracted by his talk with Synthia and the terrible events of the past few days.

But he was wrong; his focus came almost immediately. The hurricane of static in his head helped him concentrate on the task at hand. It was like Tamara was running with him; her ghost trailing behind him in whispers on the wind.

Everything was set; the preparations made. There were no worries left, just execution.

When he returned to the locker room to begin the long process of dressing in his armor, Grids was waiting for him. "I'm a genius," he said.

"You got it to work?"

"Did you have any doubt?"

"No." Jonathon opened his locker and began to pull on his bodysuit. "Now I want you to leave," he said.

"Simsense is complex data," Grids said, "so I had to do more than just tap into Dougan's frequency. I had to modify the datastream itself to make it look like a normal data-packet. But it should have the same effect as simsense. There's no time to test it, of course."

Jonathon was putting on his Kevlar-3 jacket. "Did you hear what I said?"

"What?"

"I want you to leave now. Take the limo and drive to

the airport. Go to the Bahamas or Fiji or wherever you've always wanted to go. There's a half-million nuyen on certified credsticks in the limo. Don't come back for at least six months."

Grids furrowed his brow and took a step back. "I've been good about not asking exactly what you're going to do, but—"

"Don't. It's better if you don't know."

"But—"

"Shh, just shut up and go before I have security throw you out."

Grids picked up his satchel and walked away. Jonathon ignored a tug of emotion in the pit of his gut and concentrated on getting the new polycarb slats into his armor. Soon the feeling gave way to the business at hand and the rising wind of Tamara's whispers.

Sounds of the trideo drifted from the other room where Ion and Smitty were watching the pre-game hype. Jonathon caught the announcer's words in snatches as he finished the meticulous job of assembling himself.

Millions worldwide watched. And the ratings had continued to rise since the news had leaked that both Jonathon and Dougan had showed at the stadium. Everyone anticipated the coming confrontation between the two best linebikers in the world.

Jonathon let the hype wash over him. Remained unaffected by it. Once upon a time he'd actively pursued fame, desired to be what he'd now become. Now, he just wanted out.

Scenes of Tamara's death came on the trideo and Smitty punched it off. Then the dwarf turned and walked over to Jonathon. "We're all primed that you showed today," he said. "We would've won anyhow, you know. But with you it'll be easier."

Jonathon finished slotting the plates into the Kevlar pants, then sat down to stretch. He listened to the crowd outside grow louder and louder, until it was time to don his helmet, get on his bike, latch in, and rumble out into the maze.

The crowd screamed when they saw him. He made one complete circuit through the maze of concrete barriers. Assuming the role of superhero for the moment because soon it would all be over. As he rode around the twists and turns, he checked his retinal display. He noted the ghost shadow of the five-second timer for the detonator under his seat. And he saw the tiny gray chip-shaped icon in the lower-left corner of his vision. Grids's little addition to the occasion. Jonathon would activate it when the time came.

Suddenly the crowd started hissing, and a wave of jeers and boos traveled around the stadium. Jonathon saw a small yellow dot on his display that indicated Dougan Rose had entered the maze.

Thank you, Grids.

"Dougan, this is Jonathon, can you hear me?"

"I copy, Jonathon. What's the deal? We shouldn't be able to communicate."

Jonathon accelerated toward the ramp of the skyway on his side of the maze. "Just a little patchwork by a chummer of mine, designed to speed up our inevitable confrontation."

Dougan laughed. "I see," he said. "What's on your mind?"

"Head to head on the skyway, chummer," Jonathon said. "Just you and me."

"Before play begins? I like it, I like it."

Jonathon knew that the referees and the comtechs were probably following their communications at this very moment and trying to shut them down. "Let's go now," he told Dougan. "I'm prepped."

"What weapons, chummer?" Dougan said.

"All out," Jonathon said. "Anything you got."

"To the death?"

"That's what the fans are here for, *neh*?"

"Frag the fans," Dougan said. "What do *you* want?"

"To the death," Jonathon said.

"It's your funeral," Dougan said, laughing long and low. Then, "Okay, I'm in position and prepped."

Jonathon took one breath.

Hearing the charging crackle of Tamara, setting his hair on end.

Another breath.

Then . . .

"Go!" Jonathon said, then he cranked the accelerator on his Suzuki full out into the red. His wheels screeched beneath him, rocketing him up the narrow ramp toward

Dougan. The crowd screamed around them as everything closed on the moment.

He saw Dougan's Yamaha cresting the downward curve of the skyway ramp. Dougan riding in full combat armor, his Roomsweeper in one hand, his whip in the other.

Jonathon raised his empty fists toward the sky as the crackle of static rose to a deafening scream in his head. He needed no weapons. The crowd was a blur around him, the skyway's pavement ripping by underneath his wheels.

He focused on the closing distance, mentally calculating the narrowing gap of time to the clash. Who would dodge? Who would flinch at the last second?

Jonathon held his course, aiming himself straight into the heart of the inevitable. He rocketed up the ramp, an angel of vengeance. The moment of finality rushing toward him like Hell's minions reaching up from the deep to take him. Taking him to see Tamara once again.

Tamara's face fluttered in the windy spaces of his mind. *It's time,* he thought, then mentally engaged Grids's rigged simsense pulse. The chip-shaped icon on his retina changed from gray to red as the data went to Dougan Rose.

Payback time.

Dougan's bike swerved slightly as the simsense engaged. He would be experiencing the wet-feed recording of Tamara's death. As his bike hurtled toward Jonathon, Dougan would see himself through Tamara's eyes. Right now, he was feeling his cyberspurs slicing up into her neck. Smelling the iron tang of her blood filling her helmet.

Jonathon engaged the five-second detonator at the same time he unclamped his legs from his machine and disconnected from it cybernetically. This was his one shot, his only chance.

Dougan unjacked himself from his bike to cut off the simsense feed. "That was unfair—"

Jonathon stood on his seat and jumped at the last second, flying through the air at nearly a hundred klicks per hour. He sailed up and over as the bikes met in the sharp crashing of metal and plastic.

The explosion hit him like a concussion of fire, a tsunami of searing heat and a spray of sharp shrapnel that blew through his armor like rice paper. He flew up, flailing and twisting in the afterimage of the blast.

Jonathon soared, a limp ragdoll in the air. Tumbling. And as he flew, he saw the huge fireball lifting up from the wreckage behind him, and he remembered his house in Redding. He saw the grandfather clock and the bassinet in the billowing flame. He heard the sobbing cry of his mother and the wail of his sister in the flame.

And for just a second, he imagined the hiss was gone from his head. The dead air silenced.

The pain began when he came back down. Agony like nothing he'd ever known bathed him, and it seemed his skin had melted from his body. He hit the concrete and bounced, hearing his bones snap and pop before feeling the split second of pain.

When he finally scraped to rest, up against the far wall, he knew he was dead; he wished for it to come quickly and take him away from the pain. Take him over the edge of fadeout.

And as the blackhole edge dopplered toward him, he reached for it. Throwing himself into the abyss. Plummeting into absolute silence.

To be with Tamara again.

55

A thunderous boom echoed around her, shaking the world.

Maria faded into an awareness of her surroundings. Inside the passenger compartment of a rented Toyota Elite limousine. Black synthleather upholstery, trideo, small refreshment case.

She looked out into darkness. Ah, nighttime had finally come. But something was wrong and it took her groggy, drug-affected mind a few seconds to realize she was underground. In a parking garage.

At the stadium, if the sounds of the crowd were any indication. *But what was that loud boom?* Maria punched on the trideo to see a male-biff newscaster with a plastic face and spray blond hair talking about an explosion at the combat biker match.

"A bomb implanted into one of the bikes has exploded," the man said. Behind him, Maria could see the accident. The two bikers slamming into each other at phenomenal speed, the slow-motion of the trideo showing a close-up of Dougan as he tried to serve away at the last second. Showing Winger jumping up and over, the explosion blowing from his bike in frame-by-frame clarity to engulf Dougan and send him hurtling off the skyway in pieces.

"Preliminary evidence indicates that Jonathon Winger planted a small explosive device into his motorcycle. It is believed Winger's motive was revenge for the death of Tamara Ny in last week's New Orleans match.

"The two players have been rushed by DocWagon helicopter to UCLA Medical Center. However, both are presumed."

Maria sank into the comfort of the limo's plush seat and opened up one of bottles of chilled spring water. *You got what you deserved, Dougan,* she thought. The cool, clean liquid soothed the back of her throat and cleared her head a little.

She decided she would stay right here for a few minutes, letting her senses sharpen inside the car as the drug wore off. She wanted to make sure Dougan was dead. Because if he wasn't, she would find him at the medical center and kill him herself. And after that, she would go back to her house in San Bernardino and see her kids. Frag, it would feel great to go home.

56

Hendrix stood in the stands of the LA Coliseum and looked at his hands. Dark brown skin with augmented muscle underneath. He turned them over to see his palms, white and callused. How many people had he killed with those hands? Too fragging many. He'd spent his entire life in the death business.

Time to get out. That was his inner voice talking to him. The same inner voice that had told him to leave the merc unit during the El Infierno invasion. That time it had saved him from being skinned alive and hung from a lamp pole.

He missed Layla, and he wasn't sad to see Jonathon Winger blown to shreds in the blast. But he was glad he hadn't needed to kill Winger himself. He was tired of killing.

The announcement had just come over the loudspeaker that Winger was confirmed dead on arrival at UCLA Medical Center. Dougan Rose had somehow survived, but was in critical condition.

Hendrix glanced up through the macroglass in front of him to look at the woman he'd been watching for the past few minutes. Synthia Stone, Jonathon Winger's love. The woman Hendrix had originally planned to kill in revenge for Layla's death.

Her short-cropped red hair caught the light like a shimmering fire. Her delicate features belied a hidden power. Hendrix had seen some of that power, but it wouldn't deter him from shooting her if he so desired. But he'd hesitated; he didn't want to kill anymore. And now that Jonathon Winger was dead, it didn't matter.

Synthia Stone sat hunched over in obvious shock from seeing the explosion. Tears streamed down her lovely cheeks as she stared into space. She blinked in slow motion and turned her head to look at Hendrix.

Her eyes were the color of a washed-out sky. Her features much like Layla's, petite and delicate—a deceptive mask for her hard core. A fraction of a second passed before Hendrix saw a spark of recognition. She remembered him.

He moved fast, his old instincts kicking in. Any hesitation might give her the chance to fry him right now. At jacked-up speed, he stepped past the opening to her private-seating box and brought his silenced Predator II to bear. It was his discreet weapon, better for crowds. But it would kill just as effectively.

She saw the gun and just sat there for a second as Hendrix crossed the small space between them. Then, as the pistol snapped into perfect aim, she broke into laughter. And her laughter grew into a hysterical cackle that made Hendrix hesitate, and for the briefest of moments, she reminded him again of Layla.

"I'm already dead," she said, then doubled over with laughter. In seconds her body shook uncontrollably. Her arms and legs shivered as she tried to stand and take a palsied step toward him. "Already dead," she said, then fell to the concrete steps.

"What's wrong?" Hendrix asked, holding his gun at ready just in case this was some elaborate deception.

Synthia shook violently. "A toxin in my blood," she said. "Nanites and symbiotes, you wouldn't understand."

But he did understand. He understood all too well. And as Synthia curled into a fetal ball, Hendrix decided that his inner voice was right once again. *Trust it,* he thought. Then he hefted her over his shoulder and started to run.

He passed through the dazed and confused crowd. The combat biker match was finally beginning. Hendrix contacted Mole on his headphone as he ran, ordering the decker to get in touch with Sergio, the street doc who'd cleaned the symbiotes from Hendrix's blood so many years ago.

Hendrix carried Synthia out of the stadium, running as though the salvation of his soul was at stake. He wanted to save a life, just once, instead of taking one. Sergio was the best. He'd have no problem with Synthia's nanites. No problem at all.

57

Sounds came to him in his sleep. Voices. Whispers.

He lay on his back, as he had for countless days. Motionless and hazy with neuroblockers. The feeling in his skin was not crisp. Instead he felt a dull pressure around him. A gentle weight over him.

How much time had passed? He didn't know, could be weeks or months.

The sound of a door opening made him open his eyes to a room bathed in dim yellow light. A face came into view, an old friend looking down at him. A dwarf with black curls and a beard. A very old friend from his Fort Lewis days. From prison. Theodore Rica.

"Jonathon," Theo said. "It is you inside, isn't it? How do you feel?"

Jonathon opened his mouth to speak, but his throat was parched and he only managed a weak croak. "Theo," he said. "I'm alive?"

Theo brought water to his lips and let him drink. "Yes, my friend. Welcome to Mitsuhama Computer Technologies. You're no longer you, but you're alive. I know this isn't the most luxurious room, but it's a long way up from Hell."

Jonathon closed his eyes. *The plan must've worked then,* he thought. *That meant . . .*

"We nearly lost you," Theo said. "But you must've decided to live after all. After the surgery, you went into a torpor of some sort. Like a waking haze the doctors couldn't explain."

"How long?"

"Ten days. Ever since they brought you from the Coliseum. And from what the docs say, most of what you missed was depression and pain. They only cut away the bandages around your face yesterday." Theo produced a small mirror and held it so Jonathon could see his face.

But it wasn't his face that looked back at him from the mirror. The cheekbones were a fraction too high, the eyes too green and overly slanted. He sucked in breath and stared at the face of his enemy. The plan had worked in the most frighteningly possible way.

Jonathon had sold his soul. He had become Dougan Rose.

"The docs say it will be a few more months before you'll be ready to compete again, but MCT is counting on you to fill Rose's position. The Buzzsaws have to regain the championship after losing." Theo smiled. "Very few know about what we did," he said. "Most of the DocWagon techs were our people so it was easy to switch Dougan's body with yours. You killed him dead, chummer. He was blown to bits and burned beyond recognition, just a lifeless lump of flesh.

"We had to get a couple of our deckers to tweak the genetic databanks so any undamaged cellular residue would scan as yours, not his. All in all, the whole operation didn't cost that much and only a few non-dedicated personnel know about it. And most of those will experience 'memory loss' after you're gone.

"MCT was extremely grateful for the data you provided. You've actually strengthened my position here."

Theo was silent for a moment and when Jonathon didn't answer, he pulled the mirror away. "I know it must be hard, chummer," he said. "But you'll pull through. At least you're alive."

Jonathon didn't answer. He simply stared at the white ceiling tiles and thought of death. Tamara was still gone; killing Dougan hadn't changed that. In fact he hadn't killed Dougan at all; he had *become* Dougan. Dougan lived on, while Jonathon Winger had died in a ball of flame.

Jonathon had never really expected the plan to work; he'd only set it up because he'd been afraid to go all the way. Afraid to cross over and join Tamara. And now, he was isolated from his closest friends. Synthia, Venny, Grids, everyone.

I'm alone.

"Look, chummer," Theo said. "I'm gonna leave you to your thoughts. I've got biz, but if you need anything, just push the button on your bed, and I'll come." Theo's head disappeared from the periphery of Jonathon's vision, then came the sound of a door opening and closing.

The silence of the room haunted Jonathon. The absence

of sound created a stillness that enveloped him in its death. Like the icy cold nothingness of space.

I am truly alone, he thought. Even when his mother had died, Tamara was there to hold his hand. But now . . .

"You're not Dougan Rose." The woman spoke in a husky voice, stating a fact, not a question. Jonathon looked at her, standing above him. Long straight black hair and dark eyes. Olive skin and the same black bodysuit with feathers he'd seen her wearing at the shooting range in Grandma's Pharmacy and Survival. Except now, the feathers were larger, like those of a massive bird, and woven into the fabric of her arms and legs. They covered her ears and head, making her look like an owl. Her name, he remembered, was Maria.

She must be projecting here, Jonathon thought. *As Syn did in the locker room.*

"Your aura's wrong," Maria said. Then, after looking closely at Jonathon, scrutinizing with her eyes, she went on. "Is Dougan Rose dead then?"

Jonathon nodded.

"You're Winger?"

Jonathon didn't answer, but she must have known.

"I've been waiting for you to wake up," she said, and there was a softness to her eyes that drew Jonathon in. "I wanted to thank you. What you did—killing Dougan Rose—was a good thing. He deserved to die a long time ago." Tears welled in her eyes as she bent over him. "He was responsible for my brother's death. For so many deaths."

Jonathon reached up with a gauze-covered arm to brush away her tears. To caress that beautiful face. So sad now. But his bandage-wrapped hand passed through her dark cheek as though it were translucent. Touching nothing but air.

Maria took a step back and gave him a melancholic smile. "Thank you, Jonathon Winger. I hope we meet in person someday. Until then, your secret is safe with me." Then she disappeared.

Leaving him alone again with only the yellow ceiling tiles for company.

Minutes passed in absolute silence before . . .

It started in the distant reaches of his mind like a ghost. A shiver of sand, barely audible. A hiss of static, vanishingly faint. As if, perhaps, in his imagination.

Tamara, is that you?
Tamara?

Epilogue

The hiss rises in your head as Jonathon Winger's sensations fade from your body. The static grows to fill your ears, and a grainy holographic black serves as a backdrop for the closing credits.

You jack out from the console in the armrest of the sim-recliner where your flesh has been sitting during the simfeature. And the events of the story flicker in your mind for a minute as your senses return to the here and now.

But those sensations fade slowly as you exit the theater and return outside to the heat and the exhaust. All that remains of the sim is the hiss in your head. You barely notice it, but the static does not dissipate. It serves as a subtle reminder that reality is never completely virtual. That even sim can have a lasting impact.

The static crackles on in the subliminal regions of your mind. And later when you are alone in the silence of a dark night, you hear the wailing whispers. And you feel the crackle at the edge of your conscious mind as they hiss their secrets.

About the Author

Dead Air is Jak Koke's first published novel. His second, *Liferock,* will be published by FASA Corporation as part of its Earthdawn® series in late 1996. Koke has also sold numerous short stories to AMAZING STORIES and PULPHOUSE: A FICTION MAGAZINE, and has contributed to several anthologies such as *Rat Tales* by Pulphouse, *Young Blood* by Zebra, and *Talisman,* an Earthdawn® anthology.

Jak is a lab technician during the day. His work currently focuses on protein expression in marine phytoplankton and the attempt to isolate environmental markers for bloom conditions including "red tides."

Jak and his wife Seana Davidson, a marine microbiologist, live in California with their three-year-old daughter, Michaela.

Pita sat in an alley in the shadow of a rotted-out chesterfield. She'd tried sleeping on it the night before, but the springs had dug into her back. Now she leaned against its padded arm, ignoring the musty smell of moldy fabric. She took a bite of a Sweetnut Puff and washed it down with some steaming soykaf. The doughy pastry made her teeth ache, so she tossed it aside. Then she dug inside her pocket.

The alley was only faintly illuminated by the sodium light up the street. Tilting her hand to catch its dim yellow glow, Pita looked at the capsules that lay on her palm. Three pale white ovals that promised an end to the flip-flops that wrenched her stomach and the nightmares that plagued her sleep. They'd cost her plenty—an unpleasant favor for the off-duty DocWagon attendant she'd met at the local bar. She grimaced, still feeling his sloppy kisses on her shoulders and neck. It hadn't been anything like what she'd had with Chen . . .

Blinking away the sudden sting in her eyes, Pita tossed the capsules into her mouth and took a gulp of her soykaf. It was still hot enough to burn her lips, but she drank it anyway, not wanting the capsules to get stuck in her throat. Then she waited.

She heard a rustling noise somewhere to her left and turned her head. A cat with a matted coat and torn ears emerged from a recessed doorway and began eating the piece of Sweetnut Puff she'd tossed. It paused as it sensed her movement, then turned to stare at her. Its eyes were twin red moons, reflections of the streetlights at the end of the alley. Pita felt suddenly uneasy, as if the cat were looking into her soul. Somehow, the cat shared the hunger that burned inside her. Then the animal turned and scuttled back to cover, favoring one leg in an ambling limp.

A wave of warm fuzziness washed over Pita. The Mindease capsules were kicking in. Her hand drifted out in a gesture of goodwill to the cat, willing it to return and share the bounty she had offered. Her head felt like a balloon attached to a string, floating high above her body. Something hot flowed over her other hand, trickled down her arm to her elbow. The soykaf. It must have been burning her skin. Pita laughed, and raised the cup to her lips to take a drink. The dark liquid sloshed out over her chin. Her wide grin made it impossible to shape her lips around the cup, so she dropped it and watched the soykaf splash in slo-mo across the cement.

The bang of a metal door brought her head around. She frowned, peering deeper into the alley. The office buildings in this part of town had been closed for hours. Lights still burned in some of the upper stories, but only for the benefit of the cleaning crews. Were they coming out into the alley to empty the trash? Pita hunched down in the shadow of the chesterfield and giggled. This was just like playing Hide and Search, the virtual reality game she'd enjoyed so much as a kid. She even felt like a computer icon, all thin and transparent.

A man staggered up the three steps leading to street level. He emerged from the doorway clutching his shirtfront, gasping as if he couldn't catch his breath. Even though the drug blurred her vision somewhat, the lowlight sensitivity of Pita's ork eyes let her pick out details. The man was sweating profusely; the underarms of his expensive-looking suit jacket were heavily stained. His tie had been jerked loose and sweat plastered his dark hair to his head and trickled down his neck.

The man took one staggering step, two . . . and collapsed on the cement in front of Pita. He landed face-first with a solid smack. When he turned his head, she could see blood trickling from his nose. His mouth gaped open wide and his eyes rolled back in his head. A strange burning smell rose from him.

The Mindease stripped all the fears from Pita's conscious mind, burying them deep in the back of her brain. She sat up, intrigued. Giggling, she reached out a finger and poked the man's cheek. It was hotter than her soykaf had been.

A dim red light appeared in the man's mouth and nose. She knelt forward, lowering her head to the cool cement to peer inside. The smell of burning meat filled her nostrils. Then a steady rush of smoke began pouring out of the man's mouth and nose. Sweat steamed off his body.

"Mega cool," she whispered, wondering if the Mindease was making her hallucinate. Then her street instincts took over. She flipped the man over and patted down his suit pockets. The way he was dressed, this guy had to be a corporate executive, his pockets full of goodies.

The first suit pocket held a smog filter and a melted Growliebar. Pita tossed them aside. The next held a folded hardcopy printout and an optical memory chip, which she palmed. It just might have a simsense game on it. The only other thing the guy had on him was a credstick. Even if there were a million nuyen on it, Pita wouldn't be able to access a single credit of it. To do that, you had to give a thumbprint, retinal scan, or voice sample. And Pita didn't have the technical knowhow to fake any of that stuff. So she nearly threw the credstick away. But then she spotted the magnetic keystrip on the side of the stick. Maybe, just maybe, it opened a locked door with something worth boosting on the other side. She slipped the credstick into her pocket.

The man was flopping now like someone hooked up to an electric current, and his skin was nearly too hot to touch. And something else weird was happening. White light poured out of his mouth and nostrils, the beams straight as lasers. His movements jerked the light around in jittering arcs. As it did, Pita caught sight of a flash of gold around the man's neck. It was a gold chain, hung with a tiny pendant shaped like an angel with outstretched wings Pita reached for it.

"Ouch!" One of the beams brushed her arm. Even through the dulling effects of the Mindease, she felt it burn. A bright red line now creased the inside of her wrist. She jerked her arm back, afraid the beam of light would catch it again, but the man had already stopped flopping and lay still, his head to one side. The beams now focused on the wall beside her, slowly charring the cement. Still giggling, Pita experimentally held the hardcopy she'd pulled from his pocket in the path of the beam and watched it burst into flame.

Suddenly, the light beams slid away from the man's head. They merged into a single ray of light that ricocheted off one wall and did a zig-zag across the alley, bouncing back and forth from one tinted window to the next. The night was filled with strobing light as the light broke into a scattering of laser-thin beams, each a different color, then melded in a solid white flash that left Pita blinking. It was weirdly beautiful, and at the same time terrifying in its intensity. At last seeming to find its way out of the alley, the light shot up into the darkened sky above like a reversed shooting star. Then the sky lit up with a flash of sheet lightning. Pita waited for the thunderclap, but none came.

The smell of burned meat was overwhelming. Pita couldn't help but gag when she saw that the skin around the man's lips and nostrils had blackened and was beginning to flake away. She glanced down at his wrist and saw a DocWagon wristband. A winking light indicated that it had been activated.

Drek! The meatwagon could be here any second!

The artificial calm of the drug dampened her fear. She wanted to curl up and sleep. But instead she willed herself to rise to her feet. The last thing she needed was to be questioned about a corpse—especially one whose pockets she'd just rifled.

It took Pita a moment to orient herself. The Mindease was making her fuzzy, making it hard to think. One hand on the wall beside her, she staggered out of the alley. Dimly, she registered a man across the street, fiddling with a trideo camera. A tiny red light glowed above its lens. Pita smiled and waved at it, remembering how the cat's eyes had glowed red with reflected light.

The man's head jerked up. He flattened against the wall, looking wary, tucking the trideo camera in against his body. Then he relaxed, as Pita staggered past him.

"Fragging druggie," he whispered under his breath.

Lulled by the Mindease, Pita let his comment slide away like oil down a gutter.

* * *

"Hey Carla! Got a minute?"

Masaki grabbed Carla's arm, jerking her to a halt in mid-stride. Angrily, she turned on him.

"No I don't have a minute, Masaki," she snapped. "In just thirty minutes I'm doing an interview at the Chrysler Pacific showroom. It's going to take me twenty-three minutes to get there—longer, if traffic is bad. I'm already cutting it fine." Tucking the coil of cable she carried under one arm, she used her free hand to pry Masaki's fingers away.

"Spare me thirty seconds, O.K.?" Masaki insisted. "I need to show you a trideo clip I shot last night."

"Jack off, Masaki. I don't have time to give you any editing tips."

"Twenty seconds! That's all it will take!"

Carla turned and strode away down the hall. Masaki trotted after her, speaking as rapidly as he could and wheezing with every word.

"I went out last night to shoot an interview. I had a tip from a guy who was a junior exec at Mitsuhama Computer Technologies. He wanted to tell me about some top-secret project the corporation's research and development lab was working on. Some radical new tech that he thought the public should know about. He was going to spill his guts, give me an exclusive preview. He promised the story would be the biggest one of my career. He was going to give me both hard copy and a data chip with the project specs on it."

Carla snorted. "Yeah, right. So why didn't your source take it to the majors?"

"He owed me a favor. Before signing on with Mitsuhama as a wage mage, he owned a thaumaturgical supply shop down on Madison Street. I did a puff piece on the store that brought in a lot of business." Masaki sighed. "He was murdered last night before I could conduct the interview. Burned to death."

"So?" A murder was hardly unusual, considering Mitsuhama's rumored Yakuza connections.

"He was burned from the inside out."

Despite herself, Carla was intrigued. "How? Magic?"

"Maybe." Masaki shrugged. "But if so, it's something I haven't seen before, in all of my twenty-eight years as a snoopy. And I've seen some pretty weird things through the lens of my trideo, believe me."

"And the hardcopy and memory chip he was going to give you?"

"The hardcopy was nothing but ashes by the time I got there. And the chip was gone."

Carla pushed the door open and triggered her cyber-eye's built-in time code. According to the glowing red numbers that appeared in the bottom right-hand corner of her field of vision, she had just twenty-six minutes to make it to her interview. "If you really had the goods on a hush-hush Mitsuhama research project, you'd have a big story—not to mention a tiger by the tail. But it sounds like you've got nothing, now that your source is dead and your proof has vanished. So why are you pestering me?" She jogged across the parking lot to her Americar XL, then slid in behind its padded leather steering wheel and voice-activated the ignition. She revved the engine and watched the seconds scroll by on the timepiece built into the mini-cam in her right eye. She'd give Masaki thirty seconds for his reply.

He leaned in through the car's open door, talking rapidly. "I was mucking about with my portacam just before I went to meet my source. I didn't realize it was on. But it's a good thing it was. There was a witness to the murder. Remember that ork kid who wanted to talk to you two days ago, about the Humanis Policlub? I think it was her. She even waved at the camera. And guess what was in her hand?"

"The memory chip," Carla whispered. She smiled, realizing that Masaki had just handed her, on a silver platter, the story that would get her a slot at NABS She laughed to herself. Had Masaki been a little smarter, a little more cutthroat, he would have asked her for the name and address of the kid without revealing the reason why he wanted it. Oh, well—his loss and her gain

Carla cut the engine of her car. "Forget the Chrysler story," she told Masaki. "It's nothing more than a trideo op for the corporate execs. One of the junior reporters can cover it. We've got a real story to follow "